DISPLACED

BRIDGET E. BAKER

Created with Vellum

For Elijah

You cheer me on endlessly, and you are fierce, just like the best parts of both twins. You're also kind, empathetic and brilliant. May you grow in judgment and wisdom for many, many years to come. (But maybe not a thousand. . .)

I

My mom should have killed me the day I was born. In her nearly nine-hundred-year reign as the Empress of the First Family, sparing my life seventeen years ago was her single act of mercy.

Evians around the world refer to me as "Enora's Folly."

It's no wonder I'm fatally flawed, a blemish among the shining population of evians Mom rules. I spent my childhood running away from my twin sister's taunts. Maybe that's why no one on the island can catch me. On days when life feels too heavy and my heart struggles to beat without melancholy, the Kona wind blowing against my face reminds me the world is vast and full of possibility. And on days when I need that wind, but my mom's too busy to run with me, there's always Lark.

"Wait up," she calls from dozens of yards behind me.

I stop at the top of the northeastern cliffs, the highest point on Ni'ihau, and scan the horizon while I wait for her. Dolphins leap energetically in the distance. I've been on this island the majority of my life, yet every single time I stop to take in the lush island of Kauai in the distance, and every time I stand at the highest point of Ni'ihau, the majesty of my surroundings astonishes me. When Lark finally reaches my side, her lungs heave in great, gulping breaths and she bends over double. "We should've taken the horses."

"Are you okay?" I lift one eyebrow.

She waves her hand at me absently and wheezes. "Fine, you idiot. Not all of us are machines. You've got to ease up for the little people."

"You're the one who suggested we take this trail."

"I guess that makes me the idiot." She straightens next to me, her heart rate decelerating back to normal.

"As your best friend, I officially disagree with you." I grin. "You're smart and talented, Lark. People like you. Now repeat that until you believe it."

"Speaking of how much you love me..." Lark won't meet my eye.

"What's up?" I ask.

"I need help."

Most evians don't do favors, not without negotiation and *quid pro quo*, or at least a few moments of analysis to weigh the impact and risk to them. But I'm the broken heir, the defective twin, the one who doesn't view friendship as a commodity like I should.

Which is why I immediately say, "Anything. You already know that."

Lark's voice drops to a whisper. "The intelligence subsection is getting more competitive every year."

She's a year older than me and recently completed her training, which means placement for her first work assignment happens in the next few days.

"Right," I say. "Balth said it's gotten popular." Not that I care, since I'll never be placed anywhere. I'm stuck here forever.

"A few years ago, Mom could've gotten me a spot for sure."

"But now?"

"Well." She clears her throat. "She can't do much now. But if I could defeat a seventh gen in a challenge. . ."

Lark wants to fight me. And more than that, she needs to defeat me. Publicly.

"You want to stab me with a sword in front of everyone we know?" That's a pretty big ask. I mean, I heal lightning quick, but it still hurts. Plus, Lark is tenth gen. Losing to her would be a new low, even for me.

"I really don't want to get stuck working for Uncle Max."

"Oh come on. He loves fostering the young minds. He's always talking about it."

"He is." Lark groans. "The idea of restructuring corporations all day long. . ." She closes her eyes. "I'll die of boredom."

Lark has always been melodramatic. "Just submit your DNA and you'll be auto-admitted into intelligence. It's not *that* competitive. I mean, you suck at appearance modification, and your mom is pretty well known, so you'll probably be stuck human side initially, but you can buckle down and practice your modifications and you'll cross over eventually."

"But if I defeat you, I'd be automatically ranked number one in Alamecha's class."

And I'd look pathetic, being beaten by someone with three generations more genetic deletions. I open my mouth to tell her no, but her quick inhalation stops me. She can test right into a top tier Security placement with a simple blood draw. Usually only candidates below fifteenth gen resort to theatrics like a public challenge. Why would she ask me to destroy my reputation for something she doesn't even need?

"You're absolutely positive you want a Security placement?" I ask.

Her gray eyes widen and her breath hitches again. This request matters to her. She might have even orchestrated this run to ask me without interruption. Heaven knows she never wants to go jogging, so this suggestion came out of the blue. My oldest friend has never asked me for a single thing, not in seventeen years. She probably knows better than anyone else how hard things are for me, and now she's asking me to do something she doesn't really need, knowing Judica will never let me forget my defeat.

Why?

I want to shove the thoughts away and ignore the nigglings at the back of my mind. But I can't. I'm not wired that way, and I keep circling back to the same conclusion. "I can only think of one reason you'd ask me to throw a challenge."

Lark's heart rate spikes and the scent of her perspiration rises, almost as strongly as when she was running full tilt.

Unfortunately, that's the confirmation I need. "You can't do the blood test."

Her nostrils flare. "Of course I can."

She's lying to me, but I hope I'm wrong about why. Because I think she just asked me to commit treason, and she didn't even plan to tell me I was doing it.

Why does she need me to throw a fight? I rarely train in earnest, whereas she spends hours every morning with her mom. Actually, she's rumored to be one of the best fighters on the compound. "Why not simply challenge me?"

Lark's gray eyes widen.

"Come on Lark, you can tell me. What's going on?" Please, please come clean.

"Never mind. It's fine." Lark turns away from me and picks at non-existent lint on her pants.

When I grab her hand, she jumps like I electrocuted her. "Tell me."

She yanks her hand away with wounded eyes. "There's nothing to tell."

"You're half human." My words hang in the air like a cloud of gnats, impeding my vision of the future, clouding my memory of the past, a plague on my heart. I wish I could wave my hand and dissipate the reality of my accusation, but I can't. Only Lark can fix this, by denying my wild claim.

I need her to deny it.

I'm afraid she can't.

When she doesn't say a word, I struggle to breathe. Lark's father must have been human. She's only half evian. Every moment of our seventeen years as best friends shifts, recharacterized by my new knowledge. Her heaving when we run, her training alone, her reticence to travel with me. The ground beneath my feet feels unsteady, like there's been an earthquake.

"Why didn't you tell me?" I whisper. "Why didn't you confess years ago?" The realization that she didn't even tell me now slaps me hard. I had to figure this out, about my own best friend.

A tear streaks down her face and she wipes it away ruthlessly. "What will you do now you know?"

"Look at me."

She doesn't.

"I can't believe you're asking me that right now. I'd never turn you in. You think I could ever watch your execution? Lark, *look at me*."

Her lower lip wobbles. "I should never have asked in the first place. Mom was right. Why did I try to outsmart you? I'm deficient."

I can't even imagine living with that kind of fear. Why didn't her mother leave with her or adopt her out? The idea of life without Lark shatters my heart into pieces. All this time and she couldn't even risk telling her best friend.

That's reason enough for me to throw one fight. No one should live like she's had to live, and if I can create a safer space for her in our world, I'll do it.

This time it's my voice that wobbles. "Your mistake wasn't in asking, it was in withholding the relevant information. Of course I'll do whatever you need. You'll get into Security and select intelligence and then you'll leave." I realize one reason I didn't want to help her before is that her Uncle Max lives here, and I didn't want her to leave.

But she has to go.

If she stays on the island, it's only a matter of time before someone else figures it out. "Then no one will ever know."

She shakes her head. "If you figured out why I asked, someone else might guess too."

"So we stage your challenge. Someone optimistically throws one down on me at least twice a year, you know, seeing as I'm the useless twin. I always turn them down flat, but maybe you'd make me mad enough to accept. Best friends know exactly which buttons to push, right?"

The corner of Lark's mouth turns up slightly. "Even so, Balthasar might figure it out," she says. "During the match I mean. It's dangerous, too dangerous to risk, which is why mom said not to even ask you." She drops her face into her hands. "Mom's going to kill me when I tell her about all this."

"Tell your mom that you have an ally now." I smile and take her hand in mine. "I may not be *the Heir,* but I'm an heir, and beating me will be enough. Besides, once you're in the field working from the human side, you'll be away from all the evian politics. And working on the human side, you'll be safe."

"That's the plan," she says. "But when Mom finds out you know..."

"So don't tell her."

Lark shakes her head. "I can't lie to my mom. I can't. I lie to everyone else."

Her life has been harder than I ever realized. "How slow are you, exactly?"

Lark balls her fingers into a fist and swings at me. I duck easily. Her reflexes probably put a human to shame, but they're notably slower than mine. Ugh. How will we pull this off?

"I think the only way people won't notice your speed is if I'm truly horrible," I say. "Which shouldn't be too hard. I haven't reached the point of integrating active combat into my training yet, so I'm sure I'll be convincingly terrible."

"You're saying your mom's insistence on training you in old school melodics might save me?" Lark's smile reaches her eyes this time, and when her stormy gray eyes sparkle, I decide we can pull this off.

We don't have a choice.

2

"You took it easy on me." Lark accuses me as we reach the palace compound.

Cookie Crisp, my King Charles Spaniel, frolics around my legs when I turn onto the main hallway. I ordered her to wait here while we went for a jog. If I let her come, she practically keels over about a mile into the warm up. I crouch down and pet Cookie's ears to buy some time for Lark's heart rate to come down.

"Chancery," she hisses. "If this is going to work, you can't do that. You can't act a hair different than before."

I nod infinitesimally. "Fine. Now shut up."

She grins. "Good. That's back to normal."

"I've got to meet Mom for breakfast soon. So if you want to do this, we better go right now."

At her nod, I head for the Security office. When it comes into view and I notice the tall, broad-shouldered guy sitting in the front, I pull up short. "Actually, maybe after breakfast is better. I should go shower right now. I stink."

"You barely broke a sweat, you freak of nature." Lark's eyes follow mine and her mouth breaks into a grin that nearly cracks her jaw. "You're such a chicken."

She's the only person on Ni'ihau who knows how hot I think Edam is, and now I regret telling her.

My cheeks flush, but before I can invent a more believable excuse than needing to shower, Lark pushes past me toward the office. I hear voices coming toward us from the opposite direction, voices I recognize. Kegan and Voron are in Lark's class. This is the perfect opportunity, which means I can't duck out no matter how badly I want to. I nearly swear under my breath, but Mom's injunction rises to my mind, like always. *Profanity is the crutch of the ignorant.* Gah.

"Chancy." Voron stops in front of me and offers a half bow.

"How many times do I have to tell you guys to quit with the bowing?" I hate it.

"At least one more time, your highness," Kegan says, offering a half bow of her own.

"I guess Lark doesn't bow anymore?" Voron asks.

"Anymore?" I ask. "She never bowed. Unless you count the times she did it mockingly."

"You'll miss having one person around who never bows," Lark says.

"I'm pretending you aren't leaving," I say.

"Since we're being placed next week, you can't pretend much longer," Lark says. "What are you two requesting?"

Voron groans. "Political liaison. Dad insists it's a perfect fit for me."

More like perfect for his schmoozy father. Voron's going to hate it.

"How about you?" Kegan asks Lark. "I heard you wanted Security."

Lark shrugs. "Yeah, but I don't want guard duty or attack force, which is the problem, so my family's pushing me to apprentice for Uncle Maximillian."

"I'd love an exciting assignment like intelligence too,"

Kegan says. "But as a fifteenth gen, I've got less than no chance."

Lark sighs, but before she can say anything, I cut her off. "You could challenge someone," I say.

"But who?" Kegan asks. "I'd have to defeat someone top level for it to help, and I'm mediocre at personal combat."

"If you beat me, you'd be placed first," I say.

Kegan shakes her head. "And get carved up like a turkey for my efforts? No thanks."

"She's not that tough," Lark says. "Hardly ever trains."

A surreptitious glance shows me Edam's listening from around the corner. Perfect.

"I'm not tough, huh?" I ask. "You couldn't take me."

"How would anyone know? No one's ever seen either of you fight." Voron crosses his arms. "I'd pay to see that match. I bet a lot of us would."

I arch one eyebrow. "You'd pay to watch me stab my friend? You're sadistic."

He grins. "Guilty."

"Well I don't know about Kegan, but I could take you for sure," Lark says.

"Oh please." I cross my arms. "You couldn't take me with one hand tied behind my back."

Lark raises one eyebrow. "I train every morning, and you watch television every chance you get. Which one of these things makes it likely you'll defeat me?"

That's actually not a lie. Heat rises in my cheeks again, maybe because I know Edam's listening. "Even so, I'm third in line for the throne. I'd destroy you."

Lark throws a hand up on her hip. "Destroy me, huh? Or maybe you wouldn't. And if I beat you, maybe you'll spend less time watching television and more time training. Your mom might thank me."

"You sound just like her," I say.

"Judica would gloat if she pummeled you," Lark says, "but, I'd only do it to teach you a lesson."

"Pummeling me?" I raise one eyebrow in irritation. "Ha."

"Fine. I'll do it." Lark's eyes flash and she lifts her chin.

"You'll do what?" I ask.

"Chancery Divinity Alamecha, I challenge you," Lark says.

Voron's jaw drops, and he swears. Obviously his dad hasn't pounded the same proscription on profanity into his head that my mom has.

"You wouldn't dare fight me," I say. "Because when you lose, you'll look unbelievably silly."

Lark lifts her chin and strides toward the Security office. "I'm serious, and I'll prove it right now."

She pushes through the door and pins Edam with a pointed look. "I'd like to record a challenge. Lark ne'Lyssa Alamecha challenges Chancery Divinity Alamecha."

I can't quite help from inching close enough to see Edam's perfect face with total clarity. He may be my evil twin's boyfriend, but there's no law against appreciating flawless, unparalleled beauty. His close-cropped blond hair gleams, even in the dull office lighting. His chiseled jawline, his aquiline nose, his full lips, all of them working together to create the most heart-stopping face I've ever seen. If I stand too close, he'll hear my heart pounding and he'll know. So I stay in the hallway.

And Judica doesn't chop my head off for ogling her boyfriend. At least, not today.

Lark watches as he writes our names down and then ducks out of the office. When she leaves, Edam's cerulean eyes lift rapidly. He catches me staring at him longingly. Shoot.

I snap my mouth closed and spin on my heel to lope toward the breakfast room where Mom's probably waiting.

Lark owes me for that nonsense. My life is hard enough without losing mismatched challenges and being outed for secret crushes.

"Chancery," a deep voice behind me says. My heart skips a beat, and I hope he didn't notice. The hall is utterly empty though, so I don't like my chances. How did Voron and Kegan disappear so quickly?

I pivot to face him and nearly trip over Cookie. "Edam." Why did he chase me down? Was I that obvious?

"I set your challenge with Lark for eleven a.m. today, but you left so fast I couldn't confirm whether that time will work, Your Highness. Are you accepting her challenge?"

I frown. "Don't call me that."

"I apologize, Your Highness. I tried calling you properly first, but you didn't reply."

He thinks I'm objecting to his use of Chancery. I want to sink into the floor. "No, I mean, don't call me 'your highness.' I hate it."

"You're second in line to the throne."

I roll my eyes. "I'm plain old Chancery. I'm not the Heir, so you don't need to call me anything but my given name."

"Fine. Chancery, then." He draws out the syllables in my name in a low tone that makes my shoulders feel tight.

I want to hear him say it again. Which is monumentally stupid. "Right, but the point is, eleven is fine. I'll be there. But for now, I'm late for breakfast with my mother."

Edam salutes me and straightens his impossibly broad frame. "I won't keep you then, just Chancery."

My stomach flips again. I wish he would keep me. I inhale a deep, ragged breath. I'm a mess today. It must be nerves. I've never fought anyone, much less in public. Mom's going to freak out. "Any last-minute tips for someone who's never fought in an official capacity in her life?"

Edam's eyebrows rise. "You're not off book yet?"

I shake my head. "Most people aren't, not until well into their twenties."

"You aren't most people, your high—er, Chancery. I assumed— but I'm sure you'll be fine."

"Lark's going to murder me, isn't she?"

Edam's eyebrows draw together. "I don't believe she's training in melodics."

"Nope. Her mother argues with mine frequently about the benefits of sladius and limitations of melodics. That's why Mom agreed to let Judica start there. Lyssa says sladius is easier to master, which is better—"

"Judica started there so she could protect herself from birth, as Heir."

I nod. "You think melodics is antiquated?"

Edam crosses his arms. "I don't, no."

My eyebrows draw together. "You trained in melodics?"

"No, but my mother did. She was formidable. It's a subtle, refined, nearly lost art form."

I scowl at him. Art form? "My mom trained in melodics." I really hate that I'm going to have to throw this fight. It's just going to bolster all the detractors' arguments against Mom's preferred, but currently unpopular, fighting method.

"I have the utmost respect for your mother, both as my Empress, and as a warrior." Edam's eyes haven't left mine.

I should walk away, but I can't. Once, when I wasn't even three years old, I popped a habanero pepper into my mouth. I didn't know whether to spit it out and cry, or close my eyes and savor the pain. Being around Edam is like that, except there's no chance I'd ever spit him out.

"Chancy," Mom calls from down the hall, "you're late."

Edam bows his head and departs so quickly I don't even

have time to admire his retreating form before he's rounding the corner. Mom never misses a beat, so I can't moon over Judica's boyfriend or she'll notice immediately. I ruffle the fur on Cookie's head and jog over to the small dining room where we always have breakfast.

Mom takes her usual seat, and I drop into mine next to her. "How'd the party planning go?"

Mom rolls her eyes. "I told Angel no lemon cake, but did she listen?"

I lift my eyebrows. "Really?"

Mom sighs. "Technically, she says she did. She made an orange cake with chocolate frosting, which is basically lemon's first cousin."

"Oh," I say, "but that's my favorite."

"And if it were your birthday, that would make sense."

I watch as my mom picks up her napkin. Tomorrow she'll be nine-hundred years old, which is old, even for us, but you'd never know to look at her. Her chestnut hair shines, her light golden skin luminesces, and her nearly violet eyes sparkle like she's only been alive three or four centuries.

Today the world's human rulers who report to her are coming to pay their respects: The United States' President, Senate and House leaders, the British Prime Minister and the President of Mexico to name a few. Not many humans know about us, but obviously the ones we use to administer the government as our figureheads do. Tomorrow, the heads of the other evian families will show up for her real party. She's a little stressed over all the details. Sometimes when she's anxious, she focuses a little too much on things that don't matter.

"Eat your eggs, Chancery," she says, because she always says that.

I never do.

I need to distract her so she won't notice I'm only

pushing them around on my plate. "Speaking of cakes, Angel and I spent a while yesterday on it, but no matter how many times we tried, we couldn't get the nine hundredth candle lit before the first hundred candles melted down to the frosting line." I pull out my phone and show her a photo of the melted goo on the left side of an enormous tiered cake that resulted from our fourth attempt. "Guess we'll have to use those big numbered candles this year instead. You know, a clunky number nine and two zeroes."

Mom's eyes crinkle. "You know very well we won't have any candles on my cake. It's beyond tacky, and a human tradition in the first place."

"You always put candles on my cake." I frown.

"That's because you're a child. Seventeen little flames look cute."

"Eighteen this year."

Her eyebrows crinkle in consternation. "Yes, you're getting quite old."

I point at her with my fork. "You're the expert on old, so I guess you'd know."

I love mornings in Ni'ihau with Mom. We live on the only desert island in Hawaii, and while I've occasionally wished we lived on nearby Kauai instead, at least I have a nice view of the lush, tropical island from our breakfast room. My mom doesn't seem to care about the view, since she always sits at the head of the table with her back to the windows. The sunlight streams down through her hair, just as bright in March as it would be any other month. The seasons don't really impact Hawaii like they do the rest of the world. The light illuminates her face in a sort of halo. I look past her toward the abundant vegetation of Kauai and sigh. In a moment the world will intrude, but for now she's all mine.

"Alora can't make it to my party," Mom says.

"She told me." Evian gatherings make my much older sister claustrophobic, but nine centuries is a big deal. I'm annoyed she's not coming to support our mom. She's not the only older sister who isn't coming, but she's the closest one to me, and the one I'll miss the most.

"She'll come visit sometime next week. We can celebrate together without all the political nonsense." Mom scrunches her nose. "Wait, when did she tell you?"

I try to act like it's no big deal. "She called me yesterday."

Mom's eyebrows rise slightly. "Alora did? When?"

Mom and I are usually together. "I stepped out to talk to her during the Military Council, remember?" And I don't really want to talk about Alora right now, or what I ducked out to ask her. I want to wait until after Mom's birthday so she'll be in a good mood when I make my request. I change the subject to the one thing I couldn't care less about. "Did I miss anything in the Council meeting?"

Mom shakes her head. "Not really. Judica petitioned for incursions against China again."

"What's her obsession with that?"

"She wants to make her mark. It's the only part of the world that isn't under direct evian control. That makes it an attractive target for all six families, but Judica's plagued by the burning desire of youth to prove her aptitude."

Poor China. I wouldn't wish Judica on anyone. "It's so hard, it'll be difficult to effectively administer. It's why we've failed in the past."

"True," Mom admits. "But our American branch owes the Chinese quite a lot of money currently. Judica may have mentioned that if we invade, we wouldn't have to pay it back."

"What's her plan this time?" Last month she wanted to

bomb them, and the month before that, she suggested an alliance with Vela, whom no one would suspect.

"She's proposing trade sanctions to soften the area. Divide it among all six, but heavily in our favor, of course." Mom chews and swallows more of her omelet. "She's learning."

"Why bring that up during Military Council?" I ask. "Seems like an economic initiative to me."

"If the US defaults on its debt, China will react, and that means military force. It would mostly be human lives at stake, but that still has an economic impact on our bottom line, and our strength in relation to the other families." Mom takes another bite and then glances at me sideways. She has realized that I distracted her. "What did Alora call about?"

At least she hasn't noticed that I'm not eating my eggs. A tiny win, but I'll take it. "Nothing much. She misses me. She called to invite me for a visit in New York. I still haven't seen anything on Broadway, and you promised."

It's funny that my sister feels closed in and unsafe here, on our tiny, mostly uninhabited island, but completely at home in New York, which is teeming with humans. She loves Broadway and theater productions, packing into a room full of people like sardines in a can. But the vast majority of humans don't know what we are, or even that we exist, which means she walks among them as a veritable goddess, and they have no idea. Very different than interacting with hundreds of other evians, all of whom want something from you, and all of whom are analyzing your every word, breath, and heartbeat.

Mom leans back in her chair with less relief than I expected. "Between my party tomorrow and yours in a few weeks, I've fallen behind. I doubt we can take a trip until late summer or early fall. Sorry little dove."

I've just stuffed a big bite of fruit in my mouth. I wait

to swallow it before responding. “I think she meant just me.”

Mom sets her fork down. “You’ve never gone anywhere without me.”

“True,” I say.

She frowns. “You’re too young.”

I don’t meet her eye. I’m not that young.

“Do you want to leave?” she asks. “Is there a reason she invited you?”

Uh, yeah, but if you don’t know, I’m not going to tell you. “She’s got a new show, I think. Chill, Mom. I told her I probably couldn’t go.” When I take another big bite, this time of toast, Mom takes the hint and changes the subject.

Even so, I can’t quite give up the dream: a long, simple visit to New York. No fear I’ll be attacked, because humans don’t know who I am. They just muddle along around us with their mediocre existences, producing more things for Alamecha to trade or sell to other countries. They go to war when Mom points, and they work at her bidding, without even realizing they’re doing it.

And if I could simply blend in among them, it would be amazing.

“Have you chosen your gown for my party?” Mom asks, tearing me away from my daydream of normal life.

I shake my head. “I was waiting for you, so we can match.”

“I wasn’t sure if you still wanted to.”

“Of course,” I say. “It’s our thing.”

She smiles. “Eventually you won’t want to match me anymore.”

But for today, I still do. “What’re you going to wear?”

“Maybe I’ll try on some gowns after breakfast and you can help me choose.”

It’s as good a time as any to confess. “I’d love to help you, but I’ll need to do it this afternoon.”

Mom wipes her mouth with a pristine linen napkin. "You are full of surprises today. What do you have planned after breakfast?"

"So, Lark and I got into a discussion in the hall earlier, and I might have goaded her a little bit. I'm not sure what came over me."

"What's going on, Chancy?"

I clear my throat. "She challenged me. Probably because I don't know how to fight very well, and if she can beat me, she'll be ranked first in her class and get whatever placement she wants." I hate how my voice shakes near the end of my explanation.

"I'll talk to Lyssa. I find the ingratitude appalling."

I shake my head. "I didn't have to agree, but with a few other kids around, I figured refusing would look...weak."

"You'll destroy her."

Oh, no. Mom and everyone else needs to believe I'm a bumbler and that's the reason that I lose. "Mom, I've never fought anyone. Not ever."

"Which is why she should never have challenged you. It was selfish and extremely inappropriate."

"She's my best friend."

"She's not acting like it." Mom frowns. "Why aren't you upset?"

I gulp. Mom needs to believe this too, more than anyone else, actually. "We knew it would happen at some point, that I'd have to fight in some kind of formal situation."

"You're my daughter, only seven generations removed from Eve herself. Your genetics are as pure as anyone alive. Whether you've trained in melodics or sladius is irrelevant, whether you've gone off book yet, whether you're nervous or not, you will defeat her."

I glance around the room. "Is Judica in here and I didn't see her? You're talking to *me*, Mom, and I love Lark. So if I can help her place first, and I'm unlikely to win in any case, where's the harm?"

Mom purses her lips but doesn't argue. Because more than anyone else on the island, she knows who I am. The kind-hearted Alamecha daughter. The weak twin. The one who probably couldn't win if her life depended on it. And she needs to believe I'm a loser, or she'll see right through my act and the stakes are far too high for that. Lark and her mother would almost surely die for this secret, and maybe me too.

After a few terribly long seconds, Mom places her hand over mine and squeezes. She knows me for what I am, and she loves me anyway. Glaring flaws and all.

Mom doesn't chastise me or give me unhelpful last minute tips. She knows I haven't ever fought anyone in a real match, and I might lose. We have zero time to prepare, so there's no point stressing over it. She refocuses on eating, and unlike me, she loves eggs. Her gold-rimmed plate is piled high: two boiled eggs, two fried eggs, and the last bite or two of an omelet. Evian bodies need protein, lots of protein. Long life, incredible strength, and quick intellect are a few of the gifts of our pure DNA, but compared to humans with corrupt DNA, we have to eat a lot. Trade-offs.

I grab a few pieces of ham to make up for skipping Mom's favorite food. Mom notices but doesn't complain. In light of my confession, dickering over my egg consumption probably seems pointless.

"Which dresses are you considering?" I ask. "You need to make a statement this year, clearly."

"Should I be wearing a funeral shroud do you think?"

I roll my eyes. "You've got decades and decades left. You're healthy, wise, and strong."

"Decades and decades, huh?"

No one has ever lived past a thousand years. It's a sore

point for evians, or at least, once they reach their last century it is. Everyone knows that once you start showing any real signs of age, you've got a few years left at best, or maybe only months. Good thing Mom hasn't gone gray, sprouted crows' feet, or started sprouting liver spots. "You know what I mean."

"I do, and I'm mostly teasing." She smiles. "I was thinking about the new Chanel—"

The solid wood entry doors fly open and slam against the wall on either side, effectively halting our conversation. There's only one person who wouldn't knock, so I already know who barged in, but I glance up anyway.

Judica.

My sister is the worst.

No, I mean, really. A lot of people have probably thought that over the past six thousand or so years, but I'm pretty sure I'm right. She started pulling my hair and biting me in utero, and my mom has the ultrasound photos to prove it. That was, quite literally, just the beginning. You'd think by seventeen, I'd have toughened up a bit, but she still hurts my feelings pretty often.

I'm lucky when that's all she hurts.

I grit my teeth as she strolls in, flanked by her tall black Doberman Pinscher, Death, and the head of her personal guard and boyfriend, Edam ne'Malessa ex'Alamecha. Only two places are set at the breakfast table, but that doesn't stop my twin from dragging an empty chair over near us and sitting down right across from me. She's wearing her typical knee-high black boots laced up over tight black pants. Her white button-down shirt is pristine, which makes me feel bad about my sloppy t-shirt and denim shorts.

Not that it's a competition, because, of course, I always lose.

Her hair is pulled back into a high ponytail that falls in

a cascade down her back. She wears hers straight most of the time. It compliments her broodiness and severe looks. Our faces may be identical, but I've tried to set myself apart a little. I never bother straightening my waves and curls, which helps, and as soon as I learned how, I darkened my skin tone and changed the color of my eyes slightly to keep people from mixing us up. I still change my eye color every few weeks, actually.

Even so, I hate sharing a face with someone so hateful.

"Good morning Mother," she says.

Death stretches before curling up at her feet. Edam steps back to stand unobtrusively by the doorway. His eyes meet mine for a split second. A little zing runs up my spine, but I refuse to shiver or turn away. The corner of his mouth turns up ever so slightly before he breaks the connection and looks out the window as if evaluating the waves outside for any potential threats. His golden hair is perfectly mussed, and a muscle in his jaw twitches slightly.

I try not to stare at him. I don't succeed, but I try.

"Good morning Judica," Mom says.

I force myself to say, "So glad you could join us."

She half snorts by way of response, which I take as a sign she's having a very good day.

"There are over a hundred petitions to hear," Judica says. "They all came a day early for the party."

My mother's Empress of the First Family of Eve. It has some great perks, but it carries a load of downsides, too. Ruling on disputes when the Alamecha family arbitrators have failed is one of the worst, but today it means an awful lot of the people here will be loitering around in the throne room.

Normally I wouldn't care, but if they're in the throne room either being heard or watching the proceedings, they're not around the ring watching me throw a fight to Lark.

"Really?" I force a fake groan. "Great present, right Mom? Happy Birthday, now please settle my petty arguments."

"It's certainly not the best part of my birthday each year," Mom says.

"Maybe you can split them up," I say.

Judica lifts one eyebrow. "You think *you* can settle their petitions?"

I shrug. "I might not get them all right, but for instance, I do feel bad for the women having half-human kids. I've been meaning to talk to you, Mom. Maybe we can stop banishing them. Corrupt DNA or not, they're half-evian. Surely Alamecha can use them somehow, even if it's just in a spy network, where clearly they'd be an asset on the human side. Since we force them out, frequently their mothers go with them, and we lose full evian women forever. It's silly."

Judica snorts. "The law is clear, and there's a reason for all of it. Half-evian children are gods among the humans, but keep them here, train them with the sons and daughters of Alamecha? They'd be nothing, less than nothing. I wouldn't condemn any child to that kind of guaranteed failure."

"We could set up a separate curriculum," I say, "only children with—"

Mom clears her throat. "You're right Judica, that particular law is for the good of the children and for the safety of our family. And on top of that, without repercussions, the risk of interbreeding becomes too commonplace. We must keep our bloodlines pure."

Interbreeding? It's not like they're dogs and we're people. We're all people. I just don't have the guts to argue any more. Not with Judica here to swipe at me.

Oh how I despise it when Judica gloats.

"But perhaps as my Heir, Judica," Mom says, "you could

start the petitions alone today. Begin with the lower echelons and work forward. By the time you've reached the petitions from seventh, eighth, and ninth generation family members, I'll be present to help. Perhaps I'll be there even sooner. I have some business to attend to beforehand." Mom glances sharply my way.

Ugh, she's going to watch my match. At least she's maneuvered Judica out of watching it.

My twin pales slightly, but her heart rate remains steady. Her control's amazing. I need to practice hiding my emotions. I stink at it.

Judica inclines her head slightly. "As you wish, Mother."

"Chancery and I are going to choose our gowns for my party this afternoon after I complete the petitions. I assume you're wearing your signature black?"

Judica's face is blank. "I'll wear whatever you'd like. It's your birthday." Her heart rate doesn't increase, and she isn't sweating or I'd smell it. She means it. She doesn't care what she wears. I'd be upset if my mom matched Judica and not me, but she's indifferent. Sometimes I think she's broken inside.

I reach for the last pancake, but Judica snatches it from the platter first. She loads up her plate with fresh fruit, bacon and toast, and then pours syrup over the top of all of it.

I clear my throat, but she doesn't glance my way.

"Do you need me to do anything else?" Judica asks.

Mom smiles. "After petitions and gown selection, you'll both train. Other than party preparation, petitions and accepting homage from the human dignitaries, today is a normal day."

I notice two triangles of French toast on a plate at the edge of the table and reach over to spear them, but before I can, Judica slams her pointy silver fork into the back of my hand and keeps shoving until the tines have rammed through skin, sinew, and bone, and sunk deep into the wood of the table. The pain radiates up my arm as my blood spurts downward and spreads outward across the white linen tablecloth. Judica lets go of the fork and tosses the French toast I wanted on the ground.

To her dog.

Death snaps up both pieces without batting an eye. I grit my teeth so I don't whimper when I use my left hand to yank the fork out of my right. I flex my hand to make sure the muscles knit together properly and the bones don't need to be rebroken. Luckily, they seem fine. I watch as skin grows across the puncture holes. Once I've healed, I use my napkin to wipe the blood from my palm and the back of my hand. There's not much I can do about the ruined tablecloth, or holes in the enormous oak breakfast table that are probably permanently soaked with my blood.

The worst part is, now all that's left on the serving dishes are eggs, which Judica knows I hate. I've finally restored my composure enough to glance at my mom. I wait for a moment to see if she'll do anything. A glance, a harsh word, or even a hand on my arm to tell me she's sorry Judica's so awful.

Predictably, Mom acts like nothing happened.

Something dies inside me, not because this is different than any other day, but precisely because it isn't. No day will ever be different. Judica was born thirty-six seconds after me. To preserve the bloodline and maintain our genetic supremacy, the youngest daughter is always Heir. My whole life was ruined by thirty-six seconds.

Mom will turn a blind eye to the actions of her Heir forever.

Beneath me, Cookie whines. I want to whimper too, but it isn't worth it. It just isn't. I look at Judica's plate, piled high with everything but eggs and I consider trying to pilfer something from her plate, but that's not me. I never sink to her level, and I never bait her. I'd probably just get my hand stabbed again for my efforts. Or maybe she'd bop me on the nose with a newspaper.

"You seem quite taken with your silverware, Chancery. Eggs?" Judica holds up the bowl of boiled eggs and feigns passing them to me. Her eyes gleam and I want to slap her face.

Instead, I stand and rub my freshly healed hand against my cut-off shorts. "I'm not hungry. I'll see you in a bit, Mom."

Mom stands up, too. "No need. I'll walk with you." My mom and I walk out, and I can't help but glance back over my shoulder. Judica isn't even looking my direction, and I hate myself for checking. But Edam catches my eye and half grins, half grimaces.

I whip back around and practically jog from the room. What does his expression mean? Is he laughing at me? Or maybe he feels sorry for me. The wheels in my brain whir around so fast, I'm worried Mom will hear them. Or notice the cartoon smoke pouring out of my ears.

"It was a very imprudent thing you did," Mom says.

Huh? Staring at Edam?

"I've been mulling it over, and you may be right. It's extremely unlikely you'll defeat Lark. Melodics doesn't work like that. Until you're ready to go off book, you're more of a dancer than a fighter."

Duh. She's worried about me looking like a moron in front of, well, everyone we know. And the pain of all the stabbing and slashing while I'm losing, well, that's going to suck, too. "She didn't say this explicitly, but I think she needs this, Mom. She wants to do intelligence, but she's crap at changing her appearance. She needs another leg up, or she'll end up pulling guard duty for the next decade."

"Would it be so bad to have her around the palace a while longer?"

Mom wants Lark to stay. Of course she does, and so do I, but not if it makes her miserable. Besides, now that I know her secret, I understand why she needs to go, and why her mother is pushing her toward her reclusive Uncle Max and his never-ending number crunching. Her odds of being caught rise dramatically if she stays at Alamecha central command, but hiding in a dark room, staring at a computer screen is her best option to go unnoticed.

Lark's biggest problem is that the difference between evian and half-evian will become more and more obvious as she advances in her training.

"Of course I'll miss her, but I want her to do what makes her happy," I say. "Everyone should want that for the people they love."

Mom frowns. "Well, not only will her departure make you miserable, but losing this challenge to her won't make things easier for you when she does leave."

I've toyed with this idea for weeks, and the only person who knows is Alora, but something about my mom's criticism of my decision pushes me over the edge. "Which probably won't matter."

"Excuse me?" We've reached the door to Mom's room, guards at attention on either side of it. I won't miss the complete and total lack of privacy here, that's for sure.

I shove past them and after Mom follows, I close the door behind us. The familiar color scheme soothes me. Gold brocade curtains with pale pink swirls. An ivory and pale pink embroidered bedspread. Shaved and contoured carpet so thick it's practically springy. Portraits on either side of her colossal four-poster bed. I'm smiling in mine, but Judica isn't.

This room is so familiar, I could sketch the entire thing without needing to close my eyes and recall any memories. I breathe in and out once, then twice. It smells like my mom. Like safety. Like home. This is my center.

But not anymore. Lark's moving on, and it's time for me to do the same.

"Mom. I have something to tell you. Something you may not like."

Mom's eyebrows rise. "Something other than news of the challenge you rashly accepted?"

The one Mom expects me to lose? I swallow and forge ahead. "I want to move to New York and live with Alora."

3

Mom doesn't blink when she orders kings and presidents around. She never falters when she chastises friends and political allies, or enemies and rivals. She's utterly stoic as she sentences criminals to death.

But right now her lips part and she splutters in a satisfying way. "For a few weeks?"

I shake my head. "For the foreseeable future."

Mom's eyelids flutter like I've wounded her. "Why?"

I don't want to break Mom's heart. I don't even want to crack it. Maybe I should just keep soldiering along. But then I think about Judica stabbing me with a fork today while Mom looked on impassively. Not a raised eyebrow, not a cluck or a murmur.

"It's not that I want to leave you," I say, "but I have a lot to learn, and I can't stay here forever."

"You're learning everything you need to know from me."

What she doesn't say is that I don't really need to learn anything, not really. Because I have no purpose here. Not like Judica, or Lark, or every other evian I've met. I have no future. I just follow Mom around, keeping her company, like a really sophisticated and interactive pet. I can't do it forever. I need to find a place where I can grow, stretch, learn. And that place can't be anywhere near my twin. It can't.

Mom's grandfather clock chimes and I realize I only have half an hour before I need to check in for my challenge with Lark. "Can we talk about this later? I need to prepare to be decimated right now."

"You're far faster than she is," Mom says. "All you need to do is focus on your strengths. And stab her with the pointy end."

"Thanks for the vote of confidence," I say.

"Oh I think I can offer more than encouragement. I've got a few tips to share to help you prepare."

I lift my eyebrows. Mom's advising me outside melodics? "Uh, sure, great."

Mom ducks into her closet and comes out wearing training gear: white pants and a white shirt. She tosses me the same. "Put these on."

I do, quickly.

"We're fighting in your bedroom?" I glance at her pristine furniture, carpet, and bedding.

"Of course not." She tosses her head toward the courtyard and snags two swords from a rack above her door, handing one to me as she walks toward the back door.

My eyes widen. Alright.

She steps out onto the cobblestones barefoot, and I follow her lead.

"Your forms are perfect, your melodies precise and true. Think of what you've learned like making cake batter. You've got the basic ingredients, and you've mixed them up. You just haven't baked it all together or frosted it yet. But you're close, and that part is easy once you understand the method."

"Meanwhile Lark can open her own bakery."

Mom shrugs. "As a warrior, Lyssa's technique is flawless. I'm sure she's passed that skill and focus along to her daughter. Ironically, no one's seen Lark fight before to know, just like you." She closes her eyes briefly, as if she's praying silently. "I'd slap that little brat right now if she showed up in the doorway."

"Good thing she won't," I say.

"I suppose that's true. I love her mother, and I always thought she kept Lark out of the public eye to take the pressure off of you."

"Why didn't you train me publicly?" I wish the words back almost immediately. I'm not sure I want to know the answer.

A gentle smile steals across Mom's face. "First it was that I was greedy and didn't want to share you, but then as you grew older, I didn't want to draw Judica's attention to your development. Your upbringing diverged so much that I didn't want her watching you, preparing herself to defeat you specifically."

Emotion surges in my chest. Mom did want to keep me safe. She did try to protect me from Judica.

Mom drops into andante, one of the warrior poses, and begins to circle me slowly. "You know the proper positions. Normally I'd wait a while before adding blades, but who knows what may connect or when? My mother insisted no melodics master truly succeeded in going off book without being forced. She challenged me herself on my eighteenth birthday, and our fight was a terrible mess." Mom shakes her head. "I suppose we all meet our trial by fire at some point. And maybe I'd never think you were ready, you're so precious to me. I hate to see you struggle, and I know that has held you back from rising to your potential."

"I'm not ferocious like Judica, but I'm still your daughter." I drop into andante and hold it, opposite her, lifting my sword arm in mimicry of hers.

"First thing you do is assess your environment. You'll be in a ring, so raised from the floor, with only small ropes to hold you in place. A natural skylight overhead and people watching."

I nod, because duh. I've seen challenges before. Maybe she's talking to herself, preparing herself by starting at the beginning.

"Keep moving, because that's how you find openings and keep changing the target you present to your opponent."

"Okay." I shift the heavy hilt in my sweaty palm.

"You've got a heavy sword there, so grip it with both hands. I wish we'd had time to test you with a variety of blades, including short swords, broadswords, daggers, scythes, and the like. Everyone has a natural propensity for a particular offensive method, but for now, you get one of mine."

Maybe I can blame my failure on using the wrong blade. "What about deflecting?"

"Your grandmother preferred to use two swords, one to block and the other to attack. I prefer vambraces. I'll give you a pair."

I glance at my mom's shiny metal cuffs. She's worn them my entire life, and I almost forgot she had them on. "Thanks."

"Now, keep your sword here, at the ready." She angles sideways so I can see hers, at a forty-five degree angle from perpendicular. "You can move it up or down, right or left from here. Choose your lead, probably right for you, and keep that foot forward, just like you hold your hand in the second and third arias."

"We're short on time, Mom."

"I know that, and I have a point. I'm trying to

connect a few dots for you first. For instance, you know your eight basic angles of attack, you just may not know you know them because you haven't ever used them. Your goal is to drop into the music of the room, without hearing any."

I shake my head. "I have no idea what that means."

She smiles. "I know, but one day it'll click."

"Very helpful."

Without warning, Mom leaps toward me, sword extended. I shift sideways, acting on pure instinct, but my sword is heavy and it slows me down. The edge of Mom's sword slices my right forearm near my wrist.

"Oww," I complain.

Mom swings around, her sword halting an inch before my throat. She laughs. "And you're dead."

"Okay," I say, my arm healed. "Let's try again."

She does, lunging at me from a basic andante and waiting for me to block. I do better the second time, and much better the third and fourth.

Then she stops and drops the tip of her sword. "But you don't win by blocking."

"Okay." I have no intention of even trying to win, but she can't know that.

As if she can read my mind, Mom's sword arm goes slack. "Do you even want to beat Lark?" Her eyes fill with compassion. "Be honest."

I shrug. "I've never been a warrior. It's not part of who I am like it is with you or with Judica."

"You're stronger than you know, Chancy. Truly."

I wish strength didn't mean hurting people, but for us it does. "Well, lay it on me then. How do I win?"

"It's not the same for everyone, but your hurdle will be overcoming your disdain for causing pain. You can really only win a fight on the offensive. Defense just prolongs your defeat. It may help you to know that a quick win is much less painful than a protracted one. So a few calculated injuries may be the most merciful course."

"I need to strike you quickly and with purpose. That's what you're saying."

Mom's lips compress grimly.

Before I have time to think it through, I swing at her, and she's close enough that my borrowed blade will connect. She doesn't block or make any move to stop me.

Horrified, I pull back. "Mom!"

"And that's the crux of your problem."

I frown. "What is?"

"You can't bring yourself to hurt people, Chancy. Until you can, it doesn't matter whether melodics clicks for you or not. You can't survive among our people without hurting anyone, and you certainly can't leave me and go to New York City until I believe you're capable of defending yourself."

Great. Now Mom will use my loss to Lark as ammunition to keep me here, under Judica's thumb. Or fork, as the case may be.

I glance at my watch. "Five minutes. I better go wash off this blood and get ready to be destroyed."

At least Mom won't think it's weird when Lark beats me, which is my real goal. I wish it didn't bother me that everyone will think I'm as pathetic as Mom does.

I jog through the doorway to my adjoining room and change clothes, tossing the shirt and pants I borrowed from Mom into the corner. I pull on a fitted white shirt and tight white pants for the challenge, and then tug my hair into a high ponytail. I consider removing my purple stone necklace. It's large and ornate, and I'm worried it may get in the way during the challenge. On the other hand, Mom made me promise never to remove it. So in the end, I leave it alone.

My heart races as I lace up my shoes, and I focus on

calming it. I can't have every evian in attendance knowing I'm agitated. Why did I agree to this again? Oh, right. Lark needs me.

I can do this for her. I can. Maybe if I repeat that over and over in my head, it'll be true. Poor Lark deserves a better friend than me.

Ironically, if I were better, I couldn't do her this favor. It's only because I'm pathetic that people will believe my defeat. Take that, fate. I listen for my Mom next door, but don't hear anything. She's either still in our private courtyard, or she's already left her room. She doesn't typically attend private challenges, but I have a feeling she's coming to this one.

My room is simpler than Mom's, but features the same colors. Hardly surprising, since she designed it for me, remodeling my father's old room to be a nursery and then updating it again when I turned ten. At least Mom's consistent in what she likes. I pad across my thick, contoured carpet to the exterior door and yank it open. My heart's beating at a normal rate, and I'm holding the sword Mom loaned me. I'm as prepared as I can be, and there's no point in being late for something I've agreed to do.

I walk briskly down the long breezeway to the combat hall. I really, really hope it's Mom's War Lord Balthasar officiating, not his second-in-command. Edam's already seen me look pathetic. Twice. I'd rather not add a third instance in the same day. So of course, when I walk through the enormous doorway into the room, Edam's standing up on the raised dais. His eyes meet mine and my heart picks up speed. Dang it.

And then I glance around and notice the entire hall is packed. Why have this many people turned out for a simple challenge? Probably because we've both been trained by our mothers in secret for seventeen years.

Sometimes evian life can really suck.

Lark's already standing on the platform behind Edam. Her face would look blank to anyone else, but I notice the tension between her eyebrows and the tight set of her mouth. I glance around at the people I've known my entire life as I walk up the stairs, waiting to watch and pass judgment.

Once I'm close enough that she can hear me, I whisper. "I didn't realize how boring things had gotten around here."

I may not be the scary twin, the powerful twin, the warrior twin. But at least I'm funny.

"With my birthday celebration tomorrow and dozens of humans in attendance today," my mother says quite loudly behind me, "I'm surprised more of them aren't attending to what I assume are pressing duties." Her words scatter at least a third of the audience, which I appreciate.

Mom changed out of her simple white pants and shirt, and is now wearing a rich, chocolate taffeta evening gown, with a stiff, high collar. She rustles as she approaches the ring. "Good luck, little dove," she whispers.

I'd rather everyone on the island stay, if only Mom wouldn't watch herself. I should just be grateful Judica's not here. I wonder why Edam didn't mention it to her. She'd hold off on hearing petitions to watch me be humiliated every day of the week and twice on Monday.

"Where's Balthasar?" I whisper to Lark.

Before she can answer, Edam does. "He's reviewing last minute party plans for your mother's gala tomorrow. I figured that was more important than a friendly challenge. Lark indicated it's to first major injury. Do you concur?"

Spine, head, heart, severed limb. I nod mutely. Those all sound plenty bad to me.

Edam raises his voice so everyone can hear. "Lark ne'Lyssa Alamecha has challenged Chancery Alamecha, second heir to the throne of Family Alamecha, seventh removed from Eve, to first major. The results will be determined by Empress Enora Alamecha. We are honored by her presence." He bows.

"We are honored by her presence," the audience repeats.

My mother nods my direction. "They've selected blades?"

First major injury by hand-to-hand combat could take hours. Gross.

"Yes," I say at the same time as Lark. I lift my longsword-on-loan and Lark lifts her weapon, a curved sword that looks much lighter than mine. I wish I had a weapon of my own.

"I'll count them off." Edam walks to the edge of the platform and claps four times, followed by chanting, "Three, two, one." He flips over the edge of the platform and lands on the balls of his feet outside the arena.

I should have been paying less attention to Edam and more to Lark, clearly. Her sword arcs down toward my right side, about to strike my right shoulder.

When I step aside from her cut easily, I realize we may be in trouble. I thought she'd destroy me since I haven't done any actual fights, but she's slow. Really slow. And if I don't figure out how to make this quick, everyone else is bound to notice.

"Afraid to hurt your friend?" I ask, trying to play off her speed limitations as reticence. That's believable, right?

Lark narrows her eyes at me, and slams her sword toward me directly, much faster this time. I block it, but the force slams me back several steps and I bump into the ropes. I press back, and she parries several blows by me before twisting her curved sword around, hooking it under mine, and shoving it wide.

When she yanks backward with hers, it clips my ribs and the sharp edge of her blade splits the side of my body open. I nearly drop my sword. Blood pours out of the slice and I focus on healing it. Unfortunately, that distracts me from Lark's next attack, and I don't block it. Her blade slams into my right arm, and this time I do drop Mom's sword when I spin away from her.

No sword, two wounds, no time. I agreed to throw this match, but at this rate, I'll be a laughingstock. And no one even knows she's half human. Good grief. I drop into andante and slowly edge away from Lark, even though I know she's driving me to the opposite side of the dais from my blade.

That's fine. I don't need my blade when I can take hers. She jabs, but this time, instead of blocking, I let her stab me in the stomach. I grab her blade and yank, toppling her into me. I know pain. Judica hurts me all the time, but even so, I didn't expect the lancing agony when Lark's scimitar pierces both my liver and my kidney.

Spots dance in front of my eyes.

I am evian. I can do this. I stomp on her foot and pull harder on her blade, wrestling for control. I toss it in the air and catch it in my blood-slicked hands, ready to do some damage. And then it hits me that Lark may not be able to heal a major wound. I can't chance it. I have no idea what she can heal, or how long it takes.

We should have taken at least a day to prepare.

So when Lark springs away from me and inches backward toward my sword, I act like I don't even realize she's doing it. I advance on her directly, backing her right into her last chance. I feint left and then cut her right arm. Not deep, but I better do some damage or we'll never sell this. Then I cut at her from the right, hard, and she drops into a crouch to snag my sword. When she stands back up, I don't pull back. She pivots and brings her new blade straight up into my belly.

It slides through my stomach and shoves onward, severing my spine. I collapse on the floor of the ring like a marionette with cut strings, blood bubbling up into my mouth. When I cough, I spray blood all over Lark's pants. I've healed the slice on my side and my arm, and my hands are nearly healed, but it feels like a fire poker is incinerating my insides. At least I can't feel anything from the waist down. I've always heard that's the best thing about spinal cord injuries.

Edam leaps onto the platform, his feet on either side of my face. He shifts me slightly, gauging the damage. "Her spine's been severed."

The audience doesn't shout or hoot or murmur. They're utterly silent. I take my nearly healed hands and grasp the blade and tug. It doesn't budge. I'm supposed to remove the blade myself, but I'm not sure I can. I close my eyes to try and steel my resolve.

Everyone's watching. I grit my teeth and turn so that I have a better grip on the blade, and I yank again. It shifts two inches and blood gushes from my stomach onto the mat. It also bubbles up into my throat. I cough again to clear my airway and spit it out next to me.

Lark pales and her eyes widen in concern. I hope she gets it together soon, or attract undue attention. I shove up on one elbow and use the angle to force the blade out the rest of the way. Then I focus immediately on healing my spinal column. It only takes ten seconds or so, but they drag on and on.

Once I've fixed that, I close my eyes and sink back to the mat to focus on the rest. Stomach, abdominal muscles. "I'm fine," I say. "Lark beat me, well and truly."

Mom stands up and brushes off her immaculate skirt. "I have work to do." She spins on her heel and marches out of the room. The rest of the audience begins to whisper after she leaves, but I don't listen to a single word. As I heal up all the minor wounds and seals things off, I can't quite suppress a small smile of relief. Mom may be annoyed or embarrassed, and I will surely catch crap from Judica, but Lark is a lock for an intelligence placement where she'll be safe. We did it.

When I open my eyes, Edam's watching me, and I don't like his pensive expression.

"What?" I ask softly.

"Most people don't look happy when they lose."

"I'm not happy." I force myself to sit up as the skin of my abdomen closes up. "I'm relieved I'm not hurting anymore. That's all."

"Your sister becomes downright hostile." He offers me a hand, which I accept.

"I heard she never loses."

"Everyone loses sometimes," he says.

"Speaking of Judica, why aren't you guarding her? Aren't you head of her personal guard?"

Edam shrugs. "I run the guard roster, and I take my turns, but I'm not watching her all the time. Besides, my duties as Balthasar's second take precedence, and he asked me to moderate this." He reaches for my blade.

I snap it up off the floor before he can.

"I can clean it for you," he offers.

"No," I say childishly. "I always clean it myself." As if it's not completely obvious to everyone in the room it was my first time ever using a sword. It's like my IQ drops fifty points around Edam.

"As you like," he says. "But for the record, I didn't think you did badly at all." His voice drops to the barest whisper. "In fact, I really thought you had her."

If Mom hadn't drilled it into my head that swearing is a sign of low intelligence, I'd say a horrible word under my breath. Because I just healed my severed spine, and I thought we were in the clear. My only play is to act like I have no idea what he means.

"I thought so, too. Overconfidence, maybe. I've clearly

got some hard training ahead of me. Mom looked... displeased."

Edam studies my face for a moment, his eyes travelling from my mouth up to my eyes. "I'd be happy to help, if you ever want to try any other training methods."

Studying with my twin's super hot, uber intense boyfriend? Umm, I really want to say yes, and I also want to run away screaming. Lark notices I'm drowning and jumps in to drag me to shore. "We both better get cleaned up. Thanks for moderating."

Edam straightens and assumes the expression I'm used to seeing. Total absence of any emotion. "Of course. It's my job." When he straightens, I notice my blood on his pants and sleeve.

"Uh, you might need to change clothes," I say. "Sorry."

He shakes his head. "Part of the job. I'm glad you healed up so well." He salutes and heads for the office, presumably to record Lark's win.

When I make for the exit, no one tries stopping me. Once I've showered and cleaned up, I tap on Mom's door. No response, but I push through. She's not there, so I leave. No guards outside her door means she's already en route to the petition hall. I groan and hang a right.

There's no part of me that wishes I was Mom's Heir. If I've learned anything in the past seventeen years, it's that being an empress sucks. But the worst task of all, in my opinion, is making decisions about how to punish whiny people who can't get along. And evians have got to be the world's most entitled group of complainers. Luckily, I reach the petition hall at the perfect time.

"That's everyone on the docket," Mom says. "Unless there are any petitioners who didn't file formally?"

In seventeen years, I've never seen anyone register an informal complaint. These petitions are prepared, researched, and evidence is assembled in advance.

"Your Majesty." Balthasar steps toward Mom. "There has been an anonymous complaint filed." He hands her an envelope.

"What is this?" Mom looks around the room expectantly, waiting for a petitioner to step forward.

"Did you read this?" she asks him. "Anonymous complaints aren't allowed."

He shakes his head.

"Who brought it to you?" Mom's eyes flash and her fingers tap on the armrest of her throne. "I have half a mind to toss it in the trash. If someone can't be bothered to speak their complaint, why should I take the time to hear it?"

No one responds.

Mom sighs and slides a finger under the seal of the envelope. Fear spikes through me. What are the odds that something like this happens on the very day I let Lark defeat me?

"Wait," I shout. "Think about the precedent this will set. Toss it, and let them bring a formal complaint in the future or nothing at all."

Judica raises one eyebrow, scenting blood obviously. "I'd like to know what it says."

Mother's already reading, and her face drains of color. The only time I recall seeing her react this obviously was to communications from my older sister, Melina. Surely it's not a birthday card from Melina disguised as a petition? Or worse, a threat from her?

"Lyssa ex'Alamecha," Mom says, her voice sepulchral.

I close my eyes, as if this might all disappear. I snap them open, in case anyone is watching me. But all eyes are on Lark's mother.

Lyssa stands up from the second row of the audience and turns back toward me briefly, her eyes questioning. Even if no one saw me close my eyes, people noticed that look. I glance surreptitiously around, looking for Lark, but I don't see her. What are the odds that Lyssa's summoning is unconnected to today's challenge? My stomach turns and I want to expel whatever is left of my breakfast onto the swirly white and gray marble floor. That kind of reaction would draw far too much attention my direction.

Lyssa kneels at the foot of Mom's throne. Judica shifts uneasily in her smaller throne next to Mom. I should be sitting on Mom's other side, but I'm frozen in place at the back of the room.

"It has been alleged, and a DNA test has been provided as evidence, that your daughter, Lark ne'Lyssa Alamecha, is half human."

My hands shake and I force myself to still them. Was it Edam? Did he figure us out? Did he notice where the blood spatter from the one injury I caused to Lark landed? Did he commission the test? How could it have been completed this quickly?

Is this my fault?

"That's ridiculous." I stride quickly toward the thrones. I step up into my place at Mom's side, forcing myself to look impartially at Lyssa. As if I don't care. As if I'm not crumbling to pieces inside.

Mom ignores me. "Lyssa ne'Davina Alamecha, answer my question. Is your daughter half-human?"

Lyssa bows her head. "She is, Your Majesty."

"And you hid this from me for more than eighteen years."

I silently will her to say she didn't know. If she'd only claim she suspected, but didn't believe. Perhaps she could claim she recently discovered the truth.

Give Mom something to work with, Lyssa. Anything.

She obviously doesn't hear my urging, and she isn't thinking along the same lines. Her whispered defense won't help, either. "Lark had no idea."

"She knew nothing?" Judica grins. "Which means nothing, since you're saying she *had* no idea. Which means she knows now. Unless you're claiming she anonymously turned herself in. Whether she knew for an hour or a decade without immediately surrendering, the punishment is the same."

I roll my eyes. "You can't really mean—"

Judica shouts. "Lyssa's been training her daughter in private for years. Obviously that was to cover this abominable lie."

"I train alone," I say.

"Because you're pathetic." Judica sneers. "I honestly don't know which is worse."

"She asked me why she trained alone," Lyssa's voice wavers. "I told her it was to preserve the mystique of her skill, Your Highness."

Judica stands up and steps down so she's eye level with Lyssa. "You told her she had to train alone because otherwise the entire evian world would see her for what she is." Judica's face twists. "Trash." I never realized how much she hates humans.

"I did not," Lyssa says. "She never knew."

"Liar," Judica says. "You're compounding your crimes by trying to protect her."

"Step back, Heir," Mom says. "This is my interrogation."

Judica's fists clench, but she steps back and sits down.

"Why did you keep her?" I ask softly.

"Because I loved her. From the moment she was born and I realized she wasn't Paolo's child, I knew she was half-human. But my love for her kept me from giving her up." She meets my mother's eye, and I don't know what she sees, but Lyssa flinches and looks back down at the ground.

"You should have left with her," Mom says. "You know the law."

"I do," Lyssa whispers. "I broke it, and I will accept your judgment."

"Others knew," Judica says. "They must have. Didn't Lark have some kind of challenge today? I just heard—"

"Lyssa ex'Alamecha." Mom cuts Judica off. "I convict you of treason, compounded by eighteen years' time and unmitigated by confession. I take no pleasure in this, but I sentence you to immediate death by beheading."

Mom draws her sword from the sheath at her side with a snick and before I've even stood up to protest, she beheads her best friend of more than eight hundred years with a single stroke.

4

Enora the Merciless.

That was Mom's moniker for almost nine centuries, but I could never make sense of it. Mom nursed me herself. She held my tiny hands in her own while I learned to walk. She fed me spoon after spoon of pureed peas and carrots. She swung me up in the air and rained kisses down on my cheeks, the bridge of my nose, my forehead, and my mouth. She changed my diapers without complaint, and when it was time, she taught me to go pee in the potty. Mom tucked me into her bed every night, until I was old enough I wanted to sleep in my own. And then she complained that I was growing up. She rocked me and read to me and watched human movies with me.

Mom's the opposite of merciless.

She has always been the epitome of mercy, forgiving my weaknesses and flaws before I even realized they existed. She kept peace among our lands and protected our people. She taught me everything I know, and she gave me everything I needed. Always. She was a gracious friend, a doting mother, and an excellent ruler.

I never understood how people could call her merciless.

Until today.

She killed her friend without a thought. No hesitation, no regret.

My heart breaks, the light goes out of the room, my knees shake, and I can't even process the scene before my eyes, but Mom doesn't pause. She marches down the aisle between petitioners and strides to the door. I follow her numbly, passing Lyssa's fallen form without looking. Judica walks along next to me, head high, eyes flinty, as though Mom acted exactly as she ought. My best friend's mom keeps one tiny secret and *off with her head?*

It's like we're in a demented scene from *Alice in Wonderland* and my mom's been possessed by the Queen of Hearts. Only it's real life and no part of this was drawn with ink or created with CGI.

When we reach the exit, Mom tosses a command over her shoulder to Balthasar. "Call Larena for clean up, and find Lark. She stands trial here in fifteen minutes. I'm taking a small break to confer with my daughters."

Confer with me? I have nothing to say to her. I can't believe she killed her best friend. I can't believe she's really about to try Lark for the crime of being born.

Mom doesn't stop until she reaches her room and we're all inside. She shuts the door carefully, not showing the least bit of anger, frustration, or grief.

"How could you do that?" I ask, the second the door's closed.

I wish I hadn't. Mom's shoulders sag, and her face looks older than I've ever seen it. Lines crease her forehead, and crows' feet crinkle around her eyes. She sinks onto the bench at the foot of her bed and Judica puts an arm around her in a shocking move. Judica never comforts anyone.

"I did what I had to do." Mom turns watery eyes toward

me. "And you will follow my lead in a few moments with your friend."

Wait. Is she implying that I'll behead Lark?

I stumble backward, bumping into the door. "I will never kill my friend."

"This is your fault," Judica says. "Lyssa as good as said she kept Lark because Mom kept you."

"Excuse me?"

Mom drops her face into her hands and I hear a sound I've never heard from my mom in my entire life: sobbing.

I want to shove Judica aside. She couldn't comfort a brick wall, much less a human. I settle for walking around Mom's other side and taking her hand in mine. "I'm sorry if this really was my fault."

"Don't be ridiculous. *I* chose to keep you, and *I* knew the risks, if not the price." Mom squeezes my hand. "I'd pay it again if I knew. I don't regret keeping you, and I never will."

"Is that really what caused this?" My voice sounds surprisingly small. I'm supposed to be comforting Mom, not soliciting reassurance myself.

Mom shakes her head. "There was no law that required me to kill you, Chancery, as you know. It became common practice after the Hundred Years' War, but there's no rule. Every time twin heirs are left alive, they battle for the throne." Mom pauses. "But the two things have nothing to do with each other, and Lark was born before you. Lyssa made her decision *before* I made mine. Lying about Lark, keeping her among us, she violated that law. Among other things, that decision left her susceptible to influence from the other five families. On top of that, it was dangerous for Lark, and for the rest of us. It's one of our oldest standing rules, and it's inviolable."

"Even so, you might have simply exiled her, but..." Judica trails off.

Mom couldn't look weak, not after keeping me. Not after everyone talking for the past seventeen years and eleven and a half months about Enora's folly.

"So it is my fault."

Enora closes her eyes. "I'm not worried about looking weak. Let the other families attack. I'll raze them to the ground." She clenches her fists. "But Judica." Enora stands up, pivots on the ball of one foot and slaps my twin full across her face.

My jaw drops.

"If you ever, ever again try to steer an interrogation toward the implication of your sister in a crime, I'll execute *you*. And you'll deserve it for disloyalty to me and our family. Do you understand?" Mother's eyes flash, and her body shakes with suppressed rage.

Judica's voice raises goosebumps on my arm. "Yes, Mother. I understand perfectly."

What had Judica been asking when Mom beheaded her friend? She'd been pressing Lyssa for who else knew. Which means...

Mom knows Lark knew, because Mom knows *I knew* Lark's secret.

Judica realized it too? And was angling toward making sure I was punished. How did I wind up in this family? I'm so dense compared to everyone else.

Because I'm only now realizing that Mom executed her oldest friend without a reprieve, without letting her say goodbye to her daughter or her son who are both in residence... because of me. Not in a roundabout way, because of an old decision, or because Mom keeping me emboldened Lyssa to hide Lark. No, Mom executed her friend to keep Judica from implicating me in the whole mess.

Mom killed Lyssa to cover for a mistake I made today. Mom protected me: the weak one, the stupid one, the deficient one. Same as always.

She really should let me go to New York. Her life would be much better without me around to ruin everything.

Mom brushes off her skirt and steps toward the door. "We need to return. They'll have located Lark."

No, no, no. Not Lark. I whimper. "We can't, we cannot execute her, Mom. It's not her fault. She had nothing to do with the decision to stay."

Judica's cheek isn't even red, but she's on the war path anyway. "She *is* the decision. She must die."

I look at Mom, desperation freezing my muscles, tightening my jaw, forcing my hands to shake uncontrollably. "No, no. There's something we can do, right Mom?" A sob escapes before I can clamp down on it. "You can't kill her too. You can't."

"If Lark knew," Mom says, "then the law is the law."

"But she's so young," I protest. "You can't hold someone to a law when they're a child. She's barely an adult, and we have no idea when she found out. Don't you think killing her mother is enough punishment for just, I don't know, being who she is?"

The lines on Mom's face pull at my heart. She's resolute. "She's eighteen, almost nineteen."

Great tears stream down my face and I brace for Mom to yell at me, or maybe even slap me. I know I need to pull things together. I can't walk into a trial sobbing like a baby. But Enora the Merciful is here in this room, and she draws me carefully into her arms. "I'm so sorry, little dove. So very sorry. If I'd had any idea, we could have worked out a way to avoid all of this, but it's far too public now, which means our hands are tied. If she knew, our hands are tied."

If I'd trusted my mom with Lark's secret, she could have done something, avoided this. But I didn't. I thought I could help Lark myself, and I wanted to be the one who kept her safe. I thought I was helping, but something about that fight must have triggered someone to pull a DNA test.

I'm so stupid.

"Wait," Judica says. "You weren't hearing petitions with me. Someone tested her DNA after she won a match..." Judica's eyes widen and her mouth gapes. "Was Lark fighting you?"

Mom's nostrils flare. "That has no bearing whatsoever on the hearing we are about to hold."

The corner of Judica's mouth turns up. "Doesn't it? I'm not asking anything in an interrogation room, but I hope we can be honest with one another in private." She crosses her arms. "Which is it, sister? Are you so pathetic you were defeated by a human? Or did you know her treasonous secret and commit treason yourself to help her? I'm not even sure which is worse."

I've never seen Judica smile quite so big.

"Your sister," Mom says, "had no idea what her friend was. I watched the entire thing. But as you know, Chancery detests violence, and I haven't yet taught her to handle a blade. Those things hampered her in a challenge against her dearest friend in the world. We're aware of the deficiencies and are working on a solution. It's not of your concern."

Judica scowls at me before she jerks the door open and storms out, stomping toward the petition hall. Before I can follow her through the doorway, Mom places a hand on my arm. "We will talk about this later, but tell me you understand the importance of your ignorance."

I nod numbly.

"I'll burn the world down to protect you," she whispers.

Or cut off her best friend's head without regret, apparently.

Her hand tightens on my arm painfully. "But I'd prefer it never comes to that."

Me too. And I really hope Lark survives this. I'm afraid

if I beg for her life, Mom will decide to teach me a lesson or something.

Judica's already seated when we reach the petition hall. The gathered crowd has swollen to an absurd degree. Every seat is taken, and dozens of evians are standing in the back of the room. My heart sinks. This hearing won't go unnoticed. Even if her body has already been removed and all evidence of her decapitation expunged, word of Lyssa's sentence has clearly spread widely.

Mom ascends the steps to her solid wood throne, carved to look like a tree, its branches spreading out to the right and left over the smaller thrones for Judica and myself. I take my place to her left side without saying a word. Unfortunately, even from where I'm sitting, and even though she's kneeling on the hard marble floors a dozen feet lower than me, Lark's stricken face is directly in my line of sight.

Her gray eyes are full of unshed tears, and she looks decades older than she did an hour ago. Her mother was right. She never should have asked for a favor from me. I doomed them both.

I inhale deeply to keep from sobbing in front of hundreds of my mom's most important subjects. I need to hold it together right now, because Mom's affection for me gives Lark her only chance of surviving this. I wrack my brain, scrambling for any idea that might save her.

I can't think of a single thing.

"Lark ne'Lyssa Alamecha, daughter of Lyssa ne'Davina Alamecha," Mom says flatly, her words reverberating off the fifty-foot ceiling, "you are half-human."

Lark doesn't speak, but a tear rolls down her cheek. She's standing trial for who she *is.* Her mother died for Lark being different than the rest of us, but Lark is the exact same person she was yesterday. Everyone liked her just fine then.

This is wrong. The certainty of that washes over me. How can it be treason to be who you are? I want to stand up and scream it to the rooftops, but that's exactly what Mom cautioned me not to do. I've made enough mistakes today to last a lifetime, so I keep my mouth shut, but I'm howling inside.

"You don't contest my statement."

Lark shakes her head and bows deeper, until her nose nearly presses against her chest.

"Lark, look at me," Mom says.

Lark slowly raises her face. She knows she's about to die, I can see it in her eyes. But what hits me in this moment is that she welcomes it. Her mother is gone, her secret is out, and Lark wants it all to end.

"Did you know you were half-human before you received word of your mother's treason?"

"Of course she didn't," I say. "She had no idea."

Lark's eyes turn toward mine, toward my voice, but she doesn't even register that she knows me. Her entire face is blank. "I've always known."

I grit my teeth. "But she couldn't have done anything about it, not before, and not once she turned eighteen. She wasn't given a choice. How is her *very existence* a crime?"

Mom turns toward Judica. "Heir?"

"She should have turned her mother in. If she had confessed, she'd have been spared. Cast out, but not killed. But she didn't do that. She tricked my soft-hearted sister into accepting the mockery of a challenge I hear she lost." Judica sneers. "Lark's as traitorous as her mother."

Rage and despair flood my body in equal portions. How can I do nothing? How can I say nothing while Lark pays for my mistake? But what can I do? I couldn't even defeat a half-human. Never in my life have I hated the core of who I am as much as I hate it right now. If I weren't so weak, if I were a warrior, maybe I could do something to save my only real friend. But nothing I do will help, because I'm useless. Worthless. Weak.

"Lark ne'Lyssa Alamecha, I sentence you to death by execution. My daughter Chancery Alamecha will carry out the sentence."

I try to refuse, but no words emerge because my throat closes off.

"I'll allow twenty-four hours for each of you to prepare. Chancery is the only person allowed to see or speak to Lark in her cell during that time. I grant you each the mercy of saying goodbye." Mom swallows. "And the execution will be conducted privately, not here in the petition hall."

Murmurs from the gathered crowd fill the space, rising like smoke toward the rafters. I don't know many things, but I do know one for sure.

There's no way I am going to execute my best friend.

Two guards yank Lark to her feet and march her down the middle of the room and out the door. Mom stands up and begins her descent, beckoning for me to follow. Judica hops up, but Mom turns back and shakes her head. "You need to train. Chancery's going to help me select a gown for tomorrow's gala."

"I need to train?" she whispers. "I think you have me confused with someone else."

Mom's eyes flash, and Judica bobs her head stiffly in acknowledgement. When I walk past her, my steps wooden and shaky at the same time, Judica slams her shoulder into mine and nearly sends me sprawling down the steps. Of course she has no empathy for me. She has no friends of her own, so she couldn't even imagine how I feel right now.

Once we walk through Mom's doorway, I close the door, and it's like that motion snaps something inside of me. I collapse into a pile, tears streaming down my cheeks to soak the carpet. Cookie frolics around me, darting toward me repeatedly to lick my face and bump my hands. She can't comfort me, because nothing will make this better. I know I'm way too big to fall apart like this, but Mom doesn't chide me. She sinks down next to me and pulls me against her chest. I clutch at her, not sure what can possibly be done, or what could ever make things right again.

I wish I'd come straight to her room and told her the truth. Why didn't I trust her to fix everything? Mom always fixes everything.

When the tears let up enough for me to form any kind of words, I hiccup, "I can't. I can't do it, Mom."

Her hands stroke my hair. "I know you can't."

Wait, what? I straighten. "Huh?"

"You won't kill your friend, but everyone needs to believe you have."

5

Her words are a single ray of sunlight after a terrible storm. Broken branches, downed trees, rubble and shattered glass, but I cling to the one isolated beam of hope.

"What?" My voice cracks on that one word.

"It's the only way I could think to spare her life. She'll go into intelligence like she wanted. I couldn't spare her mother. She had to die publicly, or no one would ever believe we executed them both." Mom presses a kiss to my forehead. "I couldn't tell you, little dove. You'd have given it away. I thought about not telling you at all, not yet. People need to believe she's gone, and you have no experience with dissembling. But I couldn't let you believe she was dead, not when it was killing you in front of my eyes." Mom's voice drops to a whisper. "Not when you'd hate me for it."

I shake my head and wrap my arms around her waist. "I could never hate you."

"I am so sorry about how this has all transpired, but if you do exactly as I say, we can sneak her off to join my network."

"Yes, yes, yes," I beg. "I'll do anything, say anything."

"Lark will struggle," Mom says.

"I'll do anything she needs. I'll give her anything she wants."

Mom shakes her head. "You can't do anything. As much as she needs help, as much as she's hurting, this is her trial by fire. And you need to know, Chancy, that it may consume her. Some people emerge from their life trials cleansed of impurities, and some people burn to ash. When we help her escape, we've done everything we can for her. She'll make it, or she'll give up, and whatever the outcome, it's not your fault."

I think of how I'd react if my mom died and I shudder. "I'd burn."

Mom strokes my hair. "You never know your own mettle until you're tested, but I hope that's decades into the future at least."

I can't even contemplate my mom dying. She may be merciless, she may be fierce, she may even be cruel sometimes, but never to me. And she's the best ruler Alamecha's ever had. I'm so glad she's still strong and healthy.

"Now, we'd better actually try on a few gowns so I won't have to attend my party naked."

"That would make quite a splash," I say. "People might stop talking about Lyssa and Lark." I choke up just saying their names aloud.

"That's a noble goal, but even that won't wipe this slate clean." Mom holds me for a few moments before standing up and crossing the room toward her vast walk-in closet. She turns the corner and disappears from my view, even the sound of her heartbeat fading to non-existence.

I know we can't cancel her party. I know that the rest of the world doesn't care what punishments Mom doles out to her friends. I know that Mom can't spare the time to sit in her room and sob, or call off her nine-hundredth birthday party.

But I still think she should.

Life can't just march on after something like this. You can't shake it off and pretend you didn't just execute your oldest friend.

When Mom emerges a moment later in a tight-fitting ivory gown with pink and gold trim that matches the décor of her room, I know I'm expected to give her feedback, but I keep seeing the replay in my mind: Mom's sword connecting with Lyssa's neck.

I close my eyes.

Mom raises her eyebrows. "Is it that bad?"

I swallow. "No, it's fine."

"So I should wear this tomorrow?"

I inhale deeply through my nose. Who cares what she wears? Lyssa will be wearing a funeral shroud. "Um, if you want."

"You're supposed to be helping me choose."

If Mom hadn't killed her, Lyssa could offer her input too. A flare of anger consumes me, and I bite my lip. Mom was protecting me. Because I'm such a weak mess that I need protection. She did what she had to, in spite of the pain it surely caused her. "You look stunning in that," I say, "but you wore it two years ago."

She frowns. "I wore the black Versace two years ago. I may be old, but I'm hardly senile."

"You wore the black Versace to *your* party two years back. But you wore that Vera Wang to Nastasia's birthday two years and two months ago."

My mom tsks. "You're right. Why's it still in my closet?" She pivots and walks back inside. I hear her slide the gown down her body and toss it out onto the bedroom floor. I hop off the bench to snatch it up and walk across her room to the door that connects to my bedroom, Cookie Crisp on my heels. I throw it onto my bed, a miniature of my mom's bed right down to the coloring of the silk duvet, and walk back, confusing Cookie. I've only been able to fit into Mom's hand-me-downs for a year, but I love every one I've snagged.

This time I flop backward on her enormous gold gilt bed to wait. I sink into the thickly embroidered duvet and try not to think about Lark, or Judica or Lyssa. I wish I could run an eraser over my brain so my heart would stop aching.

"Maybe I could help Lark," I say. "If you let me go to New York to live with Alora, I'd even be close to her. But I'll need my own network at some point. Why not let Lark be my first operative? It might give her purpose, and I can be close to support her when she struggles."

"You can't do anything out of the ordinary right now. Nothing that will draw attention." Mom's voice is muffled from inside the closet. "Besides. Running away from Judica won't make anything better. Seven hundred years ago, Lenamecha gave birth to twin daughters, Senah and Denah. She thought it would be fine. It wasn't."

I roll my eyes. "I know, Mom. Her death sparked the Hundred Years' War, and that's why the next two empresses with twin daughters both killed one immediately."

"The older girl always dies, but when I saw you, I couldn't do it." She pauses silently just inside the closet, and then steps out slowly, her dress rustling with every step as she makes her entrance. I guess after nine centuries of formal events, you develop quite a flair for the dramatic. Even without staging, the green silk ball gown with pink embroidery would be stunning. "What do you think?"

I look her over as I ponder her question. Her curly, light brown hair is swept up into an elegant twist with no traces of gray. Her nearly indigo eyes sparkle with life. Crow's feet, small wrinkles by each eye, are the only real sign that she has aged at all.

"You look great, Mom," I say. "You could easily still pass for six or seven hundred."

The lines around her eyes relax. It's nice to talk about normal things. Until I remember what happened today and I think about Lark, shivering in a cell, waiting for me to kill her. And the fact that she'll never see her mom again. And then I think about Lyssa, her hand on my shoulder, her light, airy laugh. A sound no one will ever hear again.

Mom clears her throat. "This one's bad too?"

"I don't know about that dress," I finally say. "And if I'm being honest, this isn't very fun, what with Lark waiting for me to behead her down below." I drop my voice to a whisper. "And knowing Lyssa's gone."

Mom sighs and sinks onto the bench. "I know." She closes her eyes. "As soon as everyone has turned in for the night, we'll go down and dismiss the guards. I'll arrange for transport off the island shortly, and we'll incinerate a goat in her place. This isn't my first false execution, little dove. Lark will survive this, and right now, there's nothing in her cell she could use to do herself harm. She's physically as safe as she can be."

"Wait, you've done this before?" I thought I knew Mom so well. I'm beginning to wonder whether I know her at all. She's really trying hard to protect me, and Lark. I need to do my part. I force myself to study her dress.

"It's awful for me too, you know, choosing something to wear to a celebration moments after losing my dearest friend." Mom folds her hands in her lap. "But I have to pick something, and my gown sends a message. Everyone will have either witnessed or heard about what happened today. I can't wear something that hides it, nor do I want killing my friend to be the focus of the evening."

The green gown swirls around her, hugging every curve, and fans out below her waist to a skirt that cascades in full swaths down to the carpet around her feet. While her figure looks amazing and the dress is to die for, the color isn't the most flattering for her eye color and complexion, and emerald green feels... disconnected.

"Are you planning to change your eyes or darken your skin tone for the party?"

She grimaces. "I'm not. Not all of us can do that as easily as you, and it's become even harder for me in the past few years."

I ignore her comment about things becoming harder. Mom's not old. "Then what about the burgundy ball gown with the silver brocade? The Marchesa." I slide down to the floor where Cookie's curled into a fluffy ball and rub her back. "Because that color is almost..."

"Like dried blood."

I nod. "You'd be addressing it without saying a word. Telling them you know what they're thinking and you're not afraid of it."

Mom frowns.

"You didn't like it though, right?" I rub Cookie's tummy and my mom's dog, Duchess, whines, so I rub her ears with my other hand.

"It caught on my ring at the final fitting, and I worried a pull would destroy the delicate overlay. Last week Edward fixed the loose prong on my ring, and I realized that might have been the problem, not the dress. Just in case though..." Mom tugs and tugs on the ring she wears on her right middle finger. It finally slides off and she sets it on her nightstand.

I gape. In almost eighteen years, I've never seen the ring off of her finger. I recall Edward complaining as he repaired the prong while it stayed in place. Mom suffered through moderately severe burns in the process, but they didn't even discuss the possibility of her removing it.

Mom tsks at me. "Don't be so melodramatic. I've taken

it off before, I just don't do it often, and only in front of direct family."

"When? When have you ever taken it off?"

She shrugs. "Plenty of times, but usually when no one else is around to see."

I stare at the ring. "Is it...?" I look up at my mom and then back down at the ring. The rainbow sparkle in the stone fades, and the stone darkens to a solid black.

"It's fine." She looks at me fondly. "Everyone knows staridium sparkles when it's in contact with someone with pure DNA, but very few people know it turns pitch black when it isn't."

My mouth hangs open and I close it with a snap. "Is it magic?" I regret the words as soon as they leave my mouth.

Mom raises one eyebrow. "You know better than to ask me that. Humans are quick to label things magic, but really, they just don't grasp how it operates. Staridium is the only stone of its kind, but it's not magical."

When Mom walks back into her closet, my eyes go to the portraits hanging on either side of her closet door. One of Judica, one of me. The photo of my twin was taken last year during one of her training sessions. She's holding a broadsword, her muscles straining, and she's bringing it up and over her shoulder. The photographer captured her perfectly, her face so determined that it's practically feral. Her hair is pulled back tightly, but a few stray strands stick to the sweat on her brow. Instead of looking unkempt, it looks fierce, like she's been honed to as sharp an edge as her blade.

My portrait hangs on the other side of the door. I'm sitting cross-legged in my favorite pair of jeans, barefoot in the shade of the huge banyan tree in Mom's private courtyard. I'm hunched over a good book, so enthralled I didn't realize the photographer was even there. My hair's down, loose curls obscuring part of my face and eyes, almost covering the high cheekbones, square jaw, and aquiline nose Judica and I share. Mom chose photographs of each of us doing something we love, but it doesn't paint a very flattering picture that I love to sit around indulging fantasies while Judica could hack the entire cast of *Game of Thrones* into bitesize bits.

If you asked a hundred of my mom's subjects which twin was born to rule based on these photographs, every single one of them would pick Judica.

Including me.

I hear rustling inside the closet as Mom changes gowns. I stand up to get a better look at the black stone in my mom's ring. As I bend over it, I realize this is my chance. I'll never be queen and I'll never wear my mom's ring by right, but a desperate desire grips me to watch it change from deepest black to a sparkling rainbow of colors on my finger. I want visual evidence that my blood is as pure as Judica's, even if we don't share any talents or even similar temperaments. I reach for it greedily.

"Chancery?"

My hand freezes and blood rushes to my face. Even worse, I know Mom senses my elevated heartbeat. "Yeah?"

"What are you doing?"

How'd she change clothes so fast? Her heart pounds steadily one step behind me. I yank my hand back and look up at her guiltily.

Maybe some well-deserved flattery will distract her. Because if the last dress was beautiful, this one is breathtaking. "Oh, Mom, you have to wear that. Georgina and Keren outdid themselves."

She lightly touches the overlay on the gown. "You may be right."

My heart sinks when she reaches around me to pick up her ring. She holds it in her hand for a moment and then extends it toward me, the metal band clasped between her thumb and forefinger. The simple platinum band shines dully, encasing a black rock that looks flat and unappealing.

This time it's my turn to ask, "What are you doing?"

"Go ahead and try it on," she says. "It's been an awful day, and I'd like to see it on you. I've only seen it on one other person's finger in my lifetime, and that was many, many years ago." She looks sad.

"Your mom," I guess.

She nods. Since the youngest daughter inherits the throne, a new empress rarely has a chance to know her mother for very long. Mom was only 27 years old when her own mother died. It must have been hard for her to rule alone at such an early age.

"Go ahead, little dove." She waves it in my face.

"Are you second guessing your decision to make Judica Heir?" I joke.

"I'm not changing my mind." Mom smiles to soften her words. "But I've come to realize how much Judica needs you. And one day, when I die, you'll be her Heir. Don't let titles determine your value."

"Mom." I roll my eyes. "Judica will probably pick a Consort five minutes after she's crowned and then have a child each year until she births a daughter."

Mom shakes her head. "Crass."

"I won't be her heir for very long, okay? That's my point." I sit down, the ring forgotten. "Judica hates me, so whether she needs help from me or not, she'd never accept it."

"That's a conversation for another day when we have more time." My mom takes my hand gently and places the ring in it. "Try it on. No one else will ever know."

The ring is colder and heavier than I expected. Much heavier. I slide it on my right middle finger and look down at the stone. I always assumed it was carved carefully, like a diamond or other precious gem, to refract the light.

It's not.

It's jagged and uneven, and the rock is set so that the base of the stone rests on the back of my finger. It's the size of a large grape and even though the cold base is touching my skin, the staridium remains black. Black as pitch. Black as sin. Black as death.

My stomach sours.

Why isn't it lighting up? Where are the colors sparkling across it to prove that I've got pure DNA? I look up at my mom, whose face is riveted to the rock in a way that is not reassuring. Even after a full five seconds, the stone is still utterly dark. Even if I'm not the Heir, it should respond to me, right? I mean, Mom's only six generations removed from Eve, which makes me seventh generation. Plenty of other empresses are seventh generation, and their stones sparkle on their hands right now.

A horrible thought grips me. What if our line somehow suffered a major deletion, generations early? We all know it's inevitable. One day even our DNA, perfect, royal, evian DNA, will falter.

Suddenly I'm angry. I may not be as vicious as Judica, and I may not be my mother's Heir, but I'm not damaged. I'm as good as Judica. I glance up at the portraits. Looking at them, it finally hits me. I'm *not* as good as she is. Maybe I really am deficient. We may be twins, we may even look identical, but perhaps there's something wrong with me.

I want to read instead of fight, and I love baby animals. I've always binged on human television, books and movies. I'm not good enough, not strong enough, and I'm not fierce enough. I'm glaring at Judica's portrait, about to yank the cursed ring off my finger, and I'm fighting the urge to hurl it to the ground, when I feel something. Something strange.

There's a pressure inside my head, like my ears need to pop, like there will be a spark the next time I touch something. I smell ozone. And then a second later, like a lightning strike, like an explosion, like fireworks on the Fourth of July, the rock flashes. The room is bright with a blinding light, like the force of the sun for a single instant before my vision goes dark and a flash of heat explodes outward from where I'm standing.

I blink several times while my retinas heal and realize that all the lights in Mom's room have gone out. If sunlight wasn't shining through the stained glass in her big bay windows, the only light in the room would come from the ongoing pulses of bright, angry light emanating from the stone on my finger. Well, that and the flames currently licking up the side of Judica's portrait.

There's a pounding at the door. Mom's guards.

Mom says, "Everything's fine in here, Frederick. Check in with Balthasar and secure the perimeter before you return."

What's she saying? Nothing is fine. The wall is on fire, for heaven's sake.

Mom steps toward me, one finger pressed to her lips and the other grabbing my wrist. She stares for a moment, marveling along with me at the bright, bold, clear flashes pulsing angrily from the ring. The staridium looks like someone stuffed a rainbow down inside it that's desperately trying to claw its way out. I tear my eyes away from the ring and look at the burning portrait of Judica.

The ceiling sprinklers should have kicked on to put out the fire, but they haven't.

"What happened?" I ask. "And what do we do about that?" I point at the wall. The flames from Judica's portrait are licking the paint on the wall above them when a low humming noise begins somewhere far behind us. "What's that sound?"

"The generators are finally kicking on," Mom says.

"The generators?" I look around the room. The lights

still haven't come back on. "Why do we need generators? And if that sound is the generators, why aren't the lights working?"

Before Mom can answer, the sprinklers in the room pop down from the ceiling and put out the fire, soaking us in the process.

Mom ducks into her closet to keep from ruining the gown she selected. She comes out in slacks and a silk blouse just as the sprinklers shut off. She's lucky the sprinklers inside her closet didn't go off, too. When I meet her eyes, they're full to the brim with sorrow. A shiver shoots down my spine. I have no idea what just happened, but I really wish I'd never touched her blasted ring.

Her voice is soft, but it cuts through me like a sword. "You definitely aren't going to New York, Chancy. This changes everything."

6

Duchess whimpers, and I relate to the sentiment. Cookie never, ever jumps up on me. Never. But she leaps up on me now, paw pads catching on the embroidery on Mom's bed.

Mom shoos her away and collapses next to me.

When she speaks this time, her voice is almost normal again. "Maybe you'd better pass my ring back. More people are coming."

I hear the faint footsteps after she points them out and slide the ring off my finger. The stone barely darkens before it's back in place on her hand, accompanied by its usual swirl of pastel color. Not two seconds later, there's another rapid knock on the door.

"May we enter, Your Majesty?" Frederick sounds frantic.

"Yes, come in." Mom shoots me a stern look and puts a finger to her lips before she turns to address the guards. What's she telling me not to say? I have no idea what just happened. It's not like I could tell them anything at all.

Frederick's eyes scan the room, starting with Mom, moving to me, and then widening as he takes in the charred wall and drenched carpet. His uniform is bone dry. Apparently there wasn't a fire in the hall. "There's been an attack, Your Majesty."

Mathias crosses the room to check the windows. He ducks inside the bathroom, examines the sitting area and then inspects the closet. When he returns, he says, "Clear," and takes up a position on the other side of the door from Frederick.

"What type of attack does Security believe took place?" Mom asks, utterly calm.

Heavy footsteps pound down the hall toward us. "Mother?" Judica and Death round the corner of the doorway simultaneously, and Judica's face relaxes visibly when she sees that Mom's unharmed. Her eyes fly wide as she takes in her blackened portrait. She pins me with a glare, her lip curling.

Mom steps in front of me. "We're both fine, and everything is okay."

Mom's Security Chief, Balthasar, enters the room as she finishes her statement, Edam on his heels. Mom inclines her head toward Balthasar. "Is the attack ongoing?"

Both men bow, and Balthasar says, "Too early to know, Your Majesty. We were hit with a strong electromagnetic pulse of unknown origin. The EMP wiped out most of the electrical circuits in the palace and at least a few hundred feet on either side." He notices our wet hair and looks around the room. Edam and Balthasar both do a double take at the sight of the torched portrait.

Judica swears. "What happened in here? Did a lightbulb explode?"

"Language," Mom says. "Expletives are the crutch of the uneducated."

Judica rolls her eyes. "Why is my photo the only thing burned?"

"Well, that and half the wall," I say.

"You did this." Judica takes a step toward me.

Mom doesn't ignore her this time. She holds up her hand. "Stop and listen for once in your life."

Judica flinches like Mom slapped her.

I suppress a smile.

Mom turns toward Balthasar. "What do we know?"

"We don't know how anyone came into range, and we've been unable to detect any other intruders or threats. We have reason to believe it originated locally, perhaps the work of a counter-agent among us."

My mom sighs. "Oh good. You can all take a breath."

"Take a breath?" Balthasar's stormy eyes widen. "All our heads of state are here, or arriving shortly, as well as hundreds of evians from all five families. Someone wiped out our communications, as well as most of our day-to-day electronics. We don't have a clue who did it, and you think we should take a breath? These might be some of our last, which means I've failed you, miserably. We have no leads on who set off the EMP, and no idea how it could have been done, and worst of all, we can't fathom why. Which means another attack is likely imminent. EMPs are preparatory strikes."

"Balthasar, relax." My mom quirks one eyebrow, seemingly amused by his agitation. It almost looks like she's enjoying herself. At least her heart rate has slowed.

"Your Majesty, I appreciate your show of faith in me, but I cannot relax. I have work to do, and I will do it. Now, please explain how the wall caught fire so I can ensure there's no additional threat, and then I'd like your assurance you'll remain confined to your room until I've worked out a few more—"

Mom shakes her head, "Your work is done. Larena can handle electronic cleanup for the main building, and you can focus on getting our security systems back up. We have a plan in place for recovering from the effects of a targeted

EMP. This will be a good opportunity to test out its effectiveness. Consider this a drill."

Balthasar's face turns bright red. "Unless you're removing me from my position, I beg your pardon, but I'm not done, Your Majesty. Not until we know details about—"

"There is no outside threat," Mom says emphatically. When Balthasar's eyes widen again, my mom sighs. "I set it off, okay?"

"How could you—" Edam begins, his vibrant blue eyes intent.

"I am Enora Isadora Alamecha, Empress of the First Family." Mom squares her shoulders and her eyes flash. "Do you doubt what I say?"

Edam scowls instead of cowering. Impressive, because I'm scared and I'm her daughter. Before my mom can say anything else, Judica jumps in. "Of course he doesn't Mother, but Edam's the head of my guard and Balthasar's second-in-command. He's entitled to question something that wiped out the whole island, even if you knew about it. I want to know what's going on, too."

"I didn't say I knew about it, I said I personally *set it off*. And he's not entitled to anything." My mom narrows her eyes. "And neither are you."

Edam bows. "I apologize. It was not my intention to question any action you have taken, Your Majesty."

Balthasar says, "Well, I'm not afraid of you, and I bloody well want some answers. How do you have an EMP I don't know about, and why would you set it off the day before—"

"The day before my ninth centennial birthday celebration?" My mom sighs heavily. "It was bad timing, but then we didn't quite expect it to work, at least not to this degree, did we Chancy?"

I have no idea why Mom's acting like we planned this—I'm not even sure the EMP came from me. I'm scrambling furiously for any possible reason that makes sense, but nothing materializes, so I shrug noncommittally, hoping that will satisfy Mom.

"I'm not entitled to know a thing, but Chancery helped plan it?" Judica practically gnashes her teeth and I can't quite hold back my grin, even if I'm nearly as lost as she is.

"It was her idea to begin with. I could hardly exclude her from the execution." Mom beams at me like she's proud, which only deepens Judica's scowl.

"Well it's terrible timing." Balthasar runs a weathered hand through his salt and pepper hair. "With everyone arriving here tonight or tomorrow, I don't know how we'll spare the personnel to prepare for dinner and the celebration, and simultaneously make necessary repairs."

Mom's eyes soften. "We have extra circuits and everything else we need inside the Faraday boxes. We always knew this would be a good pre-emptive strike tactic from a rival family. I really am sorry about the timing, Balth. I didn't intend to drop such a mess on you, but now that it's done, I need you to initiate the proper protocols. Find out the precise range on the EMP, with the knowledge that the pulse originated here in my room. The EMP generated a surprising amount of localized heat, which caused the fire."

Judica, Balthasar, Edam, Fredrick, and Mathias all glance around, clearly looking for a device.

"The device has been... disposed of," Mom says. "And if I had notified you in advance of our efforts, we wouldn't have had an accurate picture of the damage, or known the extent of the additional preparation necessary to withstand something similar in the future."

Balthasar grunts, but after a moment of staring at her, he bows and heads for the door.

She interrupts before he leaves. "One last thing, Balth."

He turns back. "Yes?"

"I need you to wait fifteen minutes before you open the Faraday boxes and begin repairs. Can you do that?'

"No! Until our monitoring equipment goes back up, we're vulnerable, defenseless even."

"I wouldn't ask if it wasn't important, and I swear no one else has any idea this is going on."

They stare at each other for a moment. Mom and Balthasar have known each other for almost nine hundred years. Mom's first Consort, Althuselah, was Balthasar's older brother. He's been her Chief of Security for as long as she's been Empress. Finally, he nods slowly.

Before the door closes, he mutters, "It better be important."

Judica stares daggers at me. "You know nothing about weapons, and even less about electronics, so what was this idea you had? What did you do? Use nail polish and a curling iron to make a bomb?"

I shrug again, feeling even dumber than usual.

"You don't know everything about your sister." My mom crosses her arms. "If you spent a little more time with her—"

"How many hours do I need to play dolls with Chancery, Mother, before you two invite me to join your super special club? Showing up uninvited to one of your breakfast club meetings every few weeks obviously isn't enough."

Judica spins on her heel to leave, but Mom grabs her arm. "You're always welcome to eat with us."

"Am I? That must be why there are always two place settings, unless I've been specifically invited. You know what? Save it." She wrenches free of Mom's hand.

Mom's face falls. "Wait. Judica, you can't leave yet." Mom's head snaps toward Edam. "Bring Inara to my rooms. I need to speak to all three of my daughters." She glances at the guards. "Alone." They nod and silently leave the room after Edam.

"What's going on, Mother?" Judica asks. "Edam's not an errand boy. You can't just send him to fetch people."

Mom pinches the bridge of her nose. "Judica, let's scale the hostility back to a Defcon seven or eight, okay? I'll explain what's going on after Inara arrives."

I sit down on the bed and pick at the soggy, embroidered duvet cover while we wait for Inara. I'm already drenched, so sitting on a wet bed doesn't make it any worse. Judica glances around for a place to sit, but remains standing. She shifts from one foot to the other and then begins pacing. I breathe a sigh of relief when there's a knock from the other side of Mom's carved wooden door.

"Enter," Mom says.

Inara's heart rate is elevated and she's perspiring. "What happened, Mother?"

Mom inclines her head to Edam. "Thank you, Edam. I know you're too important to run errands, but with the communications down, I had limited options. I appreciate your willingness to help. You may return to Balthasar at the command center now. I'm sure he's missing you."

He glances at Judica and she nods her head. He's second-in-command to Balthasar, but he's also captain of Judica's personal guard, so he takes his orders from both. It's got to be an uncomfortable tangle to work out. After he's gone, Mom sighs and perches on the edge of her bed next to me. My poor mom. Ever the ruler, always on guard, even with only her own daughters present.

Mom steeples her fingers. "I'm going to ask the two of you to do something strange, and I need you to promise not to talk about it to anyone."

Inara's brow furrows.

Mom slides her ring off her finger and the lights in it wink out again. She pinches the metal between her thumb and forefinger and holds it out to Judica. "Please put this on."

Inara clears her throat. "Are you stepping down?"

Mom shakes her head. "No. I just need both of you to try on my ring."

"What does any of this have to do with the EMP?" Judica asks.

Mom purses her lips. "I'll provide more information when it's time. For now, put this on."

Judica shakes her head. "Inara first."

Mom sighs heavily. "Fine." She holds the ring out to Inara, who takes it calmly.

Inara slides it on and smiles, like somehow her world is finally complete. I know how she feels, happy to pretend, even for a moment, that she might be our mom's choice, her successor, instead of irrelevant. The ring fills with gentle light, colors swirling through the stone slowly. Inara stares at it with complete attention, and we wait. Ten seconds. Twenty. After a full minute with no other reaction, Inara looks at me. "What's this for? Somehow this ring caused the EMP?"

She's too smart. What did Mom expect? She purses her lips. "No."

Uh, okay.

Mom holds out her hand and Inara takes the ring off with a sigh. Mom turns her attention to Judica, staring her down. Judica snatches the ring from Mom's hand and gazes at the black stone, dumbstruck.

"Slide it on your finger," Inara says. "Go ahead. It won't bite."

Judica startles, but she doesn't snap at Inara or scowl at me. She simply slides it on. The stone remains black for a single instant, and then fills with the same pastel colors as on Mom's finger and Inara's.

"So are you going to tell us what's going on?" Inara asks.

Mom stares intently at the ring. They know something is up, and Inara already figured out that it's somehow the cause of the EMP.

"Did Chancery already put the ring on?" Judica asks. "Because you aren't asking her to do it, and I know there's no way you two decided to assemble an EMP in your spare time."

Mom sighs, and I glance her way. She's aged a hundred years in the past half hour. The dark circles under her eyes tighten my chest. She closes her eyes for a long moment and opens them again. "Chancery set off the EMP with my ring inadvertently. It was an accident, but the event has... significance. I wanted to see if either of you could do the same."

Judica's eyes narrow. "Why were you even wearing the ring in the first place?"

I open my mouth, realize I don't really have an answer, and snap it shut.

When my twin's face turns toward our mom, I imagine for a moment I see sorrow, or pain, but just as quickly, any emotion is gone. Her heart doesn't miss a beat or speed up, not even a hair. I don't smell perspiration. I wonder what that kind of control costs her. Or maybe she really has very few strong feelings. Judica pulls the ring off and shoves it toward me. I stand and take it without thinking, but it's heavy between my fingers. I want to drop it, or better yet, throw it.

"Put it on," she says.

I shake my head.

Judica narrows her eyes. "I want to see what happens when you put it on."

I shrug. "I didn't do anything. I put it on, and it stayed black. I thought maybe there was something wrong with me—"

Judica snorts.

I clear my throat. "But then, I guess I got a little mad about feeling that way. Suddenly, I felt this buzzing or humming feeling and then *wham*. Heat flew out of me and the picture caught on fire."

"Anger at me, then?" Judica asks.

I shrug again. "Maybe. I don't remember exactly."

Inara looks down at the black lump of stone in my hand expectantly. The same phrase keeps repeating in my head: *This changes everything.* What did Mom mean? The EMP changed everything? Or the fire? Either way, why would my reaction to the ring change anything at all? What did Mom mean, it has *significance*?

I glance down at it, the ring I've seen every single day of my life, lights usually flickering in its depths on Mom's hand. Now, it's completely black, heavy, solid. A chill slinks down my spine and I suppress a shiver. I try to hand the stupid thing back to Mom.

"I don't have a good feeling about this." I shake it at her. The dead and lifeless stone fills me with an inexplicable terror, a sense of foreboding I can't explain. The image of Lyssa, dead at Mom's feet, floods my mind and I drop the ring. An ominous certainty that putting it on again will change our future forever grips me, and I hope it hits the ground and shatters. Which is highly improbable on the carpet.

Mom snatches it out of the air before it even has a chance.

She puts her hand on my arm and I glance up at her face, expecting her to be angry. Instead, her voice is small, quiet. "None of us know how much time we have left." Before I can object, she continues, "But Judica's right. I need to see you wear it again." She places it into my unwilling palm.

I shift from one foot to the other for a moment, but I finally slide the ring back on my finger, shoving down the inexplicable sense of doom. The stone still feels more like a burden than a treasure, like it's loaded down with expectations. It remains dark again, and the sinking feeling stays with me. What is wrong with me? Why doesn't it fill with simple, gentle light like it does for my entire family?

Mom touches my arm again, and I expect something big to happen, something shocking, something electric.

Nothing does.

"Maybe you drained it, like it's a battery," Inara says.

I close my eyes and think about the weight of the stone and suddenly I feel something faint in the back of my skull. Like a small cup is sitting there, slowly filling with liquid. That's wrong, it's not a cup, and it's not liquid, but I can't think of any better description for it. My shoulders tighten and my neck shivers.

"What?" Judica asks. "What now?"

Mom squeezes my arm. "Stay calm. If this has anything to do with emotion, we should tread carefully."

"What else do we know about this?" I ask. "I don't want to freak anyone out, but a bucket in the back of my mind is filling and it's near the top. I don't know what happens when it overflows." I try to pull the ring off, but Mom stops me.

We all wait. The sensation that power is oozing into that space is odd, and I can't explain it, not even to myself. But finally it stops. And the ring begins to flash with light as the power overflows the cup. Not the gentle rays of light that sparkle when it's on Mom's hand, or Inara's or Judica's. This is different. It flares and flashes like burning chunks overflowing the top of a contained fire. Mom, Inara, and Judica all stare at it, their mouths dangling open in almost the same fashion.

"It's gone," I say. "I can't feel it anymore, the filling sensation I mean. What do I do now?"

Mom shakes her head. "No one knows. To my knowledge, no one else has ever done anything like what you did earlier."

"Maybe I haven't either," I say. "Maybe there *was* an attack earlier, a real EMP."

"The flash came from the ring on your finger at the exact moment of the EMP," Mom says. "If nothing else, Occam's Razor demands the assumption that you set it off."

I sigh. "You and your scientific postulates."

"It's a principle, little dove, not a postulate."

Judica huffs.

Mom ignores her. "Think about the light the ring is giving off. That's coming from you. Even without any kind of electromagnetic pulse, that's a very strong reaction, much stronger than mine has ever been."

"You've been wearing it for a long time. Maybe it's excited for someone new."

Mom tsks. "First of all, it's not alive. Don't personify it. Secondly, I've seen lots of women wearing their rings over the past nine hundred years and I've never seen this reaction, including its reaction to both Judica and Inara a moment ago. They say the stronger the ruler and the purer the DNA, the brighter the light."

Judica growls, but Inara looks thoughtful.

"That makes no sense," I say. "The reaction should lessen over time if that's true. Any way you look at it, the three of us are farther removed from Eve than you."

Inara clears her throat. "Unless God included junk DNA at the bottom of our strand. Perhaps the purest DNA requires a few deletions of extraneous materials. You're seventh generation. Sevens come up a lot in the records and prophecies. It might be significant."

"Loads of empresses are seventh generation right now. Plus you and Judica are, too," I protest.

Judica balls up her fist, and her arm trembles. I know that look. She wants to punch Inara in the face.

"Maybe you haven't decided what you want to do," Mom says. "Channel your thoughts into something. Give the energy, or whatever it is, a purpose."

"Okay. But what?"

"Well, we know the sprinklers are working," Inara says. "Why don't you try and set your photo on fire. Then maybe Judica will forgive you for targeting hers."

I roll my eyes, but I don't have a better idea. I focus on the picture of myself and will it to catch fire. Nothing happens.

"It's not working," I say.

"Failure is a choice," Mom says.

It's her personal motto. Every time I said I couldn't do something when I was little, I'd hear "Failure is a choice, Chancery."

I grit my teeth and look at the stupid portrait of myself reading. I stare at the useless, irrelevant kid who gets to sit around and read while the important people do stuff that matters, like weapons training, strategy, studying history of warfare, and diplomacy. I mean, I hate the idea of having to do all of that, but it sucks that I'll never need to. I look at the girl in that portrait, her face unconcerned, her legs crossed at the ankle, flip flops skewed. Her life doesn't matter, and the image is an accurate reflection of reality.

My life doesn't matter.

I was born before Judica, but that's not why Mom chose her. She chose my twin because I'm not good enough. I'm not the one Mom thinks is strong enough, not the one suited to rule. I'm too soft, too kind, and too weak. I focus on it all, on the ring I'll never really have, the position I'll never take, and the world I'll never inherit. The power in that little cup flares to life, and the flashes from the ring intensify.

I feed the flames with my anger and frustration, and then I push on it with my brain, clamping down on the bucket until the ring flashes again. Not like it did the first time, but darker, hotter, and sharper. The fireball that flies out of the ring heads straight for the wall and blasts a hole in it, burning a path through the right side of my mom's closet.

"Oh no! I'm so sorry!"

I race into the closet before Mom can stop me, plowing right into the burning clothing. The flames lick against my skin, tasting my wet shirt and shorts. I stare at the mess I created with horror, willing the damage away. Then, just as quickly as the fireball burst out, I suck the flames back. The fire around me snuffs out and the ring bursts once and then scales back to smaller, less insistent flashes again.

The plush, shaved ivory carpet under my feet is singed and smoke billows into the room in front of us. I glance around the closet and breathe in a huge, smoky breath, but at least the Marchesa for tomorrow was on the left side of the closet. I'm staring at it dumbly when Mom takes my arm and pulls me back, away from the closet. The sprinklers don't go off and I wonder why.

"No sprinklers?" I ask numbly.

"I think you blew the generator," Mom whispers. She slides the ring from my finger and gently pushes me toward her bed. Balthasar, Mathias, and Frederick burst in the room without even knocking.

"What's going on in here?" Balthasar's eyes flash and he waves his sword in the air. "Give me the EMP, Enora, just hand it over." He holds out his free hand. "You've blown the generator now. Unless there's a backup generator no one told me about, we are screwed."

Mom sinks down on the edge of her bed with a sigh. "I hadn't thought about that."

Balthasar's face darkens. "You hadn't thought of it!?"

"I'm sorry. I promise there won't be any more EMPs today. They're kind of a single use thing and the last one has been used up."

Balthasar notices the closet and expletives pour from his mouth. I listen closely and make note of a few new ones.

"That's quite enough, Balth." Mom grabs his arm and he pulls up short.

He leans toward Mom and whispers, "Are you alright? What's going on?"

"I'll fill you in on more details later. You'll recall I asked for fifteen extra minutes. I'm done now. You can begin replacing circuits in the generator first and work your way out from there. I'm truly sorry for the confusion and frustration."

Balthasar opens his mouth as if to say something else, then rethinks it. He turns on his heel and marches out the door, dragging the others behind him. Edam turns and glances over his shoulder. Directly at me. His intense, deep blue eyes meet mine questioningly. The pulse from Mom's ring didn't burn through me that hotly.

I break eye contact with Edam, and he jogs down the hall to catch up with the others.

Once we're alone again, I explode. Figuratively this time. "Don't ask me to do that again, ever."

"No kidding, freak," Judica says.

"Judica, Inara, you may both return to your duties, but remember. Not a word about this to anyone. Ever. Chancery and I need to talk."

Judica stomps out the door, Death on her heels. Once he's gone, Cookie crawls back out from under Mom's bed and curls up near my dangling feet. Inara walks calmly to the door, and as she ducks out, she turns back and throws me a double thumbs up. "Very interesting development."

Normally that would make me smile, but with Lark

decimating me today, and Lyssa's execution, and now this, I can't summon any humor. I'm hollowed out like a gourd.

Mom wraps an arm around my shoulder and I collapse against her, sobbing. She hugs me close and lets me cry on her for the second time today. Eventually, my tears lessen. I gulp in deep breaths and sit up.

"What do you need to talk to me about?" I ask.

"For starters," Mom says, "after my party is over and the guests have returned home, I'll be drawing up new heirship documents."

"Excuse me?" I ask.

"I won't lie to you. I still think Judica's better suited to ruling, Chancy. Nevertheless, you're my new Heir."

7

"Wait, I don't understand," I say. "So what if the stone reacts only for me? Why does that change anything?"

"My ring is staridium."

I nod. "Yep, the stone cut from the mountain, I know. God barred Adam and Eve from the Garden of Eden. Afterward, as a sign He still loved them, He broke a piece from the gate in the wall and gave it to them so they could find their way back."

Mom says, "Eve gave the stone to her youngest daughter, and then when Mahalesh's daughters were on the brink of destruction, she gave each one a tiny piece of the stone and divided the earth between them to end the fighting."

"Except for Shenoah," I say.

"Correct. Mahalesh's older sister by just one year was her dearest friend. Mahalesh gave the smallest piece of the stone to her. And she carved out a chunk of land for Shenoah, too."

"You know, if Mahalesh hadn't given a stone to Shenoah, we'd be mahaleshians." I tut. "Evians sounds much better, so I suppose it's good that Shenoah was an amazing sister."

Mom raises one eyebrow. "Focus, Chancery. The point is that there's a prophecy given by Eve herself that empresses do not often share. It predicts that one day, thousands of years after Eve's death, one of her line will—"

"Isn't everyone technically 'one of her line'?"

Mom's not in a joking mood, judging from her scowl.

"Sorry. One of the empresses will do what?"

"This isn't a joke."

I shake my head. "I know. I am sorry. It's just hard to believe that any prophecy from thousands of years ago is really predicting anything that will happen, up to and including my strange reaction to a rock."

"Nevertheless, the prophecy states that an empress will reunite Eve's descendants and regain admittance to the Garden. By so doing, this empress will obtain salvation for all mankind."

I try my best to look like I believe in any of this, but I have to ask, "Salvation? From what exactly? Avarice? Elitism? Too much perfection? Oh, I know. Overdose of preservatives."

Mom's lips compress tightly. "Mother had lots of theories, but ultimately, we don't know."

"Why's this special prophecy such a big secret? Seems like keeping it quiet is a good way to possibly lose it."

"Shenoah and Mahalesh's daughters agreed to keep all of Eve's prophecies secret. Only the current empress of each family has access to them. I'm violating that rule to explain this to you."

I can barely force out my next question. "Why?"

"For generations, as soon as she reads the prophecies, every new empress has believed she would reunite the families and claim the right to re-enter the Garden of Eden. I know I certainly did, and Mother's journals confess she did too."

"And you think, somehow, I'm actually the one."

Mom's expression is grim. "No one has ever succeeded in uniting two families for more than a few days."

"Clearly I was chosen for my strong leadership skills, my ferocity, and my deft political skill."

"You have depths you don't yet fathom," Mom says. "And hopefully you'll have decades with me to prepare before you need to take over."

"I don't even want to take over."

Mom slams her hand down on her dresser. "I don't care what you want anymore. We have an obligation, and you may be the only person who can save all of us."

My eyes widen. Save the world? Me? By unlocking the entrance back to the Garden of Eden? Preposterous. "Do you even know where it is? The mythical Garden?"

Mom shakes her head. "I thought it might be on one of the Hawaiian islands. After all, they're perfect almost all year, but I've combed them, and Puerto Rico, and every other paradise I could seize." She leans against the dresser. "No one alive knows where the Garden is located as far as I know. Eve, if she remembered, took that information to her grave. In fact, as the world has shrunk with new technology, I sometimes wonder whether it's not more of a vault of sorts, holding only answers. It's awfully hard to hide locations these days of anything with any decent size."

"Which means that even if I bring the stones together, it won't help. We have no idea what to do with them."

Mom takes my hand. "Chancery, the prophecy identifies the queen who will reunite the kingdoms specifically."

As much as I want to dismiss her words, my heart falters. The EMP. The fire. The ring's odd reaction. What if it means something? What if I'm suddenly expected to *do* things? Save people. An overwhelming sense of despair seizes me. That stupid rock chose the wrong sister. I can't even save myself or my half-human best friend.

"You may recognize bits of it. Eve's original journals

refer to it, and it's referenced again in the few copies we have of Mahalesh's journals. There are even obscure references elsewhere. Obviously someone couldn't keep quiet about it and told their Consort, and so you see mention of it in public places too, like Isaiah chapter five. 'And he will lift up an ensign to the nations from far, and will hiss unto them from the end of the earth; and behold, they shall come with speed swiftly... And in that day they shall roar against them like the roaring of the sea: and if one look unto the land, behold darkness and sorrow, and the light is darkened in the heavens thereof.'"

"Umm. I'm pretty sure that doesn't say anything about a woman reuniting the world, or a ring or an EMP." If her prophecy is this obscure, I feel way better about my chances. I just need to convince her that it doesn't say what she thinks it says. Bless prophets for being so obtuse all the time.

My mom turns and gazes out her window at the waves crashing against the rocky shore, lost in thought. I wonder if my lack of understanding disappoints her. Am I already failing in my new role as Alamecha's salvation?

"Isaiah never makes any sense," I mutter. "What does that even mean?"

"You're being too literal." My mom turns back to face me. "Isaiah's writings are about symbols. He was describing things he'd seen from so far in the future that although he understood them, no words he could have used would have made sense to the people at his time. How would you describe an iPhone to the early Jews? Or a helicopter? How about a nuclear bomb?"

"Pictures might help."

"Be serious. An EMP wouldn't even have done anything a few hundred years ago. It's an electromagnetic pulse. It destroys electronics and wiring. I was born in a time so different from now that the people I knew then, my mother for example, would be utterly confused were they dropped here among my subjects today."

"How old are the writings you've got from Mahalesh? Wasn't she born in 3226 BC?"

"She was," Mom says, "but they're copies of copies at this point."

I raise my eyebrows. "Are you at all worried that they've morphed?"

Mom stares at her ring. "Do you know how the stone was broken? The stone cut from the mountain was whole when God scooped it out, one solid piece."

I hadn't really thought about it. It makes sense, though. A shattered key seems pointless. "Did Eve break it?"

Mom shakes her head. "No, Mahalesh's sisters hated her, except for Shenoah, but Eve passed the mantle of leadership directly to her anyway. It was smooth. She received an intact key, a complete chunk of staridium that would grant her access to the Garden."

"Then how?"

"As Mahalesh neared a thousand years of age, her five youngest daughters, born within decades of one another, fought bitterly for control over the earth and its people. Their discord broke her heart." Mom turns toward the window and when she speaks again, her voice sounds sad, as though it isn't ancient history to her. "Shenoah proposed a solution—split up the land. There was plenty to go around. But Mahalesh feared it would eventually be divided too far. She felt the division would need to be limited."

I knew this part. "Mahalesh couldn't choose one of her daughters to rule. Shenoah suggested Mahalesh break the stone and give one piece to each daughter. Divide up the earth and let them each rule a portion to stop the fighting."

"You're right," Mom says, "but no one could break the stone, not by any method they tried."

"Then how?" I look at the ring.

Mom whispers, "I'm not sure whether I believe it, but those were different times then. Amazing times, if the records can be believed. Mahalesh prayed and asked God to break the stone, to help her end the fighting among her daughters. She asked for peace among them before she died."

"And God did it?" I ask.

"We assume so," Mom says. "It doesn't say. But in the next entry it speaks of how the stone was split among the daughters. Mahalesh gave the pieces out in order, with the largest piece to her youngest and wisest daughter, Alamecha. Thus your great, great, great grandmother became the Empress of the First Family."

"Do you think God broke the stone?"

Mom shrugs. "I don't know. Our family received Mahalesh's actual journals, and I've read her first-hand account. The heads of the other four families have copies that were made at that time, and Shenoah's line has her records."

"Do you believe we're God's chosen?" I ask.

Mom shakes her head. "I wish I knew. I believe we're God's creation, and I believe God struck that stone. Even if He's not very involved in our world now, He was then, and He may be again. Especially if what I believe is true. If you're her."

"You think I can reunite all six stones?" I ask.

Mom closes her eyes. "Mahalesh asked God to split the stone into five pieces, one for each of her daughters. God split it as she asked, but not into five pieces."

"I know, he split it into six."

"No." Mom shakes her head. "The records report seven stones."

"Wait, what?" There are six families. One for each of the five daughters, and one to Shenoah the Peacemaker. My heart rate picks up.

There's another stone somewhere? Why? And where exactly?

"We have the biggest stone, and we rule North America, the United Kingdom, Cuba, and Puerto Rico. The second, third, fourth, and fifth families are descended from Mahalesh's older daughters in order: Malessa rules most of Europe, Lenora rules South America and Greenland, Adora controls most of the Soviet Bloc countries, Mongolia, Thailand, and Indonesia, and Shamecha rules the Middle East and India. Mahalesh gave each daughter a ring and a territory to rule. She gave the smallest stone to her sister, Shenoah, as well as the entire continent of Africa to rule. The Shenoah family, through Adika, still rules most of Africa today."

Mom's stalling. I learned exactly what each family ruled and how they held each of their nations while I was still drinking from a bottle.

"And the seventh?"

"No one knows. My mother believed God kept it for Himself, to give to a worthy queen at the appointed time. My grandmother believed it never existed to begin with, that there was some kind of transcription error."

"What appointed time?" I ask. "When did your mom think God would award this extra credit stone?"

"According to Mahalesh's journal, God told Eve that the stones would one day be shattered. He told her that one of her descendants would be able to regain admittance into the Garden by uniting the families and their stones. Only this Empress could gain admittance."

"Can I see the actual prophecy?" I ask. "Or is that not allowed?"

"Only I can enter the archive, but I'll quote it for you." She closes her eyes as if seeing the parchment in her mind's eye. "'In time of great peril, when the lives of women and men shall fail, the Eldest shall survive certain death to unite the families. She comes in a time of blood and horror, in a world overrun with plague and warfare. She shall command the stone of the mountain, be it small or large. Its power shall destroy the vast hosts arrayed against it. With the might and power of God, the Eldest shall destroy all in her path, and unite my children as one. Only through her blood can the stone be restored to the mountain. Together, with the strength of her strongest supporter, she shall open the Garden of Eden, that the miracle of God shall go unto all the Earth to save my children from utter destruction.'"

The Eldest?

"I always assumed the 'Eldest' referred to the empress who lived the longest. So far, that's Eve, at nine-hundred and seventy-one years."

"Which means, you hoped it might be you."

Mom shrugs. "We've all hoped. Everyone wants to be special."

Not me.

"But what if it doesn't mean the eldest empress to live? What if it's referring to something else? What if God knew we would start killing the older twin, and no "eldest" sister eligible to rule would exist? Until you."

"That's a stretch," I say.

"Is it?" Mom throws her hands up. "It makes more sense than the eldest empress. And look at the other evidence. You commanded the stone today, and it *destroyed the light*. It's talking about you, Chancery. Our people, and perhaps the whole world, will need you, and I don't intend to fail them."

"The world isn't overrun by blood, plague, or warfare," I protest. "There's no eminent destruction."

"Not yet," Mom says, "but I very much fear it's coming."

"What about all the destruction you and your rivals

have caused over the years? Where was the salvation of the earth then?"

"War, famine, plague. Those are commonplace. An apocalyptic event, something that could wipe out the evian race, that's the real threat. Judica has been awful to you, but now I'm beginning to believe things happened as they did for a reason. You survived certain death to be here, spared by the most merciless of rulers. I deserved my reputation. I meant to kill you, you know, but I couldn't. Something stopped me and I spared you, the eldest twin. And then you survived again, by sheer luck. Or possibly providence."

She's referring to my ninth birthday.

"Although I become more certain the prophecy refers to you with every breath, I think Judica serves a purpose too. I think she could become your strongest supporter. You may need her skillset to save everyone. I think, like Mahalesh's daughters, my precious daughters need to make peace before they can unite the other families."

"That's a nice hope," I say. "But I'm afraid the only way Judica's ever going to help me is into an early grave."

8

"We may have to force Judica's hand," Mom says. "The more time you spend together, the sooner she'll see what I've known for ages. Your many amazing qualities more than compensate for your weaknesses."

"Wait," I say. "What does that mean?" I know I'm not strong, but it still stings to hear my mom throw out the words "deficiencies" and "weaknesses" like everyone knows just what they are.

Mom sighs. "Right now we have guests arriving. We need to distract them long enough for their rooms to be prepared."

I follow Mom into her throne room, but I stop ten feet from where Lyssa fell this morning, cut down by my own mother. The white marble floor is pristine, not a single speck of red, or even a hint of orange. It could've happened last month, or last year. Except it didn't. It happened today.

And my best friend Lark is still locked away in a cell.

"Chancery, come and greet our guests." Mom's command cuts through the fog in my brain.

"Right." Because none of them can know what evian life is really like. They're merely the humans who serve us. The best, the brightest, and the only ones who even know we rule the world.

I make small talk with the current US President, the Prime Minister of England, and a handful of powerful senators and justices, barely stumbling over my own words at all. But when Larena, Mom's Chamberlain, pokes her head inside the throne room to let Mom know the guest rooms are ready, I breathe a heavy sigh of relief.

"Can we free Lark now?" I whisper.

Mom shakes her head slightly. "We have more pressing business, but I haven't forgotten. I told Frederick to put things in motion."

I frown. "Put things in motion? How long will it take? Won't people become suspicious?"

"Timing matters, Chancery. And right now, we must begin other things. Something we'll work on daily."

Mom drags me down to the family bunker where I practice setting off EMPs with her cursed ring. I guess a lead lined bunker encased in tons and tons of rock is the only place to limit the damage from my reaction to the dumb thing. It's not exactly how I'd like to spend an afternoon, but it could be worse. I could be stuck hearing more petitions with Judica. I'm not very successful, only setting off three more over the course of more than an hour, but I do set the wall on fire. Twice.

"As your great grandmother Corlamecha always used to say," Mom says.

I grumble. "Yeah, yeah, Rome wasn't built in a day."

I guess she'd know.

I reach the top of the ladder and climb out of the bunker and onto the ground. The giant banyan tree keeps the entire courtyard in front of Mom's bedroom in the shade. I inhale deeply of the ocean breeze that whips across every inch of the small island of Ni'ihau. Being stuck hundreds of feet underground gives me new perspective on the value of fresh air. My mom presses a few buttons in a hidden keypad under a rock, and an enormous boulder rolls back into place without so much as a whir. I guess that means the iron in the walls of the bunker kept the newly-repaired electronics out here safe. Cookie and Duchess cavort around our feet, glad to see us again. Dogs aren't allowed in the bunker.

"Time for your training as Heir to start, little dove," my mom says.

I suppress a groan. "You haven't thought this through, clearly. And do we need to start today, with all the repairs and leftover petitions and whatnot?" And Lyssa's death, and my friend's spirits sinking lower and lower in her cell?

"Melodics was fine when you had nothing but time, but sladius is much more effective for making quick progress, and we need immediate progress. I'll be making the announcement soon, which means it's necessary to expand your instructor pool, yes."

"Wait," I say, "you're not training me anymore?"

"Actually, I'm required at a meeting with Inara and Larena right now, so for today you'll be training with an expert in sladius."

"Balthasar?" I ask.

She shakes her head. "He will be there, but he wants to see you in action before he begins training you himself."

"Then who?" I ask.

"Judica."

My jaw drops. "You're kidding."

"No, I'm not. You two are going to have to learn to work together, and there's no point in delaying it. I already told Balthasar you'd be by around three o'clock. Change quickly."

I haven't trained with Judica in almost eight years. Not since before our ninth birthday.

"Sounds like a great plan. The only way this could be worse is if you told Judica you're making me the new Heir." Oh crap. "Which you will have to tell her at some point."

Mom nods. "But not today. We'll tell her together, after my birthday."

"Phew. Because I'd rather she not know the first time you send me into a ring with her and tell her to whack at me with a sword."

"You'll be fine," Mom says.

Easy for her to say. She's not the clownfish being dropped in a tank with the biggest shark in Ni'ihau.

"Your face has gone completely white. Don't worry. You heal fast." Mom's smile is mischievous. "Accept the world as it is..."

I grumble. "Or do something to change it. I know, I know. But do I really have to change it? I was fine with things before today. We need a new family motto. How about 'be true to yourself.' That sounds like a good one, probably because it's so vague that no one understands what it means."

Mom laughs. "Go."

I wait for a moment to see whether she'll change her mind, but when she glances my way, one eyebrow arched, I know she's annoyed. I head to my room to change clothes and have to immediately throw open all the blinds. Repair crews clearly prioritized the guest rooms and haven't reached mine yet.

Cookie's lapping at her water bowl and I'm lacing up my Merrells when there's a knock on my door. I tie the bow on my second sneaker and walk over to answer. My heart's working fine until I open the door. Then it flutters in spite of my Herculean efforts to keep it steady.

It's Edam, and for once, he's alone.

I usually have to avert my eyes so he won't notice me studying his face. Or worse, so Judica won't notice. I live among the direct lineal descendants of Adam and Eve. All of us have nearly flawless DNA. We're the most perfect people on Earth, and every single one of us has unblemished features, clear skin, bright eyes, shiny, curly hair, symmetrical and well-proportioned bodies. Even surrounded by sparkling gems, Edam stands out. Strong, square jaw. White blond hair that practically shines. Deep, sapphire eyes over high, prominent cheekbones and rich, dark golden skin that glows. And when he's standing this close to me, I have to crane my neck to see his face at all. Not that staring at his perfectly sculpted chest is bad.

"Your Highness." His intense eyes are trained on the ground.

"We've been over this. Please call me Chancery." My voice emerges high and squeaky, so I clear my throat. "You spent enough years on routine guard duty, taking your turn watching me scamper all over the island. I think the 'your highnesses' are unnecessary."

"Things were different then," he says.

It has been seven years since he was assigned to watch me, but the only real change I've noticed, other than his rapid rise in rank, is his dating status.

"You know what? Call me whatever you want. I'd hate to cause a fight between you and your sweetheart." I slide past him into the hall, Cookie on my heels, and slam the door shut.

"Balthasar sent me to bring you to the arena." He pauses. "Chancery."

His eyes meet mine, and my hands shake. "I know where the arena is. I don't need a babysitter."

He bows stiffly, a quick bob of his golden head. "He wasn't sure whether you were coming." Edam glances at his watch pointedly. "It's already three-eleven."

"Mom and I were caught up—" I gulp. "Well, I'm running a little late. I'm sorry."

I'm not sure how Cookie will react if I'm injured during training today, which I assume is a given, so I open my door again and signal Cookie to stay in my room. She whimpers, but she listens. I wonder as my rubber soled shoes squeak their way across the marble tiles of the hallway, how Annihilator, Lyssa's wolfhound, is doing. Not that I can do much about it.

Is Gray down with Lark? Or did they stuff her greyhound and Lyssa's wolfhound in the same kennel?

I barely notice when Edam falls in beside me. He doesn't speak, and I have no idea what to say to him, so I don't breathe a word either.

We zig and zag around work crews replacing lights and circuits in the massive lobby. The entire palace has only one floor, but with twenty-foot ceilings, it looks two stories high from the exterior. It sprawls over most of the center of the plateau on the island, which gives us visibility on all sides if any aircraft, boats, or even submarines approach. With today's technological advances, we could probably move somewhere with less visibility, but after today's EMP, Mom will probably be less inclined to rely on tech than ever. She knows the five rival families will never stop vying for control, and Alamecha is at the top, which makes it everyone else's number one target.

Edam and I don't have to walk in awkward silence for long, because the training arena is right around the corner from my room. One wall of the arena is composed almost entirely of glass so we should have enough light to train, even if the circuitry replacements haven't reached this area. Judging by the lack of overhead lighting, they haven't. I brace myself as Edam pushes the solid wooden double doors open and we walk through into the cavernous room. It's a good thing I do, because I immediately see what the door was blocking, the only thing worse than Judica.

Judica brandishing a broad sword.

"Sister." She glares at me from the center of one of the training rings.

"Well met." It's a traditional evian response, but I don't even try to sound like I mean it.

Balthasar tosses something at me and I catch it by reflex, then stagger back almost into the doorframe from the unexpected heft. I'm lucky he tossed the sword hilt down or I'd have sliced my hand in the process. "I don't really fight with a sword," I say. "The challenge today was my first time to use one, actually. I prefer to work on target practice with a handgun, a bow, or a slingshot—"

"We've used swords for six thousand years," Balthasar says. "Are you saying you don't value tradition?"

"Of course I do, but I'm suggesting that training should be tailored to a person's strengths."

He scowls. "And after your pathetic display earlier, no one would ever mistake swordplay as one of yours."

My face heats. "I never claimed it was." I lift my arm and groan from the effort. "And even if I had, this thing weighs a ton. I'd choose a lighter weapon."

"It is massive." Balthasar selects another sword from one of the racks that line the back wall, an even heavier one, and holds it aloft. "Do you know why these swords all weigh a ton?"

I shrug. "Because they're made of metal?"

He snorts. "Indeed, but the weight helps us. With our perfect muscles, if we exercise them properly, the weight isn't burdensome for long and it increases our momentum. You may be good with a handgun, but do you have any idea how many bullets I can take without slowing down?"

I shake my head. "Five? Ten?"

"I've taken more than twelve without noticeably

changing my speed. You want to stop a member of one of the pure evian bloodlines? You better have a sword. Chop off their head, sever their spine, or remove a limb, or they'll keep hacking at you." He slams the sword, point down, into the black mat that covers the arena floor. "Let's not waste any more time. Your mother told me you're competent with basic forms, but you haven't spent much time integrating weapons into combat. Is that true?" Balthasar's hair is streaked liberally with white, but his face is still unlined and the muscles in his arms ripple with strength as he crosses them.

"The Empress is never wrong. I'm passable at hand-to-hand and projectile weapons." I square my shoulders and step up into the sparring ring. He doesn't want to waste time talking, huh? Fine. "Our cue will be?"

Judica chokes out a laugh.

Balthasar looks confused. "Your cue?"

"Melodics uses cues." Edam's eyebrows are raised. "But surely you know that sladius doesn't."

I will not blush. "I didn't know that, but I won't apologize for being trained traditionally. The Heir of Alamecha has been trained in melodics for six thousand years. You mentioned tradition as the reason for the sword."

Judica practically growls. "You aren't Heir."

I shrug. She's right, at least, as far as she knows. And I don't want her to be wrong. "I'm sorry. I said the 'Heir,' but I didn't mean the Heir so much as the children of the queen, as in anyone who is an heir."

"Melodics suck," Judica says. "Everyone tossed them as a training method over a century ago when the first Sword Master not trained in melodics won the Centennial Games. Even Inara wasn't trained in melodics."

"Melina was," I say.

Judica scrunches her nose. "You're making my case for me."

I can't quite keep my nostrils from flaring, but I don't allow my heart to race. And I don't clench my fists or grit my teeth.

"Mother only indulges her nostalgia with you because *you don't matter*."

"Mom has a reason for everything she does."

"Enough talking," Balthasar says. "No musical cues, Chancery. Your mother instructed me to catch you up. Here we cross swords, sweep back and begin. On my mark."

Mark or cue, it's all semantics. Something starts them off. They're just being obnoxious.

Balthasar claps three times, and suddenly I'm bringing my sword up to block Judica, who's swinging at me with an ecstatic grin and a maniacal glint in her eyes. I duck and dive her blade a time or two, but those moves back me into the edge of the dais quickly.

And she's still slashing at me like a gas-powered weed whacker. I turn and block, the impact of her strikes shaking my entire arm. Since I received my first lesson at age five, I've never fought without musical cues, other than my match against Lark this morning. Thinking about my loss, Lyssa's subsequent death, and Lark's current imprisonment crushes any energy I had for this stupid exercise.

I hate every second of this.

I'm already sweating pretty badly when Judica slices my forearm wide open. Blood mixes with sweat and runs down my arm to drip on the mat. Red blotches stand out against the khaki colored mat like hibiscus blossoms.

"Yield?" Judica asks, grinning like a feral cat.

I step back against the wall for a moment and look down at the gash on my arm. The white of my bone gleams, distracting me, so I close my eyes and ignore the pain. I focus instead on the blood, the vessels, and the muscle tissue. I open my eyes and watch the miracle happen. I've always loved watching evian bodies in action, but healing my own injuries sucks. The distraction of the pain nearly eclipses the wonder. Even so, my muscles knit together, my skin regrows in front of my eyes and seconds later, my arm is still covered in blood, but is otherwise completely whole again.

I look up at my sister's triumphant face and I say, "Yield to you?" I think about Lark and how Judica didn't even care that her mother died. How she fully supports all the horrible rules we evians live by. How she hates Lark for being half-human. "Not today."

She growls and hacks at me again. I clench my hand around the hilt of my huge sword and block. Several minutes later, I'm still on defense. I'm backing in tight circles while Judica thwacks away after me, occasionally nicking my hand, my shoulder, or my arm.

"Melodics," Judica mutters. "Mother's a moron, and you're even worse."

For the first time since beginning our session, anger overwhelms my sorrow. Judica may fight better than me in this barbarous way, obviously, but that's not Mom's fault. I'm angry with Mom for killing Lyssa and leaving Lark defenseless, but Mom didn't have a choice. Mom always does the best she can. How dare Judica criticize her?

I feint left, which my twin sees coming, but when she brings her sword in a sweep toward me, I step in closer to her and slam the pommel of my sword into her face. I try not to shudder at the crunch from breaking her nose.

"Yield, sister?" I mock.

She spits blood in my face and knees me in the gut. I double over in pain, focusing on healing my bruised rib while she repairs her face. Seconds later, I'm standing again, sword ready.

"Why are you even here?" Judica whispers so quietly

only I can hear. "Shouldn't you be with Mom, gloating over your little party trick?"

I stumble back. "Actually, just this morning I begged Mom to let me leave and live with Alora. I still want that."

I don't know quite what I expected. Gratitude? In my wildest imagination, maybe even a hug, or a gentle smile? Judica never does what I expect, so I'm not sure why I thought she'd start now. Something I said got through to her, but not in the way I hoped.

"I should thank you, then." Judica isn't whispering now. She's practically shouting. "Is that what you want? My undying gratitude?"

I'm in trouble. Judica was taunting me earlier, but she wasn't angry, not really. She was having a bad day, sure. She was cranky, but she wasn't angry. I'd been fighting a semi-pleasant Judica, or maybe even a nervous and unsure Judica, all without realizing it. Now, even through the blood smeared across the lower half of her face from where I broke her nose, it's clear she's pissed.

Suddenly I'm fending off an angry bee, and I keep getting stung. She slices my right arm and then before I can heal it, my left. And my cheek, my left thigh. Each injury drains me, but she doesn't let up, not for a split second.

I successfully block a jab aimed at my right lung, but she's so strong that the impact causes me to stumble backward. That's when she takes her shot. She sideswipes me and kicks my knee cap. Pain from the shattered knee suffuses me as I crumple in a heap. I knew she was angry, but her next move is still a shock.

Her sword arcs downward at full speed, aimed at my exposed throat. Time slows, and I realize she's going to kill me, here and now. Evians heal from most anything, but not severed heads.

Another sword stops her blade inches before it separates my head from my neck.

It's not Balthasar's sword.

Judica screams in Edam's face. "How dare you!"

"This is a training session, Judica, not a duel. You're not supposed to kill anyone." Edam pushes back with his blade playfully and Judica steps back, but the glare she gives him is not forgiving.

He leans over me and offers me his hand. I knock it away because after that, I need to stand on my own. I inhale deeply and take the opportunity to heal all the slices and nicks my body hasn't finished repairing. I wipe my hands, slicked with sweat and blood, on the remnants of my tattered jeans. I focus on my knee next, bringing the shards of bone together slowly and repairing the ligaments so it will hold my weight. While I heal, Judica cleans her blade dispassionately, not looking at all bothered that she nearly cleaved my head from my body.

Balthasar finally speaks, spluttering a little as he does. "I certainly hope you were planning to stop your blade, Judica. You certainly knew this was a training session."

Judica smiles. "I guess we'll never know."

"What's your game here?" Edam stares at Judica, and cocks his head to the side, probably listening like I am to her smooth, steady heartbeat. She's completely calm, nonplussed. My blood runs cold. Mom wants me to take the throne from her? Or even worse, share it with her? She almost beheaded me, and she's not even agitated.

Judica glares at Edam, a look I'm familiar with, and says, "I wanted her to see how unprepared she is for an actual fight." She laughs and the sound makes the hairs on my arm stand on end. "Not that she needs the lesson from what I hear. Beaten by a half-human." She spits on the ground.

"I think that's enough sparring for today." Edam grits his teeth and crosses his arms.

He and Judica are locked in some kind of unspoken conversation. It upsets me in a way I'd rather not study.

Balthasar interrupts them, which I appreciate. "That's not your call yet, my boy. You may instruct the rest of the men, but I'm still the Security Chief last I checked, which means I'm the only one who manages the Heir's training."

Edam blushes and inclines his head slightly. "My apologies, Sir."

Balthasar's steely gray eyes take in my state of bloodiness and soften just a hair. "Insubordinate or not, Edam's right, Judica. I think you'd better call it a day."

Except I can't stop, not now, not after she's made fun of everything Mom taught me, and then proven her words by practically ending me. Judica can't get away with calling Mom old, outdated, and past her prime. And as much as I don't want to be here—even Mom only wants me as Heir because some rock reacted to me—I need to improve, and if I walk away like I want to, I'll never be anything but the victim everyone sees when they look at me.

Surely if Mom chose to train me in melodics she had a reason for it. There must be some value to my training and abilities.

"No." My voice wavers and my stomach ties in knots, but I remain firm.

"No?" Judica scoffs. "You're not done? That wasn't painful enough for you? I didn't realize you were a sadomasochist."

I raise my sword arm and turn to Balthasar. "She hasn't defeated me. We'll go again. On your mark."

This time, when he claps, I'm ready for it. I bring my sword arm back with as much enthusiasm as Judica. I was too busy the first time to listen for it, to feel the rhythm of the fight.

I feel it now.

When Judica attacks me, I hear triads, sharp, clear, and defined. I defend with a sweeping scale, ready for her. She may not know melodics, and we may be dancing without music, but she moves to her own song. Her melodic line's choppy and confused. I breathe through my nose and monitor her movements until I sense the best melody for my attack. As I watch her jumping around, a pattern emerges and my avenue becomes clear. I begin with a simple run. A parry, a swipe, a jab. And then I show Judica just what our mom taught me. An arpeggio. An aria. Suddenly, she's the one blocking, running, and backing up. I rage. I rail. She cowers, and I revel in it.

Melodics are dead? Eat my blade, Judica.

She almost does. I slide under her block and smash her toe with the heel of my boot. She winces and I slam the flat of my blade into her shoulder. She drops her sword and I kick it away.

"Do it," she says.

"Do what?" I ask. "You're unarmed. I've done it already. You're finished."

"You haven't even drawn blood. We're just getting started." She shoves herself against my sword until the end pierces her skin and blood oozes out.

What is wrong with her? "Maybe for you this is the start, but I'm not that bloodthirsty." I hurl my sword toward the corner of the ring, where it lands against hers with a clatter.

"You're a coward." Judica leans back and I notice the wound she inflicted on herself has already healed. I've never seen anyone heal so fast. "You're never willing to hurt anyone, never willing to inflict even a little pain."

"Pain's overrated."

Judica laughs. "Spoken like someone who doesn't understand it."

"And you're an expert?"

Judica's eyes flash. "More than you'll ever understand. But here, let me offer you your first lesson." My only warning is a flash of silver near her ankle before she rams the knife up to the hilt into my stomach.

I fall backward and land on my butt. Of course Judica keeps a concealed blade. I'm awash in pain now, but I have enough sense about me to know I need to pull the knife out before I can heal the damage. When I try to yank it out, Judica leaps above me, covering my hand with her own, and twisting the hilt. My vision blacks out and my body begins to shake.

"Enough." This time it's Balthasar who pulls Judica away.

Edam yanks the knife out of the gaping hamburger meat that used to resemble my stomach and lifts me up. He wraps an arm around me to keep me upright. "Are you okay?" he asks softly. "Did she puncture anything major? Should I call Job?" Pain rolls outward from my stomach in waves, but his hands on my shoulders still draw half my attention.

Judica snarls at me as Balthasar pulls her toward the back corner of the room. I ignore them and focus on my stomach, filling holes, repairing the torn and sliced bits. I push the pain back, one second at a time, and clench my fists until the worst recedes.

"I'm fine." Despite my words, I don't pull away from Edam and he doesn't release me. He's staring down at my face when I finally look up. I'm healed, but the process has drained me right down to my bones.

"I think I'm done for the day," I mumble. I'm not sure I can stay on my feet without help.

"I was wrong," Judica says.

I'm not expecting an apology. After years of trying, of hoping, of forgiving, I gave up completely on ever being the recipient of Judica's remorse long ago. I should ignore her proclamation and walk out, but since I can't walk, I turn toward her.

Besides, Judica has never admitted she's wrong before, so her declaration piques my curiosity. "About what?"

"You're not a coward," she says.

"No?" I'm actually surprised. She never retracts insults. Maybe my comeback actually impressed her.

"No." She smiles at me and something inside me I thought long dead surges.

Hope.

Is she sorry for what she did? Does she realize she went too far by stabbing me after our sparring ended? Maybe she regrets being so cold and cruel over the years. Maybe she wants me to forgive her. Maybe shreds of compassion exist in the inner parts of her heart. Perhaps there's a shred of hope she might be willing to help me, to support me.

Her smile grows cold and I know. A split second before she speaks again, I realize nothing has changed.

"Cowardice can be overcome," she says. "Cowards sometimes grow backbones. You're not a coward, and you'll never change. You're weak, just like our father was, and you can't fix that, no more than a housecat could age into a tiger. Even in utero, Mother knew I was the strong one. She knew you were too small, too kind, and too weak to rule Alamecha. Nothing will change that. *Nothing*."

I just healed a broken knee, a gash on my arm that cut to the bone, and the damage from a knife being twisted inside my gut. Even so, her words hurt worse. It's not even her hatred or contempt that sting. I've become so accustomed to those that they have no power over me now.

But.

What she said this time is true.

Mom chose Judica over me without hesitation or delay. The only explanation is that she saw something in me, even as a baby, that was lacking. In seventeen years, I've never heard a single soul express the sentiment that Mom might have killed Judica instead of me. It was always *me* she spared, and it was always me who was doomed to die. My innate deficiency is the one wound my perfect body can't heal. Because if I hadn't ever tried on her ring, even my own mother would still think I was too flawed to take her place.

And everyone knows that Enora's instincts are never wrong.

9

By the time I stumble back to my room, I'm done with evian politics and my sister and rings and prophecies and everything else even remotely related to any of it. I collapse on my thick, champagne colored carpet and sob into Cookie's fluffy coat. She doesn't mind one bit. Which is exactly why I love my dog so much.

Maybe I am weak, and maybe I cry too often, but he never complains.

A light knock at the door connecting my room to Mom's leaves me scrambling to sit up. Mom never waits long after her courtesy tap, so she catches me, puffy red eyes and all. Not that it matters. She could probably hear me sobbing though the walls connecting our rooms. Most evian walls are soundproofed heavily because of our sensitive hearing, but Mom wanted to be able to hear my heartbeat at night. She says she can't sleep without it.

Mom sits next to me on the floor and pulls me against her chest. "Ready to kill Lark?"

My breathing hitches, and her hand strokes my hair. "Relax. You'll be pretending to kill Lark, and Frederick will testify he saw it. I'll lead her out through one of the secret passages to freedom instead."

"Wait, we have secret passages?" I wipe my cheeks and sit up straight. "How did I not know that?"

"Duh," Mom says. "Because they wouldn't be secret if everyone knew about them."

I lift one eyebrow. "I know about the secret bunker." I wonder how many other secrets my mom is hiding.

Mom shrugs. "Need to know."

"Does that mean Judica—"

"Has no idea. True."

I beam.

"Balth told me today didn't go so well."

I shake my head.

"Well, maybe you'll feel better once Lark is safely on her way."

Yes, maybe my spirits will be lifted when I watch my best friend escape through a tunnel to a world I'll never join.

Mom's eyebrows draw together. "I know it's not what you had in mind when you woke up this morning."

This morning I thought the world was safe. This morning I knew my place. What I wouldn't give to go back in time to this morning. A single tear streaks down my face, but I wipe it away. Because crying won't help Lark, but helping free her might. I stand up and nod at the air duct. "Is that the passageway?" The air whooshing through always seemed abnormally loud to me.

Mom laughs. "Not even close." I signal for Cookie to stay in my room. Then I follow Mom through the door into her room and watch as she slides a portrait of me as a baby aside and presses her finger into a tiny scuffed spot in the wall. A bookcase that I've never seen shift even a hair slides silently to the right, opening to show a dim hallway that slopes steeply down.

"What in the—"

She signals Duchess to stay, and says, "Let's go."

I rush after her, nearly bumping into her backside before she begins to jog downward. I shudder when the bookcase slides shut behind us, closing off the last of the light from Mom's bedroom. Now the corridor is completely black. I follow my mother's heartbeat, its steady, slow *buh-bump* reassuring in the complete darkness. It's so quiet down here that I can make out the heartbeat of some tiny animal, like a bird, or ugh. I shudder. Maybe a mouse or a rat. It's beating much quicker than Mom's heartbeat, and very near.

I speed up, and stumble over a rock. It's bad timing, because Mom stops short. I bump into the back of her, and she takes my hand and places it on a rod next to me. She's been walking along with the guidance of a handrail, and I move much easier with that in my grip, even if I still feel like I can hear the mouse.

"There are normally low lights, but that EMP you set off killed them all. Move quietly, or the guards will hear. We need to wait until Frederick takes over for them. He's going to be the witness for the execution."

"You're the Empress," I whisper. "Why is all the secrecy necessary? Why not just free Lark? She had nothing to do with her mother keeping her here, and you certainly already punished Lyssa."

"You'll learn someday that what you can do and what you should do aren't always the same. I know in my heart I should force you to execute your friend, but I also know what that would do to you and to us. I'm not willing to face it. But if my people see me as lenient, well, I can't have that, either. Sometimes it's more judicious to fly under the radar. Empresses always have so many options open that it's often hard to choose. But after a few centuries, it's easier to know."

Mom stops in front of me, and there's just enough light that I can see her tilt her head slightly. She's listening, her face pressed to a wall.

Feet on the other side of the wall scuffle around, and then guards shuffle out, presumably to make their reports. This is our window. Mom places her hand on a rectangular box I can barely see, but nothing happens.

Mom swears under her breath and my jaw drops in the dark. My mother never swears. Ever.

"Of course your EMP wiped out the sensor for the door. That means we're going to have to do this the hard way."

Mom turns a corner and begins shifting stones in the dark.

"What's the plan?"

"We could have marched in and announced we were executing Lark. But it would have drawn attention, and it would have been harder to move her, and practically impossible to transport the goat we're using as cover. Sneaking down to free her lets you say goodbye, and makes this all simpler. But that door should have slid out of the way, and it can't because the board is fried. Luckily, there's an alternate method."

"That's good news."

"The bad news is that we have to shift all these stones to access it."

I crouch down and follow her lead, shifting heavy stone blocks out of the way one at a time. Once we've cleared a two-by-two area, Mom stoops and crawls through on her stomach. I try not to think about the mouse when I follow Mom into a utility closet that services the holding cells in the basement. Once we step into the center of the cell matrix, it's clear that someone has lit the old wall sconces. It's nice to be able to see.

Since we've only got one prisoner at present, it's easy to

know where to go. Lark's heart thumps along steadily in the third cell on the right, just a little faster than it should. I can't believe I never realized she was half-human. Mom beelines for her cell, with me following close behind.

At the sound of our approach, Lark stands.

Two fingernails on her right hand are broken and one is ragged, like she was prying at stones too, even though there aren't any in her cell. Her always pristine hair is rucked up on the right side, as though she's run her hand through it twenty times in the last few minutes. Which she probably has, because her mother's dead. Even though I've been thinking of it all day, the realization still strikes me like a slap to the cheek.

Lark's eyes widen when she sees me and she stumbles back a step.

Good. If she's worried I'm here to kill her, it means she still wants to live, at least a little bit. That's better than I expected based on her reaction earlier.

"Lark, we don't have much time," Mom says. "You think Chancy's here to execute you, but she's not."

Mother uses her handprint on the cell door, and it works. These electronics have been replaced. I watch Mom wipe the history on the keypad so there won't be a record of Lark's release.

"You need to follow me out right now. Frederick will come inside and monitor the fake execution." Mom's voice is so low I can barely hear her.

"Wait, what?" Lark glances my way.

"I assume I'll be killing the goat you mentioned, Mother?"

Mom nods, and Lark shoots through the door and collapses into my arms, sobbing silently on my shoulder. I wrap my arms around her and drag air into my lungs to keep from crying, too.

"I'm so sorry," I whisper.

My best friend squeezes me again, so tightly I can barely breathe, and then she lets me go and nods at me. I expected her to yell at my Mom, or sob uncontrollably and have to be carried out. But she's doesn't. The Lark in front of me is a warrior. She's been trained for this moment since birth by her mother. Of course she has.

Mom hurries back to the utility closet and pushes down on an old, rather dingy looking bottle of bleach. A panel opens and she presses her palm to it again. The secret panel reopens.

"Tell your friend goodbye," Mom says. "Frederick will be here any minute."

"Where am I going?" Lark asks.

"I'm sending you to meet one of my deputies, the head of my network in Austin," Mom says. "Her name is Marselle. She's going to mentor you, and once you've grieved and she thinks you're ready, she'll send you in for your first field assignment." Mom narrows her eyes. "I killed your mother. Can you swear loyalty to me? I must trust my agents one hundred and fifty percent. Sparing you is a tremendous risk."

Lark's lips tighten and her heartbeat accelerates.

Mom might kill her anyway, or have Marselle do it if her loyalty isn't unquestionable. My stomach twists.

"What about me?" I ask. "Do you blame me?"

Lark's face falls and she takes my hand. "Of course I don't blame you, not for any of it. You took a huge risk for me this morning."

I spin to face Mom. "I'll need my own network. I'd like Lark to be my first asset."

Mom's eyes widen. "You will need your own. Where would you send her?"

"Not Austin," I say. "I'd send her to Alora in New York. I trust Alora to train Lark. And you know, of all people, Alora won't care that she's half-human."

Mom frowns, but she knows my older sister loves humans more than she should. "Fine."

I whisper. "Can you promise to be loyal to me, one hundred and fifty percent?"

Tears well in Lark's eyes. "A thousand percent." She hugs me again. "I'm going to miss you so much."

"If there's any way I can swing it, I may move to New York yet. Don't give up on having me around."

Bootsteps and hooves sound down the hall. "Frederick is coming," Mom says. "Time to go."

Lark bobs her head and squeezes my hand before she lets go and crosses to where Mom's waiting. I want to collapse on the floor and sob again, but I can't do that. I have to execute an innocent animal. Ugh.

I turn to face Frederick. He's holding the lead rope on a dove gray goat with one black leg and two black ears. It looks as scared as I feel, but its mouth is bound with a cord so it can't bleat. When I glance back, Mom and Lark are gone without a trace. Frederick hands me a sword without saying a word.

"How can you possibly testify that you saw me execute Lark?"

Frederick bobs his dark head at the goat. "I named her Lark."

Of course he did, five minutes ago. I tighten my grip on the sword and I think about spilling Lark's blood this morning, about my mother decapitating Lyssa, and about Judica stabbing me in the gut. My stomach turns and my heart quakes. Poor Lark the goat's eyes dart from me to Frederick and back again, clearly terrified.

I can't do it.

I hold the sword toward Frederick. He shakes his head. "You have to do it."

"I can't, okay? Why can't you do it?"

His eyes are sad. "I've known you for your entire life,

Chancery. I've cared about you every day, and I've seen how happy you make your mother. Serving her has been my life's work. But it's time for you to clean a toilet, for once in your life."

"Excuse me?" I lift my chin. What do toilets have to do with this?

"Your life has been blessed. Safe. Clean and perfect. But real life isn't like that. Normal people have to clean toilets, even when we don't want to. This is partially your fault. If you'd told your mother this morning what you knew, if you'd trusted her, she could have spared Lyssa and Lark. But you tried to fix it yourself, and Lyssa's dead. Feel the weight of that mistake, and then clean this up yourself so I can tell people I watched you behead Lark without lying. Do the uncomfortable thing to keep your friend safe."

I blink back tears, tighten my hands on the sword and lift it up. I put it back down. I will never understand how evians can kill, can maim, can attack, can inflict pain on others with impunity. I adjust my steps to avoid killing beetles, ants, anything. I insisted the cleaning staff leave a birds' nest with three baby sparrows alone, even though they pooped all over the floor for weeks. I didn't actually clean up after them, but I would have.

But this isn't about me.

It's about Lark. And I need to do this for her. So I grip the hilt, my palms sweaty, and bring it up over my head. I swing it down, closing my eyes at the last second. The blade cleaves through poor Lark the goat's neck, barely slowing as it severs her spine. I suppress a shudder when the warm blood spatters my arm.

When I open my eyes, Frederick's grin is self-satisfied, like he's taught me an important lesson. I wish I could slap his smug face. It's atrocious that savagery is a life lesson for us. I hate it. I don't hand him the sword. I don't thank him, or even ask what he's planning to do to dispose of Lark the goat's body. I walk up the steps to the entrance of the dungeon, dragging the blood-stained sword behind me, leaving a trail of gore and staining my pants badly in the process.

Dozens of people line the hallway as I leave, some headed toward the throne room, some headed for the guest wing. They all freeze when I emerge, staring at my bloody sword and clothing. I wipe the tears from my face with my free hand, and my fingers come away red. I didn't even feel any of it hit my face.

"Lark is dead." My voice is flat. No one stops me on my way to my room.

I peel my bloody clothes off and toss them in the corner. If Mom had adhered to her own rules, they'd be stained with Lark's blood, not a goat's. Because ruling evians is the worst job in the world. For the last seventeen years, I've secretly felt lesser because Mom didn't pick me. Inferior, because Mom didn't think I was good enough to rule. And now that she wants me to be the one making these ghastly decisions, I realize too late that I was wrong all along.

I want to take it all back. I'd tell Mom about my discovery with Lark and never touch that detestable stone. But for all my perfect DNA, I can't reverse time. I can't undo what's been done, no matter how desperately I wish I could.

10

The next morning, my newly nine-hundred-year-old mom makes time to train with me. First, we go back down to the bunker and practice with her ring again. I'm better, but not by much. I manage to send a few short bursts of heat only, in between a handful of fireballs, and then I let loose a dozen controlled EMPs that short out some iPods Mom had brought in from Kauai.

"Better call it a morning," she says.

"Why?" I ask. "I'm finally figuring it out."

"This fire extinguisher is empty," Mom says.

Neither of us wants to count on my ability to suck the flames back in like I did yesterday in her closet. I haven't been able to replicate it since.

We return to the private courtyard outside our adjoining rooms to work on my normal melodics training. We're already running late for the normal daily routine, and with the party we can't afford to be, but Mom makes time anyway. We run through the cues we've been working on quickly, and I'm smiling by the time Mom stops the music.

"You're ready," she says.

"For what?" I ask. "Breakfast? Because I'm absolutely starving."

She smiles. "You're ready to go off book."

I shake my head. "You said it takes twenty years at least. That means I have almost a decade to go since I started at five."

"You've always shortchanged yourself, little dove. You let other people's expectations interfere with your progress. You aren't like anyone else on Earth. You're ready now, and it's good that you are, because change is upon us."

"What does that mean?" I ask. "It sounds like a movie script. Except if you said something that corny, you'd be sure to die in the next scene. At your age, you should probably be asking yourself, 'Does this sound like something someone in a Greek tragedy would say?' before you speak."

She rolls her eyes. "I'm being serious. You're ready to fight without musical cues, and we'll start this afternoon, before my party." Mom turns and walks toward the table in the corner of the courtyard, which is already covered with food for breakfast.

"Perfect," I mutter, just loudly enough for her to hear. "I was thinking a little swordplay would be just the thing to get me ready to entertain all your guests."

When we reach the table, I dig into my food. I polish off a stack of French toast, a pile of pancakes, half a pound of bacon, and I'm sliding the fried egg off my loco moco when Mom clears her throat.

"Chancery."

"Oh come on, Mom. It's so much better without the egg."

"You can choose which egg to eat. Any type you'd like is fine."

I glance between my options. Chef Angel put a boiled egg on a stand next to my plate, a fried egg on top of my loco moco, and a huge blob of scrambled eggs on a salad plate. "You do know that a chicken pooped out every single one of these. Have you been around chickens? They're gross."

"I didn't realize you were an expert on poultry."

"Besides, it's like I'm eating their baby. Even if you like chickens, that's still disturbing."

Mom sighs. "The eggs we eat haven't even been fertilized. They could never become chicks."

I groan. "Mom, seriously. Ease up on the egg pushing."

"Fine, we don't have to talk about it, but you have to pick one and eat it. I'm done with your theatrics. They're good for you, and you'll learn to eat them. Not everything in life is fun."

I stare at the one thing I hate even more than evian politics: a boiled egg. It sits there trying to look innocent with its slimy white exterior, but I know it's hiding a bulbous, chalky yolk. I shudder. I finally groan and pinch off a piece of a fried egg for Cookie.

"You have to eat it," Mom says.

"I know, but Cookie hasn't tasted it yet, to make sure it's fine." That's the official reason everyone in the royal line has a dog—they taste our food. But honestly, there aren't many kinds of poison that can hurt an evian. Even so, I use the excuse to delay consuming my eggs whenever I can.

Mom's still staring pointedly, so I'm about to take my first bite of the fried egg when my mom's chamberlain, Larena, breezes through the door. She gives us a report on the progress of the repairs, which went on throughout the night. I take that chance to feed the rest of the egg to Cookie under the table. Mom doesn't bat an eye.

Larena leaves and I beam at her. "All done?"

"Chancery," she says, "you aren't invisible because I'm talking to someone. I saw what you did."

"What? I'm supposed to give Cookie the first bite."

"Which implies you would take a second, or a third bite." My mom cocks one eyebrow.

"The fried ones are so gross," I whine, "especially the inside. The yolk is usually runny, or if not, it's rubbery."

"So eat the boiled one."

"That's even worse. The yolk is mealy."

Mom slams her hand down on the table and I jump.

"What is going on Mom? You usually think this is funny." I take a good look at her and notice faint circles under her eyes, so faint that it's almost like they've been disguised by something.

"Mom, don't take this the wrong way, but are you wearing makeup? You don't look so hot this morning."

"Happy birthday to you, too."

"It's not my birthday." I ignore her joke because I'm genuinely concerned. And because this gets the conversation off my egg eating... or not eating.

"Next year," she says, "I plan to institute a new birthday policy: no age jokes."

"Mom, I'm not joking. You don't usually look a day over six hundred. But today you look... tired. Did you sleep at all last night?"

"Not really," she says. "I have too much on my mind to sleep."

"Like what? I know you're worried about the stone and all that, but maybe I can help. I've been thinking about it, and I still think going to live with Alora is my best bet. Your prophecies don't say how exactly the reuniting queen will do what she does. Judica knows what I can do, so why can't I go do what I want, let the better twin rule when it comes to that, and then she can call me in if she needs me. I'll be like a pinch hitter. That's someone who bats for someone else when—"

Mom sighs. "I know what it is. I do think Alora could help with your perspective. You seem to be operating under the delusion that being away from Alamecha's base of operations will fill your life with boundless joy."

"You think she'll tell me all the horrible things about living amongst humans? Mom, she surrounds herself with them by choice. Plus, it's not like I haven't done my homework. I've watched a million movies and television shows. I know what humans are like. And Lark will be there."

"Movies and television shows are one image they present, but I doubt the shows you like so much accurately reflect reality. Regardless, I'm not budging on the Heirship. The ring reacted to you, which means you're going to reunite the families. You're going to save the world. The sooner you accept it, the sooner we can address any deficiencies in your training to prepare you for that task."

"Oh my gosh Mom, how can you possibly know that's what it means?"

"What we will not do is stick our heads in the sand like an ostrich. You will not hide from this, because it won't go away." Mom sighs. "Even so, it might be wise to give Judica time to process the change without you being in residence. Since I'll be changing the paperwork soon, sending you home with Alora after her trip next week seems prudent."

I smile. "That's the best thing I've heard all day. I'll miss you of course, but I think it will help. Did you hear Judica tried to kill me again yesterday? More time with her is not helping us get along."

"Agreed, but there are terms. Alora will prepare you as my Heir while you're there, a full regimen of training around the clock. You'll adhere to the same schedule Judica follows. Routine weapons training, battle strategy, political maneuvering, pain training—"

"Wait, pain training?" That sounds terrible. How have I never heard of that?

Mom rubs her temples almost like humans in movies with headaches, which makes no sense. Evians don't get headaches, just like we never get sick. "Being Heir is miserable, Chancery. I know you think my selection of Judica was a slight against you, but honestly it's a lot of awful training and even more work. Pain training is similar to healing training."

I groan. Mom explained that last week. She delayed mine as long as possible, but when I turn eighteen, I'm supposed to start. I'll be systematically injured and practice healing while being distracted with other things. Sounds horrifying.

"Similar. You must continue to fight in spite of injury or ongoing pain. There are several ways to do it, including the placement of a blade in your body, which you cannot remove, but must fight around."

So you can't heal it. My lip curls.

"You may have noticed that pain distracts us during a fight. But the more you practice fighting through your injuries, the better you become at doing it, and the less negative impact an injury will have on you during an actual challenge."

"So it's essentially torture?"

"Actually, torture training is separate, and that particular course—"

"Geez Mom, do you even hear yourself?"

"It's a lot to take in." Mom reaches across the table and takes my hand. "I'm sorry things are changing so fast, but I have one more thing we need to discuss. It's been a crazy twenty-four hours. If I thought I could, I'd put this off. But if you're leaving with Alora soon, we need to discuss it now. The thing is, I may look the same, but I'm getting older. None of us live forever, and—"

"Stop, Mom." I shake her hand away. "You aren't old. You're fine, and you'll be around for decades and decades."

"Nevertheless, getting older has side effects. It could be that I'm older, or it could be something else, I'm not sure.

But for whatever reason, this is harder than it ever has been."

I think about the bags under her eyes and I wonder what she's trying to tell me. Is Mom dying? I shake off the thought. It can't be. We have time. So much time.

"Mom, what's harder? What's going on?"

Before she can answer, there's a loud banging on the door. Mom looks at me with great sorrow. "It'll have to wait. I'll tell you after my party tonight."

"Tell me what?" I ask.

"Enter," Mom says.

Larena and Inara stomp into the room. Inara's mastiff, Brutus, lays down by Cookie Crisp under the table and whimpers a little. I reach down and rub his head. What's wrong now?

Inara and Larena sport identically furrowed brows.

"Is everything alright?" Mom asks.

Inara sighs. "Adika and Venagra are wearing the same color and they're upset. Shamecha's hiking oil prices and Adika has raised their tariffs, but whatever the real issue, Adika's insisting you loan something to Venagra. I'd normally pull something from your closet for one of them, but it all smells like smoke. If I hand over something that smells, they'll ply me with questions."

"Which we couldn't even answer if we wanted to," Larena says. "Because you won't tell us what really happened."

"In due time," Mom says, "but for now, I'd better go. Venagra will fit into something of Chancy's just fine."

They storm out as quickly as they barged in.

I don't want to wait until tonight. I clear my throat. "You said—"

"I know," my mom says, "and I will explain, but it'll have to wait until after the party. Have a little faith in me, but for now I have something pressing to take care of." She glances at her watch and then looks back at me. "I told you that you'll be training as Heir. That starts today. You have weapons training in five minutes."

"That's plenty of time," I say, "but can you tell Balthasar to lay off the swordplay? There are other weapons, you know."

"I told him you needed to focus on bladed weapons since it's your weakest area. I don't plan to revise that direction. You can't just ignore things you don't like anymore. That's not what an empress does."

"But I won't be sparring with Judica, right?"

Mom sighs. "No, not today anyway. But Balthasar's vetting security rewires and running interference on the entire party. He's too busy to handle a training session, even though it's important that you catch up quickly."

"I thought you said I've got weapons training in less than five minutes." I stab a pancake and plop it down on my plate. "Make up your mind."

Mom stands up. "That is what I said and it's true. You're training with Edam today."

I hop up without taking a single bite. "I better get going, then."

Mom winks at me on my way out. She obviously heard my heart rate pick up when she mentioned his name. Some days I really hate evian hearing.

11

I'm training with Edam alone.

Which is totally no big deal. Even though Judica doesn't begin to deserve him, I'd never do anything to ruin whatever weird thing they have. I walk through the door to my room, Cookie Crisp trailing behind me slowly for some reason. Probably because she isn't about to train with the hottest dog in Ni'ihau.

If I'm fast, I can change clothes. After all, if I'm practicing bladework, I need tighter pants and a fitted shirt. Obviously. And if I choose my nicest jeans and my favorite shirt, well, that doesn't mean anything.

I signal Cookie to stay in the room, but instead of lying down like usual, she whimpers. I crouch down and rub her ears. "It's been a rough few days, I know." Instead of calming down, she licks my hand and whines piteously, which is not at all like her. She must be anxious about all the party guests, or maybe she can feel my tension since Lyssa's execution, or Lark's departure, or the ring incident.

It's been an awful twenty-four hours.

I relent and let her come with me. It's not like Judica will be there trying to saw me in two again. What could it hurt to have Cookie curled up in the corner while I train? I glance at the clock. It's two minutes before the hour, and yesterday Edam came looking for me when I was late. I rush out the door and toward the arena.

He's sitting in the chair in front of the room's computer interface. He looks up at me when I walk in, then glances at the large, round clock mounted on the back wall. "Right on time this morning."

He's alone in the room, a room that holds six training rings, one of which is raised for formal duels. I'm dozens of yards away, but I try my best to calm my heartbeat before moving closer. Did I mention that I hate evian senses? No human girl has to worry that her pulse will give her feelings away to her crush. Every one of them can pine away without her heart betraying her. Plus, human high schools might be small, but the sheer volume of guys a human girl encounters dwarfs the tiny pool of available men when you're evian. Especially an evian in the line of succession like me. I've got a pool of three dozen guys from whom to choose any future mate, in case something happens to the current Heir and I have to step up, a pool I *share* with Judica. Which leaves me constantly trying to make sure the one guy my stupid sister is dating doesn't realize I think he's yummier than a stack of chocolate truffle pancakes.

"Sorry about being late yesterday," I say. "I'm not accustomed to training with anyone other than my mom, and we just train whenever she has time."

Edam crosses the room and stops directly in front of me. "Never apologize, Your Highness. Not to me or to anyone else."

"Excuse me?"

"You're second in line to the throne of the First Family of the Six. You should never apologize."

I raise one eyebrow. "I appreciate the advice, but I always apologize when I'm wrong. I'm not my sister."

He bows. "You most certainly are not." I listen to his tone for any evidence that he's mocking me, but I can't find any.

He looks so serious for someone so young, at least, young in evian terms. He can't be much older than I am, not more than a decade anyway. How has he advanced so fast? "You're taking over for Balthasar when he retires as Chief of Security, right?"

"If he ever retires, you mean?" He smiles. "Even if I do take over, you'll still outrank me. Don't apologize."

My heart melts. Until a little voice in my head screams, 'He's the demon-spawn's boyfriend!' I repeat it over and over to remind myself that even if he's beautiful and kind and impressive, he's still the enemy.

Out loud I say, "I'd take your advice if I agreed that I should only apologize to people who rank above me, but I think people should apologize whenever harm has been done. I'm sorry for a lot of things that aren't my fault. It's called empathy, and evians in general need to find a little more of it. Even if it makes people perceive me as weak, I won't forsake common courtesy."

"You aren't common. It doesn't apply to you."

"Changing my behavior because you tell me to would be worse than apologizing for a slight. As you pointed out, I outrank you, so even if I'm not as strong and impressive as your girlfriend, you'll have to deal with it. I am who I am."

"She's not," he says.

"Huh?" She may be a horrible person, but even I admit Judica is both strong and impressive.

Edam coughs and takes a step back, then turns toward the weapons rack. "Judica's not my...you know."

"Not your what?" I ask, because I need to hear him say it. Even so, I'm suddenly very interested in the weapons in front of me.

"We aren't together anymore."

My jaw drops. "Whoa, she dumped you?"

Edam's head snaps around toward me so fast it practically blurs. "No, she didn't end things."

"So you're still together? I'm confused."

"None of this impacts our training." Edam reaches for a long sword and I imagine it swinging down toward my neck. I suppress a shudder. His hand pauses. "What do you want to work on today?"

I shrug. "You're the one who brought it up."

He reaches for a scimitar.

"Not that," I say.

He pulls his hand back and looks at me expectantly.

"Mom says I should practice my aim. Other than that, I dunno."

"I wasn't trained in melodics, but I know a few drills. Should we start with some of those?"

"Mom and I usually do."

He walks to a cabinet and pulls out a flute case.

I laugh. "I haven't used a flute in a decade."

"Oh." He looks sheepish. "What do you do, then?"

I walk over to the computer screen he was sitting at moments before and tap a few things. "The flute is for basic runs. Triads, scales, and so on. I mastered all the variations of those by age seven." I tap the screen again. I put my selection on time delay.

"Beethoven's Fifth?" He's standing right behind me, and when he speaks, his breath warms the back of my neck. Steady, heart, steady.

"Beethoven was the last great melodics composer."

I untie my shoes and pull them off. I peel off my socks and set them on the floor by Cookie, who has curled up in a ball, fast asleep. At least she's calmed down. Her heart's barely beating. I could use some of that zen myself.

I walk to the middle of the room before inhaling and exhaling deeply a few times. Then the music begins.

Melodics ties a sequence of notes to each body motion. You learn to flow from one movement to the next, following an established method. Turn, strike down, pull back, drop, strike up, crouch, leap, kick, spin. I move from one form to another, following the pattern of the music. The great dance, that's what Mom sometimes calls it.

The song ends and Edam claps. "Graceful, but perhaps not so useful."

"Mock me if you will, but there's a reason evians have trained with melodics for thousands of years."

"Science hadn't invented guns, yet?"

"Funny. And that'll be a good argument against it when the evians update their duels and use guns or bombs. For now, we still fight it out in arenas, up close."

"But even as hand-to-hand or weapons training," Edam says, "it's outdated."

I shake my head. "It isn't. The body learns certain movements and how they connect, and it helps you read your opponent and respond without thinking about it. You *feel* it."

"Were you feeling it yesterday?" His eyes are kind, but the criticism still annoys me.

"Look, you don't drop the external music until you reach a certain point in your training. It's hard to hear the music in your head, to feel the movements and see the patterns without actually having music playing. They call hearing the music around you 'sensing the score of all things' and when you can hear it, you go 'off book.' I haven't reached that point yet, and yesterday I wasn't feeling much of anything." Except for a brief moment, maybe. But the euphoria from that blinded me to Judica's hidden blade. Not exactly a winning endorsement.

He taps his lip thoughtfully, probably to help him focus, but it has the opposite effect on me. "You improved dramatically the second time. Were you hearing it then, this score?"

I blush. "I finally did, a little, but it wasn't enough." The sympathy in Edam's eyes pisses me off. It's not like I'm delusional. I know Judica destroyed me. "So, I'm warm now. What's next?"

Edam walks to the middle of the arena until he stands so close I could reach out and touch him if I dared. I focus on keeping my heart rate steady.

Edam's voice is scratchy and low when he says, "I shouldn't have asked about yesterday. Your relationship with your sister is none of my business."

I arch one eyebrow. "It's so much simpler to just say 'I'm sorry.'"

"Touché."

"Besides, everyone knows Judica and I aren't close."

"She was out of line," he says. "You've never threatened her, and I told her that last night."

"Whoa, that didn't go well."

"It didn't," he said. "In fact, you could say it precipitated our breakup."

So she dumped him because he defended me? I should keep quiet, but I don't. "Sometimes change is for the best."

"I hope so." Edam reaches out to touch my arm and I jump back.

"So, what now?" I ask.

Edam turns away. When he turns back to face me, he's wearing a strange expression I can't read. "Hand-to-hand. Even if you don't want to work with swords after yesterday, I think you could use some practice in dueling forms."

"You're probably right." I spread my feet shoulder width apart and let my arms drop to my sides.

"Shouldn't you take your necklace off?"

"This?" I gesture to the necklace I never remove. It's a framework of silver in a 'U' shape, set with purple stones of varying colors. It circles my neck, the larger stones near the bottom. "No, I don't think so."

He raises his eyebrows at me. "Really? I could grab it and use it to take you down."

"I'm prepared for that possibility. I never take it off. Mom's orders."

He looks curious but doesn't press for more.

His stance shifts to match mine. "On my mark, then." He claps and we're off.

He's good. He pins me in under a minute.

"Again," I say.

And again, pinned in under a minute.

"Don't pin me this time," I say. "Hit me."

"Full contact?" His words practically quiver with doubt.

"I didn't do much right yesterday, but I think I proved that I heal just fine."

He grins. "True enough."

Less than two minutes later I'm lying flat on my back with a broken shin and a bloody nose. I roll over and spit blood all over the mat while I mend my shattered bone. "Why did I ask for full contact? Yuck."

Edam chuckles.

I moan as I sit up. "If you aren't better than Judica, I'll eat my boiled egg tomorrow."

"Not a fan of eggs, huh?"

I snort. "You may be the best fighter I've ever met."

Edam smiles. "Didn't you wonder why Balthasar's finally talking about retiring, after nine hundred years as Security Chief?"

I hadn't really thought about it. "He's old. He has to retire sometime, but I guess you're right. There are lots of people much more..." I was going to say more qualified, but that seems rude. "Well, there are people..." I trail off, not wanting to say older either. I also don't mention that I think it's dumb to choose someone to run all the family's non-military security interests based on how good they are at one-on-one combat. A lot of evian traditions don't make sense to me, which is another reason I'd make a terrible empress.

"I know I'm too young and I'm inexperienced. Everyone's thinking it, but none of them can beat me in here, and I doubt anyone else could defeat Balthasar either, no matter how old he is."

"Can you?" I ask.

He smiles. "I can't take over until I do, and I won't challenge him until I'm sure."

"I hadn't thought much about it."

"My point is, don't feel too bad about losing to me."

"You're just that awesome?"

He grins ear-to-ear. "Something like that, Your Highness."

"I thought we were past that?"

"My apologies. Chancery."

The sound of my name coming from him warms my heart. "I should probably practice my aim, now that I've been beaten so soundly in hand-to-hand."

"I think I should teach you a few moves first. Melodics or not, there are some sneaky holds and a few strikes you ought to know."

He demonstrates several moves I mastered long ago. I repeat them anyway, pretending to pay attention. Finally, he shows me a pull and strike combo that would have broken his elbow if I'd used it earlier.

He grabs my arm. "Now, you show me—"

I execute it perfectly. He grunts and straightens, and I watch in awe as his elbow mends. He heals fast, much faster than me.

"You obviously already knew that one," he says, "so why didn't you do it earlier? When I struck you on the left."

"I hate it." I look at the springy black floor of the arena, unable to meet his eyes.

"That strike? Why?" He's trying to meet my eye, but I'm too embarrassed.

"No, not that strike, just the noise." I swallow.

"Wait, do you mean the sound of a bone breaking?" He raises his eyebrows.

"Yeah."

"I heal too, you know. I may not be from Alamecha by birth, but Malessa's not a bad family. It's the second best in fact, although if you ever tell my sister I said that, I'll deny it." He grins.

His smile is so contagious I can't help grinning back.

"I'm seventh generation just like you, and I can heal a broken bone in half a second."

"Wait, you are?" I'm surprised. Seventh generation is pretty rare. I assumed he was eighth, son of Analessa, the Malessa family's current queen.

"I was Senah's last child. She died when I was three. I have few memories of her."

"How do you remember her at all? Weren't you sold at birth?"

Edam shakes his head. "Nope. My mother kept me, I guess because she'd gotten nostalgic, but my sister Analessa sold me after she died."

"Wait, really?" Most empresses sell their sons, because if they don't, other rulers won't sell theirs to them. It's sort of a *quid pro quo*. Each family wants to raise any possible consort for the new Heir themselves, to ensure loyalty, so they all sell any sons of the current queen to other families. Occasionally, if a queen had already sold quite a few boys, they'd decide to keep one. It happened more often at the end of their lives. I guess it makes sense. People get sentimental with age. Even so, the idea of being sold at the age of three horrifies me. He would have remembered every single thing about his family, and being sold would have felt like a major betrayal. Combine that with losing his mother and. . .

As if he can sense my horror, Edam says, "Your mother was kind, for what it's worth. She met me at the funeral and when Analessa announced she was selling me, your mother brought me home personally. She clipped me in right next to her on the jet. I believe she had just lost your brother Moses."

Mom told me once she meant to keep a son, but it was too hard because it reminded her of all the boys she had given up. She sold Moses when he was twenty-five days old.

"Kind of sucks your sister sold you. Your mom died and then you got dumped in a new family at the same time."

He shrugs. "I hated her for a while, but I'm sure Analessa had her reasons."

"I'm still sorry."

"Don't be. I'm not sorry to be here." His eyes meet mine and I can't breathe.

They're so blue. And his jawline is criminally chiseled. Oxygen. I need oxygen. I force a breath in and then out of my lungs.

Edam nods, as if he's been considering something and come to a conclusion about it. "Look, you hate hurting people and I get it. You want to fix everything and everyone, but I don't need fixing." He stares at me with something very much like a challenge in his intense, stormy eyes.

He's not the one who needs fixing. "I've always hated causing pain."

Edam doesn't say anything else, but I'm sure he agrees with Judica that I'm weak, maybe even fatally flawed. He crosses the room to another cabinet and pulls out a simple slingshot, which he passes to me.

"Let's work on your aim."

He presses a button and the targets pop up across the

room in varying places. The targets differ in size and height. He drops a bag full of irregularly shaped pebbles into my hand.

"Timed?" I ask.

"Of course."

"On your mark then." He claps three times and I start shooting. I hit the closest ones first and then fan out. I shoot the last one and drop my hand. "Done."

He looks at the screen, reading impact, precision, and timing. He doesn't say a word, but he makes me do the same thing with moving targets. Then he makes me try a more complicated slingshot, a bow, and finally a crossbow. I'm equally good with all of them. He reaches for a gun, but then he notices the time. "I guess we can practice with guns tomorrow."

I try not to show the shiver of excitement that races through me when he says tomorrow. "Sure."

"You're amazing at that," he says.

"I know. Forget Goliath, I'd have taken out most of his army too, right?"

He smiles because I may suck at hand-to-hand and I may hate hurting people, but I dominate all projectiles. I glance at my watch. Five minutes after eleven. I should get cleaned up.

"Well thanks," I say. "It's been interesting."

Edam smiles at me. "That it has."

Do not freak out. Do not race, heart. Do not. But it's not lost on me that he's not dating Judica anymore, and he's smiling at me. Maybe it's not awful if he hears my traitorous heart racing along a little bit. . .

I turn to go and snap my fingers at Cookie. I reach for the handle on the door before I realize she didn't get up. She's still asleep. Weird. I walk over to her and shake her a little.

Nothing.

It takes me several seconds to register the import of something I don't hear. Something I've heard every day for seven years. I can't hear her familiar heartbeat because it's not beating. I was so distracted with Edam that I didn't notice until just now. I crouch down and cradle Cookie's head in my arms. My sweet little dog is dead. She was in perfect health this morning. She came on part of my run, ate as much as always, but... she was acting oddly in my room before we came here. Almost as if she felt sick.

Or as if she'd been poisoned.

Seconds later I'm screaming a name and I'm not stopping until I get my pound of flesh. Judica, I'm coming for you, and this time I will relish the sound of every last crunch.

12

"Judica! JUDICA!"

I'm raging. She isn't in her room, the ballroom, the throne room, or the kitchen, and I don't know where to look next.

"Sister." At the sound of her quiet voice, I spin around. Death is at her heels as always. And probably in response to the threat in my voice, the fur along his back is raised and his ears are up. Judica's wearing a burgundy gown that matches Mom's Marchesa almost perfectly, but with a burgundy overlay instead of silver.

I can't quite keep the tremble out of my voice when I accuse her. "You killed my dog."

Her eyebrows rise and her eyes widen in surprise at first, but no. Maybe I imagined that because her arched eyebrow and cold words confirm my suspicion. "Pity it was only the dog."

I scream and run toward her. I don't know quite what I'll do when I get there, but my fingers are curling up and I'm itching to sink my fingernails into the skin on her face. Someone pulls me back just before I reach her, and I spin around to face him or her.

It's Edam.

"Let me go," I say. "You don't understand!"

"I understand your dog died and you're upset, but you have no evidence Judica had anything to do with it."

"You're defending her?" I snarl. "She killed my dog." My voice cracks. "Again."

Judica's laughter chills me to the bone.

Edam's voice is a low rumble in my ear. "I'm not an expert on dogs, but I'm pretty sure they can't die twice. Unless Cookie was a zombie dog."

I appreciate what he's trying to do, but his attempted joke enrages me more.

Quiet or not, Judica must have heard him, because she says, "I killed Fruity Pebbles, her first spaniel, on our ninth birthday." Judica's still standing in the exact same spot, completely calm, seemingly unconcerned. "No zombies that I know of, canine or otherwise."

"This isn't a joke," I grind out between clenched teeth. "Cookie is dead." My voice wavers even though I try to keep sorrow out of the equation. How can she still hurt me after so many years?

"A pity," she says.

I strain against Edam's arms, but they hold me firmly.

"She said it's a pity." Edam's looking right at me, not even bothering to glance at Judica. "See? She's sorry. It's some kind of misunderstanding."

"That's not what she means." I growl. "She meant that it was a pity she killed my dog on our ninth birthday, because she meant to kill me instead. I didn't eat her disgusting poisoned cookies, but Pebbles did."

Edam doesn't speak but he lets go of me, his brow furrowing. I assumed he knew. I assumed everyone knew the story. It seems like something Judica would gloat about.

Judica's lip curls, but I'm not stupid enough to think it's really a smile. "I didn't know about your distaste for sweets then and I miscalculated. An understandable oversight, since you named your mutt after a sugary breakfast cereal."

Rage swells inside me as I think about Pebbles' cold body, and now Cookie's. "That's your problem, Judica. You didn't know me then and you don't know me now. If you'd spent five minutes with me that weren't forced upon you, you could've killed me then and saved yourself all this hassle."

"Oh, I think I learned my lesson. Believe me sister, if I wanted to kill you now, I wouldn't make the same mistake." Death growls as if to emphasize her point.

"You'd just decapitate me during a training session, is that it?" I clench and unclench my fists. "But when that didn't work because Edam stopped you, maybe you'd give poison another go."

Edam looks from me to Judica and back. He gestures at the people who are gathering in the hall to listen. "Let's all calm down. Maybe we can find your mother and talk to her about this. In private."

Judica turns on Edam. "I'm surprised you can look me in the eye after yesterday." Judica's eyes flash and I need to know what exactly happened. "I don't take orders from you. I haven't had this much fun in months, so go away and leave us alone. You're good at that."

"What happened yesterday?" I ask. "What made you dump him?"

Judica's face turns bright red and it's suddenly clear to me. I'm grinning like a fool when I say, "Whoa, you didn't." I shouldn't gloat, I know that. But I can't help it. "He dumped you."

I might be imagining it, but Judica sounds a little bit broken when she says, "As much as I wish I could, I can't take credit. I had nothing to do with your dog's death. Was that all you wanted from me, Chancery?"

I want to demand that her dog die this time, too. She

needs to pay, but I realize it's not Death's fault. She should have to pay herself. "I'm going to challenge you."

"You're challenging *me*?" She laughs bitterly. "Do it, I beg you. I've wanted to challenge you for years, but Mother would never forgive me. If you challenge me, I'll finally be rid of you, and it won't even be my fault."

"Fine," I say. "I, Chancery Divinity—"

The door to my room opens and I jump. No one ever goes into my room without my permission. Who could be coming out of it?

When Mom emerges with tears streaking her cheeks, I'm confused. She never goes in my room unless I'm there, too. Her voice is soft, but cuts like a knife. "Would you break my heart, Chancy?" She stands just outside my door, Duchess beside her. "On my birthday? My two beautiful daughters at one another's throats?"

My mouth opens, but no words come out.

"I was leaving a gown on your bed. I wanted us all to coordinate for my birthday ball, but then I heard you yelling in the hallway."

An answering tear rolls down my cheek. Dang it. I can't cry, not now. Not in front of *her*. The words feel torn from me. "She killed Cookie, Mom."

"Is that true, Judica?" Mom asks.

"I didn't touch her mongrel, I swear it." Her smirk makes my blood boil.

"She might not have touched him, but she poisoned him. She always lies in a way that sounds like truth. Gah, listen to her—"

"Chancery, please." Mom glances at the audience that has gathered and my face flushes. I know better than to act like this in front of guests, no matter how angry and hurt I am.

"I want something from you both," Mom whispers. "I want you to stop fighting for just one day."

I know I shouldn't argue, but my heart is broken. I can't help it. "But, Mom," I say, "she—"

She shakes her head sharply. "No. Tomorrow you can hate her again, but for today, please be at peace." She pleads with her eyes and reinforces it with her words. "Do this for me, little dove."

It's more effective than any order ever could be. It's her birthday, and she never asks for anything. She looks so sad and so tired. I've never seen her look so old. I can wait one day. When I think of my poor, sweet Cookie I simmer inside, but I love my mom more than my dog.

"Fine." I bite off the end of my words. "One day."

Judica laughs. "This is rich."

"You can go—"

"My birthday," my mom says sharply. "Chancy, come try on your dress. It's nearly time for the party."

I follow her back into my room. She looks even worse than she did at breakfast. "Mom, are you sure you're okay? You don't look like—"

"I'm fine," she says. "My twin daughters were hurling death threats at one another in the hallway, but otherwise, things are great." Her face looks almost haggard, her lips compressed into a thin line. Judica poisons my dog, and I'm the one who has to suck it up to make peace. Typical.

"I'm sorry," I say simply. And I am. Above all things, I never want to cause Mom pain.

She's only asking for one day. I breathe in deeply through my mouth and out through my nose. I can give her that. Besides, her request probably saved my life. Not that I'll ever admit that.

She waves at my bed. There's a gown similar to hers, with the same silver overlay, but with silver cloth underneath instead of burgundy. "I wanted each of you, my identical angels, to reflect a part of me. Will you wear it?"

"I guess," I say. "Judica's already wearing hers." I can't seem to stop myself from sulking.

"Please don't pout. I am very sorry about Cookie. Sorrier than you realize. What an awful two days for you." Mom sits on the edge of my bed and puts her face in her hands. "I don't know whether she killed him, but I know she goads you. She starts fight after fight, and I see her do that too, but can we pretend to be a happy family for one day? We can take things as they come after that."

I nod. "Yes, I'll let it go until tomorrow. I'm sorry for causing a scene." I walk back to the door.

"Where are you going?" she asks.

I choke up. "I need to get Cookie, Mom. I can't just leave her lying on the floor of the arena."

"I'll take care of that." Mom stands. "We'll do a service for her tomorrow when all this is over. I promise, little dove." She lowers her voice. "And I'll ask Job to do an autopsy to determine cause of death."

Job is going to hate that, autopsying a dog. I look my mom in the eye and see that she understands. Duchess bumps my leg and I crouch down and sink my face into her shaggy white fur. The royal family mostly has dogs to taste our food, but we come to love them like family. Mom's enormous Pyrenees will miss Cookie as much as I do. I turn away from my mom to head for my bathroom. "I'll meet you in the ballroom at noon?"

Before I can escape, she pulls me toward her and into a hug. I'm still angry about Cookie, but it's not my mom's fault. When she finally lets me go, she smiles at me, but it's not as stunning as usual. The circles under her eyes look worse, and there's so much tension in her mouth. Even her skin looks almost... sallow. I'm doing this to her, Judica and me.

I squeeze her hand. "One long day to celebrate you, and then everyone goes home and we go back to normal."

"Normal," she says. "I'm not sure what that is anymore."

"Me either," I say, "but more than ever, I think going to live with Alora is my best plan." The thought of leaving Mom behind stabs at my heart, but I shove it down. Staying here and dying by Judica's sword would be worse than living apart from Mom for a while.

She sighs heavily and I worry she's changing her mind.

"I'm still going, right? To New York?"

"Alora will be here soon," she says. "We can discuss it then."

"Wait, what does that mean?" I ask. "Are you rethinking it?"

"It's been a busy few days. I need to read some of the prophecies and think about them all in context with what has happened."

Prophecies? There's more than one? I groan inwardly.

"I won't make you promises I can't keep. You reacted to the ring, and it's not crystal clear what that means yet. Besides, there's more going on than you know."

"But if I train in New York and give Judica space—"

"I need some time to consider everything."

"What did you want to talk to me about earlier?" I ask. "Can't you just tell me now? I'm dying to know."

She shakes her head. "It requires a longer conversation." She touches the side of my face gently. "It has been a horrible, exciting, and scary twenty-four hours. I'm sorry about Lark and Lyssa and Cookie. I'm sorry you reacted to the ring, because that pulls you down a path opposite from the one you wanted. I'm sorry your sister hates you. I fear it's my fault, and that I handled everything wrong, but we have time to make things right, and I promise I will."

Mom leans forward and kisses my forehead. Then she slips out.

I rush to shower and style my hair, toweling off with moments to spare. I pick up the dress from my bed, startled when something heavy rolls out from under it. My old flute case falls to the floor.

I used it for years when I was learning melodic forms, but I haven't looked at it in a decade or more. Who got it out? I pick it up and shove it back onto the far corner of the top shelf of my closet. I put on my dress and twirl once in front of my mirror.

"Look Cookie," I say. "It's perfect, right?"

Except, Cookie isn't there. She never will be there for me again. I can't sob into her fur when I'm sad. She'll never again lick my hand. She can't eat all the food I don't want. She can't curl up at the foot of my bed, or walk so close to my feet that I trip over her.

But it's 11:57, and I don't have time to lose it right now. I need to survive one last party, and after that, no matter what Mom says, I'm headed for New York to escape evian politics for at least a few weeks. I close my eyes and imagine that none of the misery of the last twenty-four hours ever happened. Lark's safely in New York, and her mother's with her. Cookie is safe in my room, hiding under my bed because the guests are making her nervous. And I'm mad at Judica as usual, but I have nothing in particular to be angry about.

Surprisingly, it works. My heart rate slows, and I reach calmly for my door knob, ready to head to my mom's nine-hundredth birthday party. But before I can touch it, the knob's already turning.

13

I back up against the wall, my body tense, my nerves humming. Who would open my door without knocking first? I can only think of one person, but Mom never enters from the hallway. She always comes through from her room.

I grab a ruby handled dagger from my chest of drawers and swing it around in front of me as the door opens. Edam inhales sharply before twisting the knife out of my hands and flipping me face-down on my bed.

"A decorative knife?" Edam asks. "Really?"

I shove backward and he lets me stand. He drops the dagger on the floor and holds up his arms.

"Sorry," he says. "When someone points a weapon at me, I react first and explain later."

I guess so. He barged into my room, then disarmed and shoved me down in less than a second. I eye his tuxedo. At least he's a really good-looking jerk. Even better looking dressed up, and knowing he dumped Judica yesterday doesn't hurt either.

I'd probably be into a gorilla if it had recently broken my sister's heart.

"I grab a weapon when someone enters my room unannounced. Why'd you come barging in without knocking? I could've been naked."

He doesn't laugh or smile. His eyes don't even light up. I try not to fret that I've misjudged everything. "Why were you breaking into my room?"

He looks like he really doesn't want to be here. His voice is low and concerned when he says, "It's your mom."

"What about her?"

"She collapsed."

My stomach lurches. "Let's go, then."

He turns and runs out the door and I follow him, lifting my full skirts to keep up.

My mom is fine. My mom is fine. My mom is fine.

Thinking the words over and over doesn't quite convince me. My mom looked sick. Evians don't get sick. Our bodies gobble up the viruses and bacteria that infect normal humans and spit them out. She's probably sleep deprived. But adults don't need much sleep. An hour or two and she should've been fine.

Something was wrong, and I shouldn't have left her side.

"We're going to the ballroom?" I ask.

Stupid question. We're standing outside the doors already. Edam pushes them open.

My eyes scan the room. I can barely see the wooden parquet floor for all the people. Representatives from all six families are milling around murmuring in low voices. Tables laden with all the food my mom and I selected line the walls. The entire room is decorated in gold, pink, and ivory flowers, beautiful fabric crepe, and ribbons. The chandeliers cast a perfect champagne light over everything. It's enchanting, and it's perfect for her birthday.

Until I see the person we're celebrating.

Mom's lying on the parquet floor as still as Cookie was,

but with a gorgeous burgundy and silver ball gown spreading out all around her like a puddle of gilded blood.

"No!" I run to her side and reach for her hand. It's still but not stiff. If she was dead it would be stiff, right? People stand all around me, looking at one another, at the floor, anywhere but at my face. Some frown, some scowl, but no one says a word. And no one moves toward me or my mom. Why aren't they trying to help? Why are they all standing around uselessly?

I scramble across the floor so I'm close enough to lean over her face. I lift her head and cradle it in my arms, but she doesn't respond. I gently set her head down and press my ear to her chest, as if I don't already know, as if I can't already hear what every other evian in the room hears.

She has no heartbeat.

I feel stupidly for a pulse like human doctors do on all their TV shows. "What's been done?" I ask. "Where's Job?" I scan the crowd. "Where's Job?!"

"I'm here, Your Highness." Job's built like a brick wall. He's not the kind of person you don't notice, but he was standing right behind me, and I didn't even realize he was in the room.

"Why aren't you doing anything?"

"I tried." His sky blue eyes widen, urging me to believe him. "She can't be revived."

"You just gave up? What are you, a moron? Crack her chest open and shock her heart. Humans do it all the time. You've got to be the worst doctor in the history of the world. Evians heal so well, you basically sit on your hands and do nothing. But obviously you need to be doing something now. Do it. Get over here and save her!"

Job's mouth turns down, his eyes clouding with sorrow and something else. I finally recognize the other emotion.

Pity.

Because he can't bring my mother back. No one can. She's dead, like Cookie. Like Lyssa.

Job's lips are moving, words pouring out, but my mind's no longer processing the data. I've cut him off, because I'm unraveling from the inside out. How can this be happening? I saw her a few moments ago. She stood across from me and hugged me. She can't be gone. I'm shaking all over and I'm hugging Mom and crying. Duchess is frantic next to me, licking my hand and barking and licking my mom's hand. Someone around me is screaming, but I don't know who. They sound exactly the way I feel. Like their insides were run through a blender and there's no healing the slurry of their heart.

I'm rocking back and forth, cradling my mom to my chest when they come for me, Edam and Balthasar and Inara. They try to pull me away and the screaming cuts off abruptly. My voice croaks, "No! Get away from us."

"You need to let go, Chancery." Inara looks at me like I've cracked, and I realize she's right. I am broken. Lyssa's death hit me, and Cookie splintered the ensuing crack. Now this, Mom's ... I can't even think the words. Mom in my lap with no heartbeat has shattered me into a million pieces and there's not enough glue in the world to put me back together.

I can't. I won't. It's too much. They don't understand, none of them do.

I wrench my arm out of Inara's hand. "You let go! Get away from me, all of you!" I shake off their hands, the hands trying to take my mom away from me. I glance around at an ocean of perfect faces, none of them quite right, none of them her, all of them unwilling to meet my glare. The hands return, but I slap at them. "Leave me alone!"

"Chancery Divinity Alamecha," a voice says, a voice like

winter. A voice that returns me to temporary sanity. A voice I hate from the depths of my soul.

I turn around to glare at Judica.

"What?" I stand up slowly.

Her eyes shine like she's been crying, but I've never seen Judica cry. Not in seventeen years. Not when she's injured, insulted, sad, hurt, angry, or disappointed. Not ever. "Step back from our mother. Act with decency. Never forget that you're evian."

"What do you know about how to act? Mom's dead and you're pretending nothing is wrong. We're all gathered here to celebrate a birthday for a dead woman, and you're not even upset. What should I be doing? Making small talk with possible allies? Sizing my head for her crown?"

She flinches. "No matter what we think or feel, our duty lies before us." She gestures around her. "The world is here, spinning on its axis, its leaders all watching while you sob on the floor like a child."

Hundreds of faces, all blurring in front of me. Hundreds of people who don't matter to me, not now, not after this. They matter to Judica, though. Everything matters to her. Everything except Mom's death, apparently.

"You aren't even acting, are you? You really don't care." I'm suddenly so angry I could scratch her eyes out. "You're not even upset because now you're Empress, you sadistic freak."

Her eyes widen and she inhales sharply. She takes a step back involuntarily, as though I've thrown a knife in her stomach and twisted the hilt. Thanks to her, I know exactly how that feels.

Finally, she speaks. The words sound forced. "I'm as devastated as you, but I won't wallow and scream and sob, because queens endure. I'm acting with decorum, in a way taught me by Enora herself. By our mother."

"She didn't teach you anything. You learned from

tutors." I take a step toward her. "You were never around. You didn't even know her."

She clenches her fists and her eyes flare. "I am standing here, ignoring your insults for one reason. My mother asked me for a birthday present. She asked me to get along with my twin for a day, for one single day." Judica closes her eyes and reopens them. "I choose to honor her last request."

She looks carved from stone, and her words are so final. *Her last request*.

I sink back down to my knees and pull my mom's body back into my lap. "Fine," I whisper. "Fine. It's what you wanted, Mom." I turn back toward Judica. "I'm sorry. You're right and I'm sorry."

Judica walks over to where I'm slumped on the floor and crouches down by Mom. "How did this happen?"

"I don't know," I say. "She was tired this morning, but she seemed fine. It wasn't until after breakfast that—"

Like the first rays of sunlight eradicating the night's darkness, the truth dawns upon me. I put the pieces together slowly, but when the last one falls into place, I know beyond the slightest doubt.

I sit up straight and look Judica in the eye, all her pretty words about honoring last requests and the world going on ringing hollow in my ears.

I slap her, hard.

Judica's eyes flash and her hands clench, but she doesn't strike me back. Her voice is low, deep, angry. "How dare you?"

"How dare you?" I gently set Mom's body on the ground and stand. I speak loudly enough that the crowd gathered for Mom's birthday can hear me, but I'm talking to Judica. "I was there at breakfast this morning. Duchess hates eggs, and I hate eggs. But Mom? Mom loves them. Boiled eggs are her favorite. When Mom tried to give the first bite to Duchess, she'd never have eaten it. Cookie ate whatever

Duchess wouldn't. I also gave Cookie my entire fried egg." My hands shake with fury and righteous indignation.

Judica looks at me blankly. "And?"

"That's why Cookie died first."

Judica looks legitimately horrified. "But nothing that took time to kill a dog would be strong enough to kill our mother."

"Mom ate way more than Cookie did because she loves eggs. You know, because you take breakfast with us sometimes. You might have ignored my preferences, but you'd remember hers."

"I would never harm our mother. Never."

I shake my head. "A few days ago, that might have been true. I don't know. But after yesterday?" I don't elaborate, since no one else knows about my role in the EMP. "You were nervous."

She's smart enough to know the EMP and my modified training schedule meant something. Judica was clearly furious when we sparred, but I'm not a threat, not yet. Not unless Mom made me into one, and she was waiting until after her party.

But Judica couldn't take that risk.

"No." Judica shakes her head and stands up. She backs away from me, almost involuntarily. She's convincing, I'll give her that. If I didn't know her like I do, I might believe her, but I do know her, far too well. Which is why I know what she wants more than anything, and how far she'll go to keep the throne.

"Judica Angelica Alamecha, I name you mother slayer."

14

Eyes fly wide all around me and several people gasp.

Inara grabs my shoulder and whispers in my ear. "That's a significant and very public allegation."

Her heart rate speeds up, and I smell her perspiration. Whether I've panicked Inara or not, I won't retract my claim.

"It's true." I feel it in my bones. Judica killed our mom because she couldn't stand the thought of me becoming Empress instead of her. Maybe Mom even told her about her plans in a misguided attempt to prepare her.

The irony is that Judica didn't have to do it. I didn't have any desire to rule over this pack of jackals.

Inara whispers, "Be that as it may, you might have waited to talk to me about what proof we might find before shouting it in front of enemies and friends alike."

"I'm sorry," I say flatly.

But I'm not, not really. I'm destroyed, I'm broken, I'm livid, I'm scared. I am full to the brim with feelings right now, but not a single one of them is apologetic.

Judica stares the members of the murmuring crowd

down one at a time. "My sister has named me mother slayer. It isn't true. I loved my mother, and I would never have harmed her. But, it doesn't really matter either way, does it?" She speaks slowly and her words dispel the fog that has settled into my brain.

She's right.

It's awful, it's horrible, and it's every kind of hideous, but she's right. Even if she killed my mom, it doesn't make a bit of difference. She's the Heir. For six thousand years, two categories of people have had the right, by law, to kill an empress. Another empress as an act of war, or the empress's own heir. Judica, as the Heir, had a right to do it. It was a law put in place to ensure that if a monarch fell ill or was incapable of governing, the parts of the world she controlled wouldn't languish. Which means my allegation is meaningless.

I watch, numb, as Judica bridges the gap that separates her from Mom's body. She leans over and presses a kiss to Mom's forehead, and then she leans forward and pulls the sparkling ring from Mom's finger. It slides off easily, without any pulling or yanking.

Judica holds it up over her head and proclaims, "I'm Heir to Alamecha by right as the youngest female of the royal line, and by record Mother made eight years ago. I hereby take my place as Empress of the First Family." The ring sparkles briefly in the sunlight, the colors reflecting from it and filling the room with tiny lights. When Judica shoves it on her finger, the whole room sighs, because it's done. The murderess has taken control. Heaven help us all, but me more than anyone else.

Before anyone can speak, Job steps forward. "I'm sorry to interrupt at such a critical time, and I tried to tell Chancery this before, but technically Judica may not be the Heir."

Judica drops her hand. "What?"

Job ducks his eyes and shuffles his feet. "I attended to your mother in her last moments, and she was quite clear and very lucid when she told me that she revoked Judica as Heir and named Chancery in her place. She said it several times. I'm sure the other people present heard it too." Job glances around him, and several heads nod in affirmation. "So you see, if Chancery has evidence that Judica poisoned Enora... there may be sufficient cause for a trial."

Judica looks stricken, but not ready to admit defeat. "She can't just name a new Heir. It doesn't work like that."

Inara clears her throat. "She cannot, not when the Heir has been declared in a formal document witnessed and sealed by her Council." Inara gestures to Mom's chamberlain and whispers, "Larena, bring the Charter. I hate that Alamecha's family business is being handled publicly, but there's no way around it now."

Silence like a blanket shrouds the masses gathered while Mom's willowy chamberlain crosses the room, the thick folds of her canary yellow silk gown swishing as she walks quickly toward the exit. Once she's gone, people shift and murmur in tones so low that even other evians can't make out their words. Moments later when Larena returns, even those whisperings die off. Inara shoves hors d'oeuvres and silver dishes out of the way on an ornate serving table near the end of the room, and Larena plonks a solid wooden box with the Alamecha family crest carved on the lid onto the cleared space.

Judica and I move toward her, everything happening in slow motion. We stand in a loose semicircle around Inara as she opens the box.

She pulls a stack of yellowed papers from it. The Alamecha Charter.

"How's this going to help us?" I whisper.

"It's not the Charter Judica needs," Inara says. "It's the Declaration of Heirship."

"Right," Judica says. "It sits just below the Charter."

Larena clucks. We all lean over the box and look down to the space below. A sheaf of thick white paper lies in the bottom of the box. Larena lifts it up and reads aloud. "Before us this day, the representative heads of the Council of Alamecha attest that one Enora Isadora Alamecha has declared her intention to name an heir. Having given birth to two daughters on the same day, she desires to eliminate all confusion that may result from the event of her death. Enora Isadora Alamecha names her daughter, Chancery Divinity Alamecha to rule the First Family of Eve, as Empress and Queen of all the lands and properties hereby appurtenant. Lest any should contest this statement, the below listed members of her Council set their hand to testify to the truth and veracity of this declaration."

Judica states the obvious. "It's not signed."

"Not by the Council," Inara agrees, "but Mom signed it."

When would she have had time? She must have known something was wrong and rushed to get it done this morning. It must have been where she went after breakfast. But it's not enough.

"Between the destruction of the prior documents, this partially executed one, and the statement to Job in front of witnesses," Inara says, "I imagine the rest of the Council will agree with me. Chancery is the Heir."

Can Judica actually be tried for what she did?

"Mother was sick and lost her mind." The words emerge as the barest of whispers. Judica closes her eyes and for the first time ever, she looks wounded, pained even. When she speaks again, it's even softer. "Oh Mother, why?"

I'm torn in two. I want nothing to do with ruling Alamecha. Judica can choke on it for all I care, but the only way to make Judica pay for killing Mom is to become Empress and convene a court. If I abdicate, then Judica becomes Empress and that possibility evaporates. We'll never really know whether she killed our mom, or even if we do find out, we won't be able to do anything about it.

The only way to make Judica pay is to become Empress myself.

As if she can read my mind, Judica says, "I did not kill her." She grits her teeth. "But I almost don't regret her death. She was obviously making bad decisions. She lacked the capacity to make such an Heirship change." She picks up the new document and looks it over with disgust.

"Curious." Adika Shenoah, the current Empress of the Sixth family has slunk so close that her heart pounds steadily right next to me. "One twin challenges the paperwork executed by her own mother this morning, and the other accuses the displaced heir of murder. I'm delighted I didn't send Vela in my place. I'd have missed all this fun." Adika's teeth gleam brightly against her deep brown skin, and a chill slides down my spine. The predators sense our weakness and are circling. The worst part is that we invited them into our home to witness this devastation.

"This Declaration is trash." Judica throws it into the box and glares at me. "I'll fight it to the end."

"What about Mom's birthday promise?" I ask. "Mom would never have wanted—"

"Then she shouldn't have replaced the Heirship documents," Judica says. "This is on her head."

"It's on her head?" I ask, practically spitting. "It's her fault that she happened to get the documents drawn up, but not fully executed before you *murdered her*?" I choke up, torn between horror, despair, and a murderous rage.

"She lied to us both," Judica says. "She named me Heir. She trained me, she promised me I would rule after her, and now that she's gone, she's left me with nothing."

My laugh sounds a little crazy, even to me. "You kill

Mom as some kind of a power play, and you're upset she broke her promise to you from almost nine years ago?"

Judica lunges for me and her hands wrap around my throat. I'm so surprised that I put up no opposition and she knocks me back and pins me against the heavy wooden box with her body. Her hands squeeze my esophagus, cutting off my air.

"I won't say it again," she snarls in my face. "I didn't kill her. I loved her."

Edam pulls Judica off me and twists her arms behind her back. "Do not attack the Empress, Judica. It's not befitting of the Heir."

I rub my neck and speed the healing from where her hands nearly choked me to death. "Thank you, Edam." I stand up and watch Judica struggle against him. He won't release her hands because he knows she'll pull a dagger and stab him.

A single tear rolls down Judica's cheek, as surprising as water springing from a stone. "Just because you screamed and sobbed, that doesn't mean you love her more. It means you didn't learn a thing from her example while she was alive."

"Wrong again," I say. "Killing her proves you didn't love her, and no amount of decorum, or savagery, or statesmanship will ever erase that sin."

Edam lets Judica go and pulls the two of us close. He has one hand on my wrist and one on Judica's. He whispers so softly that I can barely make out his words. "This is not the time or the place. You two need to talk about this, but not here, not in front of everyone. It's past enough."

Judica shakes his hand off of her wrist, but she whispers softly, too. "Get your hands off me, you lying—"

Edam frowns. "I never lied to you, not once."

"It's not that simple," she says, choking up. I don't know why it surprises me, but she seems more upset about

Edam dumping her than she does about our mother's death.

"Oh, boohoo for you and your little romance gone awry. Our mom's lying right there." My broken pieces shake at the thought, and I suck in a big breath. "Is this really the right time to play the sulky girlfriend?"

"She's not my girlfriend," Edam says.

"No, I'm not," Judica spits. "No Consort of mine would ever take her side against me."

"Oh, please. You never gave me a choice in any of it." His words have the ring of an old frustration.

"You didn't have a choice?" Judica tries to whisper, but shrill sounds carry.

"No one can refuse the Heir."

Judica's eyelids flutter rapidly and her breath comes in shallow, rapid pulls. I almost feel sorry for her, before I remember she's pure evil.

She raises her voice. "For crimes against the Heir, I order Edam ne'Senah ex'Alamecha's death. The sentence will be carried out as soon as I've... as soon as all this," she gestures toward me and the Charter, "is worked out."

The guards seize Edam and he doesn't resist, but his eyes are wounded.

"This is beyond absurd," I say. "Your boyfriend dumps you, so you order him to be executed? Even for you, that's a new low. And unfortunately for you, I'm Empress, not you." I cross my arms. "I countermand your order."

Judica addresses the guards with a voice that brooks no refusal. "Take him to the holding cells pending resolution of the line of succession. Whether I'm Heir or Empress, I certainly have the right to order a trial of someone whom I accuse." She spins around to take in the whole room, daring them to challenge her.

The guards don't know what to do, so they keep him restrained, but don't take him anywhere. They glance at

Balthasar, who grunts and looks from me to Judica and back. "Take him down. We can deal with it later."

"No," I say. "You all heard Larena. I'm the new Empress, and all Edam did was take steps to ensure my safety. He will not be punished for those actions."

Before anyone else can speak, Melisania Lenora, Empress of the Third Family steps forward, a sparkling crown atop her curly mass of hair. "Things are obviously a little confusing right now. You're lucky we're all here to help. You two are grief stricken. We'll convene a court of the Five, evaluate the evidence available on the circumstances surrounding your mother's death, and vote on which of you will ascend the throne." Melisania turns to Adika and begins issuing more orders.

"Wouldn't you love that?" Judica barks. "To see the First Family thrown into turmoil and choose which of us rises?"

She's right. Five sets of eyes bore into me when I glance around the room, none of them friendly. Every other family sees this situation as an opportunity, and they've wanted nothing more than to tear us apart and gobble up the pieces for thousands of years. If we allow it, they'll be dividing our lands among themselves like a brokered deal in a game of Risk by the end of the day.

Judica wrenches the ring from her hand and holds it out to me. I don't reach for it, much less grab it.

"Take it."

"I don't even want it." But my sister needs to pay, so I snatch it from her hand.

I'm shocked Judica's willing to hand the throne over to protect it. I didn't expect that kind of selflessness. I wait for the trick, the double cross, the sting in the tail.

She raises her voice and spreads her hands in front of her so everyone will hear. "While we appreciate the kind and considerate concern of the Five Families in this time of deepest grief for Alamecha, we respectfully decline your invitation to convene a court on our behalf. The First Family will handle this on its own. Chancery Divinity Alamecha is our new Empress, named by our mother in the seconds before she died, and attested to by several others. I will voluntarily rescind any claim I had to the throne."

"Now do your part to show them we can work this out," Judica mutters. "Tell them to take Edam below."

If Judica can accept me as Empress peacefully, Edam can spend a night in a cell.

"Take Edam below," I say. I can always free him after everyone leaves tomorrow.

Judica smiles. "Please respect our grief and return to your rooms."

The guests slowly filter out, hesitant to leave in the middle of the show. Eventually only our guards, Job, Balthasar, Inara, Larena, and a few other Alamecha people are left.

Judica turns to me with the smile that portends the reveal of her plan.

"But of course, if I deem you unfit to rule. . ."

I finally understand.

She's okay with me being Empress, since that leaves her as my Heir, one of the two categories of people who can challenge an empress at any time. Oh Mom, what were you thinking?

Judica says, "Mother may have temporarily lost her mind, but it's reparable." She meets my eye, searching for something in my face.

I wish I knew for sure whether she killed Mom.

Judica's voice interrupts my thoughts. "Chancery Divinity Alamecha, I formally challenge you to a Duel of Ascendance to determine who rules family Alamecha."

How did I not see that knife coming?

"I'll allow us both the night to recover and to honor Mother's wish, but in the morning, we settle this." Judica glances one last time at Mom's body and strides out of the massive doors.

I glance around the room at the faces of the people I've known my entire life. None of them will meet my eye, which means they expected this. I really am a bumbler, too weak and too stupid to rule. If I can't even predict the actions of my twin sister, the most predictable person in my life, how can I possibly lead our entire family?

I doubt I could have screwed this up any worse if I'd tried. Edam's imprisoned for sparing me, the Five will be plotting their attack on our family on their flights home, Lark's hiding in New York without a mother, and Cookie and Mom are both dead.

And my options tomorrow morning are to murder my sister or die by her hand.

I cross the room and kneel in front of Mom's body. I lean toward her and whisper into her hair, "I tried Mom, I really did. I'm so sorry I let you down, but that stupid staridium obviously chose wrong."

15

I'm not sure how long I lay with my head on Mom's body before the housekeeping staff shows up to retrieve her. When I glance around, everyone has left except Inara, Job, and Frederick.

"What can we do?" Inara asks.

I sit up, startled by her expectation that I'll simply head for my room to prepare for tomorrow's challenge, abandoning my mother's body to be prepared for burial. When I do stand up, I long for Mom's room, and her smell, and her things. I want to be around something that reminds me of her. Duchess snuggles against Mom, taking the spot I vacated, and my heart contracts again.

I lean over and ruffle the fur on Duchess's head, and then I force myself to square my shoulders. Each step toward the door feels like a betrayal, like I've given up on her, like I'm walking away from her and not the other way around.

Even though I know she's already gone, it destroys me to let her go.

By the time I reach the door, I recognize what else feels off. I miss the clicking sounds of Cookie's claws following me. I miss the soothing and commanding presence of my mom, and no matter where I go, I'll never feel either one again.

When I reach the door to her room, I pull up short. I can't go inside. I can't. I spin around and nearly run into Inara, Frederick and Job only a pace behind her.

"I want to be alone right now." The words emerge as a croak.

"You're the Empress now," Frederick says. "Your mother would want me here. You need protection."

"You sure kept her safe, didn't you?" I snap.

Frederick stumbles back like I slapped him. Mother's most trusted guard. He only left her door to sleep.

"I'm sorry, Freddy, I know it's not your fault." Tears threaten to fall again. "I'm really sorry. You can wait outside."

I shove past him and take the dozen steps to my own door, Inara and Job on my heels. I stop on the threshold and rest my forehead on the solid wood of my door. "Why are you both following me?"

"I need a private word," Job whispers, and glances sideways at Inara.

Frederick takes up his position next to my door, and I meet his eyes. I'm curious what he thinks about Job's request.

He shrugs infinitesimally, which means he doesn't consider Job much of a threat. If I had listened to Job earlier when I was still drowning in grief, I wouldn't have been blindsided about Mom changing the documents. I motion for him to enter my room. "Do you need something too, Inara?"

Her eyes cloud. "I'm here to help you with anything I can. And I thought you might need this." She leans toward me, her arms wrapping around my waist. I collapse against her. I forgot, in my utter desolation, that Inara is basically a carbon copy of our mother. Strong, kind, intelligent, caring, ferocious, and brilliant. And she didn't follow Judica out. She stayed with me. Which means when Judica kills me tomorrow, she'll likely execute Inara, too. I shudder and pull back.

"Give me just a moment with Job, and then we can talk."

Inara's lips tighten into a thin line, but she doesn't argue. She takes up a position near the doorway, on the opposite side from Frederick.

I walk into my room, marveling how different the room looks from the last time I entered, when Mom had just told me to put on a dress to match her.

The whole world looks different now that she's gone. Drenched in darkness, covered in cobwebs, and dipped in desperation.

Even after the door closes, Job doesn't speak. He looks down at his feet and shuffles them a bit. He's been my mom's physician for centuries. Losing her was hard for him too, and he probably feels to blame. I sympathize, but I'm exhausted and stressed and not up to the job of consoling anyone else right now. "What is it, Job?"

He meets my eyes. "Your mother told me repeatedly that you were her new Heir. But that's not all she said. Right before her heart stopped, she told me 'Tell Chancy I sent... something... to Alora.' I asked her to repeat what she said. I couldn't understand the word. She could barely talk. But she didn't hear my question. She was gone, Chancy. I'm sorry to be delivering an incomplete message. But in case it's important, I wanted to tell you everything I know."

She sent what to Alora? Alora's coming here any day. She couldn't have meant the declaration, since it was here, partially executed. What else could she have sent to New York and why? It makes no sense.

Job's heart rate is elevated and he looks pale.

"Are you okay?" I ask.

He nods. "I am sorry, so sorry to have failed you. I should have done more when I noticed how tired she looked, I should have—"

"I tried to talk to her about it too, Job. It's not your fault. Mom thought she was bulletproof and obviously she wasn't."

He reaches toward me and then pulls back, clearly unsure how he might offer comfort. Finally he shoves his hands in his pockets and heads for the door. He's gone in a blink.

I wish I could escape the mess of my life so easily. Inara slips through the doorway as he leaves. She looks at me like I looked at Lark earlier. Pity. Empathy. Sorrow. Gratitude floods my body at the knowledge that my amazing, strong, brilliant big sister followed me instead of Judica. I have no idea why Inara's on my side, but, inexplicably, she is.

"I feel as flayed as you look," Inara says, "but we need to be triaging right now."

"What's the point?" I ask. "There's nothing I can do to prepare for tomorrow. I'm either going to beat her or die trying, and we all know which is most likely. In fact, while I love you for it, it was monumentally stupid for you to follow me in here."

"You need more time," Inara says. "If you had a month, or even a full week, you might stand a chance against her. But that's not what I meant by triage. There's something more pressing than tomorrow's challenge."

"What now?" I sink down onto the edge of my bed.

"The ring," she says.

"What about it?" It's still clenched in my hand. I was afraid to put it on in front of all those people. I open my palm and look at my mom's ring, the cursed thing that started this whole mess. It's sparkling and beautiful ... when it should be black and ugly. I gasp. It shouldn't be refracting the light from my window, but it is.

Because it's a fake.

The stone in this ring sparkles whether it's in contact with a member of the family or not.

"Mom told me once that she had a fake made, in case she ever needed to hide hers." Inara looks at the ground. "I guess she decided it was time."

"What's it made of?" I ask.

"Mystic topaz. The funniest part is that it's essentially worthless. That's a manufactured stone. You can buy one online for less than a hundred dollars."

"Wow," I say. "I guess we should initiate a lock down and force an immediate search. That will be extremely unpopular with our guests, but we can't risk one of them flying out with it."

"Mom was wearing the fake," Inara says, "which we know because we saw Judica pull it off her finger. I doubt anyone else knew about it, other than me and whoever made it for her. I don't think it was stolen, because the thief would have needed the forethought to bring a fake and change them out. I think the more likely explanation is that Mother hid it herself and was wearing the fake intentionally."

"But why?" I ask. "It makes no sense." I held the ring earlier today, the real one.

Job's words hit me. Mom sent something to Alora. Would she have sent the real ring? Why? It's not logical.

Inara throws her hands up in the air. "Nothing makes sense lately." She ticks things off on her fingers. "You tell Mom you want to leave, and she agrees and sets up a trip to visit Alora." Inara shoots me a 'you're crazy' look. "Then you try on her ring and blow up the island."

"I hardly blew up the island," I say. "I set off one little EMP."

Inara doesn't laugh. She doesn't even smile. "Chancery, that is the weirdest thing I've ever seen. An evian set off an EMP with the stone given our family by Eve herself. Using only a rock, you wiped out our communications, security, and electrical systems. Not to mention, you set the wall on fire. And then blasted a fireball through Mother's closet wall."

"I know." I drop my face in my hands. "Which made Mom name me as Heir. None of that would have mattered though if only..."

Inara sits next to me and pulls me close. "If Mother hadn't died. I know."

"I was going to say, 'if my sociopath sister hadn't found out and murdered her,' but you're technically correct as well."

In spite of my attempt at a joke, tears stream down my face again, and when I turn to Inara, she's crying too. Judica may be a monster, and Mom may not have had many daughters in the last few centuries, but at least I have two amazing, involved sisters who love me. It's more than some people have.

"Now the ring is gone, and Judica's already challenged me to a duel in the morning. I wish I cared more that I'm about to die."

Inara straightens up and squeezes my hand. "Mom knew she was sick. She had to have known. I asked her about the circles under her eyes, and I'm guessing you did too. She was brilliant, and always thought a hundred moves ahead. She hid the ring, and she tore up the heirship, but didn't call her Council to witness the new one. She might have run out of time on that, or maybe not." Inara closes her eyes and looks upward. "What did you think would happen here, Mom?"

"She wanted me to rule with Judica's help. Why didn't

she change the forms to say that instead?" I ask. "It might not have made Judica as angry."

Inara shakes her head. "She'd have been just as upset. Plus, there's no precedent for joint leadership among the families. No, I think Mother knew you wouldn't challenge her if you were Heir, and that you wouldn't want to kill her if she challenged you. I think Mother may have hidden the ring for this very reason."

"For what reason?" I ask. "So when Judica kills me, her rule won't feel legitimate?"

Inara shakes her head. "No, to give you a chance to broker a deal between the two of you." Inara's face suddenly looks hopeful. "Which means *you* must have some idea where the real ring is. Otherwise, this will never work."

I shake my head. "I'm as shocked as you." Besides, if all it takes to broker a deal is that I have the ring, well, Judica already believes I do.

"Think," Inara says. "Did she hint at where it might be hidden? Because with that knowledge, we could demand Judica delay her challenge. She'd have no choice. Especially if you make it public that this one's fake."

Do I tell Inara? She followed me, but can I truly trust her? And even if I can, how far? She's always been there for me, but she loves Judica too. "Mom and I practiced with it this morning. I know she was wearing the real ring then," I say, delaying. The more I talk, the more uncomfortable I feel with disclosing everything I know. I can always fill her in later. "I have no idea where she'd have hidden it. Could Judica have it? I mean, she knows the ring is the reason Mom changed her mind. Could she be worried I'll let Alamecha know, and win the people over? Maybe she switched the rings when she took it from Mom's finger?" A chill shoots from my shoulders to my toes. "She could have poisoned her, taken a fake to the ballroom, and then switched them when we were distracted."

Inara and I both close our eyes and replay the earlier scene. It's painful to think about Mom dying and the moments after, but when I go back in my mind, the ring is sparkling on Mom's hand from the second I walk in. "Would it have gone black when she died? I mean, it's still touching her."

Inara shakes her head. "I wish I knew. But think back on when Judica took it off. It was sparkling then, separated from Mother entirely. I was watching when Judica forced it off. It was always a fake Judica took from Mom's hand. So if she switched it, she did it before Mom died."

Blast. "If we knew Judica had it, at least we'd know it's close."

"You think it might not even be in Ni'ihau?"

I suppress a frown. "No, I mean I have no idea where it is. But I mean that Judica couldn't have taken it, or sent it, anywhere since this morning."

"We need to tell her." Inara jumps off my bed and takes a step toward the door. "We go in and tell Judica what's going on with the ring, and tell her you aren't really Empress yet, and she's not Heir officially because we don't have the ring. We can't have the investiture without the ring."

"I doubt she'll care," I say. "But if Mom knew she was sick and was worried she was dying..." My voice shakes. I need to get it together. "Maybe she wanted to give us something to buy us more time. That's totally a move she'd make. But the Five will leap on any excuse to try and step into the middle of our business."

"That's why we must approach Judica with this in private."

I nod. "Okay, let's go."

Frederick follows me to Judica's room. I try not to be

irritated that two guards are standing outside her room. I try really, really hard when they refuse to let us pass.

I finally raise my voice, sick of being polite. "I'm Empress. Judica proclaimed it herself. Now step aside, or Frederick and Inara will separate your bodies from your heads."

Maybe there's wisdom behind the Heir having a personal guard. It makes the transition much easier for her, knowing already who she can trust. My only personal guard was Cookie. I swallow the ball in my throat and charge through her unbarred door.

When we walk in, Judica's face down on her pillow. Is she crying? I didn't think she cared enough about anything to cry. It pisses me off, actually. When you kill someone, you forfeit the right to cry about it. Before I can think of anything fitting to say, Judica leaps up, wiping her eyes so quickly that I wonder whether I imagined the whole thing.

Judica scowls at Inara, Frederick, and then me. "Get out."

I practically spit the words. "Thought you'd like to know that the ring you shoved at me is a fake."

"What?" Judica holds out her hand and gestures for it. "No way."

I plonk the ring down on her palm. "See for yourself."

She clenches her fist for a moment, and then hurls it at the wall. It lodges inside the drywall with a thunk. "Who took the real one?"

I throw my hands up in the air. "If I knew, do you think I'd have come straight here?"

"I never have any idea how you'll react to anything," Judica says. "You tell me."

Inara steps between us and spreads her hands out wide. "Stop. We came to alert you to an issue, Judica. We believe Mother may have hidden the real ring to force you two to spend time together to fix this problem. We can hardly schedule the investiture that officially makes one of you Empress if we don't even have the Alamecha family ring."

"Which means I'm not Empress yet," I say, "and you're not my Heir, and so your challenge was invalid." I have no idea whether that's true, but it sounds legitimate.

Judica narrows her eyes at me. "What exactly do you two want?"

"It's not what I want," I say. "It's what Mom wanted. She wanted us to rule together."

Judica laughs. "You've lost your mind. Even if Mom wanted that, she's not here anymore. So what she wanted doesn't matter much. And I don't care whether it's valid. As soon as it is, I'll restate my challenge, and you'll look ridiculous for delaying." She leans toward me. "I know facing things head on is counterintuitive for you, but you'd look less cowardly if you simply fought me in the morning."

I take slow steps until I'm standing less than a foot away from her. "The last few days have shifted everything for me, and I know it's been hard on you too. I'm pretty sure you killed Mom, but I'm willing to try to forgive you." That's hard to say. And I'm not sure it's true, but I want it to be. "Because it's what Mom would want. Don't you think ruling beside me is better than dying tomorrow?"

Judica stares me in the eye for a moment before she says, "I won't ever say this again, because I'm tired of no one listening. I didn't kill Mother. I would never have done that. You didn't own her, nor did you have an exclusive on affection for her. I loved her. But you're missing one big thing in your little inspirational 'kum-ba-ya' speech. It might be better to rule with you than die tomorrow, but I'm not facing that choice. My choice is whether I'd rather rule with you or kill you tomorrow and rule alone, and I've been meaning to kill you for eight years. I guess it's time I get around to actually doing it. So thanks for the offer, but I'll pass on sharing the throne with a halfwit while she tries to forgive me for something I didn't do."

"Are you really this hateful?" I ask. "If you truly didn't kill her, then why not give this joint rule a trial run? All you have to do is work with me to try and locate the missing staridium. Besides, you can always kill me next week or next month. What's the rush?"

"Other than the fear you'll get up the guts to have someone assassinate me?" Judica asks. "Don't think that hasn't crossed my mind. Anyone can bribe a guard."

How is she this dead inside? How can she not care about me at all? Will it really not bother her to kill me? I don't know what else to say.

Inara says, "Haven't we had enough death for one week?"

Judica sits carefully on a wooden chair, her hands folded calmly in her lap. "I don't have a choice."

"We always have a choice," Inara says. "You're just making the wrong one."

"You have no idea how this feels," Judica says.

"You're wrong," Inara says. "I know exactly how it feels to be displaced."

"I was unaware you had a twin," Judica says.

Inara lifts her eyebrows. "I didn't. But I was Heir for over a hundred years, and then my father died. Mother swore she would never take a new Consort, and I assumed I'd be Mother's last daughter. Everyone was sure I would rule eventually. Everyone. Until one day, she completely reversed her decision and took a new Consort, a man she barely knew. A man she didn't respect or admire. Not long after that, she had another daughter." Inara paces. "In the blink of an eye, the train of my life jumped its track. I chose that day how to react, and stayed the course every day thereafter. I could have killed my half sister Melina or my mother in jealousy or rage or out of a fit of injustice, but I didn't. I embraced my new life, and my half-sister, just as I embraced the two of you."

"You gave up." Judica looks out her window.

"You're facing the same choice I did," Inara says, as though Judica didn't just insult her. "Mother didn't choose another Consort and have another child, but she got new information and decided it would be best if you two ruled together. Now she's gone and she can't explain her reasons or her plan, but you could choose to try and honor it for a few days before you kill your sister, or you can make irreversible decisions now."

Judica looks from Inara to me and back again. Without any further argument or explanation, she says, "No."

"So that's it, then?" I ask. "You won't even consider it?"

"Do you think we're the same?" Judica asks. "Because we aren't. We look alike, sure, and we even sound alike sometimes. But you know nothing about me. You're too weak. You'd drag me and this entire family down with you, exactly as you did with Lyssa, and even Mother. I have an obligation to every family member in Alamecha to deny your request, to ignore Mother's delusional hopes, and to prevent implementation of the insanity she was spouting at the end of her life. So, no. In fact, with the ring missing and the pair of you trying to pressure me into changing my mind, I've decided I'm not willing to wait for the morning. I think we should have our duel right now."

My mouth drops open. "You can't. You already said we'd wait for morning. Plus, it's not even a valid challenge."

"I'm either Empress or Heir. Either way I can challenge you." Judica sneers. "You should have spent a few hours reading our laws, sister."

I splutter.

"If you had, you'd know that as the challenger, I have the right to choose the time. You, as the defender, have a right to choose whether we fight hand-to-hand or with blades."

"I knew that," I say, "but you already chose the time. Tomorrow morning."

"I don't want to wait," she says. "I'd rather kill you now."

The door opens and we all turn to see who the guards allowed inside. For a split second I worry that one of the Five has come after us and we may be facing attack. I don't even have a single weapon.

Judica draws a blade, of course.

When the intruder walks through the doorway, I relax. Dark hair falls in gentle waves to her waist, framing striking golden eyes, russet skin, and long willowy arms and legs.

"Alora!" I leap toward her and she hugs me tightly.

"Little dove. I am so sorry, so very sorry."

I'm sobbing, and she is too. Inara is great, and she's helping any way she can, but Alora has always been the person I love most, second only to Mom.

"Touching reunion." Judica's voice is flat. "You didn't get to see Mother before she died, but at least you got to see Chancery one last time."

Alora lets me go and turns toward my twin. "You're hurting, Judica, so I'll forgive you for acting like a total brat." She gestures for Judica to come to her for a hug, but Judica stands as still as a statue, shoulders square, chin high, eyes flashing.

"I was just telling Chancery I won't wait for morning. I insist on her answering my challenge now."

Alora tsks just like Mom used to. "Stop being ridiculous." Before Judica can respond, Alora holds up her phone. "Listen to this."

She presses a button and Mom's voice fills the room via speakerphone. "Alora sweetheart, you must be in the air already. I'm so glad you're coming after all, although I wish it was under better circumstances. I know everyone told me it was a mistake not to kill one of the twins at birth, but I love them both so dearly. I couldn't have done it then, and I could never live without either of them now. They are fighting terribly and everything I try makes things worse. Chancery begged for permission to come and live with you. Against my better judgment, I agreed. That's the reason I called back and begged you to come to my party last minute. I want you to bring her home to New York with you when you return. I've promised her a few weeks to decide whether she wants to forsake the family entirely and live among the humans like you. I won't lie and say I want her to go, but I'm losing them as it is, and maybe the space will help things settle." Mom lowers her voice and I strain to make out her last words. "I'm leaving you this message because I've been... sick. I don't know what's wrong precisely, but I fear I'm being poisoned. It's getting worse, Alora. I don't know how much time I have left." There's a sharp click and the voicemail ends.

Hearing Mom's voice is too much. I sit down on the ground and start to sob. She can't be gone. She can't. I know in that moment, I cannot fight Judica. I just can't. I can't kill my sister. Mom would hate that we're here, about to fight each other over her throne.

But I'm certain Judica killed Mom, or else why would she feel so guilty? Act so very angry? She found out Mom's plan and decided she wouldn't wait for it to be official. She took Mom from me forever. Suddenly I'm so angry I want to jump across the room and strangle Judica with my bare hands, which horrifies me.

Clearly I have no idea what I want.

Alora crosses the room and takes Judica by the shoulders. "You aren't going to kill your twin, Juju-bee. Not on your mother's birthday, not when all she wanted was for you two to get along."

"How quick everyone is to rush to her defense." Judica shakes Alora off. "Why isn't anyone rushing to help me?"

"First of all, Chancery isn't threatening to kill anyone. But beyond that, Mother named Chancery this morning as her new Heir," Alora says. "That makes her Empress, and you're the one challenging her moments after Mother was killed. I'm sorry if you perceive that as me rushing to her side." So quietly I can barely hear her, Alora says, "I'm here by your side, too. I want what's best for both of you, and for Alamecha. That's why I'm taking her home with me to New York."

"My sister Chancery," Judica practically spits, "is the new Empress, as you so helpfully pointed out. She isn't going anywhere."

Inara sits down next to me on the ground, her skirt belling around her, and pats the floor. Alora sits down cross-legged, but Judica continues pacing.

"We haven't had the investiture yet," Inara says, "which means Chancery's still only Heir now. We don't even have the ring to use for it."

"Wait," Alora says, "the ring is missing?"

I nod. "It's a long story, but we think Mom took it off and put it somewhere she thought it would be safer. We don't know where." I shove my guilt about lying down deep. I have no idea if what Job said was reliable, or whether it even refers to the ring.

"Regardless," Inara says. "What if you let Chancy spend her month in New York with Alora and you rule in her absence as her heir, the heir to the Heir. It's been done. There's precedent. Melamecha took decades off, several times in fact."

"What a brilliant plan," Alora says. "You wouldn't need to kill Chancery if she decides to abdicate anyway."

I almost offer to abdicate right now, but when I think of Mom lying there on the parquet, I can't. "If you'd agree to stand trial," I say, "just for the Council. Or even just for Alora and Inara. If you're found innocent of poisoning Mom, I'll abdicate."

"Our family is at risk right now," Judica says. "The Five sense blood in the water. I'm not going to agree to stand trial, and I'm not going to send you off to train for a month, either. I'm not the stupid one, remember?"

"You've been training hard for almost eighteen years. You think I'll catch you in a month?" I roll my eyes. "I didn't expect you to be afraid of me."

"You'll never defeat me." Judica huffs. "But that doesn't mean I want to prolong the inevitable, either. Mother is dead. Whether this happens now, or in a week, or in a month, that fact won't change."

"I didn't want to bring this up," Inara says, "but you're forcing my hand. Chancery named you mother slayer, Judica. Because Chancery is ascending as the new Empress, she would have held the trial to determine whether there is evidence that you killed Mother. That inquest must take place. If Chancery is alive, as Empress of Alamecha, she conducts the inquest. A direct challenge from the next in the line of succession takes precedence, so by challenging Chancery, your duel will take place before any inquest."

"I know," Judica says. "I've read the Charter."

"But you neglected to consider what happens after you win," Inara says.

It sort of stings that everyone assumes Judica will beat me, even if I agree with them.

"I take my place as Empress," Judica says.

Inara shakes her head and Alora frowns.

Alora says, "No, you don't. Inara's right. The demand for the inquest against one other than the Heir accused of killing the Empress still stands. You can't conduct an inquest against yourself, and with Chancery gone, the Five will convene the court."

"So even if I kill her, this mess won't be over." Judica collapses onto the edge of her bed. "The Five will intercede in our affairs either way, thanks to her thoughtless and baseless allegations."

"If they're really baseless, then agree to a trial now," I say.

Inara clucks. "There is a way out."

Judica looks down at her. "What is that?"

Alora sighs. "Chancery can voluntarily rescind her accusation."

I shake my head. "Why would I do that? She can deny it until the end of time. I know she did it and why."

Inara spears me with a glance. I know what she's suggesting. I rescind my accusation in exchange for time to train before this duel. Without time, I'm dead in the morning, but at least I'll die with the knowledge that my mom's killer might be brought to justice.

Although, the Five will do whatever they believe is politically expedient. I can't really trust them any more than I trust Judica. Gah, I hate politics.

"Fine. But if I rescind my accusation, do I have the right to reissue it after the challenge?"

"You're an idiot," Judica says. "The only way you could reissue it is if you win, and if you do, I'll already be dead. I'd think that's punishment enough, even to satisfy your anger."

Alora puts her hand on my shoulder. "You can always reissue an accusation. Judica is right that in this circumstance it doesn't seem that it would be necessary."

"So if I rescind my accusation, you will swear to delay the duel for a month, while I decide whether to abdicate?"

"Wrong. I'll give you a week."

"A week isn't time to decide, it's a holiday," Inara says. "She needs to spend time contemplating a non-evian life.

Not to mention, we're all grieving here." Bless her for trying to get me more time.

"Alamecha doesn't have weeks to spare," Judica says. "The sharks are circling, and our family needs to show it's strong. With the ring missing, it's even more important this be resolved quickly."

"Obviously we won't tell anyone it's gone," Inara says.

"One week," Judica says. "That's my limit."

"I don't agree to that," I say.

All three sets of eyes turn to me, each one reflecting shock at my refusal.

"I don't think I can decide in a week. I need two."

"Absolutely not," Judica says. "That's too long."

"I'll agree to ten days... if you also release Edam." Because with me gone and Judica in charge, he'd be executed in the morning. I can't have that on my conscience. She only hates him because he stood up for me.

Judica snorts. "No."

"He comes with me, and—"

"Wait," Judica asks, "where are you going? I assumed you'd stay here."

"If I stay here, there's no reason to leave you in charge in my stead. I'm going with Alora to New York," I say. "To see what it's like to be human. I've never liked or agreed with many things about evian life, and if I abdicate, I'll be living with humans forever. I'd like to experience that before I decide." Plus, I need to look for the ring. "You rescind the charges against Edam and let him come with me, or I'll stay here and fight you tomorrow. When I die in the morning, as everyone seems quite sure I will, I'm sure you'll enjoy hosting the Five while they look for evidence of how you murdered Mom."

Judica glances from Alora to me and back again. Finally, she says, "Fine, Edam goes with you for ten days, but I won't make any promises about charges against him being dropped. If you abdicate, he'll be exiled along with you. If you return, fight, and lose, I can kill him any way I choose." Judging by the set of her jaw, it's the best offer I'll get.

"I accept. But you freeze Mom's body, and if I abdicate, I can attend Mom's funeral before leaving."

"Fine," Judica says. "But I'm not doing this for you. I'll agree to your terms as a final gift to Mother."

Alora smiles as if she's brokered the peace deal of the century instead of simply delaying my demise. "Lovely. Just lovely. Now let's hammer out the details so we can all get some rest. Chancery and I will leave in the morning."

16

Inara knocks before the sun rises. When I open the door for her, Frederick's awake and alert outside, a small bag on the floor next to him. She's carrying a bag, too.

"Good morning." I rub my bleary eyes.

"Are you ready to go? Alora's plane is preparing to leave."

"I've been thinking about it," I say, "and I think you should stay."

Inara drops her bag. "Why?"

"I'll have Edam and Alora to train me, and you could stay here and look for the ring while I'm gone."

"Judica will already be looking," Inara says.

"Exactly. I'd love to have someone here I can trust not to simply schedule the funeral and investiture without me, and you could maybe try to warn me of any assassination attempts headed my way."

Inara frowns. "I can protect you better if I'm near you. And I can't counsel you at all, not from here, not with any confidence that no one else knows what I'm telling you."

"I need someone I trust to put the family first here, in the heart of Alamecha."

Inara sits on my bed, her lip trembling. "I miss her, too. I want to do what she wants me to do, but I don't know what that is."

I sit next to Inara and wrap my arm around her. Her dismay tears at the gaping hole in my heart, but I can't fall apart when she needs strength from me. Not when she's been so amazing.

Inara wipes at her face and straightens. "You need me here?"

I nod.

"Then I'll stay. Maybe I can provide something, information or, I don't know, something helpful from here. If nothing else, I can work with the people to make sure they soften toward the idea of you as their ruler."

I'm sure they hate the thought of me taking over for Mom. No one who doesn't know about the EMP thinks I'm the right choice. They're probably all right.

Inara must see the pain in my face, because she bites her lip. "That's not what I meant. I'm sure people are pleased. Everyone loves you. They were just surprised, is all. I can help them adjust to the idea."

"Might be a huge waste of time," I say. "I may just abdicate. If we can't find the ring, it won't matter that I reacted to it."

"There's a prophecy about it, right?" Inara asks. "Mom mentioned it once to Adika when I was much younger, but I overheard. There's some queen to rule all queens, and she thinks it's you."

I have no idea why it's supposed to be such a secret, but I see no reason not to confirm Inara's guess. I nod. "Something like that. It's ridiculous."

"Maybe. Or maybe not."

I stand up and grab my bag. "I guess I don't have time

to brush my teeth and shower, not if Alora's plane is about to leave."

Inara stands and hugs me again, so tightly I can almost hear my bones creak.

"Careful," I say. "I know we heal, but it still hurts."

She rolls her eyes. "Oh please."

I grab my bag and head for the door.

"Wait," Inara says.

"Yeah?" I ask.

"Give me your phone."

I shake my head. "How else will I call you?"

"Judica can look up that number on her system here. She can track you with it if she wants to. It's not safe."

"She agreed to ten days," I say.

Inara shrugs. "Fine, trust in her good nature."

Crap. I hand her my phone. "How will I contact you?"

She passes me an envelope full of cash. "You can buy a new phone, or if you trust Alora completely, have her get you one. At least no phone she provides will be monitored by the main Alamecha security protocols."

I hadn't even thought about all of this. It's making my head spin. As Empress, I need to learn a lot more about security and espionage. I glance at the stack of books on my bedside table. Mom was always piling me up with light reading about the world, telling me I'd need to integrate all that information at some point. I snag five of them: *Hacking Exposed, The Art of Deception, Thinking Strategically, Why Nations Fail,* and *Sladius Today: Decimate your Opponent.* At least I'll have something to read on the flight to NYC.

The pain I feel when I walk away from Inara, my mother's mini-me, is nothing to the ocean of sorrow when I think about the fact that she's gone. But it still hurts. I glance over my shoulder and she smiles broadly at me and waves.

Frederick, of course, trails on my heels. "Is this going to be a new thing?" I ask.

"What? Me following you?" His dark hair falls in his face, and he uses his free hand to brush it back.

"I don't need a shadow."

"I disagree," he says. "But I haven't had time to thoroughly vet enough of the guards. That will have to wait. For now, I've chosen ten I trust completely to accompany us."

I open my mouth to argue.

Frederick sets his jaw and clenches his fist, and I don't have the energy to argue with him, not now. Not after the last two days.

"Fine."

I survey his approved guards on the runway outside. Seven men and three women. I know them all, of course, but I only know four of them well enough to carry on a conversation of any kind. I'm surprised how many of them are young. Like, only a few years older than me.

"How did you pick these guards specifically?" I ask as we climb up the steps to board the jet. "I've barely met a few of them."

"I wish I could have simply transferred your mother's guard to you." He shakes his head. "But I felt it was safer to recruit only people I was one thousand percent sure supported you specifically."

"I think she was poisoned." I blink back tears. "I doubt the guards were to blame for that failure. More like one of Angel's staff."

"You can be sure Judica will conduct a thorough investigation there."

Unless Judica poisoned Mom herself. I see that register on Frederick's face, so I don't bother saying it. Frederick's guards split, half in front and half behind me. I wait patiently at the top of the stairs for them to clear me to board. Alora's jet only seats twenty, and I notice there's already one guest on board. It's not Alora.

Edam's sitting in the window of the first row on the right side. He doesn't smile at me when my eyes meet his. In fact, it almost looks like he's scowling. Did I imagine the flirty interchanges over the past few days? I expected a little gratitude for getting him out of a holding cell at the very least.

"Hey, Edam." Even with the awful day I've had, his face brightens the room.

He grunts.

Why is he grunting? What did I do? Maybe he hates anyone in line for the throne. "I'm glad you're safe and onboard."

"I wish I was." He crosses his arms, the muscles in his forearms rippling, and leans back in his chair.

"Umm, are you saying you wish you weren't safe? Or that you weren't on board?" I ask.

He lifts one eyebrow.

I sit down on the seat next to him, and he leans slightly toward the window and away from me. What the—? "What's wrong with you?"

"If Your Majesty finds me lacking in any way, I apologize profusely."

"Knock it off with all the majesties and whatnot. Why are you upset?"

"No reason. No reason at all. And now that Your Majesty is Empress, I certainly can't justify using a more informal address." Edam pulls a book out of his bag and pointedly sticks his nose into it. *Sein Und Zeit.* Great. He's reading Heidegger's *Being in Time*. In the original German. Instead of talking to me.

"A little light reading for the flight?" I thought my stupid security, economics, and game theory texts were bad enough.

He answers without looking up. "We're joining the humans for a while. I figured I should brush up on my studies of human morality."

"Are you kidding me right now?" I ask. "You're reading an old German philosopher so you can connect in New York City?"

Edam plonks the thick, leather bound book down on his lap. "What would you prefer for me to do, Your Majesty? I'm sure that your wish is my command."

"I thought, since we're in this together, you might talk to me. We could formulate a plan or something."

"We're in this together?" The corner of Edam's mouth quirks up.

"Well, aren't we? You came to my defense, which landed you in a cell, and I struck a deal with my sister, one requirement of which was that she free you."

Edam closes his eyes for a moment. "I dumped your lunatic sister, who by the way, never asked me if I wanted to date her in the first place. That really pissed her off royally. Then I kept her from decapitating you, and later, from strangling you. That certainly didn't help, but she wouldn't have killed me, not really. Especially if I groveled, which is all she's wanted from the beginning."

My mouth dangles open stupidly. "Are you saying you wish I'd left you imprisoned? Awaiting execution?"

Frederick snorts behind me, and I feel a little vindicated at least.

"I wasn't given an option. Again."

This time, when Edam opens his book and begins reading, I almost don't interrupt. But I can't have him thinking I'm the same as Judica. If I'd known he wanted to stay with her, I never would have negotiated to bring him along. "I'm sorry," I say quietly. Then I stand up and go to the bathroom, just so I can change seats.

The bathroom stall winds up being a nice place to cry in

silence. It's not like Edam being mad at me even rates on the general barometer for horrible events in the last few days, but somehow, his anger at my attempt to help sends me over the edge. The plane's about to take off when I finally emerge, and there's a seat open near Alora. Thankfully.

"Inara made me leave my cell phone behind," I complain.

Alora lifts one eyebrow. "I hope everyone on this plane did the same."

Heads nod all around me.

"I've made arrangements. You'll all be provided with new phones upon arrival, or if you'd prefer, I can show you to a location to procure your own."

I manage to read all five books during my flight. And I stick to Alora's side like glue when we exit the plane, not that steering clear of Edam is hard. I'm surrounded by guards like a crystal vase cocooned in bubble wrap for international shipping.

It doesn't take long for Alora's sleek black car to reach her enormous brownstone near Gramercy Park. When I walk up the steps, I almost forget that Mom's not climbing up behind me. The last day has passed in a haze, with no Mom, no Cookie, and no Lark or Lyssa. I don't even have Judica around to restore some balance.

When the front door opens, I almost expect to see Lark shoot through and hug me. But of course, she can't be seen by the guards without giving away the fact that I never executed her.

Alora walks through the large front entry and starts up the stairs that curve up and to the right. "Chancy, you and Edam are this direction."

Frederick and one of his guards, Arlington, follow on my heels quicker than Edam.

"I doubt she will need a door guard in my household,"

Alora says. "I vouch for each of my indoor staff, and I have a fully functioning security crew. I promise we will keep my sister safe while she's in residence."

Frederick frowns.

"It's fine," I say. "Let him do his job."

Alora bobs her head and continues onward. We walk up the stairs and follow her down the hallway to the right, passing several of her guards along the way. She points at the first door on the left. "This one's yours, Chancy." She indicates the door across the hall. "That's Edam's. I figured you'd want him close, since you worked so hard to secure his release."

I glance sideways at Edam, but he just walks into his room and closes the door. I do the same, and Alora follows me inside.

She gestures at my bed, where a brand new phone is sitting on top of a basket of other basics, like shampoo, towels, granola bars, and mineral water. "Edam's angry."

I bob my head. "I saved his life. Who knew that would piss him off?"

Alora's mouth turns up into a smile, but her eyes are full of pity. "Would Judica really have killed him? Or was she angry and hurting and looking for someone to blame?"

"Even so, best case scenario, he'd be sitting in a cell if I left him there."

"And now?" she asks. "Now he's, what?"

If I return and die, he does too. And if I abdicate, he'll have to run. Which probably looks bleaker than a cell to Mr. Perfect Evian Posterboy.

She sighs. "Your heart was in the right place."

Which is exactly why I ought to abdicate. Having a good heart does not qualify me to rule Alamecha. In fact, from what I've seen so far, it makes me less suited to the job. "He was in line to take over for Balthasar before all of this happened. Which means my mom's death and the fallout was nearly as bad for him as it has been for me." I drop my bag on the ground and collapse onto the enormous sleigh bed in the middle of the room.

"What's done is done," Alora says. "He'll either forgive you or he won't, but you can't worry about it. Right now you need to focus on training. You have to do your best to be ready to fight your sister in ten days. I can't have you abdicating because you think it's your only choice. I've already ordered my staff to clear the entire ballroom on the fourth floor and to clean that room as often as necessary."

"It's equally important that I spend some time with humans to find out whether I want to return to evian life at all."

Alora smiles. "I've arranged for that too. I enrolled you, Lark, and Edam in a local private school. If you think you can trust him. I assumed you could, but if I'm wrong. . ."

I think about how he saved me, and then I consider our recent interactions. "I do believe I can trust him. I don't love his attitude, but at least he's not pretending he's fine with things when he's not. And now, like it or not, his fate is kind of tied to mine."

"Unless Judica asks him to kill you, and he does it to get back into her good graces."

Shoot.

A tap at the door, in the corner I assumed was the closet, startles me.

"Come in," Alora says.

The door opens, and Lark walks through. She rushes toward me, a mournful expression on her face. I don't even realize I'm sobbing against her shoulder until she pulls back. "I'm so sorry, Chancy. Even with how everything went down with my mother, I didn't wish that for you. I truly didn't."

"I know."

Three days ago, we had moms who would kill for us.

Now we're both alone. Alora excuses herself, and I catch Lark up on everything. For the first time in almost twenty-four hours, it feels like there's enough air in the room for me to breathe.

A tap on the door to the hallway makes me jump. Lark hops up and points at the door she came through earlier. "I'll head back to my room," she mouths.

"How?"

"Passageway," she whispers.

Wow, my family likes their hidden corridors. "Fine."

After Lark has shut the door behind her, I count to five. I'm walking to the door when there's a louder, stronger, more insistent knock.

"Hang on, I'm coming. Geez."

I'm expecting Alora or Frederick. I am not expecting a broody Edam, white t-shirt molded to his perfectly sculpted chest. I do not sigh, or breathe deeply, or widen my eyes. Or at least, I try not to.

"What do you want?" I ask.

"I assume you're ready to begin training," he says.

"Training? I've been here for fifteen minutes."

He nods. "Right. I allowed you some extra time in case you needed to use the restroom."

My cheeks heat. "You're training me? I thought Alora would be the one—"

"She's a melodics master." Edam snorts. "You have ten days. If you want to die, suit yourself."

"You think you can teach me enough sladius to compensate for more than ten years of *subpar* melodics training?"

"I think I'm your best option."

"Alora mentioned the ballroom is also her training arena."

"She has a ballroom in Manhattan?" Edam asks.

"Ballerina," I say.

"Fine. Let's go then."

I shoo him out the door so I can change, and a few moments later I'm standing across from Edam in a vast ballroom that's at least as large as Mom's outdoor courtyard. Last week I hadn't spoken ten words in the last five years to the man the world assumed would marry my wretched sister. Now he's trying to teach me to kill her.

He extends a knife toward me, holding the blade with two fingers so the hilt is out.

"We're using daggers now?" I ask.

"Hand-to-hand, bladed weapons, we need to mix it up. You will choose the mode of combat, but you can't make that choice until we've isolated your strengths."

"I certainly hope no one chooses hand-to-hand for a battle to the death. That sounds... protracted," I say. "But I'm not very good with swords."

"That's why we're starting small. We can work our way up. I'm going to focus on teaching you moves that will use your current skill set and improve upon it, things you can learn quickly. If you want to defeat Judica, you'll have to triple your past efforts."

"But three times zero is still. . ."

Edam rolls his eyes. We start with one knife each and move to two. Every time I try to throw them, he stops me. "We need to work on your weaknesses, not your strengths."

We identify plenty of those. An hour later, I'm exhausted and covered with blood from a million swipes with his daggers. Alora's ballroom looks like the set of a bad slasher movie. "How long are we planning to do this?"

Edam pulls a sword from the weapons rack and hands it to me. "All day today. You're way behind."

"So far you've been slicing me to ribbons, but I haven't learned a thing."

"That's not true. You're healing faster."

I think back to what my mom said about pain training. I guess I'm getting the integrated version.

Edam starts swinging his sword around in circles.

"What are you doing?" I ask. "You look silly." Or he would if Edam could ever look bad.

"I'm warming up," he says. "Our other main goal today is ferreting out your natural talents and skills so we can develop the right overall strategy. Ready to show me what you can do with a sword when you aren't busy arguing with your sister?"

Without any further warning, he comes for me, slicing, pulling back, spinning around. He moves so fast I can barely follow him, and I use my left forearm to deflect his strikes as often as my blade. The spray from my last block reaches the chandelier, and I pause for a moment to consider who will clean that up. When I glance back down, Edam almost severs my arm above the wrist. My focus narrows to the present. I really don't want to regrow an appendage. I hear it's the worst.

About half an hour in, Edam pauses in his attack and pulls a long knife from his right boot. He tosses it to me and bends over to pull another from his left boot. Before I can ask why he's given me a second blade, he comes after me again.

Without thinking, I stop using my forearm and begin to use the long knife to deflect his strikes, attacking with the sword one-handed. I struggle through another half hour of attacks and subsequent healing, but my legs quiver like jelly, my right arm throbs, and I practically whimper when Edam calls for a halt.

I sink down to the ground and slump over my own knees. "Am I a lost cause?"

Edam sits across from me and looks me dead in the eye. "Do you trust Inara?"

I bob my head. "Yeah."

"You need to ask her to send you videos of Judica fighting over the past few months. Your mother trained you in your private courtyard, so no one has ever seen you, aside from that debacle with Lark and the one match with your twin, but Judica trained in the arena. There are security feeds in there that anyone with top level clearance can access. Larena, Balthasar, Inara. You would have access too, if you were still home. If we can get those files, you can learn how Judica fights. Instead of me telling you she favors her left arm and her right leg, you can watch how she pulls back on kicks with her left. How she pauses before striking from her right with a sword. We have to focus on every single weakness, because you're going to need to exploit *them all* if you want any hope of surviving this. And we have to watch the fight the two of you had that last morning, because that will also be invaluable."

"I'll call and ask Inara, but even without videos, I improved a little today, right?"

Edam sighs. "She'd kill you in under two minutes if you fought her tomorrow."

Ouch. "Still that bad? Really?"

He averts his eyes.

I jump up and start to pace. "Why are we even wasting our time, then?" Tears well up in my eyes. Can I get pruney cheeks from crying too much? If so, I'm sure to have them soon. Maybe my only real choice is to abdicate. It certainly feels easier. Would Mom want her murderer to rule? Maybe she would, since it's her daughter.

But Mom chose me. I'm so confused.

"I want to help you, Chancery. I'm on your side." He clenches his fists. "Even if I didn't decide to be myself."

"I'm sorry about that," I say. "Yesterday flew past at a million miles per hour. It seemed like the right thing to do. I guess I should've known you'd be fine without my intervention. With your history, Judica wouldn't really have killed you, but I swear that didn't occur to me in the moment." I doubt Edam can hear my last words, they're so quiet. "I was bleeding out last night. I wasn't thinking straight."

"Actually with our history, she might have gone through with it. We'll never know." Edam stands up and grabs my hand, turning me to face him. "If you'd asked me, I'd have chosen to come with you. If I were a better person, I'd have realized that sooner and spent less time sulking about it. You need help, and you're a good person. You didn't deserve my temper tantrum." He squeezes my hand quickly and then releases it. "With everything that happened to you yesterday, I shouldn't have gotten upset. Forgive me."

My heart picks up the pace. It's hard to look at him without that happening, but this time it's not about his face. It's about his words. "Thank you."

"I'm going to say something now and I want you to think about it," he says. "Don't dismiss it out of hand. And try not to get offended." He tugs me back down to the ground and sits across from me. He looks right into my eyes. "You have a big decision to make, and you can probably guess that I don't want to be exiled. I'm evian down to my bones. I would hate living away from our people, but that's not why I'm offering this, I swear that to you. I really think you'd make a better ruler than Judica. I think your mom realized that and it's why she changed the documents. I don't know exactly what's going on in your head, but I've spent a lot of time with your sister."

A tear slides down my cheek, and then another. I can't seem to stop it, not this time. And it's not even about my mom, not specifically. It's Edam's words, his faith in me. He's the first person to say that I'd be a better ruler without knowing about my reaction to the dumb ring.

He scoots over until he's sitting right next to me. He pulls my head over on his shoulder. "I'm sorry," he says. "I don't know if I've told you that. There's never a good time to lose your mom, trust me, but that had to be the worst timing in the world."

I'm not sure how long I cry on his arm, but eventually I stop and lift my head. I slide far enough away that I can look at him again without craning my neck.

"Sorry to interrupt your tough love moment." I hiccup. "What was your point? I'm ready to hear it."

He offers me a half smile. "This is going to seem strange, but like I said, think about it before you turn me down. It's an option you might not have considered or even known about. Right now you're contemplating two very different paths: either abdicate and live with Alora as a human, or return and fight your twin to the death. If you win, you become Empress."

He doesn't say I'm unlikely to win. We both know that already.

"Okay," I say. "That sounds right."

"Here's where I need you to remember not to get upset. I think you'll be a good ruler, I really do. You may not have been trained as the Heir, but you spent every waking moment with one of the best evian rulers of all time. You surely learned principles of justice and mercy and when to apply each. You had to have learned about warcraft and political management, even if what you learned was only high level from watching your mother. You can be taught the basic elements quickly because you've seen them all in application. I have no doubt you can handle Alamecha's affairs and do a fine job. You told me before it seems silly to choose a Security Chief based on his combat prowess. Similarly, it seems barbaric that our ultimate ruler is sometimes chosen by a duel to the death."

I agree. It's the dumbest method possible to choose someone who will dictate the order of the world, but it's always been our way. It's not like I can change the Charter to make it a history test or a bake off.

"If you go back, you're going to lose. Judica will kill you easily. I'm going to do my best to improve your skill and teach you to beat her, but I'm not overly optimistic. It's almost certain that if you return, you'll die."

This hardly seems helpful.

He reaches out and takes my hand in his. "Please listen to my point. I'm not trying to hurt your feelings. I'm being honest, and offering you a third option. Choose me as your Consort, marry me, and let me fight her for you. You know I can defeat her, as surely as she can defeat you. Let me do what you can't, so that you can do what's right for our people and avenge your mother."

I've imagined the man of my dreams proposing to me a dozen different ways. That is *so not* how any of them went in my head.

17

I call Inara the second I reach my room to ask about the videos, but as soon as she answers, I find myself telling her about Edam's offer instead. It's stupid. She's with Judica, and this call might even be tapped, but I can't help myself. I want to talk to Mom about it, and Inara is as close as I can get.

She doesn't respond. Not a single word. I wonder whether the line went dead.

"Are you still there?" I finally ask.

"Yes."

"Care to share your thoughts?"

"I don't know," she says. "Choosing a Consort is a big decision. Evians don't divorce."

"I could always have him executed," I joke.

"That would literally be your only option if choosing him is a mistake."

I was kidding. "Uh."

"You're not even eighteen for two more weeks," Inara says. "Mother would freak out if you told her this plan."

"I'm in this mess because she isn't here to freak out

about anything anymore." I clench my hands into fists. "What would you do?"

"I don't know," Inara says. "I just don't know. Do you feel like your combat skills are improving?"

"I think so, but Edam says it's not nearly enough."

"It's your first day."

"Even so, we don't have many more."

"Regardless, you've got at least another week before you need to make any major decisions."

True. "By the way," I say, "he wants you to send me as many videos of Judica fighting as you can get your hands on, including our fight the day of the you know what." If anyone is listening, no reason to give them anything specific. "Do you think you can do it?"

"Judica won't like it," Inara says. "I'll need to do it without her knowledge. I wonder what Balthasar will make of all this. He's devastated about Mother, and he misses Edam. And you, too, of course."

"Don't tell him if there's any way around it."

"He has all the videos and the log of who accesses them. Security section protocol," she says.

"Isn't there a way around that?" I ask.

"I'll see what I can do. Let me think about the Edam thing." I hear rustling in the background and then Inara says, "I've got to go, but before I do, tell me this. Do you like him? Would you want to spend a thousand years with him by your side?"

"Yes," I say. "I do like him."

"Well, I guess that's better than the alternative. Accept the world as it is," she whispers.

"Or do something to change it," I say, but she's already hung up. I worry about her, hopping off the phone, whispering, unsure what she can do for me. I hope she's safe there.

She can't be in too much danger, since she sends me a batch of videos while I'm in the shower. I hunt down Alora before I dive into watching them. I find her in the library. "Sorry we made such a mess in the ballroom."

"How did the training go?" she asks.

I shrug. I ought to tell her about Edam's offer too, but I'm pretty sure she'll freak out and tell me it's a huge mistake, so I don't bother. "It could have gone better, but it's early days."

She bobs her head. "It is early."

"I need to talk to you."

Frederick catches my eye and glances at Arlington, whose chocolate brown eyes are downcast. I'm not buying it. He's listening to every word.

"Freddy, can you secure and close the door?"

He bows and does it, a half smile on his face. I'm learning, even if I'm slow. Freddy may trust his people, but there's no reason they need to hear everything I discuss.

"What's wrong?" Alora asks.

"It's not that something is wrong per se. Or at least, nothing more than you already know. It's that Job gave me a message. Mom told him she sent something to you. Something I will need, something important."

"You're hoping it's the ring."

I nod.

"Why would she do that?"

"No idea, but I can't think what else she might have sent. Can you?"

Alora's brow furrows. "No. I'll conduct a thorough search, and I'll alert my people to be on the lookout for anything that might turn up. If it's here or on its way to us, I'll get it to you."

A tiny weight lifts from my shoulders. I believe she will. "Thank you."

"Hungry?" she asks.

"Starving, and I need to replenish some volume too, but can you have food sent to my room? I've got some research I need to do on Judica. Inara sent me some files of her fighting."

Alora smiles. "Wise, very wise."

"It was Edam's suggestion," I say. "Wish I could take credit."

"You're too honest to play those kinds of games. That might be more impressive than having the inspiration in the first place." Alora smiles at me and I duck out.

Her staff is efficient, too. I've barely reached my room when a short girl with dark curly hair arrives with an entire platter of sandwiches and two pitchers of lemonade. Frederick and Arlington follow her into the room. She curtsies, and her heart races. She's human. My eyes widen. "Thanks."

I take the tray from her and set it on the table. She scurries out so quickly I don't even have time to ask her name. Maybe next time. I reach for a sandwich, but Freddy clears his throat.

"What?" I ask.

"Your dog is—ahem. You need a taster."

Cookie's gone. No more hand licks or fur balls curled up at my feet. But also, I need someone to ensure I'm not poisoned.

"I can call the maid back," he says.

I shake my head. "Not her. She's human."

"Weaker is better," Arlington says, "because they react faster if there's a problem."

"Yes, thank you, I know that." I think about that poor girl, writhing on the floor, or dead with her mouth foaming. I can't handle that.

"I'll do it," Arlington says. "Frederick's too important, and no one else is near."

Before I can stop him, he snatches an egg salad sandwich, the most likely candidate for poison with the saucy filling, and stuffs half of it into his mouth. He swallows and smiles at me. "Tastes good."

I turn up my lip at the egg salad. I move my turkey sandwich toward my mouth, but Frederick clears his throat again.

"What now?" I ask.

"He only tried one of the sandwich types. And you need to wait at least several minutes," he says. "To make sure Arlington's not negatively impacted."

"Oh for heaven's sake." I huff, but I wait and watch while Arlington eats part of each sandwich.

And while I wait, I think about school tomorrow. Lark's going to enroll too, which means the security staff will see her. And Edam will too. Will she be safe? Will my secret make its way back to Judica and the rest of Alamecha? Should I send her away?

The thought slices through my wounded heart, but that's not a good reason to risk her life or my tentative control over my family. If I even have tentative control.

"Frederick?" I ask.

"Your Majesty." He lifts his eyebrows.

"You said you chose guards who were utterly loyal to me."

He nods.

"How did you ascertain their loyalty?"

Arlington clears his throat.

"Yes, Arlington. Would you like to weigh in?"

"You spared my sister, Your Majesty."

I frown. He has eleven sisters, by my count. I think about them each in turn. "Fontaine?"

"When Judica advocated for execution, you pushed for exile."

I close my eyes. My mercy, always my mercy. "And Frederick knew you would appreciate that decision?"

Arlington shrugs. "I love Fontaine, and she'd have died if you hadn't stood up to Judica. I believe in black and white, Your Majesty, but sometimes the two mix. Your sister doesn't see gray anywhere. In my experience, if you make no room for gray, the world swims in red."

I think about the other guards. Bellatrius requested approval to marry into the Shenoah family while we were at war with them, and I supported her. Her petition was declined, but over my objection. Lucas' mother was exiled five years ago for carrying a half-human child and refusing to give it up. I've been vocal in my opposition of that particular law.

"All of my selected guards have sworn an oath to serve you," Frederick says. "It's essentially the basics of the Empress' oath, which usually happens at the investiture, but given the circumstances." He spreads his arms. "I thought you should have your own guard, even if it's small. Had you been Heir last week, you'd have one already. Judica does."

"Then you think I can trust them?"

Arlington bows his head slightly. "I only speak for myself, but you can trust me completely."

"They're all willing to follow you into exile, if that's your choice," Frederick offers.

"Even you?" I ask him. "You've been head of my mother's guard for three centuries. And you'll follow me into exile and live among the humans if I choose to abdicate?"

Frederick drops to one knee. "Your mother was the best monarch I've ever seen, and I've seen quite a few in my position."

I arch one eyebrow. "She's been Empress the entire time you've been alive."

"But I've seen many others from the other five families," he says. "None of them could touch her, and she chose you as her successor."

"She chose Judica first," I say.

"She changed her mind. That's enough for me." Frederick grips the hilt of his sword with both hands. "I Frederick ne'Francesca Alamecha swear to serve and obey you, Chancery Alamecha, seventh daughter of Eve, and to place your health and safety over that of my own. I swear never to betray you in act, thought, or deed, and to support and assist my brothers and sisters in honoring their vows."

Frederick stands.

"I guess that answers my question," I say.

"Which was?" Frederick asks.

"Whether Lark will be safe out in the open, with my guards around." I glance at Arlington. "I didn't execute her like Mom ordered."

"I gathered that much, Your Majesty." Arlington's lip curls up on one side. "I'm glad, for your sake. You were always quite close."

"It would be a terrible scandal," I say, "and most citizens of Alamecha wouldn't understand or support my decision."

"There's no reason for them to know," Arlington says. "But you might be wrong about how many would accept it. You've been vocal about your positions, and more people support you than care to admit that publicly."

I wonder how much truth there is to his words. I want to believe in my people, but I haven't seen any evidence of his claim. "Lark will attend school with me. I hope I can trust my other guards with the knowledge that she's still alive."

"We'll find out soon enough," Frederick says. "Since we plan to accompany you to school tomorrow."

"Excuse me?" I lift one eyebrow. "How will I have any hope of blending in with the humans if I have guards following me around?"

"Alora arranged jobs for us around the school," Frederick says. "Arlington is the new janitor, and I'm the new head of security."

"How'd she do that?" I ask.

Frederick grins. "The school appreciates its largest donors."

"Well, I think there has been plenty of time for any poison to take effect." I eye the sandwiches greedily.

"How do you feel, Arlington?" Frederick asks.

"Fine. Wonderful." And finally, the men approve the food and leave my room.

Lark ducks through the closet door a moment later. "Good news," I tell her. "You're fine to come and go in the normal hallway and enter the room even when you hear other voices."

"Huh?" she asks.

"I cleared it with Frederick. My personal guard knows you're alive, or they soon will."

She blinks rapidly. "Are you sure that's wise?"

I nod. "Positive. It's not like people could really think much less of me than they already do on that regard anyway."

"What about Edam? He's Judica's ex. Are you sure there's no residual loyalty there?" Lark grabs a sandwich from the platter.

I think about Judica ordering him to the holding cell, and then his anger that I brought him with me. "I don't think there's a lot of love lost between the two of them, but he's still a wild card, that's for sure." I don't mention his offer, and I'm not sure why not.

"Speaking of, he wants me to review videos of Judica fighting."

"Oh, good idea," Lark says.

I hold my phone out in front of me so she can see it, too. "Glad you're here. Maybe you'll notice something I miss."

"Doubtful," she laments. "I'm deficient, remember?"

I eye her sideways. "You're nothing of the sort, and I appreciate your help."

The first file is dated just a month ago. February 14. I press play on my phone, and the video springs to life. Judica's training in the main outdoor courtyard, but the angle of the camera is strange. I can only see the fight in the very corner of the screen.

At the beginning of the match, Judica's smiling. She even laughs when her partner trips, and she gives him time to recover. Then she freezes, staring at something, people walking by in the main hallway.

Her entire body tenses, and her nostrils flare. She clenches her hands so tightly on the hilt of her sword that her knuckles turn white. Whatever she saw upset her, and everything about the fight shifts. She spins faster, sharper. She's all lines and angles and spinning blades. At the end of the match, she trips over something, and Death leaps into the edge of the screen. I can't make out exactly what happens, but there's incoherent shouting, thanks to the video quality.

It's clear enough that I see her sever her partner Fesian's hand at the wrist. Evians can regenerate limbs, but regenerating a hand takes several hours. It's also agonizing, but Judica doesn't so much as acknowledge what she's done. When she walks out of the arena she passes right under the camera, which is the only reason I notice her wipe the tear from her cheek. If I hadn't seen it myself, I'd have said it was impossible given what I know of her.

Another viewer might not ever understand Judica's emotions, but with perfect evian recall I can guess exactly what Judica witnessed. She saw me that day. February 14 is Valentine's Day, my favorite day of the year with my mom. Mom always called me her little lovey dovey, or eventually as I grew older, her little dove. Mom kept me because she loved me and for no other reason. All her other daughters were trained to be her Heir immediately, and she sold her sons to other families so they'd sell their boys to her and her heirs would have a suitable group of options from which to select their consorts.

That February, Mom gave Judica and me both bright sundresses and forced us to eat breakfast together. We had fluffy pink pancakes and bacon, tall glasses of orange juice, and even Judica was reasonably pleasant. She didn't stab my hand, steal my food, or call me names. It was such perfect weather, the three of us went for a run outside. Judica won the race, because of course what began as a friendly jog quickly turned into a competition. Running is probably one of the few things I could have bested her at, but it was Valentine's Day.

I let her win.

It wasn't as pathetic a gift as I gave her in the past, but it was my version of an olive branch. I still remember the width of her grin after beating me—it almost split her face in two. After that, we separated to train. Mom and I headed to our shared private courtyard, and Judica went to the main outdoor courtyard. Mom cut our session short because she had a surprise planned. She and I walked out and into the main courtyard. She told me in the hallway that she had a surprise planned for me.

Her eyes sparkled when she said, ""I thought you might like to do nothing at all today. My gift to you is an afternoon off from meetings, training, and politics."

I had no idea Judica could see us, much less see us as we walked to the ballroom, which had been redone in honor of Valentine's Day, roses and lilies covering every table, pink drapes, and bowls of strawberries, watermelon, raspberries and popcorn dyed pink. There was even a large screen set up against the wall.

We watched an animated film I'd never heard of called

Brave. We smiled and laughed and didn't worry about ruling, or politics, or anything else. It was one of my fondest memories with Mom. I can't help the tears, remembering it.

I wish Judica hadn't heard about Mom's gift for me. But I'm even more ashamed that it didn't even occur to me how left out she might have felt, training alone while we played like that. Mom didn't exclude her on purpose, but Judica repeatedly said Valentine's Day was silly. Judica's horrible, but my heart contracts for her anyway. I make myself watch the whole video again.

"What pissed her off so badly, do you think?" Lark asks.

I jump. I forgot she was there momentarily. I swallow and say, "Mom and I passed by, and Mom had a surprise for me that day. I think it hurt her, seeing us going off together."

Lark nods. "Maybe. Or she could have seen something else. Either way, her presence would have ruined that day for you, so don't blame yourself. It sucks she was upset, but her exclusion's on her, not you."

"I guess so," I say.

I don't want to, but I force myself to watch the others. They start back in October and many of them seem to be normal days, but several others show clips of Judica reacting to my mom and I walking past, and once we even came into the room. Each time she sees us, she fights more viciously afterward, like she's got the devil himself nipping at her heels.

I notice something else in the moments after she sees Mom and me. There's a pattern there, a whisper of a dire song I can almost hear as I watch her fight. It's the beginnings of the melodic line of Judica's fighting style, but I can't make any real sense of it, and when I try and play the tune in my mind, it slips away.

I promised Edam I'd train more after dinner, so once we

finish with the videos, Lark heads back into hiding. I tell him about the videos I've watched, and then I tell him I've started to hear a hint of a melody when I watch them.

"You think you can hear her, what? Her fight song?" Edam asks, eyebrows raised.

"Don't make it sound stupid."

"I'm not trying to," he says. "Honestly I'm not."

"Look, all I'm saying is that I think maybe I should—"

"Should what?" he asks. "Write a song for her? Pick a string quartet as your weapon?"

"Stop making fun of me."

"I'm not." He shakes his head. "I get that a lot of masters learned with melodics, but Chancery, you aren't there yet. You need to do what I'm telling you to do and look for her actual weaknesses. Stop worrying about songs and patterns and look for what's really there." He holds out one hand in request.

I pass him my phone. He opens a video and points at Judica on the screen. "See that, there? Did you see how Lucas barely stumbled back when she hit him on this side?" He waits. "But he wasn't prepared and she annihilated him here?"

I nod. He's right. I don't know what I was thinking. The whisper of some kind of glimmer of a song and he's supposed to do what? Sit on his hands because one day maybe my melodics training might click? Stupid.

Edam and I spend an hour or so reviewing videos together before he taps his watch and says, "Time to implement what you've learned."

I don't improve much, but at least my healing speed continues to accelerate. I glance down at the tatters of my pants after Edam calls it quits. I'm going to need new clothes if we keep training this often. I'm utterly exhausted when I finally shower for the second time and flop into bed.

Only I can't sleep. Because tomorrow I'm going to school with scads of humans, and I'm more nervous than the first time I met the President of the United States.

After all, the kids at the high school don't work for me. Or at least, they don't know that they do.

18

I wake up to the smell of bacon, throw on a pair of jeans and a blue blouse, and look in the mirror. The face that stares back at me looks nothing like the girls I've seen in movies or television.

I study my image more closely in the mirror. Flawless skin, high cheekbones, full lips, curly hair with several different colors intermixed.

Maybe it's the hair. I can't think of a single human with multicolored strands like mine, but I've seen dozens with shiny blonde hair. I pull a knife from my backpack and lop all my hair off as close to my scalp as I can without sacrificing skin. Then I close my eyes and think about each hair follicle, willing it to grow out into a buttery, shiny blonde.

Moments later, my hair reaches my shoulders. I grow it a little longer, and then I use the end of my knife to trim off the ends into a layered, shaggy mane.

I glance down at the black, blonde, red, and brown curls strewn across my tufty carpet. I ought to have done this in the bathroom. Whoops. I hope Alora's cleaning people aren't annoyed. I look back at my reflection. Perfect cheekbones, impeccable mouth, flawless green-blue eyes, now framed by wheat-colored hair. I could easily disappear into a teen gossip magazine.

I hate it.

I focus on my eyes until they darken to a grassy green. This time, I move into the bathroom before lopping off my hair and regrowing it long and black, like a crow's wing. I trim the ends carefully below my shoulders so there aren't any blonde tips left to give away my first attempt.

Better. I look more human, but less Malibu Barbie.

I open my door to go downstairs, and Edam's door opens at the same time.

"Morning," he says. I know the exact moment he notices my new hair and eye color, because his eyebrows draw together slightly.

"Uh, good morning."

"Where are you off to?" he asks.

"Breakfast," I say, "but then I've got school today. My first day of school, ever."

He frowns. "Training should be your priority."

I glance at my watch. It's only 5:15 am. "I'll check with Alora, but I bet we have time to go a few rounds before I leave."

His hands tighten into fists. "I need more than an hour here or there if you want any hope of surviving against Judica."

I don't yell at him or remind him that I haven't even decided whether I want to go back. By force of will, I don't collapse into a sobbing ball when I think about the reason I've got a decision like this to make at all. Mom's gone, and gnashing my teeth or stabbing Edam in the eye won't bring her back. I'm heartily tired of everyone, Edam included, questioning everything I do and arguing with everything I say.

"Nevertheless," I say, "you'll get what you get and say 'thanks Your Majesty' after you get it."

When I breeze past him and down the stairs, his eyes follow me without saying another word. Take that, Mr. Bossy. When I walk into the dining room, Alora's already there, of course. Edam jogs in a few steps behind me.

Other than raising her eyebrows, Alora doesn't acknowledge the changes to my hair and eyes. "Excited for your first day of real school?"

"Nervous," I say. "And I have no idea what to wear."

Lark walks in the door, and Edam's heart rate accelerates.

"Oh, by the way, I didn't follow my mother's final command," I say. "Lark's still alive. Do you have a problem with that?"

Edam shakes his head, his heart rate already slowing to normal.

"Good. The guards already know."

Edam frowns.

"I'm wearing this." Lark smooths her wool skirt with her hands. Rich embroidery covers her dark brown shirt, gold threads highlighting the amber glints in her eyes. "Alora told me they don't wear uniforms."

"If they're going to school," Edam says, "then I'm going with them."

"I thought you might say that," Alora says. "So I've made arrangements."

Arrangements sounds ominous. "Edam's going to be a student?" I lift one eyebrow. In evian terms, he and I are nearly the same age. But to humans, the eight years he's got on me make a significant difference.

"Something like that," Alora says.

"How close to that?" Now Edam's the one lifting his eyebrows.

"As to what you should wear," Alora says to me, ignoring Edam. "Something nice, but not formal."

She's changing the subject. Which makes me want to

dig for details, but as Edam's dying to do the same, I'd rather torment him than find out myself. A sideways smile sneaks onto my face. "So, slacks and a button-down shirt?"

"That would be acceptable."

"What about me?" Edam asks. "Should I be wearing a landscaping jumpsuit?"

I snort.

Mom would be outraged at such a crass reaction. My heart falls. I'm sitting here, baiting Edam and smiling, when my Mom died yesterday. What's wrong with me? I grab a plate full of food and stand up. "I'm heading back to my room. Edam, I'll meet you in the ballroom in ten minutes."

Lark freezes with a slice of bacon halfway to her mouth. "Did I miss something?"

I shake my head. "I've got training to complete before and after school. I'm just in a hurry, that's all."

Alora stands up too. "Edam, Frederick will brief you on the position I've secured for you at Trinity."

"I don't know why he needs to come at all," I grumble.

Edam stands up. "I will keep you safe until you decide what to do, Your Majesty."

"I have Frederick and Arlington and the others for that."

"None of them are my equal," Edam says simply. "I'll see you in the training room."

Before I can follow him out, Alora stops me. "It's a strange time of year to be starting at a new school for humans, but I developed a story for you and Lark. You're fraternal twins, which I assume you can fake, and your father was chosen to move the base of operations of a large cosmetic company from Hawaii to New York to allow a better international presence."

"Is that necessary?" I ask. "Will anyone care?"

Alora shrugs. "Humans at Trinity talk about that sort of thing. Your dad's company is called Alvian."

I grin. "Like a cross between Alamecha and evian?"

"Mother loved things like that. Which is precisely why she started that snooty water company so many years ago."

"Evian?" I ask.

Alora smiles. "I miss her."

I do too. I squeeze her shoulder and jog up the stairs to change my shoes into sneakers, and then I head up to the ballroom. Edam's waiting on me.

"We only have ninety minutes this morning, so I mean to make them count," he says.

I spend half the training session in a blindfold, and the other half being sliced to ribbons while Edam tells me to heal faster. I collapse on the floor at the end, staring up at the wood paneling on the ceiling.

"If you're trying to convince me to abdicate, it's working," I groan.

Edam sits down next to me. "I'm not."

"You're this awful to everyone you train?"

He grunts. "Not at all. You aren't like anyone else. You can do more."

"Oh please," I say.

"You have to do more. And we only have a week to get you there."

"I could quit," I say. "Live my long life doing something other than hatching plots, passing judgment, and executing my friends."

"At least Judica doesn't need to worry about that," Edam says.

"What?" I ask.

"She doesn't have any friends, so she can't execute them."

I giggle. "She has that puppy dog guy who always follows her around, right on Death's heels."

"Roman's an excellent fighter and talented with strategy." Edam crosses his arms.

I sit up. "You're mad at me."

He shakes his head. "Roman really cares about her, and she ignores him. I'm mad at her, not you. And at Roman a little, for not having more self-respect."

"Or better taste." I grin.

Edam stands up and offers me a hand. "I can't be the cause of you being late on your first day." He pulls me to my feet, but doesn't let go of my hand.

My heart skips a few beats. I hope he doesn't notice. I lick my lips, my face only inches from his. Surprisingly, even after ninety minutes of sweating, and my blood spatter all over him, he still smells good. Spicy somehow, like sage. "You can slice me to ribbons, but heaven forbid you make me late?"

His eyes stare down at me, intense, calm. "You have big decisions to make. I'm here to support you in making the right one."

"What is the right one?"

He shakes his head. "Only you know that."

"What would you pick for me, if I asked you to?"

"You'll make a better empress than your sister. You care more. And you're guidable. She's rigid and uncaring."

"You want me to fight her?"

He dips his head, bringing his lips closer to my ear. I can barely make out his words, and his tone is raspy, breathy. "You already know what I'd pick."

"Say it anyway."

"Choose option C. Let me fight her for you. Then you can rule, and I'll keep you safe."

I turn to face him, wondering whether his eyes reflect the intensity of his words. They do, and I lean toward him without meaning to do it. He moves closer, too. Much closer.

"Your Majesty?" Arlington asks from the doorway.

I step back so quickly that my heel drags on the floor and I nearly stumble. Edam's arm shoots out and wraps around my hip, steadying me. My heart races and I practically run toward the doorway. "I better shower and change."

When I look back at Edam, he's beaming.

19

I pull a green cashmere sweater that matches my newly modified eyes over my head and pair it with khaki slacks. Lark arrives while I'm zipping up my knee-high boots.

"Alora's car is waiting outside," she says.

Of course it is.

"Are you nervous?" I ask.

Lark's laugh falls around me like a cascade of bells. "About attending a human school?"

"Not about the academics, I mean, but about fitting in and interacting with so many of them. Being normal?"

She shakes her head. "Not in the slightest. It'll be nothing compared to evian court."

Alora hands Lark and me each a black Prada bag when we reach the bottom of the stairs.

"What's this?" I ask.

"It holds your books and a lunch. You have to take those things with you every day."

I sort of expect to see Edam, but he probably can't show up with a bunch of students.

When I step into the car, I'm surprised to see another

familiar face. I've known Alora's driver, Bernard, since I was a baby. "Good morning, miss," he says.

I probably saw him on the drive here from the airport, but I was in such a haze I don't recall. Frederick's sitting in the back seat in a black suit and tie.

"What's your plan?" I ask. "You can't follow me around from class to class and snatch sandwiches out of my hands."

"I already tasted each component of your lunch myself," he says. "As long as you keep it in your possession until you eat it, you'll be okay."

I stifle a chuckle. "Why am I not surprised?"

"I'll be running the security for the entire school, thanks to Alora's influence, which means I'll have eyes on you at all times via their camera feeds. I'll also have guards placed at strategic points around the school so that you're always within a dozen feet of one of us."

"I want to see what a normal school environment is like." I stare at him hard and he doesn't even flinch. "I mean it."

"The school hired a new security firm thanks to a recent incident." He shrugs.

"And you're the new firm." As close to normal as I could expect, I guess. Hopefully the students won't suspect the new protocols have anything to do with me.

It only takes a few minutes to reach the school, even with New York traffic. Freddy lets Lark and me out alone, thankfully, and we walk in alongside dozens of other students who all look at us like we're a zoo exhibit.

"You guys new?" one boy with bright red hair and freckles asks.

"We are," Lark says. "Rebecca and Laura Adair. Nice to meet you."

"Uh, yeah." He keeps walking.

"He's rude," Lark says.

"We might be the problem," I say.

Lark quirks her eyebrow. "How so?"

"Alora's hundreds of years old, and she's been living with the humans for more than a century," I say. "Beyond that, she's a prima ballerina and a genius."

"Okay," Lark says.

"And she's also, apparently, an idiot. She told me to wear something *nice*." I glance around pointedly at the kids streaming past us in the hall. I grew up in Hawaii wearing flip flops and shorts whenever an event of state didn't require me to wear designer clothing. And yet today, on my first day of school, I'm dramatically overdressed. Everyone is wearing jeans and t-shirts, interspersed with the occasional sweater.

"We look like teachers," Lark whispers.

I nod ruefully. "Alora's getting an earful later."

One kid among the dozens and dozens we pass doesn't stare or laugh. He actually looks at me with something resembling empathy. "Your last school had uniforms, huh?"

Close enough. I nod.

He holds out his hand and we shake. It seems oddly formal for school, but Alora mentioned kids here talk about their parents' professions frequently. Perhaps they're all oddly formal.

"Noah Wen. Welcome to Trinity." Noah has short, straight, jet black hair that's spiky in the front, and slightly slanted eyes, indicating Asian descent in humans. When I look closer, I notice his irises are, surprisingly, a bright grayish blue. And not from contact lenses, either.

"Thanks. I'm Rebecca Adair, and this is my sister Laura. We're not off to a very auspicious start, I'm afraid."

He grins. "I'll show you ladies to the front office. But if you want to blend in a little better, maybe wear some jeans tomorrow and lay off the SAT words like 'auspicious' until everyone gets to know you."

We pass four of my guards on the way to the office. Only one of them starts to bow before catching herself.

"You're starting on a weird day," Noah says. "We got an email blast last night saying that the School Board voted to beef up security after some incident last week. I don't even know what the alleged incident was. I didn't hear about anything, but surprise! We've got guards all over the place now like we're going to school at an airport. Don't be nervous though, because I swear it's safe here."

"Well, thanks for showing us to the registrar," I say. "We appreciate it."

"The registrar?" Noah shoots me an odd look. "This isn't college. But here's the front desk, and good luck today. I'll be around if you need a friendly face."

Thankfully, the vice principal, Mrs. Nelson, doesn't seem to notice that what we're wearing doesn't exactly fit. It's as though everyone over twenty years of age is oblivious to clothing and style. She welcomes us and walks us through the school rules.

"Unfortunately, I don't have room to put you both in the same class," she says. "We're completely full, but we do try to make room for legacy students, and your cousins have been some of our favorites."

Cousins? Alora didn't tell me any of her kids came here.

"My assistant Jane will take you to your first class, Laura, and I'll walk you to calculus, Rebecca," Mrs. Nelson says.

"Oh good," I say. "Calculus."

"We'll still eat lunch together?" Lark asks.

Mrs. Nelson nods. "Lunch is determined by grade level. But your other classes aren't the same."

Lark's lips compress, but she doesn't complain. "See you at lunch."

I follow Mrs. Nelson out of her office and to the right. Lark waves at me once before she disappears from sight.

"You may find classes here quite challenging," Mrs. Nelson says.

I know nothing about calculus other than the fact that it's a subset of the mathematics curriculum. I haven't spent much time on math at home. I might be in trouble.

"Are you sure I'm supposed to be enrolled in calculus?" I ask.

The tall, bony Mrs. Nelson stops near the open doorway as students filter past us. She frowns. "I put you and Laura in as close to the same classes as I could based on your transcripts from Punahou."

I blink. "From where?"

"I'm sorry, am I saying it wrong? Punahou?" She pronounces it like 'Punawow' the second time. "Your old high school? Maybe they say it differently in Hawaii?"

"Oh, right. My old high school. Of course."

She looks at me funny. "If you weren't in calculus in Hawaii, you definitely won't be able to keep up here."

"Oh I'm sure I'll be fine." After all, how hard can a human class be?

Mrs. Nelson stares pointedly. "You let me know if there's been a mistake. We want to prepare our students to succeed in the real world by challenging them now, but that doesn't mean we throw you in and stand idly by while you drown."

Mrs. Nelson walks through the door and into the room and I follow her. "I want to introduce a new student to you, Mr. Mansfield."

"I thought we didn't allow mid-term transfers." The short, balding man with a paunch frowns at me. He's wearing khaki pants and a white button-down shirt.

"We're making an exception for Rebecca and her sister," Mrs. Nelson tells him. Then, very quietly under her breath, she whispers to him, "Their mother recently passed, and their father thought a change of scenery might help."

He nods and turns to me. Very quietly, he says, "I'm very sorry for your loss. Welcome."

Mrs. Nelson straightens her suit coat and glares at him before marching out the door just as a bell rings.

I look around to see what the bell means. The other students are taking their seats. It must signal the beginning of instruction.

"Please, take a seat Rebecca. Any empty seat is fine." Mr. Mansfield turns to face the chalkboard.

There's only one empty seat, and it's on the very back row. I walk toward it slowly. I'm accustomed to being in a room with evians. We work to keep our heart rates steady around 20 to 25 beats per minute, our body temperature around our standard 97 degrees, and we try to give away as little as possible of what we're feeling. The average human has a resting heart rate between 60 and 100 beats per minute, and a temperature above 98 degrees. These kids might as well shout their feelings from the rooftop with the staccato beat of their hearts, and the volume with which they whisper. Two girls in the back are discussing whether my chest is made of silicone, two guys near the front right are daring each other to ask me out, and the rest are unabashedly staring.

I glance back at the seat I'm approaching and recognize the boy sitting to my right. Noah Wen, the guy who showed me to the front desk. He's smiling when I glance his way. I smile back at him before sliding into the empty chair and slinging my bag over the back.

New students in the middle of the year naturally generate attention, and I'm prepared for the other students' scrutiny. What surprises me most isn't the subdued conversations, the elevated heart rates, or the dares. What I was unprepared for are the heartbeats of two of the twenty students. One of them is a tall, lanky boy sitting next to Noah, and one of them is a girl with a riot of black curls sitting on the front left side of the classroom. They look similar to the other students, and my guess is no one else knows. If I hadn't just uncovered Lark, I might not be as sensitive, but I did, and I am. Their resting heart rates and body temperatures are too low, and their features are a little too perfect.

They're half-evian, like Lark.

Mr. Mansfield acts as though I don't exist for the next half hour. I pull out my calculus book and start reading. I'm seven months late for this class, so I need to catch up. I plow through the first two hundred pages while he writes figures on the board, including both numbers and letters, and asks questions about them. Kids raise their hands and answer, or sometimes no one does and Mr. Mansfield calls on someone.

I look at the clock and offer up a silent prayer that class is almost over. Thirty-five minutes of calculus is enough to last me for a long time. I only have a week to make my decision, and studying calculus isn't exactly how I thought I'd spend it.

"Psst, new girl," Noah hisses. He points at the chalkboard.

"Excuse me?"

Mr. Mansfield clears his throat. "I beg your pardon Rebecca, but I called your name twice and you didn't answer."

Of course I didn't, because I don't think of myself as Rebecca. "I apologize, Mr. Mansfield. It's been a busy few days."

"No problem. Do you know the answer to my question?"

At my blank look, he elaborates. "What's the derivative?"

"I'm sorry, but I—"

"I'm not trying to put you on the spot on your first day,

but I am supposed to assess your knowledge level to make sure you're in the right place." He points at the board. "Do you know the derivative?"

"Uhh," I glance at the figure and then back down to my book. Nope. I have no idea. "I guess not."

"That's okay. We have a test in here tomorrow. Depending on how you do, I'll make a recommendation to Mrs. Nelson about your placement." Mr. Mansfield glances to my right. "How about you, Mr. Wen?"

Noah nods. "Sure." He glances my way. "The derivative of a curve at a point is in the slope of the line tangent to that curve at that point. Therefore, the slope is determined by considering the limiting value of the slopes of secant lines."

"I didn't ask that," Mr. Mansfield says. "I asked what the slope is on this problem." He taps the blackboard.

Noah winks at me. He was helping me figure out what was going on. "The tangent line that passes through your function has a slope of twenty-three over four."

"That's correct, Mr. Wen. Nice work. You run your mouth too much, but at least what eventually pours out is typically correct." Mr. Mansfield looks at the clock. "Alright, class dismissed for the day. Homework for chapter nine is due tomorrow. And don't forget to show your work—that's the point in here, after all. Remember that on tomorrow's exam."

I stand up and head for the door. When I pass Mr. Mansfield's desk, I can barely make out his whisper. "Welcome, Your Majesty."

I whip my head back around, but Mr. Mansfield is looking over papers as though he never said a word. Frederick's standing guard conspicuously just outside the door. I start toward him, but Noah grabs my arm before I make it two steps. One of the guards, Titus, strides my way, looking ready to eviscerate Noah, presumably for touching me without my permission. I shake my head and he pulls up short.

I yank my arm back from Noah before any of the other guards chop off his hand. I try to ignore the hurt look in his eyes.

"Thanks for your help in there," I say to soften the blow of reacting to his touch like he's carrying the plague.

"Mr. Mansfield's actually a great teacher," Noah says. "He really is probably just trying to figure out where you should be. The tenure board is giving him a hard time because he didn't go Ivy League for his graduate degree, so he's a little cranky with anyone he perceives as entitled. Which is pretty much all of us."

"Well, I appreciate your help. Calculus isn't exactly my strength."

"What is?" he asks.

"I'm not sure if I have one," I say.

Noah snorts. "I doubt that very much. Where are you headed next?"

I glance down at the paper Mrs. Nelson gave me. "I have physical education next, and I hear the gym is quite a hike from here."

"Oh, I have PE next, too," Noah says. "We can walk down together."

"Great," I say, "thanks."

"Should be a fun day. I hear we have a new PE coach today." Noah lifts his eyebrows. "The last one was caught with one of the students."

"Caught doing what?" I ask. "Was it bad?"

Noah laughs. "You're cute."

The half-evian male from class catches up to us. He's a little taller than Noah, with shaggy blond hair.

"This is Logan," Noah says. "He tries too hard, but he's actually a pretty good guy."

"Nice to meet you," Logan says. He holds out his hand,

but instead of shaking mine when I put mine in his, he lifts it to his lips and kisses my fingers. "Welcome to Trinity."

I yank my hand away and roll my eyes. "Thanks." I wonder if he knows who he is, and by extension, who I am.

We exit the main campus and walk with a half dozen other students behind the school. I notice one of the guards headed our way and glare at him until he stops.

"So what do you like to do in your free time?" Logan asks.

"Oh heck no," Noah says. "First, don't pain us with your attempts at flirting. And second, I already called dibs."

"You can't call dibs on a person," Logan says. "It doesn't work like that."

"Standard shotgun rules still apply among friends." Noah smiles, but I notice several guards are now following us, and I'm not sure where they came from.

Under my breath, I whisper to the guards, "Back off. You're starting to stand out."

"Did you say something?" Logan asks.

"Oh no, just talking to myself." I blush, and I'm not faking. I shouldn't have spoken quite so loudly. I know Logan's half-evian, so I need to be more careful. "But maybe a little less talk about weapons, with all the new guards around." I listen for Noah's heartbeat as he walks along, but it's normal. Much faster than an evian beat, and less steady. He might have some evian blood somewhere along his line, but not near as much as Logan. His hair's too straight and his heart's too weak.

"Weapons?" Logan asks. He looks confused.

"I said shotgun rules apply," Noah says. "That's what you say when you want the front seat and someone else is driving. You don't say that in Hawaii? You can call shotgun as soon as you see the car."

I raise one eyebrow. "So I'm the car in this scenario?"

Noah opens his mouth to respond, but then closes it

with a click. Smart kid. We stop in front of heavy, solid wood doors set in a tall building with a stone façade.

"So is this it?" I gesture at the entrance.

Noah pushes the doors open with an exhalation of air. "Yeah, but you're on your own getting to the track."

I follow him through the doorway into a wide hallway that opens up to the left and right.

"You'll head right," Noah says.

"Why?" I ask.

"Uh." Logan clears his throat. "That's the girl's side. We change clothes for PE here, unless you were planning on going for a jog in those boots."

I glance down at my feet and shake my head.

"Good call." Noah points left. "Logan and I go this way to the boys' locker room and we'll meet you in the gym." He gestures toward the wall.

I head for the girls locker room alone, missing Lark, and Ni'ihau, and my mom. Noah turns back and waves at me before I duck inside. If he were evian, I'd be worried he heard my heart do a tiny cartwheel.

I'm smiling like an idiot when I turn a quick corner and almost run into the half-evian girl from calculus with her shirt off.

"Oh," I say as I avert my eyes. "I'm sorry. I didn't realize the lockers are right through the doorway."

I glance up at her face and see she's smiling when she says, "It's no problem." She pulls a t-shirt over her head and sits down on a bench to tie her shoes. "Do you know what locker was assigned to you? If you need to borrow a shirt, I have a spare."

"Mrs. Nelson told me my number and combination, but I'm not sure what may be in there." I walk a few lockers down and spin the combination lock until it opens. I pull out a shirt and a pair of shorts. Alora must have told the school my size. I glance around the small cube of space. No sneakers or socks.

I glance up to see the half-evian with dark curls and chocolate eyes looking down at me. "You must have a good memory. You didn't even look up your number."

"Photographic," I say before it occurs to me I might not want to walk around broadcasting how perfect I am.

She frowns. "Me too. There are a few other kids with that kind of memory here at Trinity, but I think it's pretty rare."

Does she know about her heritage? I don't dare ask. I change quickly into my Trinity t-shirt and shorts, but I'm a little stymied when other girls start to filter out. The girl with dark curls turns back as if to ascertain why I'm lagging behind. "You coming?"

"Uh, I guess I don't have any sneakers."

"You should have told me. What's your shoe size?" she asks.

"Size seven. Do you have a spare pair?"

"Not running shoes, but I have a pair I use for tennis. They'll be better than boots. I'm a seven and a half, but I bet they're okay. I'm Raven, by the way."

"That's a perfect name for your hair. Your parents got lucky. My name's Rebecca."

"It was jet black when I was born, so they gambled." She smiles. "I heard your name earlier. Nice to meet you. You could've been named Raven too, you know. You don't see many people with completely black hair."

"No," I say. "You don't."

"Big change from Hawaii to here." She frowns. "The weather sucks, for one thing."

I follow Raven out the door and walk into the gym. Noah and Logan are leaning against the side wall, backs against one of the huge windows surrounding the black asphalt track. Three guards are stationed around the track, but no one seems to be paying them any attention. Raven introduces me to a few of the other girls. Madison, Faith, Alyssa and Isabelle. The last two were the ones debating the authenticity of my chest. I can't quite help myself.

"Nice to meet you," I say. "And Isabelle was right. They're real."

I spin on my heel and walk across the room to where Noah and Logan are stretching. I lean down and flex my calves because they're doing it. I don't really need to stretch my muscles because, evian. We don't get tight tendons or strained muscles or pulled ligaments. I doubt Logan needs to stretch either, but if he can pretend, so can I. When I glance over my shoulder, I notice Raven's also stretching.

Our PE class is larger than calculus, but still no Lark. I listen for a moment and other than the guards, Raven and Logan, I don't make out any evian heartbeats.

I'm listening closely enough that I immediately notice when the heart rates of nearly every female in the room elevate and Raven's group bursts into giggles. I turn toward the back of the room to see what's causing it, and I groan.

"Good morning," a gorgeous man in a white shirt and blue gym shorts says. He has long, slightly curly blonde hair pulled back into a low ponytail. They're obviously tittering over his chiseled features and piercing cerulean eyes. "I'm your new physical education coach, and I'm delighted to be here. I'm told we're about to start a new section on running."

"Come on." Noah rolls his eyes. "Coach Fimmel hooks up with Courtney Vanderbilt and gets fired, so they replace him with *Adonis,* here? Who's their consultant on these decisions? Homer Simpson?"

"Adonis?" the new coach says. "Hardly. Call me Coach Renfro. I can't wait to mold young minds and teach you all how to be physically fit for life."

I really wish I could punch our new PE coach. Luckily,

I'll be able to later when we're training. I have half a mind to slug Alora too, because Edam as a PE coach is an absolute joke. He grins at me and I glare right back.

"That's the spirit," Noah says to me. "Don't let the other girls pressure you into flirting with the hunky new PE coach. Buck the trend."

Logan laughs.

Edam ignores them. "Today we'll start by working on proper breathing. We'll cover more of the general techniques and posture as well as pacing later this week, but breathing is often overlooked. You need to be breathing in and out of your mouth in short, shallow breaths if you're going to run effectively."

Edam walks up to me and says. "What's your name?"

I frown harder. "Rebecca Adair."

"Would you mind helping me demonstrate, Rebecca?" He smirks.

"I guess not."

Edam is standing less than a foot away from me when he says, "Thanks. We need to learn to breathe into our bellies and not our chests. Now, breathe in and out for me, Rebecca."

I take a deep breath.

"Place your hand here." Edam reaches over and places his hand over mine and guides my hand to my stomach before he lets go. "Now, watch her stomach when she breathes." I breathe again. My hand rises and falls. "See?" he says. "Her stomach goes in and out because she's breathing in and out from her belly. Most of you probably breathe through your chest. Don't. I don't care what you do when you're not in PE, but if you're running in here, I want you breathing in and out of your belly. Now I want you to all run at least four laps. Walk along the outside of the track until time is up after you run your laps, or you can keep running if you'd like."

"Very motivational lecture, Coach," I mutter. I lean over and pretend to stretch my hamstrings. Then I squat down and stretch my thighs. Edam stares at me the entire time.

"What?" I ask.

"You'll never be normal, no matter how hard you pretend," he whispers, his breath brushing my ear. A shiver slides up my spine.

"Do you two know each other?" Noah asks.

I glare at Edam. "I've never met *Coach Renfro* in my life." I turn to Noah. "You ready to run?"

Noah shrugs. "Sure."

Noah and I start our first lap and Logan tags along, too. Noah's the first non-evian I've ever been around for more than a few minutes, excluding people like the President of the United States or Britain's Prime Minister. He seems nice so far, and I should be trying to make friends if I want to figure out whether I could live with them. In fact, Logan should be better looking than Noah by all rights, and he kind of is. But Logan's like a very watered-down version of Edam. Noah looks... different. Edam could have walked off the cover of any designer ad. His face is the perfect balance of beauty and masculinity.

Noah, on the other hand, looks less beautiful, but more broody. He has strong features, broad cheekbones, and an aquiline nose, but his eyes are almost too large for his face. If I had to compare him to something, it would be an anime character. Logan matches me, pace for pace, which doesn't surprise me. There isn't much difference between evians and half-evians until I push things beyond the limits of a school ordered jog. Logan's heartrate and mine are both barely elevated. Twenty-five beats per minute for mine instead of the typical twenty. Noah's heart has consistently hovered around sixty or sixty-five beats per minute. He's wheezing and his face is starting to flush, but his heart hasn't gone much over seventy-five or eighty beats per minute. That's impressive for keeping up with two evians for more than a mile.

"You winded?" I ask Noah.

"I come from a family of runners," Noah says after our fourth lap. None of us show signs of dropping back to a walk. "And Logan's the captain of Trinity's cross country team. My question is, why aren't you dying trying to keep up with us?"

"I run a lot," I say. "It's kind of my thing." True on several levels.

Edam joins us a moment later. "You three paid attention. You're clearly my strongest runners."

"I've been breathing from my stomach for years, pretty boy," Logan says.

I notice that once Edam joins us, our pace accelerates. As we begin our sixth lap, Edam runs faster still.

After a few yards Logan says, "I don't know what's going on, but I am not a sprinter." He waves Noah off and drops back to a walk.

By the seventh lap, Noah's puffing hard and his heart's beating about a gazillion beats a minute. I'm worried it'll explode if we don't slow soon. I glare at Edam and when that doesn't work, I drop to a walk in protest. Noah slows down, too. Thank goodness.

"Can't keep up?" Edam calls back.

I ignore him.

"He didn't run the first four laps, that's why he still has so much energy." Noah wheezes. He scowls when Edam flies past us again. Noah's face is red and his eyes look a little buggy, but his heart slowly decelerates and my fear it will burst fades. "I wonder if Coach is a former Olympic runner. The school board eats that junk up. That's probably how he got the job." His heartbeat has finally slowed down into the seventies again.

Logan waves to us and jogs over to where we're walking. "So new girl, we have a big cross country meet tomorrow. It's a five mile race. Normally I wouldn't ask anyone to join the team on their first day, but you must have run cross country back home."

"Something like that," I say.

"Any interest? We're short one girl," Noah says.

"And you're better than the two we already have without even training." Logan lowers his voice. "We're required to have two to compete and that's exactly what we have. If anything happens to one of them, we're disqualified."

"Sure." I smile. "Sounds fun."

Edam jogs up to us. "Did you say there's a cross country meet tomorrow?"

Noah sighs melodramatically. "We have a parent sponsor taking us, since we were without a coach until today. You don't need to worry."

"Oh it's no worry. If you've done okay before, imagine how much you'll improve with my help." Edam's cheesy smile is embarrassing, even though no one realizes we know each other. "Are you recruiting Rebecca? Because as coach, I think that should be my job."

I glare at Edam, but he just smiles back at me.

"They asked me to go to the meet tomorrow, and I told them I would."

"I can't think of any better way to be spending your day." I ignore Edam's sarcastic disapproval and shove past him, heading toward the locker room to change before my next class.

20

After PE, I head for lunch, practically pouncing on Lark when I see her.

"So?" she asks.

"How did we end up with opposite schedules?" I grumble. "I mean, really. I know one single person at this school, and somehow you're in a completely different classroom block than me?"

"Maybe it'll be good. We're meeting a lot more people this way. Find anyone interesting yet?"

Before I can respond, Raven pops up behind Lark with a floral decorated paper bag in her hand. "Do you mind?"

Mind what? She sits down at our table before I can ask.

Logan, Noah, and three other people I don't know drop into the remaining seats a moment later. I introduce Lark to Raven, Logan, and Noah, and she introduces me to the other three kids, two girls and a boy, all as utterly human as Noah.

The rest of the day crawls along, with very few flashes of anything interesting. I could have taught the class in history better than Ms. Fitzgibbons. In American literature, I've already read *The Scarlett Letter*, although the instructor had a lot of insight into humans on the topics of shame and penance that I appreciated. On the way home, I check my phone and discover Inara bombarded me with lots of new video files.

"How was your first day?" Frederick asks.

I shrug, distracted by scanning through the new footage to see how many files she sent. Eleven. "It was different than I imagined."

"I enjoyed it," Lark says. "I mean, I didn't learn much in class, but I learned a lot from watching them."

"Them?" Bernard tilts his head so he can see us in the rearview mirror.

"You know, humans," Lark says.

She must be even more curious than I am, since her father was human.

"Not fun?" Frederick asks.

"Not really," I say. "But no assassination attempts, no coups, and no one stabbed my hand with a fork, so I'd say total boredom is still an improvement over the last week and a half. But I have a question for you."

Frederick raises his eyebrows. "Yes?"

"There are at least two half-evians attending Trinity in my grade. I think I identified a few more in the halls. And my calculus teacher called me 'Your Majesty.' What's going on there?"

Frederick sighs. "You know Alora enrolled you because she had influence here. You didn't stop to consider why or how she might have influence?"

I hadn't, actually. I figured Alora knew everyone important in New York and didn't go beyond that. "Wait, are they her... kids? Or grandkids, or something?"

Frederick smiles but he doesn't look happy. "Some of them are. The First Family, and all the other families for that matter, have been exiling evians for millennia. They also kick out half-evians and any parent who chooses to raise an impure child instead of giving it up. Where did you think they would all go?"

"The best prep schools in New York City?"

Bernard clears his throat from the front seat. "Precisely."

"So which ones are related to Alora, and by extension, to me? And do they know who I am?" I ask.

"Do you know, Bernard?" Frederick asks.

"A few of the teachers know, clearly, but as to the others, you'll have to ask your sister about that. I'm not positive, and even if I was, I wouldn't be at liberty to say."

Ugh. Even hiding among humans, I'm knee deep in politics.

"I will tell you this." Frederick steeples his hands and rests his chin on them. "I have heard that among the human elite aware of our existence, evian blood is prized above all else. Rich and powerful human families will do most anything to bring it into their gene pool. It gives exiled evians some leverage when they leave the family for the cold, cruel world, even when they leave penniless."

Gross. "Leverage as what? A walking womb? A brood mare?" A queasy feeling in my stomach makes me wonder if this is how humans feel when they're sick.

"Living with humans might not be the break I was hoping for," Lark says.

"Even so, time at Trinity might be a great opportunity for you to recruit for my non-existent spy network," I say. "Keep that in mind."

I open the first video file on my phone and stick in my headphones to listen. I only watch two before we reach Alora's brownstone. As if she knew I'd have questions for her, she's hovering at the top of the stairs.

"How was your first day?" she asks.

"It went okay," I say, "but I didn't learn much. Calculus, especially, seems completely useless."

She laughs. "It's not so bad, and I'm a ballerina. If I can learn it, you can suffer through it too."

"I have a test tomorrow, so I better catch up at least."

"I don't think I could live it down if my little sister failed out of Trinity." Alora laughs and starts down the stairs toward me.

"Are all your kids passing? And your grandkids?" I scowl. "You know, the ones I've never even met?"

My perfectly graceful sister stumbles. "What?"

"Why didn't you tell me the school is crawling with evians?" I ask.

"Half-evians," she says. "And there are only a handful, all of which I know about and have approved. Only one of them is related to me."

"Raven?" I ask.

She shakes her head. "No, Logan Calvert."

I nod. I should've known. "Why didn't you tell me? He obviously doesn't know. What if I'd been flirting with him?"

She raises her eyebrows. "Were you?"

"No." I scowl. "But he's cute. I could have. With my own, er, what is he to me, exactly?"

"He's my grandson."

"He's only one quarter evian?" I ask.

She shakes her head. "No, his mother is also half-evian."

"This is strange," I say. "I had no idea any of this existed."

Alora sighs. "It's all far, far beneath you, Chancery. When I left the evian world, I thought I could turn my back on it all. I thought I would leave the messiness, the haves and the have nots, and sink into the anonymity of humanity."

"But it didn't happen."

"No, it didn't," Alora says. "Walk into any trailer park in America and you'll discover a universal truth. Humans, big and small, rich and poor, young and old, they all yearn for whatever they don't have. Even among people who have virtually nothing, there are haves and have nots. It's in our nature to want to have the most of something, and it's the comparison that gets dangerous. When I walked away, it changed the stakes for me. Out here, I'm an eternal have surrounded by terribly outmatched have nots."

"Is that easier?" I ask.

She leans against the column at the bottom of the stairs and I don't think I've ever seen my sister's eyes quite so crinkled or her shoulders quite so slumped. "In some ways, but in many ways it's harder. Running away from Judica won't eliminate your problems, Chancery. You might be thinking it'll be a thousand years of laying around at the beach and sipping on piña coladas, but that kind of suspended paradise doesn't exist. And if it did, you'd hate it before the end of the second week. Life is about how you deal with hurdles, because you're always jumping them. If you aren't, you're dead. Or you may as well be."

"How many of the half-evians know about us?"

"About a third of the teachers do, and three of them are part evian. Very, very few of the students know, even those with evian blood. Among half-evians it's tradition not to explain any of it until after high school graduation. Otherwise, they spend all their time second guessing everything they say or do. Logan is an exception since he's an active athlete. He needed to be told why he has to hold back."

"What about his friend Noah?" I ask. "Is he part evian?"

"What's his full name? I can find out."

"Noah Wen."

"I'll let you know." A part of me wants her to say yes.

"You like him," Lark whispers with a smirk.

I realize she's right.

"Edam's already waiting for you in the ballroom," Alora says.

I moan, but I take the stairs two steps at a time in my

rush to change clothes. I can't decide if I'm trying to minimize Edam's irritation by hurrying, or whether I secretly like the training.

I expect him to mock me for attending Trinity, but he doesn't say a word. In fact, if I hadn't been completely positive he was there today, I might wonder whether I imagined him as my PE coach.

Fine. If he can pretend, I can too. I'll never let on that I'm hot for my teacher. I snap my gaze up from his broad shoulders and try to focus on learning something.

He tosses me a sword. "I heard you got more videos."

I nod.

"Anything good?"

I shrug. "Judica favors her left. Very, very slightly."

"It's a weakness. It's faint, but it's there. Good. Today we'll practice a few dozen moves that will target Judica's weaknesses. We're going to polish them until they shine."

He delivers on his promise.

"It would help if you pretended to have any of her weaknesses, so I could see if my moves are working."

He shakes his head. "Nope. It wouldn't. You have to assume she won't mess up and fight accordingly. Then if she ever does, you'll be ready. If she's smart, she's eliminating those liabilities right now. If you count on them, she'll carve you up for it."

A pang of guilt hits me. He is really good at this, and I robbed him of his position when I ran. He'll absolutely hate being exiled if I abdicate. Of course, that guilt fades away over the next two hours as Edam repeats move after move after move endlessly.

"Muscle memory," Edam says. "It's your only real advantage in an evian fight. If you don't know what to do all the way down to your bones, then you can't do it without thinking, and that means you won't be fast enough."

"I guess," I say.

"You guess?"

"Yeah, I guess. That's the whole idea of melodics, you know. You learn how to move in a way that correlates with the music that surrounds us, the music most people don't bother to hear. Then I wouldn't have to think, just like you're saying, but not with one move or two or three. I'd move without thinking on every single strike, every single parry, every single slash. Every move would fit into a larger pattern I'd be able to read. I wish I had gotten to that point, I wish Mom had finished my training. But to you, all of it is just nonsense. I find it ironic and sad, that's all. You're teaching me the underlying tenets of melodics like it's some revelation to me."

He steps back and spears me with a glance. "Is your heart in this, Chancery? Because if it's not, I'd prefer not to waste my time."

"What does that even mean?" I ask. "I mention similarities between your method and my former training and suddenly I'm not trying?"

He doesn't reply. Instead, he raises his sword and comes after me. I grab the first blade my hand reaches on the weapons rack and throw it up to block him. He slams into me like a freight train and I do my best to get off the track. It's not long before he smashes me to the mat, his sword pressed to my carotid.

"What were you thinking then?" he whispers.

He decimated me. Obviously I suck at melodics. Or maybe everyone's right and melodics don't hold up. "I'm beginning to doubt that there's any way I could possibly beat her."

"You probably can't," he says.

I shove him off me, ignoring the slice to the side of my neck that results, and healing as I curl onto my side. "Then why bother?"

He rocks back on his heels and stands. "I want you to

have a choice. I didn't have one. But you already know what I think you should do."

"I just don't..."

He spins away from me and walks toward the door. "You find me repulsive. I'm your horrid sister's ex. I know."

I sit down, deflated by his words. "I don't. Find you repulsive, I mean. It's not that."

He pivots on his heel to face me. "Then what? Why are you considering your only options to be a suicide mission or abdication?"

I meet his eyes, hoping he can understand. "I want to be good enough myself. It's dumb to pick a ruler like this, but it's what we do. If I can't defeat her myself, how will anyone ever see me as anything but an easy target? You might be able to defeat her for me, but how can you protect me from the entire world?"

Muscles in Edam's jaw contract. After a moment of silence, he nods. "That's a reason I respect."

"You think it's naive."

"Not naive. Hopeful."

"Stupidly hopeful?" My heart catches in my throat and I work to swallow. I shouldn't care this much about what he thinks.

"Not stupid, no. And who knows? Maybe you'll defeat her."

I nearly choke on my desperation. "You think I could?"

"If you decide that's truly what you want and stop pulling all your punches, maybe. But you don't even want to beat her, not really. I don't think you want to defeat anyone."

I close my eyes and envision my sword connecting with Edam's side or his arm. I shudder. "I don't know if I can change who I *am*. I'm not like her, and I never will be. I'm not a conqueror. I'm pretty much the opposite."

He shakes his head. "You're whoever you want to be." He reaches out a hand to pull me back to my feet.

I take his hand and stand up.

"Let's make some real progress." Edam hands me a new sword that gleams beautifully. The hilt is ornamented with fancy Cyrillic letters.

I take it and swing it around a bit. "This blade sucks."

He grins. "It's pretty."

I arch one brow. "The balance is terrible." When I run my finger down the right edge, it doesn't even break the skin. "And it's dull. Like calculus."

He suppresses his grin, but it reaches his eyes anyway and they sparkle. "And this one?" He hands me the plain sword he just annihilated me with, its hilt wrapped with black cloth.

I shift it in my hand. The balance is much better, but even with my recent accelerated training, it's far too heavy.

"I can't use this one."

"Why not?"

"My arm will tire, which will slow me down. Maybe not a lot, but enough."

He nods. "Good. Your mother didn't neglect weapons basics."

"Oh we analyzed lots of weapons, and even spent a little time doing bladed movements."

"Bladed movements?" Edam asks. "Do I even want to know?"

"You'd call it dancing with a sword as a prop, probably."

He mutters so quietly I can't make out the words. He snatches the black-wrapped hilt of the heavy broadsword back, and our fingers brush.

My shoulder blades twitch and sweat slides down the skin over my sternum. I shiver. Edam's eyes meet mine and for a moment, for one brief moment, I wonder what he would do if I stood on my tiptoes and pressed my lips to his. He proposed to me, but we haven't even kissed. Doesn't it bother him?

He gestures gruffly at the weapons rack and grunts. "Pick something else, then."

The moment evaporates and my heart sinks back into my chest where it belongs.

I select a curved blade, as heavy as I can reasonably handle, but balanced well and honed to a fine edge. It's clear how little my knowledge of blades matters when Edam comes at me like he's carving a roasted turkey after a week-long fast. He decimates me, and then when I stand up, he does it again, in a new way. And again, the third time, spraying blood all the way up to the frescoes on the ceiling.

Alora's not going to like it. In fact, as I look around at the room, I realize that if the producers of *Kill Bill* and *Walking Dead* made a cinematic baby, the set would look like Alora's ballroom. Although, there aren't any corpses.

Yet.

I feel terrible for whoever has to clean up after us.

"Your healing times are improving dramatically," Edam says.

They had nowhere to go but up. Even so, he's right. What used to take concentration happens without thought now. It's not enough, but I'm getting better.

"I guess Judica was right—I didn't know the meaning of pain. Mom almost never wounded me. Since she kept me ensconced in bubble wrap, I never had to practice healing."

"You scored a few hits on me, too," Edam says approvingly.

"One hit. I sliced your forearm."

He shrugs. "Either way, I'm starving after all that work. You must be about to fall over."

"Food. I definitely need food."

Edam bobs his head. "We're done. Go ahead and go."

After I shower and change, I jog downstairs. A dozen pizza boxes are stacked on Alora's pristine marble countertop.

"She figured with all the training you two would be ravenously hungry," Lark says from the corner of the room. She's leaning against the swirly, golden marble countertops.

"She was right." I flip the top box's lid up and snag a slice. Before I can take a single bite, Edam walks through the door and practically jumps across the room. His fingers clamp on my wrist and I nearly drop my food.

In a split second, my hunger takes a turn. Suddenly instead of pizza, I want Edam. I look from his strong fingers upward, to his face. His eyes sparkle at me and my breathing hitches. My heart rate spikes. Even Lark can hear it, I'm sure.

"Not so fast." Edam's hand slides over my wrist and takes my pizza slice. "You need a taster, Your Majesty."

I gulp. I need a taste. That's true.

"I tested it already," Lark says.

Edam startles and looks at Lark as if he didn't realize she was there. He tosses the piece on the table. It lands with a thump, and he backs away like I'm toxic.

I can't keep up with his moods. "Great, good." I snatch the slice of pepperoni pizza and stuff a bite in my mouth so I can pretend I'm not confused.

The cheese is so hot it burns the tip of my tongue, just the way I like it. The tomato sauce explodes in my mouth and the edges of the pepperoni are crisp, while the center is chewy. Edam and Lark each grab a box and shift toward opposite ends of the room. The kitchen is utterly quiet, other than the sound of three heartbeats, and the noises from Edam, Lark, and me chewing.

I don't pause until I've downed two large pizzas. I polish off three slices of a third before I wad up my napkin and toss it into the trash, along with half my fourth slice.

"Lightweight," Edam says.

"I'm not even offended, greasy fingers. Because while you pig out, Lark and I have more videos from Inara to watch."

Edam leans over my shoulder so he can see too.

I try to ignore it, but I hear snatches of Judica's fight song even more strongly in the first few fights, despite the lack of anything in the videos resembling actual music. Sharp chords, dire and dramatic sounds. I'm trying to figure out what it might mean when Edam interrupts.

"You see? There." He points. "She's holding back here, favoring that side after a major offensive. It's almost imperceptible, but it's there. And here." He watches with me. "Here she's striking repeatedly, but always from the same arm."

"That's pretty thin," Lark says. "It's not even an actual weakness. It's a preference."

"It's what we have to work with," Edam grumbles. "She doesn't have any actual flaws. I trained her."

"How would you beat her?" I ask. "Using your knowledge of her preferences?"

He laughs, but he doesn't sound amused. "No, I'd beat her because I have no weaknesses or preferences. I'm also faster, stronger, and have greater reach."

I don't think before I act. My foot shoots out and kicks the leg out from under the front of his chair. Edam tumbles forward, face down. He catches himself on his elbows, but his slice of pizza lands face down on Alora's wood floor with a slap.

Frederick and Alora race into the ballroom, eyes frantically searching the room for danger. Their faces are priceless.

"Faster, huh?" I ask.

Edam's arm flies out and strikes my chair leg and it shatters, toppling me forward too. I land on his pizza slice and slide toward him, our faces inches apart when I stop.

"That was a waste of food," Edam whispers.

I swallow hard and stand up, the pizza sauce and cheese smeared down the front of my shirt.

I need to change my clothes, and I need some time to think. Because I'm starting to let Edam affect my decision making, and that's not smart. I leap to my feet. "Thanks for dinner, Alora."

Her eyes widen and she bobs her head. "Of course."

"I better go clean up."

Edam's already standing when I turn toward the door. Lark's watching us from her chair with round eyes and a slightly open mouth.

"I'll walk you up," Edam says.

"I think I can find my room alone," I snap.

Edam follows me out anyway. "What did I do to piss you off?"

I shake my head. "Nothing. I'm just on edge."

He walks next to me until we reach the hall where our rooms branch off on opposite sides.

"She won't hesitate," Edam says.

I force myself to meet his gaze. "I know she won't hesitate to slice me in pieces, but I will. And I'm not sure I'd want to be someone who wouldn't, even if it means I die."

"Your empathy is one of the things I admire." Edam's voice is low, rough.

But my empathy will get me killed. Unless I take him up on his offer. Heaven help me, but I want to, and not only because it's my best chance to win.

21

Reading two-thirds of the calculus book to prepare for tomorrow's test makes my eyes cross. Not literally, but they feel crossed. Whoever thought this was helpful information to have? Math should not need letters.

When my phone lights up, I use it as an excuse to slam the book shut.

"Inara," I answer. "How's Hawaii?"

"Breezy, perfect."

"And my twin?" I flop back on the bed.

"Irritable, apparently." Inara drops to a whisper. "This morning she *killed* someone during her sparring."

"Whoa." I swallow. "Who?"

"Nihils."

He had kind eyes and a startlingly clear singing voice. He used to write songs in his downtime. "Why? Why would she do that?"

"Your guess is as good as mine. She didn't give any reason, and it won't surprise you that she didn't even apologize to his mother. I've spent all morning calming her down, which is why I only have a minute. I've been pondering something and decided to share my thoughts with you."

"Okay." I try, unsuccessfully, to shake the ominous feeling that slithers up my spine.

"How positive are you that Judica killed Mother?"

I nearly drop my phone. Not at all what I expected her to ask me. "Uh, pretty sure."

"But not one hundred percent?"

I think back on how often Judica joined us for breakfast. She knew Mom loved eggs, but so did the entire kitchen staff. Judica was one of the few people who knew about the EMP, and she was smart enough to guess what Mom's reaction might be. Which means Judica was the one who had the most to gain from Mom's death, or so she thought. I close my eyes and replay the memory again, and again, and again. When Mom died, Judica didn't even seem upset. She looked more guilty than anything else.

"Ninety-nine point nine nine nine nine," I say.

"Which isn't one hundred," she says.

"You're really good at math," I say. "Maybe you should fly out and take my calculus test."

"You can't do it," Inara says.

"Do what? Have someone else take my test?" I sigh. "I didn't think so either, but it sure would be nice."

"No," Inara snaps. "You can't kill her. No matter what magic Edam may work, if you aren't one thousand percent positive." She cuts off and clears her throat. "I know you, little Chancy. You won't be able to do what it takes unless you're *sure*."

I hate that I'm so transparent. "Well, you and Edam agree on that."

"Even if you've improved, it won't be enough. Judica's gotten better too. Something happened to her when Mother died. She's. . . savage now, in a way she wasn't before."

I dig my toe into the carpet. She was the most uninhibited fighter I'd ever seen. What must she be like now, to have Inara describe her as more savage than before?

"Take his offer."

I don't throw the phone across the room. I don't crumple it in my hand. I don't growl into the speaker.

"Chancery? Are you there?"

"I'm here."

"Well, you'll do what you want, but my advice is that you either abdicate or take the escape hatch he's offering. And as an added side benefit, you can offload your guilt. You wouldn't be responsible for what happens to her. He would. Let him shoulder that burden for you."

"I'll think about it."

"Do that. I've got one more round of videos I managed to pull. I'll send them now, but I've got to go."

I hear a shuffling sound and then Inara's voice. "Nothing, why?" The call disconnects.

I wait for almost half an hour, but no videos ever show up. I'm climbing into bed, my eyes drifting closed when I hear a chime. The videos, finally. I should watch them tomorrow, but I can't help myself. I pull them up immediately.

I'm supposed to be studying Judica and I do, but sometimes Mom shows up. When she does, I watch the portion of the interaction with her in it over and over and over. It's scratching an itch and it's salt in a wound at the same time. It's sunrise over the waves, and a slap across the face.

And I can't stop seeking it out.

But in the third video, Judica steals my attention back. It's date stamped from the end of this past January. Edam watches me walk past the arena in the hallway, his eyes following me down the hall. As a trained guard, he probably follows everyone who walks past habitually. But because it's me he's watching, Judica strikes him.

"Not her," she says. "Look at me. See me."

I pause the video, her words ringing in my ears. It was a relatively simple interaction. She runs on the violent side at the best of times, but her words stick with me.

See me.

Obviously Edam didn't see what she wanted, since he dumped her. Based on things he's said, I'm guessing he never saw the good in her, and neither do I. Did Mom? What did Mom see? And why wasn't Mom's love enough? How could Judica spurn what Mom offered and repay her with poison? If Judica hadn't tried to poison me almost a decade ago, I'd have said she'd never use that method to kill someone.

How could Judica actually procure what she needed to kill Mom?

I need answers. I need to know. Not only so that I feel okay killing Judica. Also, because I want to make sure her killer's not still out there if I do.

There may have been nothing I could do to stop my mom's death, and my relationship with Judica has always been fraught, but when Mom died, I lost my sister too. I don't even know whether I should have.

Watching these videos, I'm realizing something that scares me. If things had been flipped, I might have turned into Judica. If I'd been the last born, I could have been named the chosen Heir. I could have been the lonely one, the one who endured the painful torture of the Heir's training. I've painted Judica as the villain for years. I blamed my mom for not standing up for me and for never choosing my side, but is life truly that black and white?

I shake my head to clear it of the churning of speculation. None of this is helping me do what needs to be done.

But of course, shaking my head doesn't help, not really. The memory of our ninth birthday resurfaces in all its gritty misery, when I lost my first dog and my relationship with Judica crashed and burned. After she tried poisoning me, Mom finally stepped in and executed formal Heirship documents. She sat us down and told us we needed to be kind to one another. I knew it was for Judica's benefit, not mine. Surely Judica knew that, too. After all, I hadn't ever done a thing to her. The following week, Judica jumped me in the hall and struck me over and over, telling me to fight back, to defend myself. I refused to hit her back, or fight with her at all. I was covered with bruises by the time she finally stopped, and I ran to Mom, careful not to heal any of it before she saw. Mom cradled me and sang to me and stroked my hair, signaling that Judica was in the wrong, confirming to me that Judica was a monster.

But she didn't do anything about it, and she took no steps to stop future attacks.

Only, maybe Mom stopped standing up for me because it made things worse. I always thought Mom backed down and let Judica's terrible treatment stand to try and make me tougher, but maybe she meant for her indifference to prevent escalation.

The only time Mom has chosen me over Judica since her attack on our birthday was when I reacted to her ring a few days ago. Mom's response left Judica angry enough to kill Cookie, another beloved pet.

But was Judica angry enough to kill our mother?

When I finally drift off to sleep, I dream of Judica saying, "See me" over and over and over.

I'm not rested at all when I hear a knock on my door.

"Come in," I say.

I sit up in bed and rub my eyes as Alora steps through the door.

"You need to leave soon," she says. "Bernard is standing by, but Edam offered to drive you. Fair warning. He may be offering just to fuss at you for missing your morning training session."

I scowl. "No offense, but riding with him won't look right," I say. "I can't show up with the new PE coach."

Inara wouldn't have understood why, but Alora does. "Right, of course. I'll tell him to go ahead without you."

"Thanks."

"One more thing," she says. "Logan didn't know about you, but as I mentioned, he knows about evians. He called me last night, and I told him who you are. I hope that's okay. He might be able to step in to help you if anything comes up."

I raise one eyebrow. "What might come up that a half-evian could help with, but my guards can't handle?"

Alora shrugs. "I didn't mean physical defense, but he may have insight. He's had a very different life than you."

"I guess."

Before I walk away, Alora reaches out and stops me. "I almost forgot. I looked into that boy in your class. Noah Wen. I knew his name sounded familiar."

"And?" I ask.

"He's not evian, or even half-evian, but he comes from the richest family at Trinity. In fact, I'm not sure why he isn't being taught by private tutors. His dad has extensive holdings in China, Hong Kong, and Japan. From what I can tell, his family knows Xi Jinping quite well. Tread carefully, but he's a good contact to have, whether you abdicate and want an evian-free place to go, or whether you don't and need political contacts."

I nod. I don't like thinking about people in terms of how I might use them, but she's right. Ironically, now that I know Noah might have value, I have zero desire to talk to him. I stink at faking things, and he'll know I'm trying to force the conversation. But China's the last large territory not controlled by the Six. Which means I can't afford to ignore him entirely.

After Alora leaves, I change clothes and jog downstairs.

Lark's shoveling scrambled eggs into her mouth. My mom would never shovel eggs. She'd never shovel anything. She was far too refined for that, but she'd be delighted if I were eating eggs with such zeal.

At that thought, something inside my chest breaks. I collapse to my knees, and a sob rips from my throat. Memories bombard me from all sides. Mom chiding me to eat a bite of scrambled eggs. Mom wiping my mouth after I'd eaten an eclair. Mom teaching me to swim, patiently holding me up, one arm under my stomach. Mom helping me decide which gown to wear for my birthday party last year.

Usually perfect evian recall is a blessing, but now I'm drowning in it. Too many moments, too many memories, and they've all halted forever, because Mom died. She'll never teach me, lift me, support me, chide me, tease me, or hug me ever again.

Lark doesn't cross the room. She doesn't put her arm around me. She knows I need to feel my grief, or even wallow. But she shoves the eggs away, and I hear her faintly whispered apology.

"Why would you apologize for eating breakfast?" I straighten and stand, wiping at the tear streaks on my cheeks.

Lark shakes her head. "Not eating. Eating this."

I think back on my breakfasts since Mom died. They've been conspicuously egg free, because Lark and Alora know. They know that I hate them and Mom loved them. My family and friends are tiptoeing around me. I don't want that.

But I'm going to get it, at least until I can watch Lark eat without breaking down and dousing the parquet floor with tears. I wonder how Lark's doing. She lost her mother one day before I did. She's just like me. Except of course, no one is gunning to kill her because they think she's already dead. And her sister didn't murder her mom.

Because my mom did that.

What a tangle. I walk stiffly toward the breakfast table, and I know I should ask Lark how she's doing. But the world is pressing in on me and my heart is raw, so I pull out my phone and watch the rest of the video files while I eat a bowl of fruit and a bagel with turkey and cream cheese. I don't reach out to my best friend like I should because it feels too hard, too raw, and unbearably big to help another human.

The first few videos Inara sent were from February, but after that, they skipped back to October and worked toward the present. The main difference between the first videos I watched and the ones I'm watching today is timing. These all happen near the end of last year or the beginning of this one, and Judica's fighting the same person in every single one this morning: Edam.

"Were there others I missed?" Lark asks.

"Huh?"

"Between Judica and Edam?" Lark lifts one eyebrow.

I shake my head.

"Why weren't any of the others between the two of them?"

"I don't know." Edam was head of Judica's personal guard and trained her whenever Balthasar wasn't available. There should have been more of the two of them than anything else.

No matter the reason for the lack before, watching them fight now is illuminating.

"He's better than her," Lark says. "No question."

"It's not a tremendous margin," I say, "but it's solid."

"It's consistent," Lark says. "And watch how he moves her where he wants her, like he's setting up a chess game."

She's a great fighter, but he can definitely beat her. If I

was forced to place a bet on Judica's fears, I'd say her biggest must be that I'll return with Edam as my champion. She has to know she can't defeat him, and knowing that changes things. If it has occurred to her that I might take Edam as my Consort, she would know she can't win that fight. Will she patiently wait for me to convince him? Or am I in danger here?

Maybe the bigger question is, since Edam wants to step in for me, and Inara thinks I should let him, why can't I come to terms with the idea?

Because I'm not good enough to rule. If I can't even defeat her on my own, there's no way I can make the hard calls alone. And maybe I shouldn't.

Until a few days ago, I never had to do anything on my own. Mom took care of everything, and that was just fine with me. I don't want to order people around or judge people or execute them. I don't want to fix every problem or determine the course of humanity, but I picked up that stupid ring and the world exploded. Mom looked at me differently, and somehow, I started to think about things with new eyes too. If Edam wins this for me, how will I ever become some epic queen from prophecy? No one lines up to follow an empress because she married well.

Edam doesn't understand what actually scares me. Mom left a legacy almost a thousand years long. I'd be a little greasy spot in history. It's not death that scares me. It's that I really may be what Judica has claimed my entire life: worthless.

Lark's voice snaps me away from my trance. "We're going to be late if we don't leave soon."

Which doesn't matter. Late to a human school. Late to pretending to be someone I'm not. Or is this really who I am? Should I always have been born to this normal, human life? Maybe it's where I will finally belong.

I walk passively to the car that's waiting for me. Frederick smiles, but I don't feel like talking, so I stare out the window.

"Was that all the videos?" Lark asks.

I shrug. "I think there was maybe one left." But they're starting to blur together, if I'm being honest. Edam defeating Judica, one carefully measured move at a time.

"Even so, you don't find something until you find it."

I sigh and pull out my phone to watch the last one. I'm unsurprised when it's another training session with Edam, but this video begins before the actual fight does. Edam stands, back ramrod straight, while Judica walks around him like he's a piece of artwork she's admiring.

She touches his face. "You're really very beautiful, you know," she says. "You might be prettier than I am."

He is, but he doesn't seem pleased by the compliment. A muscle near his temple strains.

"I could pick anyone." She circles him completely, until she faces him again. Her hand traces the line of his brow, drops to his jaw. "Mother made sure she bought every available male over the past thirty years when she decided she might have another daughter. She wanted me to have options." She smirks. "Sixty-three men in Alamecha right now ranging from fourteen to forty, all of them available to me, eager to spend time with me." She leans closer and I have to strain my ears to make out what she says. "Begging to make heirs with me."

Gross.

It suddenly strikes me that they aren't dating yet in this video. I knew things started relatively recently, but I hadn't known the date when she chose him. I look at the video date stamp. January 6. I was with mom in Budapest hosting the democracy summit. Most of the evians haven't embraced Mom's democratic model, even though she's proved again and again that greater freedom for humans results in greater productivity. Judica couldn't come because the Empress and Heir never attend the same event unless we are hosting and can control every aspect of security.

Early January and they aren't together yet, but Judica's tone is light, flirtatious almost. "Did you wonder why you've been called in to train with me every day for the past few weeks?"

"No, Your Highness, I did not."

She laughs. "You're so gorgeous, you aren't even surprised. Of course I'd choose someone arrogant like you." She touches his cheek and he flinches. Almost imperceptible, but it's there. "I admire your confidence." She laughs again and I'm surprised because it sounds real. "Don't be afraid of me, Edam. You can defeat me in the arena, and that may be the thing I like best about you, because you never need to fear me, not like that. Which means you could actually be, well, almost a partner."

His back is ramrod straight.

"Do you understand what I'm saying?"

"You've chosen me?" No emotion in his voice. The man in the video is so different from the Edam I know that I almost wonder whether he's hiding a twin.

"Yes, I suppose I have."

He inclines his head and continues to look straight ahead.

"Does that please you?" Her voice quivers a little, almost like she's nervous. I've never heard Judica sound nervous in my life.

"As Your Highness says, you have dozens of men to choose from. It pleases me that you believe I am the best option."

"Loosen up, Edam! You're so formal all the time."

Edam turns to face her, but then the video feed doesn't catch his expression anymore. I desperately wish I could see it. "You have only to tell me what you need, and I will try to give it to you, Your Highness."

She frowns and stamps her foot. "Well, for today, just give me a good fight. Can you do that?"

Moments later, the stars align in my head and I realize something. Something that's been gnawing on my subconscious for days now. The thing that's been eating at me is the underlying melody. I couldn't read Judica's melodic line because she was never really trying, not before she started fighting Edam. Someone exerting themselves half-heartedly isn't fighting pure. But now, now I hear it, like waves of music crashing in my brain while I watch. Fury, anger, rage, all of them notes, chords, runs. Judica brims with hatred, anger, jealousy, bubbling over inside of her, but underlying all of it, despair. It floods her entire being. She might be able to defeat Edam if she could get unkinked enough to flow. Edam accused me of pulling my punches. Judica never pulls a punch, but her reach is hampered by her repressed emotion.

My fingers itch to hold a blade. If I could fight her now, I would do much better.

I close my eyes and think of the videos I saw. Judica stands just before me, lips in a pout, eyes sparking. I hear her melody now, but I'm so full of sorrow for her, for me, for both of us, that I can't even imagine swinging a sword. Tears stream freely down my face. The music fills my head and my heart and I know exactly how to take her down. I hear my melody, strong, true, clear, and know just how I should move. My arms suddenly sweeping upward in an arc, then down in a strike. My leg kicks out to throw her off balance and I'm swinging over, under, slicing up.

I'm rolling down a street in New York City at thirty miles per hour, no sword, no dagger, no opponent, but I feel it, every cell in my body humming with an unwritten tune. My mom was right. I was ready to go off book. Hearing recorded melodies would be a nuisance, because the real songs lie within us, within each person, in their movements, in their words, in their goals and failures.

Of course, we reach the school at the very moment I have my big epiphany. I wipe my eyes before Lark can tell Frederick to circle. I breathe in and out deeply. I can't cry right now. Later, but not now. At least I'm dressed better today. My v-neck green t-shirt and blue jeans look like everyone else's clothes. Even though the weather has been unseasonably warm for New York, it's chilly here in March, so I brought a brown leather coat too.

I wave to Freddy before Lark and I walk through the door. The first bell rings, and we jog toward our classes. I slow down right before I walk through the doors for calculus. Mr. Mansfield inclines his head and I swear it's like a mini-bow. I wish he didn't know who I am. I wanted to get away from all the drama, not find myself submerged in evian politics lite.

"Put away your books and papers and get out a pencil. It's time for the test," he says.

I glance around. A girl with red hair taps her pencil rhythmically on the desk. A boy with dark, russet eyes bites his lip. But Logan smiles at me broadly, peeking around Noah to do it. Great. Now he knows he's my, what is he? My great nephew or something? So much for a normal human experience.

Papers are passed around and I hunker down to take my test. I'm not sure quite what to expect. It's my first written exam, ever. When I mastered French, Russian, and German, Mom took me to a meeting of the Security Council at the UN's Headquarters in New York. I had to make small talk with people in all three languages in a conference room overlooking the East River.

This test should be a breeze.

I glance around at the students around me, scritching and scratching away. Noah sees me looking around and glances up at Mr. Mansfield. I follow his gaze. Our teacher's engrossed in something on his computer.

"Here," Noah whispers. "You can look at mine." He slides his test near the edge of his desk.

He thinks I need to cheat!

I shake my head and bend over my test. The nerve. Like I'd need help from a human.

"Okay, students, your time is up. Pass your papers to the right. We will grade each other's papers, but then I'll go over them and assign partial credit for wrong questions in which you showed your work. Hopefully you'll learn something from reviewing these while you still remember why you did what you did."

Noah scores my test. His face looks absolutely shocked when he hands mine back with "100%" scrawled across the top. I notice when he gets his paper back from Logan that he missed one, but I don't gloat.

That would be rude.

Noah and Logan walk with me to PE again, but this time I know where to go. I walk quickly to the girls' locker room to change. I brought my own shoes, too. I'm learning. Raven's talking to a tall brunette with freckles and green eyes when I finish changing.

"Rebecca, have you met Lisa?" Raven asks.

I shake my head. "I don't think so. Nice to meet you."

She and Raven start for the gym doors and I follow.

Lisa says, "I hear you're on the team. Congrats. Are you coming to today's meet?"

"Anything that gets me out of history," I say.

"You knew all the answers yesterday," Raven says. "So it can't be that bad."

The human definition of success seems to be a situation where you learn absolutely nothing, but tout your superiority over others. It's strange. To me, the fact that I knew all the answers demonstrates the futility of the exercise.

Noah and Logan are already stretching when we reach the track.

"We can use you for sure," Lisa says. "Claire and I are terrible runners, and we're dragging Noah and Logan down."

"Truth," Logan says.

Lisa snorts, hops up, and starts to jog. I follow her. She seems to be jogging pretty easily, which is good news for our team.

"Where's Claire?" I ask.

"She's 'out sick'." Lisa makes air quotes. "Claire got bumped to alternate by Coach yesterday. She's a little annoyed, but she'll come around."

"Oh." I feel even worse now. "That's too bad."

"Don't feel guilty," Lisa says. Her voice drops to a whisper. "She's awful."

I don't know what to say, so I focus on jogging slowly, consistently, like a human would. I don't do a very good job, because two laps in, Lisa's practically panting next to me. I slow down. "Sorry."

Lisa laughs. "You run like a freaking robot. Are you about done? We aren't supposed to run more than a mile today, since it's the day of a race and all."

"Sorry." I slow to a walk. "Is our team any good?"

"Logan's amazing and Noah's pretty decent too. They kind of drag the rest of us along."

"Noah and Logan seem pretty nice."

"Nice?" She looks at me sideways. "Logan is, I guess, if he likes you, but I've never heard Noah described as nice."

"No?" I think about him taking pity on me in my odd clothing, showing me around, and even offering to let me cheat. He had no way to know I didn't need it. *Nice* is precisely the word I'd use.

"No."

"Okay. Care to elaborate?" I ask.

"Noah's smart, he's hot, and he's uber rich. He's not even nice-adjacent. Good news is, if he's being nice to you, that means he likes you."

"So he's usually a jerk?"

"Nah, not a jerk per se, but arrogant and stand-offish and elitist? Definitely."

"Arrogant isn't always bad." I think about... well... every single evian I know.

"I suppose he has reason to be. His dad owns, I dunno, like all of China or something."

"Really?" I try to pretend I didn't already know. "He doesn't look very Chinese to me."

"With those big blue eyes, you mean? Well, I've seen his parents at some school things, and his dad does." She laughs. "But his mom looks like a movie star. A white movie star. But no matter how he looks, he's like the richest guy at our school, and at Trinity, that's really saying something."

"Huh." Interesting. She knows almost as much as Alora. I could've just asked Lisa. I wonder what it's like to have a life that's an open book.

"Trinity's crawling with rich kids, though. And once you get past a billion or so, what's the difference? Logan's dad owns the biggest computer company in America, and Tawnya's mom runs the second biggest software company. Anna's dad's a five-star general and her mom runs a huge security firm. Conflict of interest, much?" Lisa smirks, and wipes sweat off her forehead. "Comparatively, my dad's shipping business is almost embarrassing."

"I doubt that," I say. Lisa seems genuinely kind. "I'm sure your parents are wonderful."

"I said almost." She grins. "We do alright. What about your parents?"

"They're both dead. I never even met my dad, but Mom died last week." Silence. Awkward, awkward silence.

"Oh," she says. "I'm so sorry."

Well, that effectively shut down the entire conversation. I clearly suck at girl talk. Lisa slows down and I speed up until I'm lapping her and everyone else, too.

"Hey, Rebecca," someone yells.

"Rebecca," someone else grabs my arm. "That's enough," Edam whispers in my ear.

I'm the only one still on the track. I finished my race day warm-up laps, and kept on going. A little too fast, judging by everyone's expressions.

"Dang," Noah says. "We are *so* winning today." His smile nearly cracks his face in half.

After all the excitement of PE, I'm glad to be leaving school by third period.

Trinity may be the richest school in New York, but we still ride in a little yellow school bus to the track meet. I'm sitting on a seat alone, waiting for all the students to arrive, when Edam sits down in the seat across from me. "So, turbo racer, everything okay?"

I blush. "I got distracted."

"You need to pace yourself next to someone today, and it can't be Logan."

"I know, Alora told me. He'll probably be pacing himself against someone else." I sigh.

"Not saying anything here, but on your second full day as a normal kid, you're running faster than any professional athlete."

I shrug. "What can I say? I dazzle people."

"You dazzle me." Edam's blatantly staring when Noah and Logan climb up the bus stairs.

"Uh hey, Adonis, you okay?" Noah asks. "You're kind of creeping me out. Home girl's like, what? Seventeen?"

I laugh. They're right, of course. By human standards, Edam's way too old for me. And if we weren't both going to live another thousand years, the age difference might creep me out.

"Coach Renfro was just giving me some tips," I say. "Thanks, Coach."

Lisa drops into the seat in front of us and turns around immediately to flutter her eyelashes at Edam. "I'd love some tips."

"Oh," Edam says. "Okay, well, let's talk about pacing."

Edam must have done his homework while I was studying calculus. There's no way he even knew the basic rules of cross country before we came to New York.

"So, we all run our own race?" I ask.

Lisa nods patiently. "It's technically a team sport, but really it's just scored in teams. You run the race yourself, and every single person on the team could win individually, you know, by getting the best time."

"So, you get the most points for the team by getting the fastest time?" I ask.

"Just run fast," Edam finally says, clearly suppressing a smile. "That's all you really need to know. Later this week we'll start training all of you on pacing and whatnot." He winks at me. "But if you run like you did in today's warmup, we should be fine."

We arrive at the meet and I realize for the first time it's not just a single school we're running against. "Wait, how many teams are here?"

"It's the Collegiate Invitational," Logan says. "There are teams from all over the country."

"Crap." Judica knew I wanted a week to decide, and she knew I was with Alora, but I'd rather not have my identity and location splashed all over the internet. I shouldn't have come.

We all stretch together before the race, but when they call us over to the starting line, Lisa pulls me aside.

"Hey, you shouldn't have brought that necklace." She points.

"This? I never take it off." I promised my mom and I'm

not breaking that promise posthumously. Besides, it's not safe, especially since only two guards followed us to this enormous regional event.

"Well, you can't wear it for the race. Regulations."

I tuck it under my t-shirt. "Who will know?"

"I don't want to get disqualified because you won't take off some expensive piece of jewelry."

I want a friend, but not at the expense of prudence. "I'm not taking it off."

She frowns. "Why?"

No one knows about my necklace, not even Judica. I'm certainly not telling Miss Nosey. But I'm not used to people not listening to me. I think back on the things I know about her and examine my options. I could punch her in the nose or call Edam over and make him tell her to shove it, but both would attract undue attention. To avoid that, I need leverage.

"What shipping company did you say your dad owns?" I ask.

"I didn't say." She looks at me sideways. "Why?"

I glance at her jersey. "Your last name's Brayden. So your dad must run B&F shipping."

She narrows her eyes at me. "How do you know that?"

"You probably heard I didn't know much about calculus on the first day." I imagine that kind of mean-spirited gossip happens among humans too.

She squirms. "I might have heard a few jokes."

"I spent my time studying other things. My family may not rival Noah's, but we boast varied and extensive interests. For instance, I know B&F shipping needs approvals from US Customs to import most of its valuable items. Many of your goods originate in Indonesia."

"Uh, this is getting weird."

I smile. "I also know Mr. Constantine. He's pretty

important with the CBP, so you might have heard your parents complain about him."

"What do you know about him? Or the CBP?"

"My mom and Mr. Constantine go way back. He sent me a pretty nice baby gift, if I recall correctly."

Lisa clears her throat.

"It's not a big deal if I want to wear my necklace under my shirt. I mean, it would be such a shame if Templeton Constantine decided to look a little closer at each item, delaying or refusing delivery. I mean, if things got bad enough, your parents might struggle to pay your tuition."

Lisa pales and takes a step away from me. I don't enjoy scaring her, but staying safe matters more than trying to mimic life in a high school sit-com.

Or maybe I'm a little more like Judica than I want to believe. The difference is, I won't hurt Lisa unless I have no other choice. Not that she knows that. She shoots a few strange looks my direction while we wait to start, but I ignore them. At least Noah and I are in the first heat, along with Logan.

I pace myself by staying just behind Noah. Logan lags behind a few miles in and I wonder why absently, but I don't worry too much. After all, Noah's fully human. If I'm pacing off of him, I'll be fine, right?

Running is the first thing that's felt right since Cookie and Mom died. I close my eyes and breathe. Simple. In and out, in and out. My feet pound the hard-packed dirt and my lungs process air. Noah keeps pace, his heart hammering along far faster than mine, almost alarmingly fast, but he's not puffing too badly.

"Have you ever won one of these?" I ask him.

He shakes his head. "Gotten close."

"But close means you still lost, right?"

He shrugs. "Yeah."

"Not today," I say, urging him on.

"You want to win the whole thing?" Noah's cheeks are red, and his lungs are heaving. I may be pressing too hard.

"I always want to win."

"Always?" Noah asks. "At everything?"

"If you're not a winner, you're a loser." It seems too obvious to me. You'd think a kid from a rich family would know this already.

Noah shakes his head. "There are more than just victims and Vikings in the world, Rebecca."

I don't argue, because what's the point? But I push him a little harder, helping him be more than he aspires to be, and slowly, slowly, we inch ahead of the couple of kids in front of us. And then we keep on pushing. Noah's practically purple when we cross the finish line. Which is when I notice that our entire group, other than Logan and Lisa who are still running, is whooping and yelling loudly.

Edam, however, doesn't look very pleased.

"What's the big deal?" I whisper under my breath.

"Holy crap," Logan's dad, whose name is Roy I think, mutters. "You two broke the high school record."

He and Edam share strikingly similar expressions, their lips pursed, their eyes narrowed. Which must mean he knows who I am, and doesn't like me flaunting it. Not that I meant to, or not exactly. But what if I needed a win today? It's been a hard week. Why should he care?

Alora's here, too. She's cheering, but even she looks a little annoyed. When I reach her she shakes her head. "That wasn't fair. Running that fast against these poor kids."

"I know, I know," I say. "I won't do it again."

"Whoops," I whisper to Edam when he comes over to pretend to congratulate me.

"Apparently Noah's freakishly fast," he whispers back. "Maybe you shouldn't have used him to pace. He's got to have some evian blood in his line somewhere."

"Alora said he doesn't." I frown. "His heart beat like a hummingbird's wings, and his breathing was shallow and hitched. Also, apparently his dad owns half of China."

Edam glances at me sharply.

"I know. It's strange." Somehow, China has evaded evian control for millennia. Its natural inhabitants holed up in there for so long, and communications and travel were so dicey, we didn't even realize there was a significant civilization there until a few hundred years ago. Since then, the families have fought so fiercely over it, that no one has successfully held it for more than a few months. Operatives sent there keep disappearing. Or returning in body bags, which is possibly more impressive. Killing an evian operative is difficult.

"Strange or not," Edam whispers, "he's not full Chinese. Look at him. Maybe he had a great-great ancestor who was evian. He seems below average in looks and intelligence, so maybe his speed is some kind of genetic throwback."

I roll my eyes. Below average in looks and intelligence? Oh, Edam. No one looks like he does, but Noah is definitely far, far above average in that department. He has unique, strong features, almost too strong for his face. He may still need to grow into his looks, but one day he'll be show-stopping. Even now he looks pretty darn amazing.

"Nice run." When I congratulate him, Noah smiles at me, and it's refreshing when a little of his excitement spreads to me. It must be nice not to worry about excelling at something. Or maybe it's the freedom of not having any secrets.

"Noah!" Logan calls out from across the yard. "Hey man, I just finished and I heard. Congrats!"

"Thanks, you too."

"My dad will be happy with sixth place overall," Logan says, "but I didn't break any records."

"I've never had a better motivator than Rebecca." Noah

gestures to me. "So, when are we going to celebrate? I was telling her how your dad always takes us out on his yacht."

"Uh," Logan says. "You didn't hear?"

"Hear what?" Noah asks.

"Logan steered my yacht into the dock last weekend," Roy says. "It's being repaired."

"The dock?" Noah asks, "Or the yacht?"

"Both," Roy grumbles. "Which is why Logan should be grounded, or doing manual labor."

"I did get straight As," Logan says. "And I just ran my personal best time."

"If you're not grounding your son," Noah says, "I'm willing to invite everyone to my place instead. I think today's victory deserves to be celebrated."

Edam shakes his head tightly. "No way," he whispers.

"I need to call my sister to see whether it's okay," I tell Noah. I walk a few dozen steps away, Edam pretending to take a call himself. He's ten feet away, but I can still hear every word.

I hold my phone to my ear. No reason for them to realize neither of us are actually on a call. "I could use a little fun in my life." It surprises me, but I actually kind of want to go. "Besides. Noah's a contact I should cultivate. Even Alora said so."

"I don't know," Roy is saying behind me to Noah. "Logan hasn't been exhibiting great judgment lately."

"I'll get some adults to come," Noah says. "If that'll make you feel better."

"I'll go, sir." Edam taps on his phone and turns to face them again. "To chaperone."

Roy raises his eyebrows. "Really? You'd stay all night?"

"Absolutely," Edam says.

"Did you hear why your job was available?" I hiss softly.

Edam shakes his head.

"Coach Fimmel got involved with one of the students."

I expect him to act suitably repentant, or tell Roy and Noah how respectable he is. I'm not expecting him to smile wickedly at me. "You don't say."

I'm glad I'm still facing away from the group, ostensibly on a phone call. No one sees my cheeks flush red. No one except Edam, that is.

I think about the wisdom of wasting more time on a party. I do need to find out whether I could fit in at typical human functions, and I've been dying to go to a high school party since the first time I watched a human television program. I also need to decide whether to abdicate, fight for myself, or choose Edam. If I wrap my brain around letting Edam kill my sister for me, the next question is whether I could stand being joined to him for a thousand years. Maybe a little flirting at a party is a good idea after all. I mean, in almost every human television show, the main character kisses someone, right?

And I've never kissed anyone.

I can't wait to get back to the school so I can tell Lark where we're going. This is going to be an interesting night.

22

"You need a ride back?" Noah asks.

I shake my head. "I'll take the bus," I say. "My sister Laura's still at school."

Noah scrunches his nose in distaste. "You sure?"

I bob my head. "It's fine, really. What time will your party start?"

Noah shrugs. "Sunset? That's usually when people start showing up. Logan's good about getting the word out."

I start for the bus, and Noah waves and heads for Logan's dad's car. I wait until they're buckled in and driving away before I change course and beeline toward Alora's car. I'm totally unprepared to find Edam already sitting inside.

"Uh, hi there," I say dumbly.

He half smiles at me.

"Don't you need to take the bus back to school, Coach?"

Alora laughs from the front seat. "He had Lisa's nanny fill in for him. Any approved parent can act as an official chaperone. After that blazing success, the school won't fault him for missing the full day instead of returning for the last period."

I shrug.

"You're really going to some human party?" Edam asks.

"You didn't seem to think it was a bad idea earlier." I gulp, remembering how my blood rushed to my face when he smiled at me. I'm an idiot. He only offered to be my Consort so he can kill Judica and move into the number two position for the entire Alamecha family. It's not like he *likes* me.

"I don't think taking the rest of the day off from your training is a good idea. We're running out of time."

Alora clears her throat. "Have you decided to fight her, then?"

I shake my head. "I haven't decided anything."

"You're not even considering your best option," Edam says stiffly.

"You don't get to decide what my best option is," I say. "You're not my dad."

Edam practically roars. "I should hope not."

"Sounds like you two have some things to talk about." Alora presses the button to raise the partition between the front and back seats of the car.

Edam scowls at the raising divider as if it offends him that she's giving us privacy to yell at each other. With evian hearing being what it is, it's faux privacy anyway. We both know they'll still be able to hear every word.

Edam shifts toward me on the seat and I scoot back, hating myself for doing it. I'm not scared of him. I'm not. But he makes me nervous, like a cat around a Doberman. Or a cupcake on the counter in front of a greedy child. Only, I can't decide whether I want to be eaten.

"I didn't mean that I think of you like my dad," I say quietly.

"I'm not that much older than you," he says. "Your mother was hundreds of years older than your father, for heaven's sake."

I clench my fists at my side. "This conversation has veered way off course. The point is that, I make my own decisions. You're not my war general or my boss, or even my advisor, so—"

"I'm not even your boyfriend. That's the point."

Blood rushes to my cheeks. I hate that he can make me blush so easily.

"Right, and actually you were my sister's boyfriend last week."

He speaks so quietly I can barely make out the words. "Not by choice."

I take a moment to process what he's said. I think about the video where he's standing utterly still in front of Judica. I thought he was respectful, or maybe in awe of her interest. But now, hearing what he's said, maybe he was uninterested, or worse, disgusted. Maybe he never liked her, but he didn't think he could turn her down.

Did Judica force him to be her boyfriend? I shudder. "Look, the point is, I'll never require you to do anything you don't want to do, up to and including being my Consort. Bending others to her will may be what a good ruler does, but I've never claimed to be that. I'm far more victim than..." I trail off. What did Noah say? A conqueror? No, he said a Viking. "I'm more like a victim than a Viking, and I won't make anyone else my victim, especially not you."

"Judica has no such qualms. She's a Viking until the end of days, whenever that is. Look, if you insist on attending this party, I won't try and stop you. But I do insist we train, at least a little, before you go."

"Fine."

"Fine?" Edam leans back in his chair, stretching his legs out in front of him. His eyes snap and mine are drawn toward them. Which is a mistake. Never meet the predator's eyes. Everyone knows that. But once I look at them, I can't look away. He's so... intense.

I almost forget he asked me a question, and I'm staring at him dumbly. What was it? He threw my word back at me. Fine. Fine? Ugh. I wish looking at him directly didn't reduce me to human-level stupidity.

"What's wrong with agreeing with you?"

He rolls his eyes toward the ceiling, like a drama queen in a high school movie.

I almost snort at him.

"Nothing's wrong with agreeing with me. It's that I'm having to drag you toward what you should already be focused on doing. You need to stop wasting your time playing make-believe with a bunch of human teenagers you have nothing in common with and appreciate the time you've been given. Buckle down and train in earnest, because in less than a week, Judica's going to try to take you apart." He looks out the window. Almost like the idea of Judica decapitating me upsets him. Almost.

"What do you care?"

"Don't be an idiot," he says.

"Maybe I don't need to train. Because if I'm being honest, I don't even want to go back," I say.

Edam's eyes flash. "You were born to rule Alamecha."

I shake my head. "I was born," I pause. "If we're being honest, I was born to die. Mom should have killed me the second I cried my first pitiful wail. Or before that, even. But she didn't. Every single day since then has been borrowed time. And now I have to decide whether to let my sister wear the crown she was always supposed to have or fight her for it. I hate fighting, but I like my borrowed time. I like my never-supposed-to-happen life."

"You don't have to risk it."

"You're right. I don't. I can abdicate. I really think Judica will let me walk away." If my conscience will allow it.

"I don't mean abdication. Leaving your people would be a half-life for you at best."

Which means Edam thinks he's my only good option. He thinks I'm helpless. Bubbles of anger float up inside me and burst, one by one. "Maybe it wouldn't be a risk. Because when I was watching videos this morning before school, I heard her. Judica's melodic line was clear and strong."

"Oh?" he asks. "Then show me."

I glance around the car in shock. We've stopped in front of Alora's brownstone.

Edam steps out and waves me ahead of him with a flourish. I want to slap his face for being snarky, but I save my irritation for the fight. As I jog up the stairs, I think back on our last few fights, focusing on Edam this time and not Judica. What does he do, and how can I counter him? Hearing Judica won't help me defeat him, which means I can't show him what I've learned. Melodics feels kind of person-specific in that way.

To buy myself some time to think, I select the same sword I used last time and lift it up slowly, as if I'm trying to decide whether to use it. I envision the way Edam moved, the way he slices, chops, and spins. I close my eyes and envision his movements and his melody sings in the distance, at least part of it. I don't really know Edam perfectly yet, but I can read a part of his song. It's alpha, dominant and abrasive. All the things male evians aren't really allowed to be in our society, except as directed by their monarch. I raise my well-balanced sword. "What are you going to use?"

"I'll use these." He unsheathes two short swords.

"They're too short," I say.

He shrugs casually. "Try me."

I quirk my eyebrow. "But I'll destroy you if you fight

with those, and I really want to show you what I've figured out."

He raises his eyebrows and then gestures for me to proceed. I spin once, twice, hearing my own chords, my own runs, my own intervals. He pulls back and flips his short sword around and punches me right in the face with the hilt.

Blood pours from my nose. "Edam!" I spray him with red when I shout. "Be serious!"

"I am. Look, I know you think you can hear me now, and you can feel the music behind my movements or whatever, but you can't just *flow*. You have to think smart, too. You need to apply what I've taught you. As much as you want to believe it, fighting isn't some puzzle you can unlock. You can't drop a piece into place and then magically dominate. People are more complex than that. Melodics may have clicked for you and there may be moves that are intuitive, sure, but people can always surprise you. That's the beauty of life, and the danger in it as well."

I nod, wipe my face angrily, and resume the ready position, legs apart, arms relaxed, sword pointed toward him. "Fine. Fine!"

He comes after me and I realize the pacing for the melodic line I thought I heard with him was off. I've fought him dozens of times now, and I've seen him fight Judica at the same pace, the same speed, but now I can see that he was always holding back. Edam unleashed is faster than I can follow. He practically moves at the speed of light as I try, without success, to anticipate his moves. A new line, a new pace, a new melody, surges at the edge of my consciousness, but it dances away. He destroys me like a tiger playing with his food, smirking infuriatingly the entire time. After an hour or so, I slump to the ground and toss my sword to the ground. "I yield, okay, I yield."

He bows and says, "You've improved. A tremendous amount. But you're still not there yet. Now, let's try this again with hand-to-hand and focus on the basics."

I pretend I haven't sunk into the depths of despair, but I doubt I convince Edam, much less myself.

23

I'm tapping out a text to Logan, explaining that something came up and I can't make it to the party, when Lark bounds up to me.

"Geez, what happened to you? Meat grinder?"

I glance around, eyes wide, but Edam's already gone. At least he didn't hear.

"Training, so basically, yeah."

"I thought you said things clicked."

I stomp toward the door. "Obviously not like I thought."

Lark jogs along after me like an eager puppy. I close my eyes and stop, trying not to think about Cookie, and consequently thinking about her even more. I inhale in and out and in and out to try and stave off the tears. "What's up Lark?"

"I heard there's a party later." She's practically bouncing on her toes.

"Not anymore."

Her jaw drops. "Wait, why not?"

"I can't waste time on stupid parties."

Lark touches my hand lightly. "If training isn't going

well, isn't it even more critical that you seriously consider walking away?" She drops her eyes and her volume. "It may be your best choice."

"Is it a real choice?"

Lark flinches and I realize what a jerk I am. I didn't mean that humans are beneath me and living with them would be so awful I couldn't contemplate it, but that's how it came out. If I try and clarify, this is going to get even more awkward.

I'm sick of walking on eggshells around her. It's time we talk about what happened: our moms, her dad, our friendship. But I need to show her she matters to me first, so this party just became more important. It's not about thumbing my nose at Edam, or flirting with Noah or Edam, or anyone else. It's about showing Lark that I still see her, and there's life after our moms' deaths, life that has value.

"You're right. We should go."

Her tentative smile makes it worth it, no matter how hard going feels right now.

I force myself into the shower and dress in a pair of knee-high black boots, black pants, and a hot pink top. Not that it matters when I cover it all with a long coat. Ugh, I miss the perfect weather in Hawaii. I could ignore the cold, but I'd stand out like a sore thumb among the humans, which is the opposite of the point.

I leap down the stairs two at a time, and four or five steps away from the foyer, I almost collide with Edam. He's wearing a pair of jeans and a green t-shirt that hugs his solid frame in all the right places. The Edam I know is always on guard duty, always standing at attention. He's been in uniform more often than not, or in black training gear when he's dressed casually. I don't know how to adjust to an Edam who looks like, well, an abnormally hot human.

It's disconcerting, like a panther playing fetch with a

frisbee. But it's also beautiful and confusing, and I can't tear my eyes away from him.

"I was just leaving," I say.

"We can ride together," he suggests.

"Uh, how would we explain that?" I glance at Lark.

Edam raises one eyebrow. "Are you worried what Noah will think?"

A smile lifts the corner of my mouth. "You remember his name."

He frowns. "Of course I do." He taps the side of his head. "Perfect recall. I just don't care about his opinion."

Lark smiles. "Well I do. He's hot."

Edam's voice is flat. "He's human."

I am so going to stab him in the stomach for that one later. "Humans are just as good as evians," I say.

Edam opens his mouth, glances at Lark, and closes it.

"It's fine," Lark says. "I know my human side is responsible for my weaknesses. I'm not oblivious."

"Some humans," Alora says from the doorway, "burn brighter than the sun at noon day. Some humans run circles around us, figuratively speaking. We have a lot to learn from them."

"Speaking of," I say, "I'm ready to go."

"Edam can accompany you," Alora says. "He offered to attend the party already. Just hop out of the car around the corner and no one at the party will know you arrived together."

"I'm not a child," I say. "Lark and I will be fine."

"Five of us will be waiting on the perimeter," Frederick says, stepping around the doorway. "But I'll insist on coming as your uncle unless you let Edam attend."

I sigh. "He can come."

Lark and I talk about the humans we've met on the ride over, but Noah's place is surprisingly close to Alora's brownstone. Or maybe not that surprising, since we attend the same school. The second the car stops, I grab Lark's hand, ready to dart out of the car.

"I should go in first," Edam objects.

"Give us three minutes," I say. "Then you can follow."

Edam grits his teeth, but he nods tightly.

When I pass through the gate from the car park area into the garden in front of Noah's house, I exhale loudly. I grew up in a palace, and I've visited the richest and most prestigious people in the world with Mom. Not much impresses me, but Noah's house does.

It's the size of a small palace, and it's right on the water in Manhattan. I'd expect something like this if he were evian and looking to impress others, but knowing he isn't, well, maybe Alora's right. He might be a good contact to have. Especially if I'm supposed to unite the world someday. Not that I'm in a rush, since the uniting of the world comes after blood and horror and just before terrible catastrophe, presumably.

I don't have much time to marvel at how rich Noah must be before he's standing in front of us. I've barely cleared the gate. I'm glad we ditched Edam in the car.

Noah looks different away from school. Older, with a sense of command I hadn't noticed before. "You came," he says. "I was beginning to wonder if you really would."

"I thought about bailing," I admit.

"I convinced her to come," Lark says.

I bob my head.

"Then I owe you a debt of gratitude," Noah says. "Laura, right?"

Lark blushes and nods.

We've reached the front steps by now, and the doors open without a single touch, not sliding doors, but solid, heavy wooden doors, swinging wide to allow us access. For a nanosecond, I wonder whether there's some new technology I don't know about, but then a butler in a tuxedo says, "Welcome to House Wen," and bows.

"Thanks, Chin," Noah says.

Noah and I walk through an enormous entryway with marble floors and gorgeous crystal chandeliers that opens to the right on a shiny kitchen and to the left on a formal sitting room with a waterfall built into one corner. Then we pass a study with meticulously designed inlaid wood floors and a library with floor to two-story-ceiling books and walk out onto an enormous veranda. Past that, a sleek yacht is tied to a private dock, the word 'Conqueror' stenciled on the side. Dozens of teens mill around a fire pit while loud music plays from speakers spaced at even intervals all over the yard. Probably twenty more are soaking and splashing in a gargantuan hot tub, and another ten or fifteen are flirting on the yacht. Marshmallows on sticks lean against a rack, and men and women in black pants and white shirts pass out steaming mugs of something.

"Who are all these people?" I don't recognize many of them at all, which means I haven't even passed them in the hall.

"Too big a party?" Noah asks.

"I thought the celebration was for the cross country team. I was expecting like four kids and hotdogs on a stick." I wanted to get to know Noah and Logan better, but with this many people, I'll be lucky if we spend five minutes together. I haven't even seen Logan yet.

Noah shrugs. "I only invited the cross country team, but then the yearbook photographer and the school paper people heard and wanted to come, and everyone has a friend who tags along, and then they all tell their friends. Believe it or not, this is small."

I glance around at the enormous back yard and realize he's probably telling the truth. So much for experiencing a typical high school gathering.

"It could be worse," Logan says, walking toward me from the fire pit. "Usually Noah throws keggers. He's packed hundreds of people in here before."

"I specifically didn't buy any alcohol for this," Noah says. "Although, I have some left over from my last party if that bums you out. I just didn't envision you as someone who wants to get hammered and puke."

"What does your impression of me have to do with this party?" I ask.

Logan grins, and Noah's heart rate spikes. It may be dusk, but with my evian eyes, I still notice the flush in his cheeks. "Well, nothing, except you and I both broke the record, you know. You for the girls, and me for the boys, so it's really a celebration for the two of us."

Logan laughs. "Noah planned this whole party for you. He's showing off."

Noah glares at him.

"Laura, is it?" Logan holds out a hand to shake. "And you're Rebecca's older sister?"

"Right, and you're Logan."

He bobs his head. "I am. And you look like you'd make an excellent partner at pool."

Lark beams and follows Logan toward the back porch. "I'm not very experienced, but I pick things up fast," she says coyly.

Wait, does Lark like Logan?

A waiter with a tray pauses by us, distracting me. "Cider or hot chocolate?"

I take a mug of hot chocolate. My body adjusts to hot and cold so well I don't really need my coat, much less a warm drink, but I love hot chocolate. Who doesn't?

"Was I right?" Noah leads me over to two empty chairs on the back porch that are near a space heater. "You don't look like much of a party girl."

"I like parties," I say.

Noah's eyebrows rise. "So you do want beer?"

"Oh, no, I don't drink alcoholic beverages. I didn't realize that's what you were asking." I wonder whether I could even get drunk. I've never had alcohol, but it's not out of a sense of propriety. I've never known any evians to drink it. The evian metabolism processes any stimulant or depressant so fast they don't have any noticeable effect. I could snort cocaine without side effects from what I've heard. It makes us exceptionally hard to poison.

But not impossible, obviously.

Why does my mom's death keep hitting me over and over, like a two-by-four to the head, or a crowbar to the gut without warning? When will this terrible, wrenching sorrow clear and allow me to function again? Wondering when I'll stop being sad all the time sets off another wave of despair. Because I don't want to stop thinking about Mom. Her death should hurt.

"Hey." Noah puts his hand on my arm. "Are you okay?

"Oh, yeah. I'm okay. Sorry." I am not about to start bawling at some human function.

"You look upset." His eyes have always looked too large for his face, but looking down at me with concern, he looks practically angelic. I've always been a sucker for puppy dog eyes.

"My mom died a few days ago," I admit. "It's why I transferred." It's weird to say it out loud. "My mom is dead." I have no mother. It feels more real somehow, saying it to a virtual stranger. I wonder if he'll clam up and wander away like Lisa did.

His hand tightens on my arm. "What? I didn't know," Noah says softly. "This party was a stupid idea. I'm sorry."

"I don't really want to talk about it," I say truthfully. "It's too recent, and it hurts too much." An errant, unwelcome tear springs to my eye, and I wipe it away. "I'm actually looking forward to thinking about something else."

"Alright," he says. "I won't bring it up again, but I do want to say how sorry I am. If at any point you realize you don't want to be here, I'll take you home myself."

"There are like a hundred people at your house," I say.

He shrugs. "I don't care, but they probably wouldn't even notice if I left."

I'm not sure how to respond, but a huge splash in front of us distracts me. Judging from the shouts and churning in the water, someone has fallen off the yacht and into the river.

"Think they're okay?" I ask.

Noah looks disgusted. "They're fine. High school kids are idiots."

"Why are they even on there?"

"They wanted me to take it out, but I couldn't very well do that when I wasn't sure what time you'd be here, could I? After all, I never would have broken that record without you pushing me." Noah's smile warms my heart. He seems so genuine. It's strange to be around someone who wants nothing from me.

"Is the Conqueror your dad's yacht?" I glance at the smooth lines. It does look fun. "Why didn't your dad name her after your mom?"

He glances at me sideways with another inscrutable expression. "My dad wouldn't dare name his smallest, least impressive ship after my mom. He's smarter than that."

Interesting. "Why'd he name her the Conqueror?"

Noah's eyebrows both rise. "My dad came to America for the very first time a few months before I was born. He decided on that visit to expand the family business overseas. So when he sent me here for school and bought a yacht for his house here, it seemed logical to name it Conqueror."

"Does he spend much time in the States?"

"None," Noah says. "My dad prefers home and rarely travels."

"Wait, they aren't here right now? Do they even know you're having a party?"

Noah grins. "I check in with my dad pretty often, but believe me, this isn't something I need permission to do. He wouldn't care at all. My parents both live in China, so as long as I get good grades and don't get into trouble I can sort of do what I want."

"Where in China?"

Noah leans back in his chair. "Our family home is in a small town in the Kunlun mountains just north of Tibet. Does that mean anything to you, princess?"

The word princess takes me aback at first, but then I remember that it's a common nickname for spoiled or rich kids among humans. "Uh, no. I've seen the region on a map, but I'm not an expert on China." Judica is, but I don't mention that. I doubt he'd appreciate knowing my sister salivates over the idea of seizing control of his country.

"Knowing the general region on a map is better than most people can boast," he says.

"I can't believe your parents would send you here alone."

He shrugs. "I'm the youngest son."

Like that explains it.

Logan strolls up and sinks into a chair next to me, slinging one arm around the back of it. "Noah's filling you in on his dad's plans for world domination?"

Prickles run down my spine and the hair on my arms rises under my jacket. A chill that has nothing to do with the temperature. "World domination?" I listen for Noah's heartbeat again. It's far too fast for him to be anything but human. And Alora looked into him. I force a big breath in and then out again. This isn't a plot. Not everything is some kind of manipulation.

"Hey, where's Laura?" I ask Logan.

"She's talking to some kids over there. She stinks at pool, by the way."

"So did you lose?" I ask.

Logan laughs. "Heck no. I could win with a blow up doll as a partner."

"You mean the only girl dumb enough to have you?" Noah asks.

Logan rolls his eyes. "You're one to talk. Noah's been here since he was five, off and on, and he's never had an interest in any girl for more than half an hour."

The thought makes me smile. I've never had a boyfriend, and I always figured I was behind everyone else in the world. But maybe not. "You've been here that long without your family?" It sounds terribly lonely.

"I go home for summer and holidays," he says. "And people come visit me here. My family is huge. Don't pity me, princess. I'm happy."

"Princess?" I glance at Logan to see whether he mentioned anything. If Noah knows who I really am, I want to know it.

Logan shakes his head imperceptibly.

"It fits you." Noah shrugs. "I don't know why. Does it bother you?"

"No," I say. "Whatever."

"Well if you two are done making up pet names for each other," Logan says, "there's a new poker game starting over there."

I demur. "I don't gamble recreationally."

"Recreationally?" Logan smirks. "So, what? You're strictly a professional?"

I roll my eyes. "Of course not. I just meant, I never gamble for fun."

"I know what recreational means," Logan says.

Surely Logan comprehends that my entire life is a series

of gambles right now. So much for him smoothing my way with humans.

"Oh come on," Noah says. "A few hands won't hurt."

It wouldn't be fair for me to play against these kids, even Logan. My mom's been teaching me to read people since practically the day I was born. "Sorry, hard and fast rule. But don't let me stop you."

"Wow Noah, I think your girlfriend's worried she'd destroy us," Logan says.

"She's not my girlfriend," Noah says. Under his breath he mutters, "Not yet."

"Better for Noah that you sit it out," Logan says. "He sucks. In fact, he owes me like three thousand bucks."

Noah quirks one eyebrow. "Nice try."

Logan sighs heavily. "It might be the other way around. But if we don't play, how will I ever win my money back?"

A short kid with dark framed glasses and shaggy brown hair shuffles a deck of cards at one of the patio tables. "So are we playing, or what?"

"What do you play for?" I ask, curious. "Cash?"

Noah nods. "What else?"

"I don't need money." I shrug. "Not interested."

We're attracting more attention now, and a half a dozen new kids have gathered around. Noah rubs his hands together. "If you don't need money, then let's change the stakes. What do you need?"

I like seeing what makes people tick. "How about we change the game entirely. Have you guys ever played truth or dare?"

He looks into my eyes and I can tell he's weighing something, but I don't know what. "Sure, why not?"

Noah introduces me to a dozen or so kids who have gathered around. I notice several hands of cards are strewn on the coffee table, as well as a few stacks of cash. Noah grabs one and stuffs it into his pocket and a few other kids do the same.

"So we're done with poker?" Logan asks. "That's not cool. I'm way behind."

Noah laughs. "I'm doing you a favor, man."

Logan punches his arm. "You usually don't destroy me that bad. Who were you trying to impress?" Logan looks at me and grins.

"If you have to guess, you're an idiot," Noah says softly enough that I doubt any humans present could hear.

"Can anyone play?" a girl with light brown hair cut into a bob asks.

"Princess, this is Frances, the editor of the school newspaper. And sure." Noah raises his voice. "We're going to play a game of truth or dare if anyone wants to join us."

Raven and two of her friends I've met, Alyssa and Faith, walk our way. Logan, Lark, Frances, and ten other kids I meet one at a time all drag the chairs scattered around the back porch in and around the existing patio furniture to form a loose approximation of a circle. As we prepare, more kids crowd around. Noah points and some guys drag lounge chairs from the area around Noah's olympic size swimming pool to round out the circle.

Noah sits down on the empty side of the sofa and pats the spot next to him. I sit there, and then Frances squeezes into a non-existent space on his other side. Frances' co-editor, a guy named Sven, sits down on the arm of a lounge chair directly across from her.

Logan sighs melodramatically, but he runs his hand through his hair and sits in a chair across from me. "This should be interesting."

The captain of the swim team, Todd, straddles one of the patio chairs backward. "I think you meant fun. This will be fun."

"So who goes first?" Frances asks.

"Why don't you go first?" I suggest.

"Sure, I guess. How does this work?" Frances asks.

Geez, you'd think a bunch of humans would know how to play this game. I saw it on one of their television shows. "You're first, so you pick whether you want to tell the truth, or accept a dare," I say.

"But who asks the question or poses the dare?" Frances asks reasonably.

I hadn't thought of that.

"Pick someone," Raven says, "since you're going first, but then after you go, you can pick who goes next, and you get to issue their dare or question. So once you've gone, you get to pass along the misery."

Sounds reasonable.

"I don't want to go first. How about if I just pick someone and I can issue their dare or expose their truth?" Frances asks.

I barely know her, but I've already formed an opinion. Frances is annoying.

"Whatever," Noah says. "Just start already."

Frances sighs. "Alright then, I choose you."

Big surprise.

Noah leans back on the sofa, tossing one arm behind me and leaning back so he can look Francis in the eye. "Fine. I choose dare."

"I dare you to... Hmm, what if I can't think of anything?" Frances asks.

I could strangle her. "Then you aren't very creative," I say. "Think of something he might be reticent to do, and then dare him to do exactly that. Like eat a worm you dig out of the flower bed, or parade around in his underwear, using his pants as a crown."

"Uh, don't ask me to do either of those things," Noah says. "You have a strange, quirky mind, princess."

"Okay, then," Frances says, eyes gleaming. "I dare you to kiss me."

Logan laughs out loud and Sven looks ill. Todd was right; this is fun.

Noah grins. "Sure," he says. "Why not?" He leans down over Frances and kisses her right on the lips. He doesn't linger, but it's more than a peck.

Frances' heart practically races right out of her chest. Interestingly, Noah's hasn't changed pace, not even a tiny bit.

"My turn," Noah says. "I choose you, princess." He smiles at me and the laugh dies in my chest. He wouldn't possibly be so ridiculous as to repeat Frances' dare. Right?

Either way, I can't pick truth. Not if I want to really experience this dumb game. Plus, there are too many things I couldn't possibly answer. But the thought of him asking me to kiss him spikes my pulse. I meet Noah's gaze and force the word out. "Dare."

"Audacious," he says. "I like it."

"Get on with it," Logan says. "And no kissing."

"Where were your rules a few minutes ago?" Noah raises both eyebrows. "You didn't say a word when Frances forced me to risk a case of mononucleosis."

"Oh please," Logan says.

"Seriously, I don't think you can make up rules after the game begins," Noah says.

"It's in the actual rules." Logan holds up his phone and shows it to the people on either side of him. "I got tired of you people yammering and pulled them up online. They don't proscribe kissing, but it specifically says you can't repeat someone else's dare."

"Come on," Noah says. "I was never going to dare the princess here to kiss me. If my only hope of kissing her is daring her in a game, well, that's sad."

Frances squeaks and runs off. She brought that one on herself, but I still feel bad about it.

"Nice, Noah." Sven stands up and glares at us before jogging off after her. Maybe Lisa was right. Noah isn't such a nice guy all the time.

"Whoops," Noah says. Every face turns toward him, all of us happy for a distraction. "Well I handled that badly, but don't worry. We'll get this back on track. In fact, to keep things interesting, let's make it a double dare."

"What does that mean?" Raven asks.

Everyone looks at Logan. He glances down at his phone for a moment before he says, "It means if Rebecca refuses she owes him a forfeit, but if she does whatever he proposes, he owes her a forfeit."

"What's the forfeit?" I ask.

"A forfeit is like a gift or a favor," Raven's redheaded friend Faith says. I'm surprised because for some reason I didn't expect her to be very smart.

"I know that," I say. "I meant, what *is* the forfeit if I pass?"

"I get to choose something." Noah smiles.

"What's your dare, then?" If it's not too bad, I could use an undefined favor from someone whose dad owns vast regions of China.

"I could dare you to jump in the pool, but that would be dumb since it's heated. The river, on the other hand, will be freezing right about now. So how about that? I dare you to jump in the river."

I glance at the river. Dark and cold. But that's nothing to a typical training session. I was worried he'd pick something truly hard. Even so, I need to sell this. May as well earn a decent forfeit.

Noah grins. "You going to pass?"

"What would you want from me?"

Noah's lips compress and he taps them. "Hmm." His eyes light up. "I've always wanted a pony."

The thought of Noah on a pony curls my lip upward. "As badly as I want to see you riding one. . . I'm not losing."

"Right, your thing about never losing." Noah grins. "I almost forgot about that."

I stand up and walk down toward the water. Most of the other kids who are gathered around stand up to follow.

"Whoa," Noah says. "You guys can carry on. Pick someone, princess. They can take over. There's no reason they all have to watch us freeze our butts off."

"Wait, what do you mean 'us'?" I ask.

"I'm not such a jerk that I'd make you jump in alone. What if you drowned? I'd never forgive myself."

"Touching," I say. "Who says chivalry is dead?"

"I choose Raven." I wink at her. "Logan can come up with a dare or a question for her in my place."

"Thanks, but. . ." Logan doesn't sit down. "I'll pass that honor to Todd. I'm coming with you two to make sure no one perishes."

Lark stands up and then next to her, Todd does too. At this rate, everyone may as well come.

"If you're worried about people drowning, I should come, as captain of the swim team." Todd grins at Lark and she smiles back.

"Chill guys. This isn't dangerous, I swear. Just carry on." Noah waves his hand and everyone sits down, including Lark. Logan, Noah, and I walk down to the water. I get right to the edge of the river and stop. There's just a weedy patch and a two-foot drop between me and the freezing water. Judging by the sound, it's moving fast.

"We're upriver from Conqueror, so even if we get dragged a bit, we can grab the pilings for the dock." Noah touches my arm and drops his voice. "But you don't have to do it at all if you really don't want to. That's why I didn't want everyone following us. I don't even need a boon, truly."

Noah spoke quietly, but Logan still heard of course. "You could give him, say, three thousand bucks or so," Logan says. "And tell him it's from me. If that makes you feel better."

I shrug my jacket off and pass it to Logan. "Sorry, but you'll have to pay your own debts. Noah may not want a boon, but I do." I slip my boots off, leaving my concealed dagger in its boot sheath, and then peel off my socks. Finally, I pull my t-shirt over my head.

"Whoa," Noah says. "What are you doing?"

"I'm not jumping in fully clothed, obviously." I slide my jeans down to my ankles and step out of them. At least it's dark. I thought it would be better to do this without the twenty-five or so kids playing truth or dare standing watch, but standing in front of just Logan and Noah in a sports bra and boy short underwear feels bizarre. I'm tingling all over, and buzzing with the idea of doing something stupid and pointless for no reason at all. My skin pebbles up and I'm not even sure it's from the cold. I remind myself that all the girls swimming in Noah's heated pool are wearing less than I am right now.

"I'm not waiting," I say. "I'm jumping in now."

"Fine," Noah says. "Let's go."

Noah takes my hand as I step toward the edge. I let him, and we jump in together, crashing into the water in tandem.

Noah didn't lie.

The water's painfully cold, but when you're spending half your day being hacked at by a sword, and the other half contemplating how to murder your sister or crying over your dead mother, a little cold water isn't a big deal. I expect Noah to let go of my hand once we come back to the surface for air, but he doesn't. We kick our feet and paddle with our free hands until we reach the shallowest part. I shudder when my bare feet reach the slimy, poky ruffage at the bottom of the East River.

Noah squeezes my hand. "Almost there."

I'm sincerely grateful when Logan leans down and grabs my forearms, pulling me ashore. Logan's shaking his head, but he peels off his jacket and drapes it around my shoulders. He picks up my clothes and boots, not commenting on the knife tucked into my boot sheath, and follows us back to the house. Alora was right. Logan is proving helpful.

"The closest bathroom is here." He points.

I duck behind the door and lock it.

A tap on the closed door just as the water finally heats up sets my teeth on edge.

"You okay?" Edam whispers.

"What are you doing in here?" I hiss. "I'm fine. I'm taking a shower. How will you explain hovering outside my door while I'm naked if they find you? Go back to the car."

"I'll keep watch until you're done," he says.

"Absolutely not. Go back. That's an order."

"No one is going to see me, but you can't defend yourself from anyone while you're in there." I can see him in my mind's eye, his jaw set, his arms crossed over his chest. It makes me smile.

I shower, dry off and wrap myself in a towel. Then I toss my wet underwear and sports bra in the trash and put on just my outer clothes. By the time I come out, I catch a whiff of Edam, but he's already gone. At least he's being discreet. My hair's still wet, but I'm otherwise dry. I walk to the back door and peer through the glass. It looks like the game of truth and dare is still going strong, and it seems to have attracted a much larger audience, but Noah isn't one of them.

Noah's whisper startles me badly enough that I practically climb the wall. "You warm enough?"

I scowl. "How did you sneak up on me?"

He grins. "I used to play this game with my sister. We'd see who could move the quietest. I always won."

"I bet you did."

He points toward the back of the house. "If you need to borrow clothes, I have some you can use."

"Uh, you have girl clothes?" I lift my eyebrows.

He chuckles. "My parents don't often visit, but my favorite sister flies out a few times a year."

Thank goodness he has a legitimate reason for having clothing in my size. "That's a relief."

"You were worried I had a pit or something?" Noah whines in a creepy voice, "It puts the lotion on its skin..."

I can't help my grin. No one back home watches TV or movies at all, but he's quoting *Silence of the Lambs*. I finish his line. "Or else it gets the hose again." I smile. "Gross, no, I wasn't thinking you were making a skin suit, but I'm glad to hear you have a sister. Maybe she can fix whatever's wrong with you."

"I doubt it." Noah puts his hand on the doorframe above my head. "You want to head back out?"

I shrug. "It's late. I should probably go home soon."

"Already?" Noah grabs my hand and I let him. It feels nice, even when he interlaces our fingers. Maybe especially when he interlaces our fingers. I've never held a guy's hand before now, unless you count jumping into the river a moment ago. He tugs me out the back porch door and I let him. Gusts of cold air batter my wet hair, but it doesn't bother me. In fact, nearly all my attention is on where my hand meets his.

Noah ignores the kids calling to him and steers us back down toward the river again.

"Where are you going?" Logan asks.

"Princess lost an earring," Noah says.

Evians don't pierce our ears, because they'd just heal right back up. It's pointless. But Logan doesn't comment. And this time, he doesn't follow us either.

Noah steers me with nothing but a slight shift of his hand toward the edge of the dock. There were kids on the yacht earlier, but they've all moved back toward the house, so it's quiet, peaceful even. The hissing of the water barreling past even muffles most of the sounds of the city. Noah's so easy, so uncomplicated, and even though we're probably the same age, he seems young, younger than me. He can't want anything from me, because he doesn't even know who I am. There are no politics with him, no history with my sister, and no offers to save me hanging over us.

"So. What do you want from me?" Noah asks.

A vague sense of unease grips me. I know he can't read my mind, but it's a strange thing to ask, and bizarre timing for him to ask it. "What do you mean?"

"Your boon, duh. Tell me what you want, and I'll try to give it to you. Truth or dare means something, you know."

I lift one eyebrow. "You didn't even know the rules."

"Well, now I do. And I'm honorable, unlike you Americans."

"You offered to let me off the hook, so I can't very well hold you to your promise."

"I was kidding. I'd definitely have made you buy me a pony."

I grin, not that he can see much of it in the dark. "Fine. Then I want to skip out on my life. Take me back with you to China. I'm not too big. I'd probably fit inside a checked bag."

Noah stares at me for a moment and I wonder whether he knows I'm kidding. I think I'm kidding. Although, if I decide to abdicate, China might be the only place I could really escape evian politics.

"My dad'll probably be a bit shocked, but sure. Why not?"

I exhale. "I'm kidding Noah. I can't really run away to China. It's the middle of the school year, for one."

"I really would take you back with me for a visit as your boon. And we could see a bit of the world on the way, if you want. Paris and Rome, and let's not forget Venice. Maybe even Prague."

Now I know he's kidding. But going on vacation with someone sounds nice. Too nice to be real. Visiting places, snapping photos, seeing sights like a normal person. "Would you really want to travel with me?"

Noah's not as tall as Edam, but he's taller than me by a few inches at least. Our relative similarity of height means his face is already hovering near mine when he says, "Say the word and we'll leave tomorrow." His breath blows warmly over my face.

"The word."

Noah's grinning when his mouth lowers toward mine, but surprisingly I don't feel his perfect teeth when he kisses me. When his lips press against mine, all I feel is a soft fullness. I close my eyes and sigh against him. His arms circle my waist.

My heart goes on vacation, which is fine. Heartbeats are overrated.

I turn toward Noah's warmth, my hands balling up the fabric of his t-shirt. It's soft, and I release it and splay my hands against his chest. He's bulkier than I would have guessed, corded muscles taut underneath his shirt. When he pulls back abruptly, I'm dizzy. His eyes dance as he shifts slightly and nibbles on the edge of my mouth. When he presses tiny kisses down my jaw to my neck, I gasp. He's smiling again when his hands cup my face and pull my mouth back to his. I want to fall into this exact moment in this exact place forever.

This is why people want to live a thousand years.

It has taken me seventeen years to figure this out, but not all moments are created equal. Some stretch, some fly by, and some drag miserably on and on. But some moments, like this one, make the rest worth it.

Maybe I *should* try to convince him to return to China with me and never look back.

Loud, punctuating explosions above my head pulverize my thoughts. I leap away from Noah, eyes searching the sky for a split second, until I recognize the sound. Fireworks. I watch the sky blossom with a sense of wonder. "Wow. Tell me you didn't plan that."

He points behind me. "I wish I had that kind of game, but no, that's nothing more than garden variety luck. They're rededicating Lady Liberty after the work they had to do fixing the torch. I don't know why that thing has so many issues, but I forgot about the fireworks entirely until this very moment."

"Bartholdi was a little bit in love with my mom, you know. That's why—" I choke and cough. What am I saying? Noah would think I'm crazy.

"Huh?"

Maybe he doesn't even know who Bartholdi is. "Nothing," I say.

He leans back and puts a little space between us. "If you want to talk about your mom, I'm happy to listen. About anything. Whatever."

I look down at where our fingers are still interlocked. "I don't."

"That's fine, too."

I look up at the fireworks and then down at the reflections of light the explosions cast on Noah's perfect profile. "They're beautiful, but the kiss didn't need them."

He leans closer and closer until any less space would make my eyes cross. "I've wanted to kiss you since the minute I saw you, all overdressed and lost. Now that I finally have, I don't want to stop."

"Then don't."

He pulls my mouth back to his and my hands tighten on his shirt again.

"What the hell?"

Edam's standing at the bottom of the dock, fists clenched. "Your sister called. It's time to get home, *Rebecca*."

Noah drops me and steps backward. He inadvertently stumbles against the edge of the dock and almost falls in, pinwheeling his arms to keep his balance. It might have been comical under other circumstances.

"I thought you were kidding about chaperoning," Noah says. "How'd you even get my address?"

Edam ignores Noah. "Let's go."

"Umm, did I miss something? Is Coach Renfro taking you home?"

"I should probably have admitted to knowing him earlier, but he's friends with my much older sister, the one who enrolled Laura and me." I force a laugh. "I'm pretty sure that's how he got the job."

Noah straightens up and reaches for my hand. I let him take it. "So you know him, like outside of Trinity?"

I nod. "Yeah, I just didn't want to start off at a new school as like, the friend of a teacher."

"Seriously," Edam barks. "I can't risk angering your big sister. She *is* my patron."

Noah turns back to Edam. "What's your problem? Geez. It's barely after ten. I get that it's late for a school night, but it's not like, epically late. She hasn't had a drop of alcohol. I'd think you'd be glad she's getting to know some of the kids at her new school."

"Getting to know them?" Edam glances around. "The only person I see here is you."

"I'm the best of the bunch." Noah tilts his head in a particularly arrogant way.

Edam glances down to where I'm holding Noah's hand and his anger morphs into something else, an emotion I recognize, though I've never seen it on Edam's face.

He's hurt.

I drop Noah's hand and take a step toward Edam. "It's not what you think."

Edam stiffens. "I wouldn't dare think anything at all."

I reach out to touch his arm and he steps back. I drop my hand and my shoulders slump.

"Uh, what's going on?" Noah glances at Edam before he says, "You don't act like a friend of her much older sister." Noah looks at me and then back at Edam and I can see when the realization dawns in his eyes. "You guys are involved somehow, aren't you?" His lip curls. "Ewww. I mean, how old are you exactly? Does her sister know?"

I don't say anything and neither does Edam.

"Wait, are you here with me to make him jealous?" Noah looks from Edam to me and back again. "Because that's messed up."

My tone is strong, commanding even, when I order Edam. "I'll meet you at the car. Grab Laura and give me a minute to talk to him. Now."

Edam hesitates, but finally he nods and heads for the group of teenagers, ostensibly to collect Lark.

"Noah, we aren't involved," I say, "but Edam's not that much older than me. He just finished college and since my mom died, we've gotten close. That's all."

Noah laughs. "Man, Trinity's PE department cannot catch a break. This guy's worse than the last one. But I owe you a favor, so I'll keep my mouth shut." He tilts his head. "This is significantly less awesome than a long, transcontinental vacation would have been."

I turn to leave.

Noah puts his hand on my arm. "Tell me one thing?"

"What?"

"I kiss better than the old man, right?"

"I don't know," I say.

"You don't know because you haven't kissed him? Or because you can't decide?"

I'm smiling when I walk away.

Noah grumbles behind me. "Oh, come on."

Edam's waiting for me in the back of the Toyota Land Cruiser he borrowed, but he is most certainly not grinning, smirking, or smiling. Lark's sitting in the middle of the bench seat, and she tries to catch my eye, but I'm too tired to deal with it. I climb into the seat, lean my head against the window, and close my eyes.

No one speaks on the drive back. I'm frankly surprised that Lark doesn't interrogate me. It might mean she had an interesting night of her own, but I don't have the bandwidth to figure that out either.

Once we reach Alora's, I leap from the car and race up the front step. I don't even realize Edam kept up with me until my hand is on the doorknob to my room.

Edam's door creaks behind me.

I jump. "Geez, how did you get up here so fast?"

"I'm evian too," he says.

"I know that."

"Do you?"

"What's the big deal?" I ask.

Edam slams his hand against the solid wood door in front of him and the entire frame trembles. "What's the *big deal*?"

"Yeah," I ask. "What are you so mad about? I'm trying to make some big decisions here, and I need you to lay off the smoldering fury."

"You're making your big decisions based on what? On

how good a kisser the human is? What exactly is that going to help you decide?"

"Are you kidding right now?" I clench my fists but resist the urge to hit anything. I'm not that juvenile. "My choices are to go back and fight my sister and possibly die, or, best case, kill her, my own twin, my blood. Or, in a shocking turn, I could choose to abdicate and if I hide well enough, I can lead a normal life, which for the record, is the life I've always wanted. And if I do that, I'll be dating, Edam. I'll be looking for someone to spend my time with. Don't you think it's important for me to find out whether any of the humans will even like me?"

"Like you?" He snorts. "You're perfect! You have luminous hair, a face that would make an angel weep, long legs, and not an ounce of fat on you. Even so, you have perfect curves, high cheekbones and the most beautiful smile I've ever seen. The humans will fall all over themselves to pursue you. Even among evians, you're smarter, funnier, stronger, and faster than everyone else. Guys will literally collapse at your feet if you abdicate."

"You're acting like that's a bad thing. I've spent my whole life being not quite good enough, so what you're describing sounds a little like heaven."

"You're asking the wrong questions, Chancy, researching the wrong things."

"What should I be asking?"

"Whether you like any of them. That's what you should be trying to figure out."

"That's what I said!"

He shakes his head. "Everyone at Trinity can see Noah likes you. But do you want to spend your life with him?"

"I don't know," I say. "He's the only person I've ever kissed and—"

"I'm sorry, that's one of your arguments for abdicating?" Edam asks.

"Of course not. That would be stupid."

His voice drops. It's raspy when he says, "Someone should do something about that. You need some way to compare." He crosses the hall in an instant, towering over me.

When I look up at his face, time warps and buckles all around me. I know in my brain that seconds continue to tick by, but instead of rolling past, they tumble into a pile on the floor. Because now we've stepped into a strange alternate reality, where the guy of my dreams is paying me compliments and looking at me like he needs me to breathe.

Every time I've imagined a kiss, it's been with Edam. Every time I've thought about pressing my fingers against the stubble on a man's chin, his perfectly carved face comes to mind. Every time I've made up a dreamy future, my boyfriend wears Edam's face.

He's the strongest man I know. He's the bravest guy I've met. He's the most powerful fighter Alamecha can boast. And he's looking at me hungrily, like a panther who's done playing fetch and is ready to pounce.

Noah leaned toward me slowly. Noah pressed his lips against me gently. Noah gave me time to object, to move away, to stop him.

Edam comes after me like he does in training, but this time, his hands pull me closer instead of thrusting me away. His mouth closes over mine from above, angling down hard, capturing my lips with his own. My sigh is lost in the heat of his body, pressed against me from knees to lips. My fingers run over the hard planes of his chest, and down to his abdominal muscles. My knees buckle, but his arm wraps around to hold me up. My teeth bite his lip with the knowledge I can't hurt him.

No matter what I do, no matter how much I give or take, Edam won't break.

When he finally pulls away and takes a step back, I notice that the doorframe where his free hand rested now boasts a handprint. Edam crumpled the solid wood of my door during our kiss. I bring my fingers up to brush against my mouth. My lips are swollen, but they're already healing.

I wish they wouldn't. Because I want to see evidence of this moment when I look in the mirror. I want to know that the world is different than it was, and for the first time in a long time, better.

"Abdicate if you must, but do it with all the information." Edam's gaze dips to my lips and then lifts back to my eyes. Then he slips through his door and closes it behind him.

Great. I'm never going to be able to sleep now.

24

The next morning, I wake up early. My hands shake when I pull my pants on. My breathing hitches when I yank my shirt down over my head. I'm not tired; I slept fine. But memories from last night flood my mind, and I don't know how I'll be able to look at Edam during our training session. I open my door a crack first, and then when I don't see or hear any sign of him, I swing it open all the way, my eyes drawn to Edam's handprint on the doorframe. I trace the indentations in the wood with my fingertips.

What do I do now? I can't stand here in the hallway, swooning over last night. Maybe I'll head for the training room early and run through forms for a while before our session starts.

But when I reach the ballroom, Edam's already there. He picks up a sword and meets my gaze steadily. The jittery feeling just under my skin intensifies. Will he kiss me again? Will he pretend it never happened? He crosses the room one step at a time, his eyes never leaving mine. As he approaches, my heart races embarrassingly. I know he can hear it, because I hear his thumping steadily along in his chest.

"Obviously you're not nervous this morning," I say.

"Or maybe I'm always nervous around you," he says. "So you can't tell a difference."

He's teasing me.

I like it.

He stops a little too close and leans over and around me, his palm pressing against the wall behind me for support. His free hand holds a sword loosely at his side, but instead of being menacing, somehow it's exhilarating.

Will he kiss me again? Will I be able to fight him? After that kiss, I don't see how I could. His head dips toward me, and a pit opens up in the bottom of my stomach. I swallow and turn up to face him.

"Pick your weapons," he whispers, and then he spins away.

My fingers tremble as I run them over the hilts in front of me. Anger floods into the abyss in my belly opened by desire. What's wrong with him? Why didn't he kiss me? Maybe he didn't enjoy it last night, not like I did. My hands close around the hilts of two swords. Not a long and short sword, not this time. I've chosen a pair of evenly weighted swords, not too long, but not short either. I turn back toward Edam with a scowl on my face.

Edam's blade flashes as he arcs it toward me, and I bring up both my swords to block. Instead of leaving me unwilling to attack like I feared, something about last night increases the energy of our sparring. Edam decimates me like always, but I'm faster, and I'm healing quicker still.

"Progress, right?" I ask at the end, afraid of his answer.

"You're doing better," he says. "Much better. A week may not be quite long enough, but you've improved faster than I'd have thought possible. Who knows what you may be capable of?"

A week might not be long enough.

"You know," he says, "the day your mom died was probably the worst day of your life."

I lean against the weapon rack. "It was."

"And I'm sorrier than you can know. But for me, it was the first time I've had hope in a long time."

"Excuse me?"

"Not because of your mom," he says, "but when I found out that she changed the paperwork. I never picked Judica, you know. She picked me, and it wasn't like I really had a choice. I mean, I dumped her, and she was going to execute me for it."

True.

"But when I heard the paperwork had been changed and you were the new Empress instead of her, I couldn't believe it. I know you feel like you're not savage enough to rule and maybe that's true by comparison to other rulers. I even get why the empresses act the way they do. It's a kill or be killed world. But the evian system is messed up. Something has to change, and Judica's a one-way ticket to the status quo. You're Door Number Two. No one's quite sure what might lie behind it, but I'm not afraid to find out. I'm exhilarated."

The same word I'd just used to describe my feelings about him. And I agree with what he's saying on so many levels. Exiling evians and kicking out half-evians from our society must stop. We've also allowed humans to form into patriarchal societies all over the world because men follow rules easier, but it's suppressed billions of human women. And that's just the tip of the iceberg. Without talking to others, I'll never find out how many things must be changed or come up with the best solutions. Which is why I ask, "What would you prioritize?"

"I get that women's bodies don't experience deletions to

their eggs as they age. It means you'll have as genetically perfect a child in nine hundred years as you'll have now. But that shouldn't mean that the opinions of men don't matter. Male evians have become expendable commodities. We're literally bought and sold like stallions for breeding stock. Did you know your mother paid six times for me what she paid for anyone else because I'm seventh generation, same as you? Doesn't that bother you? Like our worth has nothing to do with *who* we are, and everything to do with *what* we are?"

My jaw drops. I've been thinking about female humans for years, but I hadn't even considered the injustices to evian males. Human men mistreat and abuse women because they're stronger. But with evians, the genders are much closer in strength. Since our royal families sell their boys at birth to ensure loyalty, it leaves them without a support system, further weakening their power. My mom hated the system, but not enough to eschew following it.

"Unlike all the other empresses and heirs, you listen to opinions from everyone around you. You'd treat a Consort as a partner. Which means that you and I together could fix so many broken things."

Edam doesn't know about the prophecy. I have to remind myself of that, because he sure sounds like he does.

It's freaking me out.

"I need to think, Edam. Please don't pressure me."

"I'm not trying to," he says. "I promise."

I rush to my room to shower, but Alora's waiting for me. She's always so serene, so calm, so peaceful. I need to discover her secret, because Mom exuded calm too. I'm nothing like them. I'm nothing like Edam thinks. I can't do this, any of it.

"Chancery," Alora asks, her voice soft, her eyes gentle. "Is everything okay?"

I jog across the room and pull her into a hug. "Nothing is okay."

I sob against her shoulder, and after a short moment, her arms tighten around me and she bawls, too.

When I finally get things together, I sit up straight and wipe my tears away. "I need some advice."

Alora chuckles. "From your washed-up sister who hides in New York City?"

My jaw drops. Alora doesn't think she's good enough either? I'm beginning to think that everyone I know is secretly faking it.

I drop my face in my hands. "Fight, abdicate, fight, abdicate. I keep thinking I've made up my mind, but then five minutes later something else happens and I'm lost again."

"What are you thinking right now?" She sits down next to me. "No processing, just your current thoughts."

"I can't fight," I say. "I'm trying, but I'm still lousy. I can't beat Judica."

"So you're leaning toward abdication?" she asks. "Because you're always welcome to stay with me. You already know I have this home in New York, but I've got extensive holdings elsewhere too. I can make sure you're safe and hidden, if that's necessary."

"Maybe, but I've got a third option too."

Alora's lips compress. "Edam."

"He offered to be my Consort."

She nods. "I expected that."

"Because you knew I wasn't strong enough to fight her myself?"

"Ha! No. Because I've seen how he looks at you. That boy is smitten."

Smitten? How old is Alora? Oh, right. "I don't know about that, but he's willing to fight Judica for me. I think it has more to do with his burning desire to make things right in the evian world, but he's passionate about it. I believe he can do it, too."

"Really?" Alora's right eyebrow rises. "Edam's a social warrior? I didn't see that one coming."

I suppose I didn't either.

"Okay, same question, but including all three options. You have to pick one right now. Which is it?"

"I guess I'd abdicate. I like Edam, but I'm not even eighteen yet. And beyond that, I don't know whether I want to win at all if it means killing my sister. I hate fighting. Slashing someone with a sword until they're dead isn't who I am. I doubt letting someone else do it by proxy will be much better. At the end of the day, whatever they do is still my fault." I shudder. "Can Edam just win the fight, but not kill her? Like, hold his sword to her throat until she surrenders?"

Alora closes her eyes and runs a hand over her face. When she opens her eyes, they're sad. "You can't, Chancy. You know that."

"How do I know that? Why can't I? My older sister, Melina, the one who shares a dad with Judica and I, she challenged Mom, right? When Mom gave birth and refused to kill one of us. That's what I heard."

Alora looks at me funny. "I don't know the details since I wasn't there and Mother never discussed it, but I heard the same as you. Melina challenged Mother, and they fought hours after she gave birth to you and Judica."

"Clearly Mom won, but Melina's still alive. So why can't I let Judica live?"

Alora looks sad. "I don't know exactly what happened. No one does. Mother threw everyone out of the room before exiling her."

"But she lives in Mom's territory."

Alora nods. "She lives in Austin and can't leave, from what I understand. And Mother forbade her to participate in politics. Not just Alamecha's politics, but all evian politics. Melina agreed, and Mother trusted her word."

"Why can't I do something like that?"

"You can't forcibly remove an Heir. Judica could choose to abdicate, but do you think she would?" Alora looks at me sideways.

Judica will never, under any circumstance, abdicate. Never.

"So if I defeat her and don't kill her," I say, "she'll simply challenge me again the next day."

"And if you defeat her that day, she'll challenge you again."

I groan. "So I have to kill her or bow out."

"You won't know whether you can defeat her until you're in the ring, not for sure. Training is very different than a real fight to the death," Alora says. "It may come more naturally to Judica, but being able to easily strike another human doesn't make her the better warrior. Anyone can learn to fight. I had no taste for it, but I improved. I actually think part of what you need to know is coded into your genetic material." She smiles. "Which is how I became the best fighter in my century."

"Wait." I shake my head. "You were a fighter?"

Alora raises one eyebrow. "I don't look it to you?"

I take in her ballerina's body—long, lean lines, an arched neck, and understated grace. "No." I shake my head. "Sorry, but I'm kind of glad you don't look like a warrior. You wouldn't be you."

"I won first place in Combat in the Centennial Games in 1900."

Humans have the Olympics every four years, but evians live a millennium. We don't need a competition every four years. Once a century is quite often enough to have thousands of evians compete in four events: Endurance, Regeneration, Strategy, and Combat.

How did I not know that Alora won Combat?

"Why aren't you training me then, instead of Edam?"

Alora looks at me sadly. "Melodics can't be mastered in a week. It's not about quick tricks or smart thinking or fighting strategy. To have any hope of winning, you need to know your opponent. It's about understanding them well enough you know what move they'll make and why. And at the risk of sounding like a fortune cookie, you can only understand them when you understand yourself. I could go through the forms with you, but you can only master melodics when you master your own heart enough to see clearly into the hearts of others."

"So you think that melodics is dying because—"

"No one takes the time to understand themselves anymore, much less the people around them. Yes, I believe that's why melodics has fallen out of favor."

Wow, Edam would laugh so hard at all this, but I almost understand her.

"Chancery, you would be an excellent ruler. I think you can master the principles of combat too, but only if you desperately want to do it. And only if you dig deep. Our family motto is pretty cheesy, but it's also true. It's time for you to accept the world as it is or do something to change it."

"Do you think I should be the one fighting?"

"Fighting isn't the only way to change the world," Alora says. "And if I were you, I wouldn't fight Judica."

"You wouldn't?" I'm beginning to think I don't know a thing about my favorite sister.

She laughs. "What did Mother tell you about my life? Did she recount any stories of my youth?"

I shrug. "Not really." I wrack my memory and come up with just a few facts. I know Alora was born in 1706 and that she was Heir for more than a hundred years, until Inara's birth in 1820. Mom hadn't said much else, not that I could recall. Just a few small things here and there: Alora loves Chinese food. Alora moves with grace. Alora detests rudeness.

But no anecdotes or stories about her early years.

"I wasn't an exemplary Heir, so I shouldn't be surprised she didn't share. Actually, maybe I should be grateful."

"But it still hurts your feelings?" I guess.

"Not anymore. I passed beyond getting my feelings hurt by anything our family does long ago," Alora says.

"What's the story?"

"I fell in love with a human, a man without even a drop of evian blood."

I must look surprised, because she smiles fondly. "It wasn't as unlikely then. Mother hadn't created her island palace and humans surrounded us much of the time. We didn't always have evians cleaning, and cooking, and serving us. We used humans for those tasks. After this, she opted for seclusion, at least until the formative, early years had passed for Inara, and later for Melina, and now for you and Judica. In any case, his imperfect blood notwithstanding, you might have heard of the man who caught my eye. I'm not sure if they still teach about his life on Ni'ihau, but he's still part of the curriculum in public schools around here. His name was Benjamin Franklin."

I snort. "Uh, yeah, he's come up," I say. "He made the first lightning rod, and was born in 1706 – wow, I never made that connection before, because why would I? But you're the same age."

Alora looks away from me, her eyes glassy, as if thinking about this pains her. "We first met in London. He was brilliant, Chancy. Brilliant and imperfect and full of life and fire in a way that no evians I knew were."

"So what happened?" I ask. "I want to hear every detail."

Alora glances at her watch. "One day I'll share the whole story with you. But since it's getting close to time for school, I'll skip to the critical part. I became pregnant."

I can't breathe. "Oh." For years, I thought Mom would change her mind if she were confronted with a half-evian child or grandchild. I guess I was wrong.

"Mother presented me with my options. I could give the child up and remain her Heir, or I could leave. She made it clear that if I left her side, I would never be welcomed back."

I splutter. "Whoa, you left way back then?"

Alora's shoulders droop and her eyes won't meet mine. "The worst mistake of my life is that I didn't. I gave him up. Benjamin raised William himself, never revealing the identity of William's mother to anyone, including William himself." Her voice trembles. "I forsook the man I loved, and I abandoned my child. I can never undo that misstep. Never."

"Then why are you—"

"You're wondering why I live like an outcast now, I suppose." Alora smiles ruefully. "It's not really that bad, you know. Evians think that the rest of the earth is covered with trash, teeming with unfit people. They think humans aren't worthy of time or attention. It's true that things are harder for humans. They work harder to comprehend, to overcome, and to create. But hard work isn't a dirty word. Evians are wrong that humans' shortcomings make them unworthy. Every life has value. People are still people, no matter how short a time they have on this Earth, or how imperfect their visage. In many ways, the humans' limited time on Earth helps them remember not to waste it."

"I don't think humans are trash," I say.

"I know you don't, Chancy, which is part of why I've

always loved you. You've been fed the same stories as all the other evians, but you open your genetically perfect eyes and look around at the world as it is. You draw your own conclusions, even when they're not popular ones." Alora drops her voice. "It's the reason you'll make a better ruler than Judica."

"So you think I should fight her?"

"I think Alamecha and the world would be better off if you defeated her and ascended the throne. I didn't say it's what's best for you. And we can't live by what should be. We have to live by what's possible."

"You had to let go of the regret."

Alora nods. "I did."

"If you weren't exiled, why did you come live with the humans?" Why didn't she stay in Ni'ihau for me? I could have used her help and guidance.

"After I gave them up, I mourned. Mother thought it would pass, but it didn't. Part of that may be Benjamin's fault." Alora looks wistful. "He really was incomparable. The man never gave up on anything. Every time he popped up somewhere, I relived my mistake, regretting it anew. Mother was furious every time, but I wasn't a complete moron. When I gave up the child, I made Mother promise she would protect William and his trouble-making father as well. Mom swore, not realizing how difficult her promise would be when she saw how distracting they were to me."

"But Mom would never—"

Alora chokes. "Don't Chancy. Don't defend her to me. I know you spent every waking minute with her. You think you know her, and maybe you do, but you don't know how much keeping you changed her. Fundamentally. The Mom you knew and loved was not the same mother who raised me. She was softer after you, not as cruel, and also stronger at the same time. She did many things in her nine hundred years that would make you squirm, if not hate her outright."

I lift my chin. I won't listen to Alora besmirch Mom. She was complicated and hard to understand, and sometimes people didn't know the truth. To the rest of the world, Mom ordered Lark's execution. Who knows what else Alora saw that might not have happened. I know Mom, and that's enough.

"The point is, seeing Benjamin's rising glory reminded me over and over of what I'd done. I couldn't move past it, and after Inara was born, Mother didn't need me anymore. That's when I realized that I'd given Benjamin and little William up... for nothing. I'd spent a full century training, learning, and studying for something that never came to pass. With Inara alive and well, I became extraneous. The sacrifice I made of everything that mattered to me felt so necessary at the time, but ultimately it was meaningless."

"You were angry and you stormed out?" I ask.

She shakes her head. "My anger had long since gone cold."

"You fell for someone else?"

She laughs. "Never again, not like that first time."

My heart sinks when I think of Alora's despair spanning centuries. It must show on my face.

"Don't look so crestfallen. I've fallen in love many times since then, but it was never the same, never like it was with Benjamin. Even when you live a thousand years, love like that is rare, almost non-existent. If it hadn't been my first love, I'd have recognized it for what it was: epic. I found the kind of love that changes who you are, and coupled with my loss..." She swallows. "I never should have let it go, and humans die so quickly."

"Then why did you leave the family?"

"I couldn't bear to stay, knowing I was unnecessary and seeing how hollow everything was. Everything that I valued became meaningless. I needed a clean break. And the saddest part is, I think Mother was relieved when I finally left."

I bite my lip. "She missed you. She never spoke of you, but she kept your photo on her dresser. She would stare at it sometimes."

Alora pats my head, like she'd comfort a dog. "I believe that. I have children myself, you know. And grandchildren, great- and great-great-grandchildren, some of whom you've now met. For propriety's sake, most of them don't know I'm their grandmother several times removed. They call me Great-Aunt Alora, and even that gets confusing. Once they realize they aren't aging normally, I fill them in, at least a little bit, on what it means to be part evian."

"So William? Your son, is he still...?"

"Alive?" She stares out the window. "Benjamin never divulged our secrets, but eventually I broke down and told William who I was, and I explained his legacy. And he was loyal to me, you know, very loyal, always to me and to Alamecha, even though the family spurned him. When the colonies decided to start their little revolution, before Mother decided to embrace it and rule this upstart group of people in a new way, he fought for me, for the family that despised him. In the end, he fought the father who raised him and who loved him dearly, and he did it for me, the mother who abandoned him."

"And?" I ask.

"He died for it, Chancy. He wasn't full evian you know, and he was more... susceptible. In the end, we think it was poison. People had begun to notice that he wasn't aging, even though he had false portraits painted depicting white hair and wrinkles. There were a lot of accusations of witchcraft then, and we think someone suspected he was different and took measures."

"I'm so sorry," I say.

"I recovered from that loss long ago."

Alora can say what she wants, but her eyes swim with unshed tears.

She takes a deep breath. "I'm not sure what the future holds for you Chancy, but there are lots of teenagers like you at Trinity doing normal teenage things. Mother told me you love TV, and I know they fascinate you, the humans. You could be happy with them, especially with my help. Living your life without the burden of leadership, without the sacrifice and the all-consuming demands it makes, it will free you. I'll support any decision you make if you promise me one thing. If your epic love appears, if your Benjamin comes along, whether he's evian or not, promise me you won't let him go, no matter the price."

"Thank you for supporting me."

"The last thing I'll say is that a thousand years is a long time to regret a mistake."

I think about Alora's story while I shower. By the time I dry off, I've made up my mind. Alora's story was about a guy. And while I think Edam and Noah are both intriguing, my decision isn't about choosing what kind of guy I want to build a life with. On the surface, Alora's story reminds me of Romeo and Juliet, but that interpretation misses the point. The real tragedy is that Alora didn't find her own path. She let Mom dissuade her from it, and she couldn't rewind a clock on the human she loved, or the half-human she lost. That became her defining moment, preventing her from finding her true calling.

I think back to my life before Mom's ring wrecked everything. I fought with Judica daily, and I was desperate to break free. Other than Mom being ripped away, the essentials haven't changed. My life still sucks and only one option offers me the chance to break out of the never-ending cycle.

I'm sorry Mom, if you're up there shaking your fist at

me. I'm terribly sorry if you're hungry for justice. Judica might have killed you, but killing her, if I even can, won't bring you back. I can't live my life for you, not anymore. Alora shouldn't have lived for you either. I have to live for myself. I don't know how I feel about Edam or Noah yet, but I know how I feel about myself, and I know I don't want to kill my twin.

I'm going to abdicate.

25

I ought to run downstairs and tell everyone that I've made my decision. But I don't. Alora told me to be one hundred percent positive, and I'm only a hair away from that. It's hard to go to breakfast and ride to school, all while pretending I'm crippled by indecision. But it's so freeing to have the peace of a plan, to have my future figured out again.

I flirt shamelessly with Noah during calculus, and again while we circle the track.

"So what are you doing after school today?" he asks.

"Studying, I guess," I say.

"Ha," Noah says. "You've gotten a hundred on every single assignment."

I quirk one eyebrow. "How do you think I do that? I study."

"Well, why don't you come study at my place? Or invite me to yours."

Edam drops in next to us. "You're not forgetting about your consultation today are you, Rebecca? Forget pulling strings, I yanked on them hard to get you a meeting with Dr. Kenning. You wouldn't want to miss it."

"With who?" Noah asks.

"Oh you didn't hear me?" Edam asks. "I said it's with Dr. None of Your Business."

I roll my eyes and lie on the fly, following Edam's example apparently. "He's a running specialist. He's going to analyze my pacing to see how I might improve."

"With her time, as a female, she could be Olympic bound, and soon." Edam beams at Noah.

"What about me?" Noah asks. "I'd be happy to pay for the entire consultation, if he'd like to take a look at my pacing."

Edam shakes his head. "I pitched you, believe me, but since you're a Chinese citizen technically, it was a hard sell. Dr. Kenning works exclusively with US Olympic hopefuls."

Edam's a better liar than I gave him credit for.

Noah drops to a walk. "Another time then," he says to me.

"For sure." Once Noah's far enough behind us, I slug Edam in the arm. "Stop baiting him."

"I never have any fun. But that I enjoyed."

I should tell him I've chosen to abdicate. I should give him time to process that fact. I open my mouth to tell him. But the wrong words emerge. "What time will the famous Dr. Kenning be arriving?"

Telling people something they don't want to hear is hard. Which means abdication really is the right call for me. Being Empress would involve a lot of telling people things they don't want to hear, and I can't even make myself break the bad news to Edam.

"Ha."

"Seriously though, what time are we training?"

"Right after school. I have some new ideas, actually."

"New ideas?" I ask. "Like the one you had after the party at Noah's?"

"Not that I mind the flirting." Edam grins wickedly.

"But maybe save it for when I'm not posing as your teacher." He drops his voice. "The humans are staring."

Right. I drop to a walk and pretend I don't feel foolish while I stretch and head to the girls' room to change. I prepare myself all day to tell Edam about the decision I've made, but after school, he doesn't give me an opening. He shows me a few new moves and points out some places I can use them, but he doesn't bring up the looming decision I need to make at all.

Alora has prepared a big dinner in the dining room right after we finish. All my guards, Lark, Edam, and a few of Alora's children are present. Edam takes the spot on my left, like a Consort would. Lark takes the seat of the Heir on my right. It's strange to be sitting at the head of the table.

I don't like it.

Which just strengthens my resolve.

The next morning, I steel myself to tell everyone. I can start with Lark, who will support me no matter what, and then I'll tell Alora, and I'll save Edam for last. He won't be pleased, but he deserves to know.

I've barely finished knotting my sneakers when I hear a tap on my door. I've gotten downright casual in my school attire, and I wonder what Alora will say, seeing as she had me dressing in a suit the first day. My older sister pokes her head into my room and looks around, her eyes wide, her heart practically racing.

"Is everything okay?" I ask.

She comes over to my bed and drops an envelope on the end of it. "A letter came for you yesterday via the normal postal service. Because my name was listed first as a 'care of,' my staff unwittingly dropped it into my regular mail."

My stomach lurches. "A letter from whom?"

Alora glances down at the thick ivory envelope and I

follow her gaze to the familiar handwriting. My stomach lurches.

"It's only a letter? No package with it?"

Alora shakes her head, squeezes my arm, stands up, and walks out.

My heart beats almost as fast as a human's would. I don't know what to do. I stand up, then I sit back down. I reach for it like I might reach for a pit viper, tentatively. Scared, excited, nervous. Finally though, I pick up the letter and hold it in my hands. It's addressed to me in Mom's perfect cursive.

Chancery Divinity Alamecha.

I don't know how long I stare at it before I use my finger to carefully separate the back flap from the rest of the envelope. I pull the parchment paper out carefully and unfold it.

Dearest Chancy,

I don't have much time, so you'll have to pardon any errors or imperfections. Today is my birthday, and I've never felt like this, not in nine hundred years. Aches and pains, trembling and hot flashes, a splitting headache, dry mouth, and cramps in my belly. I hope Alora has to call me and ask why I sent you a letter. I hope she can throw this letter out with a laugh.

But smoke comes before fire.

In case I'm not being paranoid, in case I'm in trouble, there are things you may need to know. I'm supposed to be listening to a report from. . . it doesn't matter. I'm pretending to pay attention. Today has been so busy I haven't had time to tell you some vital things. I've seen far too many people die and leave the world in upheaval. I won't do that to you.

I try not to clench my fist. Nice try, but no dice, Mom. You left my world an upside-down mess.

That's why this morning I changed the Heirship documents to name you as my Heir. I know you don't want it. You want to run away. Human life seems hopelessly romantic, but it's not for you. I know this, because I know you better than anyone else. I've loved you every single minute of every single day since you were born almost eighteen years ago, and I will love you every minute that I draw breath. I know your sister Judica will struggle with this change, but I hope that you and I together can help her understand my reasons.

It's not only about the stone, you know. I've been thinking about making this switch for quite some time, now.

You're not like her. You aren't vicious or savage, and you don't act out of anger or spite. You have trouble making hard decisions and you always look for a soft solution. I've always seen that as a liability, and it would be if your job was to carve out a place for the Alamecha family, but it isn't. You're destined for more than holding our ground, or even snatching up a little more.

I had no idea of the scope of God's plan for you when you were born. In fact, I spent a lot of time full of anger that having you and Judica at the same time complicated everyone's lives. But it was all part of your destiny, to be a unifier, a merciful and benevolent ruler the likes of which the world has not seen since Mahalesh herself.

But even Mahalesh needed Shenoah. They were different, but they complemented one another.

Similarly, you need Judica by your side. No matter what she's done, you must forgive her. You are who you are for a reason. You must unite the families and locate the Garden of Eden.

If you're reading this, it means I'm sick from being poisoned and I have died. It means I hid my ring and it's probably still missing—I didn't want it to be stolen by whomever is poisoning me. You will need time to sort all of this out, and by hiding the ring, I hope to delay the investiture to give you that time. You will know where I hid it if you think about it. When the time is right, the clues I left you will make sense. But the biggest clue is that I hid it in a place with value only to you, because that ring means something in your hands that it doesn't to anyone else.

You never developed your own spy network and you will certainly need one as monarch. I would like to gift mine to you. If you're reading this, the head of my network may be compromised. You already know who that is. I fear that individual may have had a hand in my demise. I hope it isn't the case, but don't approach her. Contact my second- lieutenant instead. If you think about the one I love more than any other, you'll be able to puzzle out my keycode.

It's almost time for my party and I must close this. But before I do, I need to tell you something that will probably break your heart as much as it does mine. Judica has resented you since she was old enough to feel the emotion. You know your father died while I was pregnant with you, but you may have wondered why I never chose a new Consort or tried to have another girl.

A new daughter would have solved all our problems, you may have thought. I can't answer that simply in the time I have here, but I will say, I loved my first Consort, Althuselah, as I have never loved another since. When I met your father, I was dwindling. I was thinking of walking away from everything, of abdicating the throne and spending what remained of my time here on Earth in retirement. Your father and I didn't share an epic love, and we were incompatible in many ways. But.

He made me feel again.

When I lost him too, my heart closed off forever, or so I thought. Sometimes we don't know what we need until it's right in front of our nose. Even without finding love again, I might have tried for another daughter, but I haven't had much luck having daughters. As you know, I've had two hundred and eleven sons, and only eighteen daughters. I had no assurances that if I had more children, they would be female. After keeping you, I knew I couldn't sell another son. It's a barbaric practice we should have eliminated long ago, but I selfishly wanted you girls to have options for Consorts who had been raised by Alamecha, so I didn't ever take a stand against it.

Be very careful with complacency, my daughter. A day quickly grows into a week, and a week quickly graduates into a month. If you feel something must change, do it now. Do not wait.

I'm nine-hundred years old and have lived a remarkably full life. If I am not with you any longer, please don't let your mourning dictate your course of action. I'm sure you'll ignore this because the heart is what it is. I feel robbed of the years I yet hoped to spend with you. But the thing I mourn the most if this is indeed my time is the loss of something very small but very precious.

Last week I discovered that the baby I am carrying, against my personal odds, is a girl. I want to name her Sotiris because I believe she might be your salvation, yours and Judica's too. If only she can come into the world, perhaps the enmity between you and your sister will finally evaporate. But if not, mourn your almost sister, dear one, as I mourn the loss of my time with you both. Accept the world as it is, or do something to change it.

And I do believe you will change it, in ways no one will expect, not even you. From the moment of your conception you've been throwing things off balance. Stop assuming it's a bad thing. Stop apologizing for it. You're more extraordinary than you can possibly know.

All my love,

Mom

It takes less than five minutes to read my Mom's letter, twice, but I still can't believe what I've read. Mom was pregnant, and with a little girl. Questions crowd my brain. Why? Who's the father? And then an overwhelming sorrow knocks me to my knees. I'll never meet my sister. She didn't even have a chance. And selfishly, I mourn what her loss means to me.

Mom was right. Sotiris would have set me free.

Last night I decided to abdicate, to let Judica rule Alamecha and selfishly take control of my life for myself. I was ready to live as Alora does. I was thinking of creating a society for the half-evians. Lark and my future children would have a place, somewhere to belong.

But if Mom was pregnant with a girl, then maybe she wasn't killed because Judica realized she was making me her

Heir. After all, Judica could have challenged me and defeated me after Mom died. I wasn't much of an impediment to her ascent to the throne. A new baby is different, though. A new daughter would be an Heir who would displace both Judica and me, and if Mom was pregnant, she might have taken a new Consort. Evians have been known to have children as late as 961 years old. She might have had even more daughters. A lot can happen in sixty years. Mom might not have stood up for me against my twin, but if she saw Judica as a threat to a new baby? I have no doubt she would have taken action.

Judica knew that. I thought she killed Mom before, but now. I close my eyes and every part of my body shakes with anger and sorrow. Mom might have wanted me to forgive Judica, even for taking her life. But this is different. Judica killed Mom because she was having another child. Because we were both being displaced.

Mom can't avenge Sotiris. But I can.

I'm not abdicating. I'm going back, because Judica can't be rewarded for what she's done. And even more than that, she must pay.

26

Edam, Lark, and Alora are waiting for me in the breakfast room. Alora must have told them Mom sent a letter.

I stop in the doorway, watching the cars in the morning traffic crawl past the window. My life turned upside down when Mom died, but New York has no idea. Life rolls along out here, people going to breakfast, and driving to work, and taking kids to school. Except not my mom, and not my little sister. They will never go to work or school. My mom will never hug me again, and I'll never meet Sotiris at all. I'll never be free of my burden, because even if I defeat Judica, I'll be saddled with guilt and obligation.

Which means Judica ruined everything like always, but so much worse.

I glance around the room. No guards in sight. "Where are the closest guards stationed?"

"I told them to wait outside," Alora says. "I thought you might want some privacy."

"Good, because this information is top level clearance only. Mom suspected she was being poisoned," I say. "And thanks to some information in her letter, I'm now certain it was Judica."

"I'm sorry," Alora says. "But are you surprised? I thought you already blamed her."

I slump down at the table. "I guess I was hoping, more than I realized, that she was innocent. The more I watched videos and saw how Judica reacted to Mom, the less I thought she could actually kill her. She denied it so vehemently. Judica is many things, but I've never known her to out and out lie."

Alora and Edam share a glance I don't understand. I consider telling them about Mom's pregnancy, but I just can't quite bring myself to say the words aloud. The question I can't resolve is, how did Judica find out Mom was expecting? If even I didn't know, how could she have discovered the secret that precipitated the poison? I think back on the tiny heartbeat I attributed to a mouse in the dark tunnel.

Maybe Judica heard Sotiris. Maybe she was smarter than me and knew the sound for what it was.

"I can't let her get away with it," I say. "I just can't. I'm going back. I'm not going to abdicate."

Edam's smile melts almost as quickly as it appears, but it's there. He's pleased, and for some reason that annoys me.

"You missed our session this morning. Ready to make it up now?" he asks.

I shake my head. "I'm eating a quick breakfast, then I'm off for school. I'm probably going to be late as it is."

Alora's eyebrows rise. "You're still going to school? Why?"

"Because Judica's watching her," Lark says.

"Exactly," I say. "If I don't show today, someone will report that I've decided to stay home. How do you think she'll react once she knows I'm not attending? I don't need to make myself a target. She gave me time to decide whether to abdicate, not a week to sit in your brownstone and prepare to kill her."

"But you're wasting time at Trinity," Edam says. "Unless...have you decided about my offer?"

I slam my hand down on the table. And my reaction tells me that I have decided. I can't take him up on his offer, no matter how dire my chances. I'll do this myself or not at all.

"I'm fighting her myself."

I grit my teeth at Lark's quick inhalation of air.

"That's a mistake." Edam's eyes flash. "You're like a terminal cancer patient insisting on full treatment. It's too little, too late, and like a terminal patient, you'll die."

"A terminal patient will die either way."

Edam huffs. "What I mean—"

"Is that really what you think?" I ask. "That I have zero chance of defeating her?"

Edam won't meet my eye, and I guess that's my answer.

I turn toward Alora. At least she'll look at me. "Do you think I'm in denial?"

Alora frowns. "I didn't say that."

"You haven't said anything about it at all. Inara told me to let Edam fight for me. Edam's my trainer and he thinks I don't have a chance, but you're a melodics master. If anyone would know whether I can defeat her with my current level of skill, it's you."

I need someone to tell me I can do this.

As though we're connected somehow, Lark says, "You can defeat her, Chancery, I know you can."

I close my eyes. I could barely defeat my half-human best friend. I love Lark and always will, but I need someone *other than her* to believe in me.

Alora sighs heavily. "It doesn't really matter what I

think, Chancery. The only person who needs to believe it is you."

"Did you see that on a bumper sticker yesterday?" I ask.

She doesn't even believe in me enough to attempt a lie. I grab a muffin and a banana and storm out of the breakfast room, bound for the car. Lark trails me, and so does Edam. When I stop, Lark continues on ahead.

"I'll tell Frederick to prepare the car," she says, ditching me with an angry man.

"Your sister won't tell you straight," Edam says. "And Lark will walk right up to the edge of the cliff and jump off with you, never once complaining. But this isn't a movie where the impossible happens because Hollywood wants to boost ticket sales. If we had more time, you could learn what you need to know. I believe in you all the way. You can defeat your twin, but a few more days won't give you enough time to get there."

"And how much time would be enough?" I hiss. "Another week? Two? A month? Two months?" I shake my head. "If you don't believe in me now, you never will. You'll always want me to need you, want me to use you. You'll never help me stand alone."

Edam flushes like I slapped him. "This isn't about my ego." He clenches his fist and the muscles in his arm ripple up and down. "We didn't speak much until a few days ago, but I've watched you my entire life." He swallows hard. "I mean that in the least creepy way possible. Ni'ihau is a small island."

"For a while, keeping an eye on me was your job."

"Exactly. Everyone watches everyone in that fishbowl. But recently I've seen you survive and rise above. I guess you're right that this is about me, but not in the way you think." He reaches out tentatively and touches my arm and a tingle zips from my chest out to my fingers and toes.

He drops his hands to his sides, his voice the barest of

whispers. "I want to fight her in your place because I can't bear the thought of losing you. Surely you know that by now."

This time when I look at him, Edam's eyes meet mine and his fear shines through. Edam's never afraid of anything. I should be swooning, but I'm not. Because his fear is based on an honest assessment of my skill. He thinks I'll lose, and that's not very heartening. I wish my mom was here, because I need her advice more than ever. How did she not anticipate Judica challenging me when she wrote that letter? A few lines telling me how to deal with this exceedingly predictable situation would have been fantastic.

Mom isn't here, but Alora is. I call her name, and her head pokes out of the breakfast room. "I need a minute," I tell Edam.

He nods, the set of his mouth grim.

I trot back in and close the door behind me. I don't waste any time with Alora. "No more vague opinions or noncommittal answers. And don't even think about telling me to follow my heart. I want to know what you'd do if you were me. Right now, with the experience you have, what would you do?"

Alora sinks into a chair. "You don't want to hear this, and so telling you will probably cause you to retrench. You're just like Mother. But you should take Edam's offer and live. No matter what other hangups you may have, if you don't defeat Judica, you die. It's a hurdle you need to clear, and Edam's a sure thing. That boy loves you. It's clear in every line of his body, every look, every grunt, every moody overreaction. I didn't tell you this before because no one else can feel what you feel. No one else knows whether this arrangement is something you can live with. But if you were ready to handle Judica yourself, you wouldn't be so conflicted."

She's right. I want to be good enough, but I'm not. Edam compared me to a terminal cancer patient, for heaven's sake. Obviously I need help.

Death of hope might be the worst kind of death there is.

"Fine," I say. "I'll do it. Before we head back, I'll take Edam as my Consort and let him handle the fight for me."

"Are you going to tell him that?" Alora asks. "Because he's right outside."

I nod numbly. "I should."

Alora calls his name, and he jogs through the door, eyes scanning the room for threats. Finally his eyes stop on me. He crouches down in front of me. "Are you okay? What's wrong?"

I shake my head. "I'm fine. And I've made my decision. I'll name you my Consort and let you fight in my place."

Death of hope for me, but the birth of hope for him. I watch it spread across his undeniably beautiful face. His eyes light up, his mouth opens in a smile, and his shoulders square. "Thank you," he says. Like I've offered him a present, or paid him a compliment instead of telling me he's stuck with me for a thousand years, fighting all my battles for me, watching my back forever.

"We can talk about details later." I can't sit here and stare at his joy, not right now. Not when it means the last supports of my world are caving in. "I don't want to be late." I stand up, and Edam steps back, dropping his hands.

His eyes find Alora's, searching for an answer. "Why are you still going to school, now that you've made up your mind?"

"We talked about this. Odds are high that she's at least monitoring my movements. I can't have her, I don't know, bombing Alora's house."

"We could fly back now. No need to wait for her to figure anything out."

I don't have a response to that, but I'm not ready yet.

"Are you sure this isn't about something else?" he asks.

"Like what?"

Edam clenches his jaw. "Are you going to Trinity to see Noah?"

I lift my chin. "What if I am?" This is a business arrangement, me naming him as Consort. Sure, maybe he doesn't want to see me harmed, but more than that, he wants to change the evian world. I'm a means to an end. I'm not the end itself, and pretending I am will only hurt us both. "It's not like you care."

Edam turns away. "I hope you don't expect me to go and watch you flirt."

"I don't expect you to come at all, Coach Renfro. I wouldn't dream of asking you to waste any more of your time on my high school drama."

I turn and head for the car outside, more agitated now that I've decided exactly what to do than I was before. Frederick and Lark are waiting when I get there, and neither of them offer criticism or advice. As though Bernard can feel my frustration and anger, he drives fast today, much faster than usual. In fact, in spite of my long discussions, we aren't even late. But before I go into the school, I pull out my phone and call Inara. She picks up on the first ring.

"Is everything okay?" she asks. "Did you get everything I sent?"

"I did, thanks."

"How are you?"

"Fine, I guess. Do you still think it's the right call to name a Consort?"

"I know you're young, and I know it's rushed," she says, "but I do. I really do. I think Mother was right. Alamecha needs you."

"Well, I've decided to do it. I'll name Edam as my Consort just before our flight leaves."

"I know it's hard, Chancy. But without the ring especially, and in the wake of Mother's passing, Alamecha needs a strong leader. Everyone knows Edam's an amazing fighter, so even beyond defeating Judica, he'll strengthen your position."

"I wish Mom was still here."

"We all do."

I hang up and jog to class. I slide into my seat as the bell rings.

Calculus may be boring now that I've figured it all out, but something about the monotony of school helps me to focus on thoughts of my future. Even so, I pity the poor idiots doomed to day after day of this kind of instruction. When Noah taps my shoulder, I drop my pencil. But then I spin around and smile at him. And I realize Edam was right. I totally came to school to see Noah.

When he leans over to hand me the pencil I dropped and our hands brush, I realize that Noah's the reason I struggled with taking Edam up on his offer. I thought it was because I wanted to handle Judica myself, but there have been plenty of great queens who simply aren't amazing fighters. There are other empresses who fight well but hate it. All of them have relied on their Consorts. And almost every queen uses her Consort when she's pregnant. He's been my best option since the moment Judica agreed I could bring him along. I wonder if she's been planning for this contingency all week.

The day creeps forward slowly. Lark grabs my arm in the hallway. "Francy Behman invited me to her house after school. I think I should go, since I'm supposed to be developing contacts. It's my whole purpose for being here. But if you're leaving right away—"

I shake my head. "Go. It's fine. I won't leave for Ni'ihau

without seeing you first. Go conquer the New York socialite scene so you can ferret out information for me."

Lark beams.

I really hope she's found someplace she will finally belong. Maybe here she won't fear for her life. I really want that for her, even if it'll never happen for me.

Noah jogs up and grabs my elbow. "You're going to be late for history, and I need you to be on time so I can copy from your paper."

I let him tug me toward class, suppressing my smile. Rationally I know he's a human teenager like any other. He's certainly no Benjamin Franklin. In fact, I barely know him. But he became my symbol for freedom, for escaping the fate I never wanted. And today I'll be saying goodbye, to him and to any chance of living a relatively normal life.

Not that Noah knows any of that.

"Hey," he says after school. "You didn't say. How did the meeting with that Olympic scout go?"

I shake my head. "He didn't even show. That coach is kind of a poser."

"No kidding." Noah snorts. "I could have told you that on day one."

"Well," I say awkwardly, wondering how to say goodbye without saying it. "I guess I'll see you."

"If you don't have any scouts or meetings today, you should come hang out with me. It's not like you need to study." He bobs his head toward the test I'm holding from history. It's really bizarre how their only real goal in school here is memorizing facts. I've known all the answers to this test since I was three, but facts alone don't prepare you for life. It's interpreting and processing information they should be learning, not lists of dates and events.

"No," I say, "I don't need to study, but I think I'm going to go for a run when I get home to clear my head."

"That's a bad idea. You're too young, and far too attractive to go running in New York alone."

I lift my eyebrows. "If I was older or uglier, then it would be fine?"

He grins sheepishly. "Maybe. Maybe not. But you'd be safer at any age if you let me come with you. In fact, why don't we run to your house. Is it far?"

I hesitate. Should I tell a stranger where Alora's house is? But I've been to his house, and Alora ran a check on him. Besides, what harm can a human really do to me? At worst, he sends buckets of roses to Alora when I don't show up at school tomorrow. I almost hope he does do something like that.

"Gramercy Park," I finally say.

"You've had a bad day," he says. "I could tell in class."

He doesn't press for any answers, and I don't offer any.

"I'll jog over with you and take a cab back here to my car." He taps some buttons on his phone. "It's only four miles. Or if you want a more scenic run, if your driver drops us off, we could jog by Gracie Mansion and walk along the East River." He cranes his neck. "Isn't that your driver?"

I follow his gaze to where Bernard's waiting on the curb. "Yep."

"Where's your sister?" Noah pays attention.

"She went home with a friend," I say.

"So... is that a yes?"

Jogging down the East River with a cute guy and driving around town. I'm not ready to stop pretending this could be my life. And it's not like I need to rush back to train, not anymore. "Sure. Why not?"

Noah waves at Bernard. "Hello there, sir. Are you familiar with FDR by the 9th Street Ferry Terminal?"

Bernard frowns. "I know all of Manhattan." Which Noah probably doesn't believe, but I'm sure is true.

"Could you drop us there so we can take John Finley down to Gramercy Park?"

Bernard looks over his shoulder at Frederick, who shakes his head vehemently.

But Frederick isn't my boss. I'm his. And if I can watch Edam kill my sister, I can call the shots on the route for a jog.

"Today is the nicest day we've had since I landed in New York," I say. "There can't be many clear, sunny, fifty-degree days like this." Besides. I don't need to train with Edam, not anymore. I have all the time in the world. "So you'll drop us off without complaint." I pin Frederick with a stare I hope is half as strong as Mom's.

Frederick nods, but he looks nervous. I whisper softly as I climb in the car, "You can have some guys trail me when we get out."

Frederick's resigned expression eats at me, but I ignore it. I'm going to be getting a lot of huffy looks in the coming weeks until people become used to the fact that I'm in charge.

When Bernard stops the car and we get out, Noah extends his arm, offering to carry my bag.

So stinking cute.

My human wannabe boyfriend is going to take my bag so my arm doesn't get tired. I shake my head. "I'll leave it in the car."

"Duh," he says. "I'm an idiot."

"You're a cute idiot."

He beams at me.

We start off at a brisk pace, and I try to watch the scenery and not the human.

He doesn't even bother to look at anything but me. "So what's going on with us?"

"Excuse me?" I ask.

"We kissed, and from my end, there were like, I don't

know, fireworks. Literal and figurative. And then you essentially bolted after that."

"Okay."

"Was it really that bad for you?" Noah bumps my hip with his and the movement is so natural, so casual, so *normal* that it physically pains me. This is what I want. Maybe not with him, but with someone exactly like him. All the things evians can't have, all the things I'll never have, that's what I long for, but is it only because I know I can't have it?

"Things in my life are complicated," I say. "Really, supremely, more-than-you-would-ever-believe complicated."

"Please tell me you aren't dating Coach Renfro just for his senior discount," he says. "Because I'm loaded. You don't need a discount with me at all. Like, I've never even used a coupon in my entire life. Not even a Groupon."

"Wait, you have money? I heard you were at Trinity on scholarship." I roll my eyes.

Noah stops cold and I stumble a step or two to stop.

"Seriously," he says. "I joke a lot, but I really want to know. Did I ruin everything by kissing you? You can tell me, and as pathetic as this sounds, even if you're not into me, I'm okay with being friends." He cringes. "Or, you know, I'll try and figure out how to be okay."

"You barely know me," I protest.

"I've seen enough."

He's seen enough. It's my appearance, I realize. My perfect DNA is hard for humans to ignore. Of course he's into me, what with raging teenage boy hormones. At least with Edam I know he likes me for more than my looks—since Judica's match mine precisely and he detests her.

"Noah, it's not—"

He kicks a soda can. "It's not you, it's me?"

"Huh?"

"Nothing," he says. "I promise not to bring it up again, okay?"

Unlike every other person I know, practically, Noah wants nothing from me except my time and company. He doesn't want power, or prestige, or position. He's not asking for a favor, or hoping that I'll owe him one in the future. Because he has no idea who I really am. It's nice pretending. Really nice.

"You miss her, don't you?" he asks. Before I can respond, he says, "I'm sorry. I shouldn't have pressed you, or badgered you to talk about your mom or us either. I'm so used to being selfish that sometimes I don't even realize when I'm being a jerk."

I shake my head. "I miss her every minute of every day. I think I always will, but you didn't know her so it's okay. No one knows how to act around me, even my own family. I get it."

"I wish I did."

"Me too," I say. And I mean it. Mom would have liked Noah's insouciance, his snark, and she would have hated it a little bit, too. Which I would have loved.

He reaches over and takes my hand with his, lacing our fingers together again and it's so easy and relaxing and calm. He doesn't say anything else, and he doesn't try to run again either. He simply strolls along the road next to me. I can almost pretend we're normal high school students walking amidst shoppers, joggers, moms with kids in tow, bike messengers, and groups of teenagers. When I look over my shoulder, I notice Donovan and Renni in black, strolling down the road. If I glance far ahead, I see Mathias and Simeon, but other than that, I can almost pretend I'm not who I am.

"It's really beautiful in the spring," he says. "In a few more weeks, these streets will be lined with cherry blossoms and, you know, leaves on the bushes."

"It's already beautiful," I say. "Look at the people on the benches, and the people running to make it to a meeting. They all have a purpose, they're all doing what they can with the time they have." Alora's right. Humans have a different perspective because their time is so limited.

"You're introspective today. If you get any more somber, I may drag you back into the river."

"You just want to see my undies again."

Noah rolls his eyes. "Duh."

I move toward the edge of the walkway and look out over the river. A fish jumps out of the water and birds swoop at him. He barely dips back under the water before a seagull snags him and flies off, wings pumping while the idiot fish flails uselessly. No control over his own destiny.

I know the feeling.

When I turn back toward Noah, he's watching me. I cross my arms and wonder what he sees.

"You look so sad." He takes two steps toward me, his heart beating faster than usual. "Almost like you're trying to figure out how to say goodbye to me. Which is crazy because you just moved here, right?"

He's far too perceptive for a human kid, maybe because he doesn't have an agenda. When you're trying to work an angle, it's harder to truly see into another person's motivations. Your desires get in the way. I want to tell him the whole truth about who I am and what happened. I want to tell him about Judica, and the ring and Mom's death. I want to get perspective from someone with nothing to gain and nothing to lose. But I can't, because... I can't really think why I can't. His best friend in school is half-evian, and if I want to use him later as a contact, he'll need to know.

"Actually," I say, feeling him out, "I'm thinking of going back home."

"This summer?" he asks.

I shake my head. "No, sooner."

He steps closer, his head hovering a few inches away, his stormy blue eyes locked on mine. "You can't do that," he whispers.

"I can't?"

He shakes his head slowly, his dark hair falling in his face. He brushes it back with one hand. "My life would sink back into utter boredom. I hate to make this all about me, but that's just how it's going to have to be." He grins at me. "You have to stay."

My stomach flip flops. Noah isn't as muscular as Edam, and he's not as commanding or impressive, but I know his intentions. I know what he wants without a doubt, even if he likes my looks most of all. And I want him, too.

"I don't have a reason to stay in New York," I say softly. "And I have a lot of things pulling me back home."

"You don't have any reason to stay here?" Noah's hand brushes against mine, his fingers rougher than I remembered.

"No reason at all."

His head dips lower. "Are you sure?"

I swallow and his eyes drop to my lips.

In the space of one blink, he closes the space between us and presses his mouth to mine. It's just like our first kiss, and it's completely different. It's the cry of seagulls, and the wind in our hair. It's the freedom of his arms, and the uncertainty of leave-taking. It's longing and resignation and desire, tangled like our hands, mussed like our hair, and urgent like his lips against mine.

"Don't go," he whispers.

I can't promise to stay, so I kiss him back instead. His arms wrap around my waist again, pulling me closer without demanding things, sheltering me without dictating my future. And somehow, in the midst of my crazy, tumultuous world, I'm safe in the circle of his human hands. Nothing can hurt me with Noah by my side.

But of course none of this is real, because I'm reinforced steel to his tissue paper. Noah can't keep me safe. His world is a sandbox compared to my lion's den.

When I pull back, Noah lets me, but the longing in his eyes tugs at my heart. I wish I'd been born into another life, another family. Then maybe Noah could be the one for me.

Noah lets me slide out and away, but his warm breath shifts my hair when he says, "Why are you really leaving?"

His murmured words distract me from a sound I should have recognized. If I hadn't been wishing quite so hard, I might have been paying better attention. I might have evaded the bullet that punches through my right shoulder.

27

The shot takes out a chunk of my arm and spins me all the way around until I'm facing the strike team. They're wearing plain clothes, but they're packing 1911s. That .45 would have stopped me cold if it had been hollow point and a little to the left. How did the idiot shooter miss my body, or even better, my head? They're wearing masks and gloves and they're dressed in black gear, but that can't disguise their frames. There are four of them, and I flog my fuzzy brain to process the data in front of my eyes.

The first is tall, even for an evian. He's got to be close to seven feet. A small blond curl pokes out from under his black mask. The second is tall but not as tall, and he's broad. I can't see any hair, but the bump in the back of his masked head tells me his hair is long, probably pulled back in a ponytail. The third is a woman whose footwear I recognize. Valentino Rockstud Boots, customized for her. I already know the soles of the boots are crossed with spider webs.

Her real name is Rivera, but she's goes by Recluse. Rivera hasn't trusted anyone since her brother died in the field. Her anger needed an outlet, and she naturally gravitated toward the angriest person I know, my twin. I don't recognize the fourth man, but if Rivera's leading the team, Judica sent them. The tall one is Deitrich, the broad man is Lorn, and the fourth could be any of her other guards. Somehow, Judica found out I'm naming Edam as Consort. The odds may have shifted in my favor finally, but only if I survive this assassination attempt.

By the time I shove Noah to the ground, I've already healed from the ill-aimed shot.

"Stay down," I say.

"Wait, did someone shoot you?" Noah tries to stand, but I kick his legs out from under him, slamming him face down onto the pavement. A broken nose is better than a hole in the head.

They fire three more shots, one slamming into my left leg, one whizzing past my head and one lodging in my left clavicle.

"Noah, stay down." I dig the fingers of my right hand into the hole in my shoulder and yank on it until I dislodge the bullet. When I toss it into the river, I glance at Noah, who promptly rubs his eyes. I shouldn't have yanked the bullet out like that, but it might have been an exploding round. Besides, I can't heal with a bullet lodged in my bone.

"Did we stumble in to some kind of gang fight?" Noah tries to stand again.

I shove him down again. "Noah, stay down and close your eyes. Trust me." Maybe we can take care of this fast and he'll think he hallucinated it.

I look back at my four shooters, clustered together against a building for cover. Hiding together is their biggest mistake. They should be coming at me from several different locations. When I glance back, I realize why they're huddling. Donovan and Renni have taken out two other assailants on the north side, but Renni is down too. A glance to the south shows Mathias and Simeon with a man face down on the pavement, but Simeon's limping.

It's good my guards are doing their job, but there's no one to take out these four.

I crouch down next to Noah, who is finally listening to me and staying near the ground.

Rivera and her crew are picking their way toward me, operating under the assumption that I'm unarmed and help isn't coming. FDR runs directly below us. I might be able to drop down and escape, but I don't want to abandon Noah. He'd break his leg at the very least from a fall like that, but if I ditch him after they saw us kissing, they might use him as a hostage. I unclasp my necklace with nervous, fumbling fingers. I've practiced for this scenario, but never encountered it before today.

"Do you think they're going to rob us?" Noah asks, eyeing my disassembly efforts.

"Hush, and close your eyes."

"You know that ostriches are widely considered the dumbest animals?" Noah says. "Closing my eyes won't keep us safe." He starts casting around for rubble and grabs a handful of rocks.

Heaven help me.

I carefully remove several of the purple gemstones and activate each one. I set the faux purple gems on the ground, slide the straps off my necklace and hook them on the edges of the pendant. Now they've been activated, each bead will take out anything in a one-foot blast radius. "Flat on the ground, Noah."

My first shot takes off Lorn's left leg. Pink mist, bomb squads call it, and that's just how it looks. The rounds are made to be almost entirely silent, but they deal maximum damage. It's going to be tremendously painful to regrow that limb, and it'll take days and days. Serves him right for attacking wherever Judica points, including his rightful Empress.

Rivera and Dietrich each break in opposite directions, but the fourth attacker heads straight for me. He gets one shot off, which grazes my side, before I explode his head. I didn't want to kill him, but he got too close. I might have survived a few more rounds, but Noah can't, and I won't risk his life.

"Oh my gosh, what just happened?" Noah asks. "Is that guy dead?"

"No, this is a dream," I say.

Noah rubs his eyes. Repeatedly.

I aim for Rivera next, but just before I release the shot, Noah grabs my arm. "Dream or not, look."

I follow his finger to the movement behind Rivera. A little girl wearing a red backpack is walking behind her. There's a sign on the faded brick building behind them that reads: Brearley School. The huddling makes even more sense. They had a plan all along. Who would attack them in front of a primary school?

If my blasts hadn't been so quiet, the kids would probably be hiding. Why didn't the gunshots in my direction scare them off? What is wrong with New Yorkers? While I hesitate, three more children round the corner. I can't risk another blast.

A tiny flash above and to the left alerts me and I glance up, right at the crosshairs of a sniper trained on my head. I cannot catch a break. I hate that Frederick was right, but this run was a terrible idea. With my back up against the rail, my options have dwindled to one: the river. Frederick is going to kill me, but this is my best bet. I just need to decide whether to bring Noah along.

It's a big drop over the rail, and Noah already looks freaked out. They haven't aimed at him once. Hostage risk aside, he's probably safer if I just disappear.

I stand up to leap over the rail, because if I'm on the move, they'll probably stay on me. Dietrich fires off another shot while I deliberate. Noah jumps in front of me like a moron, and I yank us both backward into the river, Noah's shoulder in one hand, my necklace in the other.

The frigid water slaps against my face, flooding my mouth with salt, and sending even more adrenaline into my bloodstream. I release Noah long enough to re-clasp my necklace. Then I spin him around.

"Were you hit?" I ask.

Noah should not have tried to save me. Clearly Noah is an idiot. I just hope he's not about to be a dead idiot.

"I'm not sure they were firing real bullets." Noah mouth trembles from the cold as he treads water next to me. "You seem fine, too. Is it possible we walked into someone filming a movie?"

I wonder when he'll remember that I exploded someone's leg and another man's head. Maybe he didn't notice.

"It wasn't a movie, Noah. And if we don't put some space between us and them, they'll keep coming," I say.

He bobs his head and starts swimming. I look over my shoulder repeatedly, but don't see them. After I ignore his questions for a while, he stops asking them. Probably because he's either exhausted, freezing to death, or both.

When we finally crawl out on the edge of some soccer field, parents and coaches rush over to check on us. I guess even in NYC, two teenagers climbing out of the East River is noteworthy. According to signs, we're on Roosevelt Island.

"Whoa," a lady holding a bright pink bag and wearing a green Adidas jacket says, "Did you two fall in? Are you okay? I'll call 911."

"No," I say, "it's fine. Our parents will ground us for life if they find out. Please don't."

She frowns. "We have to do something."

Noah steps in. "It was a dare. You know how goofy high school kids can be. But don't worry, we'll head straight home."

It takes him a few more minutes, but Noah calms the parents down admirably. By the time he's done, he walks back toward me wearing one donated jacket and holding another in his hand. I slide it on with a grateful smile, even though it smells like Cheetos. At least it blocks the wind.

"Your name isn't Rebecca, is it?"

I shake my head. "Chancery Alamecha."

"And Laura isn't actually your sister?"

Another shake.

"I should have realized that. You look nothing alike."

"Why aren't you freaking out right now?" I ask.

He narrows his eyes at me. "You're the one who got shot, but remarkably, unbelievably even, you seem fine. Maybe I should be the one asking the vaguely aggressive questions."

"Fair enough." I wanted to tell him before, and now I have an excuse. But we can't stand around here in the open, waiting for Judica's hit squad to catch up. I start walking toward the north end of the island and he follows, pelting me with questions.

"Who are you?" he asks. "And why don't you appear to be injured? Are we on the set of some movie? Were they firing blanks? Because I thought I saw real blood. And what kind of name is Chancery?"

I switch to Mandarin, which I assume he speaks. "You keep asking who I am, but it's less about who I am, and more about *what* I am."

His eyes widen, and he responds in Mandarin. "You speak Mandarin, and you're super duper hot." He swallows. "Are you—" He blinks repeatedly. "You're an alien, aren't you?" He bites his lower lip, the lip I was just kissing.

I laugh. "I'm not an alien. But before I explain. . . what do you know about DNA?"

"DNA?" His eyebrows rise. "Like, adenine, thymine, guanine, cytosine? That kind of DNA?"

"Yes, exactly that DNA."

"Uh, I know that it replicates."

"Good," I say. "What else?"

"Umm, it tells our cells what to do, like a blueprint so they can reproduce over and over."

"Also correct, but here's where we dip into something different."

Noah watches me more than the road as we jog toward the Roosevelt Island Bridge. "Okay. Are you going to tell me?"

"I've never told a human before."

His eyebrows rise and he stops. "A human? As in, you're *not* human?"

"You've heard of Adam and Eve?"

He nods. "Yep, they've come up. I may not be religious myself, but I have heard of the origin story that Christianity, Judaism, and Islam share."

"Okay, well, they aren't wrong. Even the Hindus still have quite a few details right. You've read the *Rig-Veda*, I assume?"

Noah shakes his head.

"It doesn't matter, really, but there's a quote in there I liked a lot. 'Whence all creation has its origin, He, whether he fashioned it or whether he did not, He, who surveys it all from highest heaven, He knows, or maybe even He does not.' So even some of the Hindus envision a single creator of some sort, whether it's a combination of Brahma, Vishnu and Shiva, or something else."

"Okay, sure. It's either that, or we came from monkeys, right?" Noah shrugs.

"Actually, evolution posits that we share an ancestor

with apes, but not that we came from them. But we're getting sidetracked. The point is that Adam and Eve did live, and they were the first humans. They also had perfect DNA, handed to them from the creator."

Noah snorts.

"You think it sounds unlikely, and that's fine. But for me, Adam and Eve were my great-great-great-great-great-grandparents."

"Let's assume I believe this, which I don't, to be clear, but assume I do. Why is it that you're only a few generations away from good old Grandpa Adam and Grandma Eve?"

I sigh. "Their DNA was perfect. With time, the DNA in your body starts to break down, hundreds, thousands, millions of replications later. Then your skin isn't as elastic, your body sags, wrinkles, and so on. You get age spots, and your body doesn't heal quickly."

"Sure, we all age."

I shake my head this time. "No. We don't all age at the same rate."

"People are always saying my dad looks amazing for his age. Is that what you mean?"

Could his dad be half-evian? "Maybe. But it's more than looking good. The average human doesn't live more than a hundred years."

"Okay."

"I'll live a thousand years, or close to it, before I begin to experience the same aging issues that you'll face in less than one hundred."

"Wait, why will you live so long?"

"My DNA is better," I say simply. "I heal more efficiently, run faster, process data better, and jump higher than you do. It's not arrogance or superiority that I'm spouting. Those are all facts. We aren't human, which is a word we developed for those with degraded DNA. Those of us with very few genetic deletions call ourselves evian, from the pure line of Eve."

Noah starts walking then, not looking in my direction, hands stuffed in his pockets. We turn on Vernon Road, and he still hasn't said another word.

"Look, the issue is that our DNA hasn't suffered any decay. But human DNA has been through thousands of tiny genetic deletions."

He stops and swivels to face me. "Deletions?"

"Yes, the very end of the DNA chain drops off the sequence sometimes when cells split. Maybe once every couple thousand replications. Maybe less, or maybe more. It's not exact, but that's why we age, remember?"

"Fine, I'll play along."

I don't scowl at him. It's natural that he doesn't believe me. "Eve's youngest daughter lived as long as Eve, but was born nearly a thousand years after Eve and Adam were created on Earth."

"Okay, sure. Why not?"

"Her name was Mahalesh, and Alamecha the name of Mahalesh's youngest daughter. She was technically the heir to all that Mahalesh had, or should have been. Alamecha was also my great great great grandma."

"So you're seven generations—"

"Six," I say, cutting him off. "I'm six generations removed, or seventh generation myself, from the woman the Bible calls Eve."

"So you're like super old?"

I laugh. "No. I'm actually seventeen, just like you."

"Are you being serious right now? You're some kind of superhuman and you call yourself evian? Like the water?"

Mom and her weird sense of humor. "Yes, like the water."

"For real?"

"My mother has a warped idea of what's funny." I roll

my eyes. "She started that company as a joke, but it's kind of taken off, and now we're stuck with it. Edam thinks it's hilarious and refuses to drink anything but Evian."

"Wait, who's Edam?" he asks.

"Right, sorry. Coach Renfro's real name is Edam."

"Oh! So that guy is one of you? He is like Eve's great-great-grandson. No wonder he looks so old." Noah smirks.

"Noah, this isn't a joke."

"It has to be a joke," he says. "Because otherwise I'd have heard something about it. People would know about this."

I shake my head. "People knew, thousands of years ago, but it caused problems. First, humans tried to worship us. That may sound awesome, but it's not. It gets really old. Then people grew envious and attacked us."

"You heal fast though, right?" His eyes sparkle. He doesn't believe me.

"Yes. We do." I grit my teeth. "Look, I'm not supposed to be telling you. We have very strict laws about this."

"You could like dominate the entire world, but you don't? You hide in the shadows, because you're so benevolent?"

Boy does he have this wrong. "No, nothing like that." I wonder whether this was a mistake. I could stop now and no one would ever believe a word. Heck, he doesn't even believe me. But he's so earnest in his mocking, and he has been so supportive up until now. I plunge ahead. "So here's the deal. My mom was sort of a pioneer, okay? We've been ruling the entire world for millennia, but once we realized how problematic it is to be different, we grew weary of dealing with human tantrums and attacks and whatnot. We developed our own societies outside of humanity, but we—"

I stop. We use them. We use the humans around us, because we don't care about them. They have no value to us. How can I say that to him, even though it's true? It sounds so wrong.

Which probably means it *is* wrong.

"Look, my mom decided that humans would be more helpful, would produce more cheerfully if we provided them with freedom."

Noah lifts one eyebrow. "Your mother's an altruist?"

Not exactly. I cringe, inwardly. "Maybe this will help. Look, hundreds of years ago Mom had a menagerie."

"You mean, like a zoo?"

"A private zoo. She loved it, but her animals got depressed, right? They moped around, did nothing, and then some of them ate nothing. It got bad enough that they died. Cheetahs first, and then others, too. She brought in specialists to figure out what was wrong. She loved the predators most of all."

"And?"

"And she discovered that while they loved having food provided for them, and they even loved my mother, they hated feeling enclosed. So she created a new park for them with habitats ten times the size of the old ones."

"What happened?" Noah asks.

"The animals flourished. They bred in captivity, they played, pounced and thrived."

"Because they needed freedom."

I shake my head. "Not quite. They needed the appearance of freedom."

Noah frowns. He should frown. Saying this out loud depresses me.

"Mom realized her humans were suffering in a similar way. They would chafe at the laws, the rules, the demands. They would even refuse to eat, figuratively. She ignored everything her mother taught her, everything her rivals did. She fashioned a new model. She decided to give them a pen that was ten times bigger. She engineered a fake rebellion that made a bunch of the humans think they were in charge. They believed they were free from England."

"America?"

I nod. "And it worked. They thrived on the appearance of freedom."

Noah tosses his hands in the air. "America is free. I've seen the elections. People travel wherever they want. They own their own homes and property."

I drop my voice to a whisper. "They love their really large and spacious pens."

"Huh?"

"Passports, taxes, bureaucracy. How much do you think humans in America pay in taxes?"

Noah shrugs.

"They pay local taxes, state taxes, federal taxes, social taxes, sales taxes."

"You're saying all of that flows through to you?"

"Of course it does. And some of the humans know it, and some of the others know something is wrong on a subliminal level. Have you heard of pork barrel spending? Humans decry the horrible waste of government. They gripe and do exposés on how terrible it is that so much money just disappears."

"You guys *are* pork barrel spending?"

"Of course we are. And on top of that, the highest level humans all know who we are, and they do what we say."

Noah shakes his head again. "What about the elections?"

"Bigger pen," I say. "They're obviously rigged. Do you really think Americans voted for that guy everyone hated so vocally? Come on." I shrug. "But humans believe their pen isn't there, so they ignore the fencing when they see it."

His mouth drops.

"Look, some Presidents have even come close to blabbing. They've walked a fine line."

"Like who?" Noah's eyes light up.

"One time, President George W. Bush was on some talk show and someone else had just taken over. People were freaking out, and they asked him, 'aren't you worried about this!?' His response ticked my mom off, but I thought it was clever. And people didn't credit George W. with a lot of smarts, but that was mostly an act. A very good act, but an act."

"What did he say?"

"He pointed to the desk in the Oval Office and he said, 'Don't worry. Whoever occupies that seat behind that desk, will quickly find out that their hands are tied and they'll end up doing almost exactly as I have done.'"

"He didn't say that. You couldn't possibly recall exactly what he said."

I shrug. "Look it up. I'm evian." I tap my forehead. "Perfect recall."

"Did he really?"

"Look, the humans all assumed he meant that the checks and balances kept them safe from sweeping change in the executive branch."

"But that's not what he meant?"

I tsk. "We control all three branches. We can do or change whatever we want. But. . ."

"Bigger pen," Noah says, his eyes shuttered.

"You're catching on."

"And it worked."

"Mom's holdings and power have only grown, because happy humans work harder, produce more, and well, they thrive."

Noah whistles.

"Except I wasn't kidding when I said my mom died." My throat closes off. "On her nine-hundreth birthday."

"Oh man," he says. "I am really sorry. I was hoping that was part of your cover."

"She was poisoned," I say. "She would've lived a few more decades at least if she hadn't been."

He stops in the middle of the path and a biker almost hits him. He glances my direction and then back at the road.

He wants to believe me, but when he's not focused on understanding, his mind rejects it.

"I get it," I say.

"You get what?" He scowls.

"I get how this feels."

"Pardon my rudeness here, but how could you possibly have any idea how I'm feeling right now?"

I lean on the hand rail overlooking the water. "When I was five, I finally wondered where beef came from."

"Huh?"

"I loved tacos, you see. I ate a lot of them. Breakfast, lunch, or dinner, I insisted on tacos. Beef and sour cream, and nothing else."

"Okay."

"In Hawaii, a lot of what we eat grows locally. Bananas, pineapples, avocados, papaya, I'd seen it all. I'd even seen cocoa beans."

"Sure, that makes sense."

"I knew wheat was ground into flour and formed into tortillas. But I'd never seen a beef plant, so I asked Mom where it came from? What kind of plant produced beef?"

The side of Noah's mouth turns up. "That's cute."

"I didn't find it cute then. When Mom told me I was eating a dead animal, my entire world turned upside down. At first I didn't believe her. That was nonsense. How could we kill *animals* and eat them? Why would we do that? Who even thought of that as an idea the first time?"

"Well, cheetahs, lions, wolves."

"Sure, but I hadn't thought it all through," I say. "I was shocked, and disgusted, and in denial."

"And then your mom explained about veal?"

I swat his arm. "Hilarious, and no. I didn't learn about that until last year, and I convinced Mom never to serve it again. Horrifying."

"Look, this is a lot to take in, more than the concept of eating dead things."

"It is," I say. "It's a shift in your entire worldview, and your place in the world. Believe me, I get it."

"Wait, my place?"

"I misspoke," I say. "What I meant was, it's a lot to take in."

"So far, I only have your word to go on," he says.

"You saw me get shot earlier. You said you did."

"I saw blood," Noah says slowly. "And I thought I saw you get shot, that's true."

I shrug my jacket down and show him the bullet hole in the shoulder of my shirt. "You did see me get shot." I put my finger through the hole. "But our better DNA makes us... well... better. It healed immediately."

He raises his eyebrows. "Wait, do you mean?" He licks his lips. "Like it healed. . . in minutes?"

"Seconds."

He shakes his head. "No way. That can't possibly be true."

"I know it sounds insane, but think it through. My body does the same things yours can do. I run, I jump, I heal, I think. It just do what you do. . . faster and better."

His mouth opens but no words come out.

"Well, it can do a few things yours can't. I hear humans can't regrow fingers, for instance, but you've seen lizards regrow their tails. It's the same concept."

"No." He shakes his head. "Now you sound completely nuts."

"You saw me get shot more than once." I point at the hole in my sopping wet jeans. "The blood washed off in the river, but I took a bullet in my leg, too." I raise the side of my shirt and show him the hole there. "And here. The injuries healed before I started swimming for safety."

Noah switches back to English, maybe without realizing it. "When I saw you pull off your necklace and turn it into little bombs you could use to protect us, I thought, this chick is bad-A. She's kind of crazy, but I like it. I was wrong though. This isn't awesome, it's unbelievable. And your evidence to support this story is a few holes." He backs away from me as quickly as he can. "I'm sorry, but it's not enough."

"Noah, stop," I say. "You have to listen to me. I know it's a lot to process."

"No," he says, "you must've given me something. Acid? LSD? What was it? This is all some kind of whacked out trip."

We aren't the only people standing on the Queensboro Bridge, and we're starting to attract more attention than the guy taking a leak on the corner. I look around frantically for anything I can use to prove my point, but I don't see anything. No knives, no rebar, and no glass shards. Where's an empty beer bottle when you need one?

I'm going to have to break a bone, which is unnecessarily grotesque, but he's turning around to leave. It's now or never. I scan the bridge quickly to make sure no one is filming us. Thankfully it's clear.

"Noah," I say, "wait. I can prove it."

He pauses and raises a skeptical eyebrow. "How?"

Go big or go home, I think. "Watch."

I brace my left arm with my right and slam it down on the railing hard enough that it snaps my radius and ulna both in two. Tears spring unbidden to my eyes and I whimper.

Noah's mouth drops open and he starts sputtering. I'm worried he may be having a seizure, so I try to calm him down by grabbing his arm reassuringly with my good hand. He looks at me like people on zombie shows look at a shuffling assailant from the undead horde.

I let go, and Noah twists and darts around me. I can't really stop him, thanks to my shattered arm.

"Two seconds," I beg. "Just watch this for two seconds." I use my good arm to reduce the breaks, my least favorite part, after which my arm heals swiftly.

Noah stares slack-jawed. It's not his best look. "Wait, what just happened?" His voice is high and squeaky and his perspiration spikes.

"I know, it happens so fast it's hard to believe right? But it still hurts, so please don't make me do it again. This is real, Noah. I'm not lying."

He reaches toward my arm, but pauses before actually touching it. He looks up at my face slowly. "This is a lot to take in."

"I understand."

Noah's face is pale, and between the river leap and the cold, I worry he might be going into shock. "Can you hear me Noah?"

He scowls. "I may not be super human, but I hear people fine when they yell."

I'm not yelling, but I don't bother defending myself. "Do you have any questions?"

"You really are leaving tomorrow?" he asks. "Nothing I can do to stop you, since you're like super girl."

"I told you my mom died," I say, "but I didn't mention that I'm heir to her throne and I have a twin sister who wants to fight me to the death to take it away."

Noah blinks and blinks. "Wait. What?" He runs his hand through his hair. "Does that mean Coach Renfro isn't really your older sister's friend?"

I roll my eyes. I clue Noah in on the truths of the universe, and he's worried about Edam.

"Uh, no," I say. "Actually, he's sort of my guard, except." I swallow. "We're getting married in two days."

"Excuse me? The old guy? You're marrying him?"

I sigh. "We'll be alive for close to a thousand years."

"Is this, like, an arranged marriage? Because he's a real drag. Plus, you didn't seem to mind kissing me. If I were engaged, I definitely wouldn't want my fiancé kissing someone like we kissed earlier." He lifts one eyebrow smugly.

"It's not arranged, no." I bite my lip.

"He proposed and you accepted, at seventeen years old? And what were you doing at Trinity, anyway?"

"I turn eighteen in a week, okay? And I'm at Trinity for —well it's a long story. But Edam did ask me, and I agreed. Things are complicated."

"More complicated than 'I'm a genetic super human who rules the world, even though no one has heard of us or seen us?'"

I grin, because this is the Noah I know. "Remember the twin sister who I said wanted to kill me?"

He nods.

"Well, she's a much better fighter than I am. Our people settle disputes between rulers through mortal combat. We've done it like that for six thousand years. Mom had named my twin as her successor, but after Mom died, the paperwork had been changed. To name me instead. My sister didn't take it well and immediately challenged me. She wants to be empress, and if I lose, I die. If I'm married, I have the option to have my, er, husband fight for me."

"Which makes Coach Renfro your meat shield."

My eyes roll heavenward. Ridiculous.

"I'm a pretty good fighter," Noah says. "My family starts training us young. I can even use a sword, believe it or not. I'd be willing to fight her for you, even if you don't marry me. I may not be super human, but I bet I could beat a girl your size."

"Yes." I laugh. "You seemed pretty impressive back there, lying flat on the ground while I shot the bad guys with ballistic beads and a necklace slingshot."

"You kicked me down!"

"Regardless, your chivalry is misguided. I can't have someone fight for me *unless* I marry them first."

We turn the corner and begin across the bridge that crosses the East river toward FDR. Noah looks down at the water. "You're headed back to your sister's house now, but then what? You fly back to Hawaii, or wherever you're really from?"

"I don't have a choice, Noah."

"There's always a choice."

"Maybe in your world."

"Let me rephrase, then," he says. "Rethink your choice. Don't marry the old guy. Don't kill your sister. I'm kind of sick of America anyway. We can go back to Beijing like you suggested. My dad would be fine with it, I swear. But maybe you should tell me your name first." He winks.

"I told you earlier. It's Chancery Alamecha."

"Right. Chancery," he says slowly, like he's trying my name on for size. "I like it. It fits you way better than Rebecca."

"Five minutes ago, you were practically running away from me screaming. Now I'm supposed to fly to Beijing with you?"

"I had to process everything," he says. "The hero gets a minute in stories to find his path. I can save you, and you don't even have to marry me. Not until you're begging to, anyway."

I roll my eyes. "So the hero in this story is a kid who has to get permission from Dad first? I'm quite reassured."

"But you agree I'm the hero," he says. "And you can't

leave the hero behind. If you won't go with me to China, take me with you to, wait, where are you going?"

"Hawaii," I say. "That was true, too. But I can't take you, Noah. It's too dangerous. You could've been killed back there."

"Or," Edam says, "he could be killed right here. I'm not picky."

Aww, crap. I've finally been saved, which isn't fantastic news for Noah.

28

Edam punches Noah in the face and I watch, transfixed, as Noah sprawls out on the pavement for the second time today.

I shove Edam. "What was that for? He tried to save me from drowning!"

"Right after kissing you," Edam says. "How do you think I found you two? I watched Frederick's feed until it lost you both, around the time you dove into the East River."

"You should be mad at me, not him. He didn't even know who you were."

Edam inhales slowly through his nose. "But I can't make myself be mad at you. I just can't."

Noah has gotten back up and is holding his fists up in the air. He looks like a 1950s boxer.

I roll my eyes. "Knock it off Noah. Apologize, Edam."

"I'm not apologizing," Edam says at the exact same time as Noah says, "The only thing I'm knocking is his head."

My life has devolved into an Acme cartoon.

I don't want to deal with it and I'm suddenly both exhausted and famished. I want to tell Noah goodbye properly, but it's not going to happen with Edam here, so I don't even try. When I climb into the car, Frederick hands me a new phone. "Yours was submerged, I believe."

I love Frederick. No punching people and no yelling. He just does his job. Edam should take notes. Noah and Edam are still yelling at each other on the sidewalk.

"What's his problem?" I ask Frederick.

"He loves you, Your Majesty. It ruins the best of us."

He can't possibly love me, not yet, but I get his point. It can't be easy for Edam to watch me kiss another guy, especially now that I've committed to taking his offer. In my defense, the decision is mostly about my otherwise imminent demise. Even so, it's not entirely about that, which means I need to talk to him about it.

My replacement phone buzzes in my hand with an all caps message from Inara. *I WAS WRONG*, it reads, and a video file is attached. I stick my headphones in and click play.

It's grainy and it's taken late at night. The video is date and time stamped. The person in the corner is talking on the phone just after midnight, less than sixteen hours after I set off the EMP. I turn the volume up as high as it goes, and I can still barely make out what the man on camera is saying.

"But why break things off with her?" the shady guy asks.

A pause.

"Of course I don't love her, but it took me a long time to get her to trust me this much. She wants to name me as Consort. I put her off to confirm it's what you want."

Pause.

"I never wanted to date her in the first place. But I want to make sure that's what you want before I throw away all that work."

Another pause.

"Fine, then what's the new plan?" His voice is muffled, but it sounds familiar.

A short pause.

"You can't be serious. Yes, I like her a lot more, admire her even, but they hate each other. That won't ever work." I know this voice. It's low, it's rumbly, but I know it if I can just place it.

Another long pause.

"Your intel better be right, because I'm the one risking my neck. What you're telling me makes no sense."

A short pause.

"Yes, okay, I told you that already, but I—"

The shady man goes quiet again.

"Fine, I got it."

Another pause.

"I said okay. If she's awake I'll do it now. If not, I'll do it first thing tomorrow." He hangs up and glances around the hall, his face briefly coming into view of the camera before the video cuts off.

Of course I know the voice. I just didn't want to believe it. The shady guy is Edam.

Inara's cryptic message —she's telling me I shouldn't make Edam my Consort. How could I, after watching that? Who was he talking to?

When Edam finally gets in the car, I shift to face the window. He sits on the opposite side and doesn't look at me either. I watch as we drive away from Noah, who looks heartbroken. I put my hand to the window and he waves back, as if we're going to see each other in the morning. Except I know we won't. It hurts to drive away from one of the only people I know likes me because of who I am instead of my genetic code.

Unfortunately, without any conversation, I have to think about what happened in the past few hours. Someone, almost certainly Judica, attacked me. The fact that it happened hours after I decided to name Edam my Consort can't be a coincidence.

Only four people knew about my recent decision: Inara, Lark, Alora, and Edam.

This morning I trusted all four of them almost unconditionally. But one of them probably told Judica. The question is, which one? The one who seems the most likely is also the one who makes the least sense. Edam stands to gain a lot when I name him Consort. If he's sure he can defeat her, why would he betray me? Unless he's been working for Judica all along. But that video. . . He broke up with Judica the next morning, just like the video indicated he would, which means the odds he's somehow playing me against her are low. He's working for someone else.

Edam's loyalties are split. How did I not see that before?

Could he have killed Mom?

I lean my head against the glass, my heart contracting painfully.

I don't know who he was talking to, but I don't think he's working for my twin. I'll have to put a pin in the question of who he called for now. One betrayal at a time.

I consider Inara next. She's the one sending me incriminating information on Edam, as if to cast suspicion elsewhere. Video can be doctored, of course, but it's hard, time consuming work. And his voice confirmed the face, not the other way around.

Inara stayed behind with Judica. I thought she was risking herself for me, but for all I know, she's been working against me all along. She's been sending me videos under the radar, helpful videos, but maybe Judica approved each one.

I think about the videos, their content, and I doubt it.

Inara did follow me to my room immediately after Mom's death. But if Judica murdered Mom, and if Inara knew, there's no telling what plan they hatched in advance. My brain scans through thousands of interactions with Inara, all of them positive. Could she really have been hatching plots all along? I can't keep thinking about it, so I move along.

I see no way that Alora benefits from selling me out to Judica. There are too many angles, and until very recently, I wasn't even paying attention. I have zero agents, no advisors and not a clue what to do.

I can't even think about Lark. She has no contacts, none that know she's alive, and she stands to gain nothing. Judica hates her. Or worse, doesn't consider her at all. She's the lowest likelihood of betrayal.

But she can't help me either, for the same reasons. I drop my face in my hands.

Edam shifts on the seat and pulls me closer, slinging his arm around me. "Relieved isn't a strong enough word for how I feel about you being okay. I should never have let you go to school alone today. Please forgive me."

I turn toward him, his arms pulling me even tighter, and I sob against his broad chest the rest of the way home. By the time we reach Alora's brownstone, I feel better. I shouldn't let him comfort me, because I don't know who Edam is, not really, but my body still trusts him. He's done nothing but protect it. Always.

When I walk up the steps and through the doors at Alora's, an old friend greets me. She towers over Alora and me both, standing at eye level with Edam. Her skin shines, almost as dark as the color of black calla-lilies. The combination of dark skin and russet hair makes the emerald sparkle of her eyes even more startling.

I run toward her, my arms outstretched. She envelops me in a reassuring bear hug.

"Marselle!"

"Little dove."

My mom's old endearment from her Field Lieutenant for her spy network brings a tear to my eye. I wipe it away quickly.

"Not that I'm not happy to see you, but why are you here?" I ask. "Is everything okay?"

Our chef back home, Angel, has run my mom's spy network for hundreds of years, but Marselle is my mom's second. She implements whatever Angel commands in the United States, anyway.

"Is everything okay with Melina?" Marselle's stationed in Austin where my other full sister lives. I've never met Melina, presumably because she caused so much trouble before I was born. She hasn't been welcome in Ni'ihau since. Marselle was tasked to Austin full time a few years ago because Melina had attracted so many exiled evians from other families. Mom thought a stronger Alamecha presence was prudent.

Marselle shakes her head. "All is quiet on that front thankfully, but there's something else. Your mother called me the day she died. She told me she wasn't sure how things would play out, but that she might need to pass her network."

Monarchs don't usually pass their network along. Typically an Heir develops her own network over a period of years from a core group of people she can trust. I should have vetted and placed each of my spies myself, allowing me to determine the reliability of each person as events transpire.

But I didn't think I needed one. Which Mom knew, and that's probably why Marselle is here. She's my mom's last gift, which means I need to make sense of Mom's final words. She said I need her keycode, and the clue she provided was 'The one I love more than any other.' Does she mean the one person Mom loves more than any other? Or who *I* love more than any other? Or does she mean a thing, like control of the family? Or something more esoteric, like security?

I'm a little conceited, I suppose, because if it's who my Mom loves, I assume it's me. It wouldn't be Chancery, though; that's too obvious. Perhaps Chancy? Or maybe Little Dove? But Marselle just called me that. She wouldn't have used the keycode so casually, would she? Or maybe she was helping me, putting the thought in my head. My brain throbs and I don't know how all this works. I wish things could be simple for once.

A sick thought occurs to me. Could my mom have meant Sotiris? Did she love her unborn child more than me already?

"Can you pardon us for a moment?" I ask Edam and Alora. "Marselle and I need to talk."

Marselle follows me to my room, and I don't waste any time. "You need the keycode."

She nods. "I didn't think we should do this over the phone. Also, I fear that—"

"Angel may be compromised," I say.

Marselle's shoulders droop. "I've reported to and worked with her for more than four hundred years. We were in the field together on our first assignment. I don't want to believe it, but she's the best chef I've ever known, which helped her get a lot of positions over the years, and she watches everything that leaves her kitchen like a hawk. I can't see how any of her food could have been poisoned without her knowledge."

"Sometimes we don't know people as well as we think."

"I loved her," Marselle says, "like a sister."

My jaw tightens. "Unfortunately, I've learned that trust doesn't always go hand-in-hand with affection."

"You're still so young," Marselle says, "but you're not wrong."

"What do you need from me?" I ask.

"Just the keycode. If your mother intended to pass you her network, she'd have given it to you."

"How many chances do I have?" Because I have a few ideas.

"Two," she says. "Otherwise people could just guess and guess forever. Two gives you one mistake."

I almost can't bring myself to say the word, but I have to know. Please, Mom, please let this be wrong. "Sotiris."

Marselle shakes her head.

I sigh in relief. Mom couldn't have expected me to guess something bizarre, like security or world peace. She must have meant a person, and it must be me. Now I need to figure out whether it's Chancy, Chancery, or Divinity. I don't think Marselle would have called me little dove if that was the code, so I rule that out, and both Chancy and Chancery are too obvious. "Divinity," I say.

Marselle smiles. "Correct, and we have a lot to talk about."

"First and foremost, what's Judica been up to while I've been gone?"

"She sent the members of each of the Five Families home about two seconds after you left."

I expected that. "Go on."

"There's a lot of movement from them. I imagine several of them would support you, including the second family, Malessa. As you know, the last ruler of Malessa, Senah, didn't have many sons just like your mother didn't have many daughters, and now that she's dead and her daughter Analessa is ruling, she hasn't had many sons either. When she heard Edam followed you—"

Suddenly it clicks. Analessa, Edam's sister, hasn't had many sons, and neither did Edam and Analessa's mother, Senah. I didn't know that. My mom struggled with the guilt of selling her sons and she had a lot, but if you only had a few, selling them off would be even more difficult. You might even keep one. If that son was only three when you died and your daughter came to power, she might sell him so that other families would sell their sons to her when she had an Heir to raise, but if that daughter didn't have any sons either, she might gain a new understanding. She might even regret doing it. She might try to bring him back to her side. And if that brother thought the sale of children was barbaric, if he raged inside over the betrayal. . . who knew whether he'd agree.

The phone call had to be from his sister Analessa or someone else from the Second Family. I would bet on it. The question is whether he's loyal to Alamecha and by extension to me, or to them. There's a reason sons are sold at birth. With our evian memories, even three years can result in shifted alliances and skewed loyalties. When I finally start to listen again, Marselle is talking about the other families and what our agents say about who they support.

"I want to hear all of this, but not right now. You're putting off something big, and I don't have time for delays. What is it?"

Marselle looks surprised. "You're right. I didn't mean to put it off, but it frightens me. Judica may officially be ruling in your place, but she's not acting like it. She wants to set the tone for her rule. She means to unite the Six, according to prophecy she says. She wants to rename Alamecha the Seventh Family once it's done. She says the uniting of all evians under one ruler would explain the obscure references in various texts to the Seventh Family. If she's going to show the other families she's strong, she needs to make a statement."

Once she has chosen a way to proceed as the new leader, she'll need to tie up loose ends. Hence the hit team on me. If she can't be completely positive she can defeat me in the ring, because I might choose Edam, she'd send her people for me. What I know of Judica, and what I've seen of her current actions, tells me her next step.

Queens through the millennia have usually started off their rule in the way they mean to move ahead. Judica discussed her plan with my mom a million times.

Before Marselle can say it, I guess. "She's launching a nuclear bomb against China."

Marselle's mouth opens and then closes. She nods.

I can't wait until the end of my ten days. I need to go back now, or millions of innocent people will die.

29

I dismiss Marselle and rush from my room to arrange a flight home, but I end up standing in the hallway like an idiot. Whose plane do I use?

Bellatrius and Arlington's presence by my door reminds me. I never even asked Frederick if my guards all survived the attack.

"Was anyone injured?" I ask.

Bellatrius bobs her head. "Simeon sustained a sliced hamstring and recovered quickly."

"And Ralph?"

"He lost his hand and is in the process of regrowing it," Arlington says.

"And being a baby about it, too." Bellatrius smirks. "Men do have a tendency to whimper more."

"Some men." Arlington huffs. "But not all."

I glance from Bellatrius to Arlington, both of whom stare at me expectantly. Arlington serves me because he's grateful I spared his sister. Bellatrius serves me because I voted for her to be able to leave the family. I had no idea either of them cared about my opinion at the time.

Or that's why I think they're here.

"Bellatrius, why did you follow me? Everyone knows Judica's stronger, fiercer, and more powerful. Why pick the losing side?"

Her eyes widen. "You're not weaker. You're merciful. The two aren't the same."

"How do you figure?" I ask.

She shifts and crosses her arms. "When I fell in love with Patiron, it was a mistake. We never should have met. I love Alamecha, Your Majesty. I love my family. But Patiron loved Shenoah, too. And sometimes, someone has to be willing to bend."

"And you were willing to bend."

"Exactly," she says. "And I could have run away with him like he asked. I could have abandoned my family. Our families were at war, so I knew Shenoah would have granted me asylum."

"Why didn't you?" I ask.

She swallows hard. "Because I wanted to do things the right way. I believed I would be granted permission to go, and so I requested it."

"But your request was denied." I recall the hearing perfectly.

"Your mother and sister didn't care at all for me or my future. They only cared about the family." Bellatrius looks at her feet.

"That's their job," I say softly. "To protect the family."

"The family is made up of individuals," Bellatrius says.

She's quoting me. I advocated for allowing her to go, because our highest calling is not to protect a group, but each person.

"We're more to you than soldiers in an army," she says. "And that's why I'm here. And that's why Ralph shouldn't be whimpering over an injury justly taken protecting you. It's an honor to be one of your guards, Your Majesty. The singular honor of my life."

I am utterly unworthy of that kind of devotion. "You're free to go to Shenoah," I say. "I need guards, but I need citizens who aren't in pain more. You may leave and join Patiron with my blessing."

Bellatrius shakes her head. "I'll never leave your service, Your Majesty. My anger over that decision faded and Patiron moved on. I'm excited to be a part of this. I want to create a new dynamic within Alamecha under your direction."

If I can even reach Hawaii alive to deal with Judica in the first place. Who can I trust? Will I ever know? I'm suddenly exhausted, but there isn't time for me to collapse in a heap and sob. It's my job to try and stop my sister before she can kill untold innocents in a nuclear blast.

I flog my tired brain. The facts are pretty simple. I decided to make Edam my Consort and let him fight for me, and I told Inara, Lark, Alora, and Edam. Then I left for school. Lark conveniently had plans and wasn't accompanying me. Then on my way home, I was ambushed. I've ruled out Edam in betraying me to Judica, probably, but he's clearly answering to someone, most likely his sister.

Did one of the three tell Judica my plans? Or did they tell someone else who told her? Or did someone bug my conversation with Inara? Or perhaps Judica realized how likely the scenario was without a heads up from anyone and decided to attack. The timing could have been coincidental. Occam's Razor would indicate it was Inara, Lark, or Alora, but I trust them all.

And now I suspect them all, too.

I don't have enough information right now, so I decide to focus on my immediate problem. Transportation. I could call Inara and ask her to send me a plane, but if she betrays me, I'll never land alive. The plane could "crash" on the way, killing me and eliminating the threat. I might survive a plane crash depending on how it goes down, but not if the person who orchestrated it has people standing by to decapitate me while I'm vulnerable.

If I ask Alora, I'm in the same predicament. Edam doesn't have a plane, not that I'd trust it if he did. If Lark had a plane, maybe. But she doesn't.

My life is a mess.

I can only think of one person who might have access to a jet and who has no loyalties to my sister or anyone else. I text Noah before I can second-guess my instincts.

Any chance I could borrow a jet? Turns out Hawaii is too far to go by rowboat.

The little dots show up, but then disappear. I stare at my phone for two minutes and he still doesn't reply. Maybe he needs to think. Or even worse, he may need to ask his dad for permission. Ugh.

The door to Edam's room opens and I drop my phone guiltily.

"What did Marselle want?" Edam asks. "She was one of your mom's intelligence officers, wasn't she?"

"Clearly a well-hidden asset," I joke.

Edam shrugs. "I was number two on your mom's security team until Judica drafted me to run hers. I worked for Marselle for a while. Besides, the lieutenants are usually more of an open secret."

Duh.

"Is she still here?" He looks past me toward my doorway.

"Uh, no. I sent her downstairs so I could think."

"Can we talk, then?"

"I don't know," I say. "Can we?"

He glances behind me at Bellatrius and Arlington. "In private?"

I incline my head and he precedes me into my room. I close the door with a click. "What's up?" I sit on my bed.

Edam grabs the chair from my desk and sets it by the bed so he's eye level with me.

"Whoa, this is serious," I joke.

He doesn't smile, and my stomach flip flops.

"What do you want to talk about, Edam? I just received some urgent news."

"Why are you kissing Noah?"

I look around the room. "Am I? I thought I was talking to you."

"You know what I mean."

I do. "You mean why did I go to school today, and why do I like him when I obviously also like you, and have agreed to take you as my Consort. Right?"

He nods. I'm actually impressed with how calm and composed he is.

"Feelings are complicated," I say. "I like you a lot, Edam, but I like Noah, too. He's different. He represents a desire I've had for a long time to escape, to be free."

"But you chose to return, and you know that I'll take care of you." He reaches over and takes my hand. "Do you doubt that?"

I don't doubt his intention. He looks utterly sincere. I think back to the videos of him with Judica. He looked like a robot: stiff, disconnected, and so formal it was unreal. He's not like that with me. But that's not the only video of him I've seen lately, and the other one generated significantly different emotions from me.

"Why did you break up with my sister?" I need to know. Even more than details about his connection to the Malessa family, I need to understand what happened between them. Because if he doesn't have a real reason for dumping her, then he really is just a puppet for someone else.

He never releases my hand. "I'm surprised this didn't

come up before. I assumed maybe you wanted to pretend it never happened."

"What did happen?" I ask. "From the videos I saw, it didn't look like you had much of a relationship."

"I haven't hidden from you my feelings about the evian royal model. It's broken," he says. "I decided when I was still a teenager and you and Judica weren't even ten that my best chance of changing things was to rise to a position of leadership. I trained as hard as I could, and I did everything anyone asked of me. I worked harder, longer, and with more ferocity than anyone else."

"I heard that," I say. "Balthasar talked about you sometimes. He called you his young lion."

He frowns. "I was assigned to keep you safe when you were a child. I was young too, and it seemed in keeping with my skill set. I only did that for a year before I was promoted and I moved up. Eventually I was assigned to train the other boys your mother purchased from other families. Luckily there weren't many new ones, since you and Judica were older. Around the time you turned thirteen, they sent me into the field. I worked with Marselle for a few months, and with a few other operatives, too. I did okay, but I wasn't nearly as good at spying as I am at hand-to-hand combat."

Not a good spy, huh? I guess not, since his phone call got caught on video.

"When I came home, you had both just turned seventeen. I was assigned to train Judica. Balthasar wanted to be able to watch her fight instead of participating himself. I know this sounds bad, but I think he's getting older and having trouble healing as fast. In any case, within a few months of that, Judica requested that I be assigned as captain of her personal guard."

"I know all of that," I say. "What I want to know is—"

"I know. You want to know when and how Judica and I

started... Look, from the time I got back, I knew I wanted to take Balthasar's position. At the time, Judica was focused on a guy named Xander, fifth family, good guy. One day, Balthasar assigned me to spar with him. I beat him in under a minute. Judica stopped talking to him the next day. She only wanted the best, and I understood and respected that. I won't lie. I wanted to be named Consort. It seemed like the one job more powerful than Head of Security to which I could aspire. Not that it's a job, but you know what I mean."

"Go on."

"When I started training with her, I wanted to like her. I wanted to, well, I wanted to want her, but I just didn't. When she touched me, I flinched. The way she spoke to me." His lips compress. "She was kinder to Death. Everything about her felt wrong to me. I knew what I wanted when I was alone, and I'd resolve again to make it work. I'd convince myself it couldn't be that bad, but when she came near, I froze up. After a while, I just couldn't do it anymore. And that day when she almost killed you? I wanted to end her. My hands shook from the effort of not cutting her throat."

"Uh, that's a little scary."

Edam grabs my other hand, too. "That's when I realized that I liked you, and I tried to project my feelings for you onto Judica, but when we were around each other, I couldn't do it. She's not like you, not at all. It upset me for years that no one ever stood up for you. I watched her bully and abuse you while your mom just watched. You could have done something about it, but you never did either. Once I realized how I felt about you, I dumped her."

He doesn't mention the late night phone call. I don't know why I thought he might come clean, but it bums me out way more than it should when he doesn't. I pull my hands from his. "That was the only reason?"

Edam sits up and stares at me intently. I screwed up. He's too smart for direct questioning, and I suck at subterfuge.

"The video camera was live, wasn't it?"

I nod.

He sighs heavily. "I came to live in Alamecha at the age of three and a half. I wasn't the only boy who struggled, but I was the only one who remembered something different, who had a family he knew. When Analessa approached me at one of your mother's birthdays I was only ten. Analessa deeply regretted selling me. She said she was young and thought she had no choice. She told me she tried to buy me back, but your mother refused. Analessa asked if she could call me from time to time. She wanted to help, to make up for her mistake, and she offered to guide me, if I was interested."

"And you agreed?" I ask.

Edam hangs his head. "I knew love and then it was gone. I missed my mother, still, and I wanted someone to care about me. None of which excuses what I did." He clenches his fists and looks me in the eye. "Yes, I've been talking to her regularly since then."

"When did she start telling you what to do instead of guiding you?"

He closes his eyes and exhales. "It was easier to let someone else call the shots, someone older who I thought wanted me. I was twenty when I told her no the first time, but she threatened to send evidence of our discussions to Enora if I refused her. I've wanted to tell you ever since we left Ni'ihau. It's such a relief that you know."

"You didn't seem too happy about coming along. Maybe once my mom died, your orders changed and my taking you got in the way."

Edam stands up. "Nothing like that. I was upset that you forced my hand because everyone has forced my hand my entire life. It didn't take long for me to realize that what you did wasn't the same. You thought you were helping, and once I told you I was mad, your reaction was to apologize. I swear to you, I haven't talked to my sister since I left Hawaii, nor do I ever care to again."

"Did Analessa tell you to stay there and beg Judica's forgiveness? Or did she tell you to come with me?"

"I don't know what she would have said," Edam says. "Because I haven't spoken to her since that night when she ordered me to do what I already wanted to do and dump your sister. And for the record, she heard news that your mom was changing her Heirship. I have no idea who her other contacts were, but her order wasn't why I did it. I'd been wanting to break up with her since we started dating."

"So you did do as she directed."

He laughs. "I'm sure she's furious now, as I haven't called or checked in with her since that night."

"Does that bother you?" I ask.

"With a little perspective, I realized she was using me all along. She never once in sixteen years asked how I felt or what I wanted. And she only called when she needed something."

Edam has been committing treason for sixteen years.

I should be angry, I should feel outraged, but I don't. My heart just hurts. How can I trust anything he says to me now? Where's the line between a sister contacting her brother and a spy? Edam's right. Our system is broken. Daughters killing mothers and sisters, siblings using one another. Buying and selling babies. It's all so wrong that we don't even realize how wrong anymore. The only reason we don't see it is that we're all born into it.

A single tear trails hotly down my cheek.

"I know your mom's gone Chancery, but you're not alone. You don't trust me now, and I don't blame you. It may take me a long time to convince you of this truth, but

I'm on your side until the day I die. For years I thought I needed to change evian society alone. My success or failure would be limited to what I could accomplish myself. But now I believe in someone else, someone who is uniquely poised to repair everything that's broken. Think what we could do together. And if you united the families behind these changes, we could redirect the course of the entire world."

A chill runs down my arms. His words echo my mom's eerily. I don't know whether to believe in his loyalty to me, but heaven help me, I want to so badly.

"What if I've changed my mind?" I ask. "What if I can't choose you as my Consort anymore? Will you support me then?"

Edam's eyes widen, but he nods. "I will. Whatever you decide, but I'll never forgive myself for putting you in danger this way."

"You didn't even confess. I caught you."

His nostrils flare. "True."

"You're not going to tell me I'm making a mistake if I don't choose you?"

"I'm not," he says. "And if that's your decision, we'll hit it hard over the next two days to give you your best chance."

I smirk. "No more terminal cancer patient analogies?"

"I'm sorry for that. I really don't want to lose you."

"You know, for someone who may be the best fighter alive right now, you sure seem to be afraid a lot."

"Not really," he says. "Losing you through my own stupidity, or losing you through your sister's. Those are basically the only things that concern me. Well, that and sharks. I mean, have you ever tuned in during Shark Week? They never stop growing teeth. Rows and rows of teeth. And they never sleep." He shudders.

I can't quite help a tiny smile. My phone bings and I glance at it. Noah finally replied.

I got the go ahead. When are we leaving? Tell me we aren't bringing the old man along.

I tap back a reply. *How many seats in your jet?*

22.

I smile.

"Good news?" Edam asks.

"You said we could hit it hard for two days."

He nods.

"What could you do in a few hours?"

"Excuse me?" he asks.

"Judica's planning on nuking China to show the Five she's tough and keep them from encroaching on her territory. Before I'm scheduled to return."

Edam groans. "And you don't want me as your Consort anymore, so you'll be fighting her yourself."

When he says it, I realize it's true. It's not that I don't want him. I do. I actually believe him. I came into this discussion not knowing whether I could trust him at all. After talking, I believe his concern for me is sincere. He really does want to protect me. I even agree that our system is broken. I may choose him one day, but not today. Besides, if I make him my Consort now, I'll never know whether I'd have chosen him without the pressure of Judica hanging over me. If I do survive, I don't want that kind of desperation and doubt hanging over my marriage for a thousand years.

"My mom died, leaving a huge power vacuum in her wake. Judica has been spawning stories of her ferocity and competency for years, and yet Judica feels like she needs to bomb China to grab the attention of the Five and shore up her rule. There may very well be empresses who use their Consort to fight every single battle. They may even be well respected, but I don't have that luxury because I don't have the stomach to bomb another country, or win a big war, and I already have a reputation for being weak. If I want to protect Alamecha and keep our family safe from encroachment, I need to do something big, something that shows the world I'm different than my reputation. Taking a tough Consort might keep me alive, but if I want to have any chance of changing things, I can't just survive."

Edam may never understand. I may be ruining any hope of ever being with him.

"I need to thrive. That's why I've got to take Judica down or die trying."

Edam compresses his lips and closes his eyes. But when he opens them, he says, "I'll do whatever you need."

In that moment, I may be breaking off our engagement, but I've never wanted to kiss him more.

30

I replace the missing stones in my necklace the second Edam leaves my room to pack. The use of my last resort ballistae makes me think. My list of powerful allies is short: Alora and Inara. Of course, Edam, the guards who followed me, Noah, and Lark are also on my side, and power and prestige aren't everything. Unfortunately, I can't really trust any of them either.

I need to figure out who betrayed me to Judica, because next time I may not survive it.

I almost call Lark up to my room, but I hesitate. She's the one person other than my mom who I'd have trusted to support me blindly without a scintilla of doubt on any point. Until my mom executed hers, and I did nothing to stop it. Until my mom ordered her execution and only allowed her to survive in secret. I don't think Lark blames me, but I'm not entirely positive.

Which leaves me puzzling out the politics and loyalties of my wannabe allies alone.

Even if I'm wrong about Edam and he is still in contact with his sister, I don't think I'm in imminent danger from her. I doubt she sees me as a threat. In fact, maybe the only universal thing in my favor right now is that, to the rest of the world, I'm the weaker ruler. That means the other empresses would likely pick me over Judica to ascend the throne, because in their minds I'll be easier to control, intimidate and ultimately defeat.

Of course, there's always a chance that my affection for and attraction to Edam has clouded my judgment.

I shake my head and move on to Inara. She's been Mom's right hand as long as I can recall. She has also been like a second mother to me. And when Mom died, I saw the pain it caused her. She wanted to leave with me, but she stayed back to defend me from afar, at no small risk to herself. I also can't think of a single reason Inara would want to harm me. She knows I'd keep her in the same position, managing many of the Alamecha affairs. I doubt Judica would do the same. And I'd rely more on her advice than my twin, too. Plus, I think Inara likes me more. And it's not as if eliminating Judica or me would land her the throne. Our older sister Melina would snatch that crown so fast our heads would spin, from what I've heard.

Which brings me to Alora. I can't think of any reason she might want me dead. Judica, Melina, and Inara would all have to die before Alora would be in line for the throne. And she's never seemed to have any interest in it. Even so, I should talk to her before I leave. She has the least cause of all to harm me, and I trust her opinion the most. I throw the rest of my belongings in a bag and race downstairs.

I find her in the library, surrounded by books and busy reading one. I clear my throat and she looks up.

I dive right into the important part. "Marselle brought urgent intel. Judica's planning to bomb China before my return."

"That's terrible." Alora snaps the book closed. "She's eager to make a name for herself."

"It's a little more complicated than that. As you know,

we control both Cuba and the United States. Evians all know that, but humans don't, which of course includes China. Mom always made Judica propose plans for what she'd do to establish herself—"

"When Mother died." Alora leans back in her chair and looks at the ceiling. "I had to do the same."

"In Judica's most recent plan, we send a bomb from Alaska, disguised as a bomb from Russia. China might reject the United States' offer of aid, but it would accept aid from Cuba. Either way, Russia looks like the bad guy, and the bombing allows her a way to slide in seamlessly and begin to develop influence in sections of China. Of course, Lainina is going to be pissed, since it implicates her holdings."

Alora stands and pulls her phone from her pocket. "I take it this moves up our timeframe. I'll call Phil and let him know we need the jet."

I shake my head. "I need you here. If this goes badly, you won't want to be anywhere near Judica. Trust me."

"At least I don't have to worry about you," she says. "I will anyway, but not nearly as much."

She still thinks Edam's fighting for me. "Actually, I decided to fight her myself."

Alora gulps. "Why?"

"Mom never made me run drills for what I'd do to prove myself, but even if she had, I'd never have come up with something that murdered millions of people."

"Humans," Alora says. "There aren't any evians in China, at least not any sanctioned ones."

"They're still people," I say, disappointed that even Alora cares less about humans.

"Fair enough."

"Since I can't do something that splashy, I'll need to do something else to set the tone of my reign." I shove down my uncertainty and doubt. I can do this. I have to do this.

"I'm going to take down the biggest dog in the place, who also happens to have murdered our mother. Two birds with one, err, sword, as the case may be."

Alora sinks into her wingback desk chair with a whomp.

I perch on the edge of the wooden chair facing her desk. "You lied before. You don't think I can do it."

Alora looks down at her hands. "I should tell you something about melodics. It's effective, and if you've started to hear melodic lines. . . it might even be enough, but. . . You know I won the centennial games a hundred and twenty years ago. What you don't know is *how I won*."

Alora stands up and removes a book from the second highest shelf in the room. She plonks it down on the table, flips it open to a page, and points at a large glossy black and white photo. "Believe it or not, this was a pretty impressive bit of technology at the time."

I glance down at the photograph of the Alamecha Centennial Games team. Alora's wearing a smart black dress with divided skirts and her hair is pulled back into a severe bun.

She flips the page and shows me an image of the Lenora team. She points at a kid near the front. "This was who I fought in my first match."

"She looks ten years old!"

She laughs. "Not quite, but she should've been an easy win. I was nervous and she was so young that we'd never even met socially. She was a nobody, barely even selected to enter. She was a last minute substitution for another candidate who became unsuitable. Everyone knew that round was a given for me, Chancery. She was *twenty-third* generation." Alora closes her eyes, reliving the match in her mind. She exhales and opens her eyes. "And she almost beat me."

Like my match with Lark, I imagine.

"No one even considered I might win the tournament after that near miss. Even worse, after bumbling my way through my first match, I had very bad luck. My next fight was against one of the top contenders, a man I had actually dated. I knew him very well. He was a much better fighter than me and everyone knew it, including Vaughn."

"Wait, you fought someone from Alamecha?" I ask.

Alora clucks. "You haven't been to the Games yet, but they don't care what family you're from. You're matched up randomly until the finals."

"Wow, so if I went, I could fight Judica, Edam, and Lark."

Alora lifts her eyebrows. "Lark isn't eligible."

Duh. "Well, Judica could have to fight Edam, then. Just like you fought your ex."

"Precisely, and the point is that I should have lost, Chancy. He should have destroyed me."

"Did he let you win?"

She shakes her head. "We ended badly, and he was angry. I am absolutely positive he did not let me win. No, I won because I knew him extremely well, maybe better than he knew himself. I knew everything about him: his pain, his pride, his anger, his joy, his every motivation. I heard his melodic line with total clarity. I anticipated every single move and wasn't off by a note."

"So I need to know Judica?" I groan. "She's the devil. We're twins, we have identical DNA but for seventeen years, I've tried to guess how she'll react, and I'm never right. If I think up, she goes down. I'm not even kidding, Alora, the other day she stabbed me with a fork at breakfast for no reason."

"That may have been the case a month ago," she says. "But now you have more in common, and I think you're looking at the past with new eyes. I hope it has given you more insight."

I shake my head. I just don't know.

"Chancery, after I defeated Vaughn, I went on to fight

more amazing, talented fighters. I researched each of them, compiling everything I knew. I watched them fight whenever I could. I managed to beat them, one after another, but my last fight was against the man who had won every single Centennial games for seven hundred years. My uncle."

My mouth drops. I thought he had simply stopped competing. I didn't know he'd lost. "How did you beat Balthasar? I heard he was unbeatable."

"He should've been. I thought my ex-boyfriend would beat me for sure, and I was delighted when I won, but I knew in my bones I couldn't defeat Balthasar. I had learned in fighting Vaughan that to win, I needed to know the person. No one alive knew Balthasar better than Mother. They'd been dear friends for almost eight hundred years. I spent hours talking to Mother about him. Then, I watched Balthasar talk to her. Mother told me a lot, but I discovered something when I watched them together."

"What?" I'm sitting on the edge of my seat, leaning toward her.

"Balthasar was in love with her. Not admiration, not high regard, not major consideration for her feelings, not respect for a great ruler. *He was in love.* Once I figured that out, his life choices, and consequently his melodic line, became utterly understandable. If I hadn't puzzled out something no one else knew, including our Mother, and possibly Balthasar himself, I never could have won that match."

"What are you saying?"

Alora walks around the desk and takes my hands in hers. "Chancy, you can beat her. But you need to know Judica better than she knows herself, and hating her won't get you there. You need to understand her. Edam may want to practice today on the flight and that's fine, but if you're hearing melodic lines, your most critical preparation will take place in here." She taps the side of my head.

Footsteps sound near the door. I stand up. "Come in," I say.

Lark's head peeks around at us.

I hadn't contemplated that I'll have to leave her. If things go badly, I'll never see her again. "Promise you'll take care of her," I whisper to Alora.

"Take care of me?" Lark asks.

Clearly I need to work on my volume levels. "I'm headed back today. Judica's moving ahead in my absence in ways I can't allow, so I'm fighting her myself."

Lark frowns. "I'm coming along."

"You can't," I say. "Mom ordered your execution and we let everyone believe it took place. You must stay here and develop into the asset I know you can be."

She shakes her head vehemently. "You need me by your side." She squares her shoulders. "You don't have that many people you can trust."

I'm not even sure she's on that list, but I want her to be, badly. "It's too risky for you."

"I don't care." She sets her jaw and I know she means it.

All the times I slid my eggs onto her plate, and dragged her along for jogs, and swam with dolphins in the surf, and painted our toenails together slam into my mind like a wave to the face. Surprising, overwhelming, and refreshing. I can't leave her here alone, not after all we've been through. She'd be safer, but life isn't worth living because it's safe.

"If that's what you want," I say.

"I do," she says. "I want to be with you."

"Then you better grab your bags."

Lark rushes out the door, and I follow her to grab my things. Edam's waiting outside, and he insists on carrying my stuff. Even if he's not my Consort, he's nice to have around. Alora meets us at the door to see us off.

"Do you want me to come with you?" she asks.

I pull her tightly against me. "No. I want you here, safe. Because I don't know how this will go down, but Judica won't be happy you supported me. I'm worried enough already."

"I can take care of myself." The glint in Alora's eye is one I've never seen, but I believe her. There's more to my older sister than I realized.

A long, black suburban pulls up behind the black sedan.

"What's that?" I ask.

"You said the jet we're taking seats twenty-two," Frederick says.

"Right," I say.

"Well, by my count, that leaves enough room for all the guards we came with," Frederick says. "And I plan to fill every seatbelt. You aren't heading home alone."

On the drive over to the plane home, Edam can't stop talking. Something about the knowledge I'm about to fight Judica has knocked a screw loose in his head.

"Another thing I forgot to mention," he says, "is that—"

I cut him off in the middle of his fourteenth tip. "Edam."

His mouth clicks shut.

"I appreciate your desire to help." I put my hand over his.

"But I'm making you nervous?"

I lean back in my seat and close my eyes. "This fight won't be won or lost from tips or tricks." I think about Alora's words. I need to win it in my head. I need to understand the enigma.

Which means I'm probably going to die.

Edam flips his hand over and wraps it around mine. "You will do it. I believe you can, truly."

"Do you not trust Alora?" Lark asks. "Is that why we're taking Noah's jet?"

I glance up at Bernard and widen my eyes.

Lark splutters.

"Of course I trust Alora," I say. "I just don't want to give Judica any more cause to blame her if. . ."

"No," Edam says. "No talking like that."

"And we're sure of *Noah*?" Lark asks. "Because we don't know him at all."

I glare at Lark and Edam.

"What?" Edam protests. "I didn't even say anything."

"You thought it," I say. "I think we can all agree he's human, and he was genuinely shocked when I told him about evians."

"I wasn't there," Edam says, "so I can't speak to that. But I don't trust him. Not a bit."

"Duly noted." I refuse to fall back into the tangle of self-doubt over who to trust. It's quicksand.

"We're here," Bernard says.

I'm relieved to be diverted from my deliberations. Even if he's not coming with us, interacting with Noah is always distracting. I climb out of the sedan and tell Bernard goodbye. When I turn away from the car, Noah's smiling at me from the doorway of the hangar. My heart lurches at the sight of his grin. I didn't think I'd see it again.

"Thanks for loaning us your jet," Edam says.

I'm proud of him for making an effort to be civil.

"Sure, happy to help," Noah says, "plus a trip to Hawaii is always fun."

Edam bristles. "You're not coming."

"Of course I am," Noah says. "It's my jet."

I shake my head. "You need to get back to school, and where we're going, it's not a vacation."

"No way." Noah crosses his arms. "I'm coming. It's my one stipulation to the loan."

Edam rolls his eyes. "Look kid, I understand you're upset, but that doesn't mean you can follow us into a hostile environment. You annoy me, but I don't want you dead."

"Why should I care whether evians are there?" Noah asks.

"We're gods compared to you," Edam says.

Noah clenches his fists.

Edam lifts one eyebrow casually and the corner of his mouth turns up into a half grin. "Are you trying to look threatening right now, cream puff?"

"Look," I say, "we're not trying to be jerks, but—"

Edam interrupts me. "A ten year old evian girl would crush you like a bug."

"I don't care, okay? I don't care how dangerous it is, or whether I'm a lowly, useless dog."

"Your hearing really is bad. I said a *bug*, not a *dog,*" Edam says. "Calling you a dog would be an insult—"

Noah practically spits. ""It's my jet and that's my offer. Take me with you or find another way home."

"Fine." Edam steps toward Noah and grabs him by the collar of his jacket. "I'll knock him out and we'll take his jet anyway."

Noah's eyes flash, but he doesn't back down, even with his feet dangling in the air. I'm almost impressed. It's easy to be brave when you're sure to win. It's harder when you're about to take an epic beating.

I shake my head. "No."

Edam throws his hands in the air, dropping Noah in a heap in the process. "Fine. Call Alora. I'm sure she'll—"

"We will take Noah's jet, and he will stay on board with his pilot when we land."

Lark taps my elbow. "Does anyone know we're coming? Because they shoot down uninvited planes."

"Not yet." I call Inara. She picks up after only one ring.

"I hadn't heard from you since I sent that last video file," she says. "I was worried."

"I'm fine," I say. "In fact, I'm coming home."

"What?" she asks. "Now?"

"Yes," I say. "It's time. Tell Judica I'm not abdicating, and you can go ahead and tell her I'm not naming Edam as my Consort either."

"I thought not," Inara says ruefully. "It still might be your best idea. I've given it some thought and—"

I cut her off before Edam can hear confirmation that she's the one who sent the footage. Although he probably guessed. "I'm only calling to ask you to pass a message along. Will you convey something to Judica for me?"

"Something happened," Inara says. "And you suspect me."

I close my eyes. "No."

"What happened? Are you alright?"

I clear my throat. "There was an attack, but I'm fine, and I don't blame you. Judica has always been a wild card."

"I'm sorry," Inara says. "And I'm so glad you're okay."

I asked Inara to stay behind for me, but I haven't spent much time worried about her. "Are you alright?"

"Never mind that," Inara says. "What can I do?"

"Tell Judica I have the ring."

"She won't even consider shooting down the plane with the ring on board," Inara says. "People don't give you enough credit."

"Think you can convince her?"

"Is it true?" Inara asks.

"Of course it is." Or at least, I know where the ring is. Same thing, sort of.

"She'll push to fight you as soon as you land," Inara says. "Be prepared, little one."

"I'll try," I say. "Accept the world as it is."

"Or do something to change it."

I press end and go to collect my bags, but Edam's already carrying them up the stairs. No one speaks as we board. It's a nice plane, roomy even, at least, until Frederick fills every seat.

"Wow," I say. "This is a top of the line jet, Noah."

"I'm blessed, that's for sure." Noah hands me a menu. "Feel free to order anything that looks good. I've noticed you don't peck at things like a bird."

"I think I'm being insulted," I say.

"All this flirting is giving me a headache," Edam says. "And we need to practice a few moves and then you need a nap."

I fill Noah in on the basics of what's going on while we wait for our sandwiches. I tell him a little more about my mom's death, how she changed the heirship documents, and how my sister challenged me. I tell him I suspect my sister killed our mother, and that she's planning to bomb an open area to cement her rule.

"Wait." The color drains from Noah's face. "Didn't you say the only open area is in China?"

He catches on too fast. "Don't worry," I say. "I'll stop her."

He lifts both eyebrows. "You also said she's a warrior and you're not."

I open my mouth to argue, but he's right. I might lose. Actually, the odds are probably stacked against me no matter how you look at it. He should worry.

Noah gulps. "Do you know where in China?"

"I wish I did."

"You're flying back to try and stop this attack, and you were going to leave me behind?"

"But I didn't leave you, and if I lose, you can warn your family immediately."

"Warn them of what?" he asks. "Tell them to hide in a bomb shelter while everyone else they know dies?"

"It's not ideal," I say, "but at least you can tell them to evacuate from any metropolitan areas."

His knee bounces up and down frenetically during take-off. Once we're in the air, he stills entirely.

Edam stands up and pulls me to my feet, too. He shows me the moves he mentioned earlier.

Noah watches us stoically.

Once I sit back down, he asks, "Do you really have a chance of winning?"

Edam growls. "Of course she's going to win, you idiot."

"What?" Noah asks. "I don't know anything about this. Last time we spoke, you were marrying Rocky here so he could fight for you."

"Change of plans," Edam says. "But she's got this." Noah opens his mouth and Edam cuts him off. "Unless you badger her with questions and she can't sleep."

Noah's mouth clicks shut, and he leans back stiffly in his chair.

I breathe in and out a few times and close my eyes before my phone starts jangling in my pocket. Caller ID says it's Alora. I'm surprised I've got reception, even with a satellite phone. I hit talk.

"Alora?" I ask. "Is everything okay?"

"Chancy? Can you hear me? Are you in the air?"

"I am."

"Marselle needed to talk to you again."

"Okay." I wait.

Marselle says, "Chancery? I've been looking into your mom's murder ever since it happened. You already know my suspicions."

Angel. But even if she administered the poison, she may just be the delivery person. My heart stutters. I think my twin killed our mom, but part of me still hopes she didn't. "What have you learned?"

Marselle clears her throat. "How much do you know about how our immune system works?"

"Not a lot," I admit.

"In order to poison one of us, the poison must be very strong and fast-acting, or it must accumulate slowly with one type, and punch through with another. If death is caused by accumulation, it requires consistent small doses to weaken the system first, then a significant dose of something strong to push our body over the edge. Accumulation is more commonly successful because usually the strong acting poisons are detectable, either through use of dog testing or smell, or texture."

"Okay," I say.

"The poison that killed your mother was exceedingly rare and difficult to detect, but it was neither strong nor fast acting. That means—"

"She was dosed over an extended period of time, and then hit right before her death with a separate toxin."

"Yes, we believe so. But the only poison registering in the examinations is the accumulation variety, a marine toxin we thought had long been extinct. I have no idea where it could have been procured, but Chancery?"

"Yeah."

"Someone very old was involved."

A chill runs down my spine. "Someone old?" Judica is many things, but she isn't old by any standard.

"It had to be administered over at least two months, which means substantial quantities over an extended period."

And the poisoning began long before I reacted to the ring. "That means it was someone who had access to her consistently. Or possibly two different people." I close my eyes, unmoored, confused.

"It would have had other side effects, things you might have noticed," Marselle says.

"Such as?" I ask.

"Most of the side effects might have been dismissed or hidden by Enora if she feared they were signs of aging."

"You're saying it would have caused fatigue or body aches?" I ask.

"Sure, but some of the side effects would have been stranger. For example, it can cause contraceptives to fail."

Which means the poisoner might have actually caused the pregnancy I thought prompted the assassination in the first place. Judica might have been telling the truth. Or she might have done it, but recruited help.

"Wait, why did you say someone old was involved?"

"The identity of that poison was difficult to figure out, but once we did, it's easier to track because it's nearly impossible to obtain. Especially in the quantities used."

"You mentioned it was rare."

"I looked into where it might have come from," Marselle says.

"Any luck?" I ask.

"We found someone who supplied about half of what would have been used."

Whoa. "That's good, right? Can they identify the purchaser?"

"Maybe," Marselle says. "If the supplier hadn't died before we could learn much. The only thing we forced from her was that the buyer wasn't young. They met for the first time more than two hundred years ago."

I want to put my hand through the wall of Noah's shiny jet. "Did you learn anything useful at all?"

"The ledger contained a single notation regarding the purchase. Does the word Nereus mean anything to you?"

"No. Does it to you?"

"No," Marselle says, "but I looked it up. In Greek mythology, Nereus is the son of Gaia and the sea. He ruled the oceans of the earth."

"So the marine toxin is fitting," I say.

"That's everything my agents were able to pass along,"

Marselle says. "But I'll keep digging. Let me pass you back to Alora."

"Okay," I say. "Thanks."

Alora says, "I'm sorry we don't know more yet," at the same time Noah's flight attendant shows up with our sandwiches.

Noah jokes with her while he takes them.

"Who are you with?" Alora asks, her voice strained for some reason.

I glance around the plane. Edam's listening and shrugs.

"Edam's here."

"Where did you procure the jet you're taking?" she asks.

"I'm safe," I say. "I'm with a friend from school."

"So you know." Alora makes a strangled sound. "That's why you didn't take my plane. I assumed Inara sent one."

My appetite evaporates. "That would have taken too long."

Alora cries softly into the phone, and the truth slaps me in the face. Alora's been my best friend other than Lark. I thought she loved me as much as Mom.

But she betrayed me to Judica.

"Why?" I ask softly.

"I'm so sorry, Chancery," Alora says. "I would never have done it if I had a choice."

So much for her advice.

"Hang up on her," Edam says.

"Chancy," Alora pleads, "don't hang up. I need to explain. You weren't Heir, so you don't understand—"

"You're right," I say harshly. "I wouldn't understand. I was never Heir. I was always a nobody. No one ever cared what I thought or did, and apparently you still don't, even now."

I hang up.

31

I don't mean to fall asleep, but I do. I wake up when the plane hits some serious turbulence. I sit up and look around. Bizarrely, Noah's awake and Edam's sleeping. He's reading on some kind of e-reader, tapping his bottom lip with his index finger. I've never been able to study him without him reacting.

I like it.

His hair is overdue for a cut, a little shaggy over the ears. He's heading into a world full of people who could snap him in half and he doesn't even seem nervous. I trail downward with my eyes, from his intense face and striking jaw, to the base of his neck where his button-down shirt hangs open, showing dark, sun-kissed skin, and a knotted black leather cord. Even lower, his shirt's untucked from his jeans, designer of course, and his legs are crossed at the ankle.

As if he can feel my gaze on him, he looks up from his book and meets my eye. A half smile and a nod of his head and I shift to the empty chair next to him. "How long was I out?" I ask.

"I'm not sure," Noah says. "I just woke up myself. Did you sleep okay?"

"Your jet is great. Thank you so much for loaning it to me at the last minute. I'm sorry you're missing school for this."

"By this," Noah says, "you mean so you can fly to Hawaii and fight your sister to either change the course of the world or die trying?"

"I guess that's what I mean."

"Why are you doing it?" he asks.

"Doing what?"

"Fighting her."

"Well, she's planning to kill everyone in your country that she can, so she can subjugate the rest."

Noah throws his hands up in the air. "I get that she's crazy and therefore the enemy. What I mean is, why are you fighting her yourself? There have to be other options. Not that I wanted you to marry that guy." He jerks his thumb at Edam. "But at least you thought he'd win for you."

"Sometimes it feels like my entire life has been on a collision course to this moment," I whisper. "Does that sound crazy? Or unbearably arrogant?"

"A little melodramatic maybe, but that doesn't mean it's not also true." Noah says, "But I still see other options. The world isn't as black and white as you seem to believe it is."

I'm supposed to be the sister who sees in gray, but maybe I'm oversimplifying too. "What do you mean?"

"You could run with me. We can warn my family and they can evacuate."

"Could you live with all those people dying?" I ask.

Noah bites his lip. "It wouldn't be our fault, but I guess not. Okay, I hate to say this, but why'd you change your mind about marrying the old man? I'd rather have you married to an ancient loser than dead."

"So *now* you're ready to support my idea, now that I've cast it off."

"What changed?"

I tap my fingers on the little divider between our seats. "I don't know, exactly."

"He did something," Noah whispers in Mandarin. His eyes meet mine and for a moment, it's like he can see straight into my soul, reading all my secrets.

I shiver and reply in Mandarin. I have no idea who can speak it, but I know that every passenger on this jet speaks English. "No, he didn't. He's great."

The corners of Noah's mouth turn up. "Something made you doubt him. What was it? You don't have to tell me, but I warn you, I'm a great judge of character, so I'm not surprised."

I lean my head back against the seat. "I found out that he's been in contact with his sister."

Noah stares at me blankly.

"She's the leader of a rival family."

"Whoa," Noah says. "Treason?"

I bob my head reluctantly.

"That is worse than I was expecting, by like a factor of ten."

"Yeah, it's kind of a mess." Lark and Edam are the two people I probably trust most, and both of them are technically guilty of treason. "The thing is, evians are complicated. I'll just say, I understand why he did what he did. If I'd been in his shoes, I might have done the same thing. Family gets fractured sometimes, because of the nature of who we are and what's expected. It's one of the things I want to work to repair if I..."

"If you survive." Noah's expression is grim.

I bob my head.

"How good is she? Do you have a chance?" Noah balls his hands into fists. "That came out wrong."

"I appreciate that you ask real questions, never pulling punches."

"Thanks, I guess," Noah says. "I'm just struggling here, thinking you're rolling the dice and hoping you can defeat her." He exhales heavily. "Killing your twin sister seems so drastic, and maybe you aren't seeing it because you feel backed into a corner. I'm good at helping people figure out how to tunnel their way out. If I were supposed to kill one of my siblings, I'd be tunneling as fast as I could the other direction."

"I've done that for seventeen years. The harder I tunnel, the faster she pursues. You told me at the track meet that people aren't all victims or Vikings, and that may be true for humans but for evians. . ." I shake my head. "Judica has terrorized me my entire life, and I'm done taking it. It's time I try to stop her for once, and if I can eliminate the threat she poses to the world then I'll be doing Alamecha a huge favor. I hope."

"You don't think she's the strongest one anymore?"

"She is strong," I say. "But Edam can beat her, so she's not bulletproof." I cough. "Well, bullets wouldn't kill her, but you get my point. She isn't invulnerable."

"But you don't trust him anymore, so you're stuck taking the risk yourself."

I sigh heavily. "It's not that I don't trust him, so much as that I need to do this myself. I've tunneled away from her for so long, Noah. At some point I have to stand up and fight back. I guess now is my moment."

Noah takes my hand in his. "I don't know her, but I've watched you, and you're strong. Maybe the strongest person I've ever met. And you're introspective. You don't just press your will on people. You listen, you think, and then you act. That's the right order, and you'll figure out the correct move for you and your family when it's time. I believe that all the way down to my deficient, unworthy human bones."

His fingers against mine feel too good. I want to sink into him and let the rest of the world disappear, which means it's time to let go of his hand. "And right now, I should eat. I'm starving. Even high end sports cars need fuel."

"Message received." Noah walks to the front of the jet and clears his throat. "Excuse me."

A tall woman with black hair and dark eyes appears in the doorway. "Yes sir?"

"I was wondering what time it is?" he asks.

"New York time, or Hawaii?" she asks.

"New York."

"It's nine a.m. in New York," she says.

Oh, no. I slept for almost eight hours and we land in less than an hour.

"Would you like breakfast?" she asks Noah.

"Please."

I think about Edam and Lark, both of whom will be as hungry as me. "Can you make enough for eight people and bring it for me and Noah and those two?" I point at Lark and Edam, who are both lifting their heads, probably due to the sound of my voice. "And I'm guessing the others on the plane will be wanting food, too. Maybe just bring out everything you have in the back. We will replenish your stores once we land."

Her eyes widen, but to her credit, she nods and ducks back into her area. I walk back to my seat and sit down, rolling my head one way, and then the other. We may not need to stretch, but it feels good sometimes.

Edam wakes up next to me, the muscles of his arms rippling as he shifts and then straightens. "Are you nervous?"

"Petrified," I say. "And regretting every second of the time I had that I didn't spend training. I'm an idiot."

Edam puts a hand on my arm. "A lot of your preparation took place here," Edam says softly, tapping my forehead with his index finger in an eerie echo of Alora.

"Thanks," I say.

"Thanks for what?" Noah yawns.

"Not you, idiot," I say. "I was thanking Edam."

"Well, you ought to thank me for letting you guys just snore away. A lesser guy probably would have poked you."

"I don't snore," I say.

"How do you know?" Noah smiles and raises both eyebrows. "By definition you can't be sure."

"She doesn't snore," Edam says. "No evian does."

"Wait, since you snore, dear Coach Renfro, does that mean you're partially human like me?" Noah smirks. "Or maybe extreme age brings that out in everyone, evian or not?"

"Stop it," I say.

They both sober immediately.

"I must be in bad shape," I say, "for you to back down so fast."

"I couldn't believe I sunk to his level," Edam says.

Noah's flight attendant shows up with an enormous tray of pastries, and another tray stacked up with bagels and cream cheese. Several other women pass out similar piles of food to the guards. Noah must be even hungrier than me, because he's the first one to take a bite.

I slather a cinnamon raisin bagel with cream cheese and bite down. "Hey," I say to Edam. "You aren't tasting this stuff first."

"It's Noah's people preparing it," he says. "And he's eating it with us, and he's human, which makes him the perfect tester."

"That's true." I take a bite, pause for a moment, and then grab my throat and pretend to choke.

"Oh please," Edam says. "You'd have to do better than that to fool me."

A thud behind us draws our attention. Noah's convulsing on the ground. His face is red, and he isn't breathing. Drool covers the bottom part of his face.

"Oh no!" I drop to the floor and open his mouth wider to check his airway, ignoring the fact that he's biting down on my fingers. It's clear, but he's still convulsing. "Could it be poison?"

"It would affect him first." Edam kneels down, trying to hold Noah's flailing body still. If Edam's worried, this is a real problem.

"Go call for help and ask them for a syringe," I say. "An evian blood transfusion might help."

Lark hops to her feet and rushes toward the front of the plane.

I lean over Noah again and check his eyes, but then the shaking stops as suddenly as it began and his eyes open. He reaches up, grabs my head, and tries to pull me down for a kiss. I slap him away.

"How was that? Convincing enough for you, oh great evian overlord?" He looks pointedly at Edam.

The laugh starts in my belly and fills my entire frame. "Oh man," I say around peals of laughter. "He really got you, and right after you said I'd have to do better. A human!"

Edam rolls his eyes, but even he looks moderately amused. "I ought to strangle you, just so I have a baseline for how it looks."

Noah smiles. "Princess needed to think about something other than her upcoming fight."

Edam quirks one eyebrow. "Princess?"

"My nickname for her turned out to be accurate. I find that ironic."

Edam coughs. "Let me get this straight. Your plan was to convince someone whose mother died from poison a few days ago that you'd been poisoned? As a joke?"

I sit back on my heels. I hadn't thought of it that way, maybe because I found Mom after it was already too late. I wish I'd been there with her when she collapsed so I could have tried to do something. Or I could have heard her last words at least.

"I'm an idiot," Noah says. "I'm so sorry."

I shrug. I'm surprisingly not upset about his prank. He didn't know, and I gave him the idea, what with mocking Edam about how he always worries about testing my food. "It's okay. You didn't mean any harm."

I do want to be up and moving, though. "Edam, you down for a little warmup before we land?"

"Sure," he says, "as long as we stick to hand-to-hand. Probably shouldn't destroy Noah's jet, at least not while we're flying in it."

Noah shrugs. "Like my yacht, it's the worst one my family owns. Don't stress."

Don't stress. I think about Noah's admonition, and realize it's an impossible suggestion. Judica's planning to kill me and cement her rule by taking over China. It will shift the entire balance of power in the families, and if they're scared enough, they might go down like dominoes. She might succeed in taking over the other families, but does it count as uniting them if she does it through brute force? It's not like any of the deep-seated disagreements, jealousies, or bad blood will be settled.

Edam interrupts my reflection by launching a series of strikes. I counter each one almost without thinking. Which leaves me plenty of bandwidth to contemplate Judica's plans.

The only way to truly unite people is to bring them together, not to shove them down into a hole. The only way I can prevent Judica from subjugating the entire world is to defeat her myself. Surely that will spook the other families enough that they'll back off while I get Alamecha whipped into supporting me.

But how can I do that?

Edam speeds up, but I'm so busy thinking that I don't worry about it. I merely counter his moves. Block, deflect, block, strike. It's almost easier to fight when I'm not focusing on it. We move up and down the aisle slowly, darting between rows of startled guards now and then. I choke out a laugh when Arlington trips Edam and throws me a thumbs up.

It's too bad I won't have anyone handy to trip Judica.

Alora said the key to melodics lies in knowing my enemy. Even if I can't trust Alora, I think her advice was sound. So what do I know about Judica? Her primary motivating force is ambition, or maybe anger. She's furious I stole Mom's time and love, and maybe impatient with how long she's having to wait to lead Alamecha. I was positive she killed Mom, but now I'm not quite as sure.

And if she didn't, who did?

And did Sotiris' existence precipitate Judica poisoning her, or was the poison the reason Mom became pregnant in the first place? And for that matter, who was the father?

How has this question not occurred to me before now?

I spent nearly every minute with Mom, and I never saw her express an interest in anyone. Why would she hide a relationship from me? And who could he be? Surely he knew about her pregnancy. Right?

Maybe Judica tired of waiting for Mom to age and decided to poison her. She might not have gone through with it, but she wanted to feel like she was in control. She might have unwittingly caused Sotiris, and when Mom told her the truth, it prompted Judica to finish things. Or perhaps it was my reaction to the ring that set her over the edge, or some combination of the two. Either way, Judica would have needed help from someone older to pull it off, someone knowledgeable with poison to locate the toxin. Of course, she has an entire guard of people who could help her and who are tasked to serve her. Presumably she trusts at least a few of them.

Edam sweeps my legs out from under me and my back whams against the floor, knocking the air from my lungs. I look up into Edam's wide eyes.

"What was that for?" I ask. "I said warm up, not take down."

He offers me a hand. "I told you we're preparing to land, but you weren't listening."

Duh. "Trapped up here." I tap my forehead. "Sorry about that."

He and I scramble back to our seats and buckle up. I hear the landing gear deploying and I take one deep breath. Edam opens his mouth and I pray he's not about to try and convince me to make him my Consort again. I feel his gaze on me and slowly turn to meet his eyes. They burn into mine, so beautiful, so strong, so sure. How could I have doubted he supports me? If he asks to be my Consort right now, maybe I should say yes.

His voice is low, steady, and confident. "You are ready. You can do this."

In some ways, it's harder that he didn't offer. Am I being an idiot? I feel like an idiot, flipping and flopping and emotional. I close my eyes and lean against my seat. I thought I was nervous before, but as the plane lands, my knee begins to bounce. Edam covers it with his large hand.

"I don't feel well," I say. "I'm not sure what's wrong."

Edam unbuckles and wraps an arm around me. "The

humans call this 'feeling sick.' You've never felt it before, but I've seen that look on a lot of their faces."

"I'm dizzy and light-headed, my stomach aches, and I'm shaky. You're telling me humans feel this way frequently?"

Noah barks out a laugh from up ahead, his head craned around so he can see me. Is anyone on this plane wearing their seatbelt? "That's pretty much Human 101."

"I'm truly sorry to hear that. How awful."

Noah rolls his eyes and turns back around.

The plane lands safely on our family's landing strip and the doors open. Frederick insists on the majority of my guards deplaning first, with Noah, Lark, and me leaving just in front of Edam and himself. As I walk down the stairs to the ground, rows and rows of guards stand at attention in the pre-dawn light. An honor guard always welcomed my mom and me home, so it feels right.

Except Mom's not here.

The moment my feet touch the pavement, Judica shouts, "Now." That's when I realize that, uniforms notwithstanding, all of the guards present were part of Judica's private guard when I left.

The guards all pull their guns. Edam pulls a gun too, and my crew springs into action. Even Noah thinks on his feet, disarming the guard nearest him and pointing the weapon at the now unarmed and shocked guard's head.

It's still not enough, not by a long shot.

"Wait," I say.

There's no way we can survive this many bullets. They'd take us down while we tried to heal the damage. I don't even want to think about what would happen to Lark and Noah.

"Didn't Inara tell you?" I ask. "If you shoot me, you'll never get the ring."

"Oh I think we're capable of searching through your

corpses until we find it." Judica's mouth turns up in the corner.

"If I had it on me, that would be true enough," I say. "But I'm guessing you didn't find it in my absence, so I doubt you'll figure it out any time soon."

"You hid it here?" Judica's eyes widen.

"If you kill me, the location is gone."

Judica's face shows not a twinge of emotion. "Why should I believe that?"

"Where's Inara?" I ask. "Shouldn't she be here with you, giving the orders to the guards while I squirm like a fish on a hook?"

"Is that what she'd do?" Judica asks. "Order your execution?"

"I think she'd insist you at least follow through on your bargain and fight me," I say. "But I wouldn't know. She stayed with you."

"Only to report back to you," Judica practically snarls. She turns around and barks a command over her shoulder. "Bring Inara."

Two guards duck out and emerge less than a minute later, one holding each arm as a struggling Inara emerges. A quick glance shows several missing fingers, in varying stages of regrowth. Judica obviously did not take the news of my return well. I feel guilty for doubting her now.

"I knew you left her as your little spy," Judica says. "But I didn't think she'd be able to send you anything helpful."

"You're wrong," I say. "She's a good sister to both of us, and she was trying to find a resolution that would have satisfied Mom."

Judica's laugh chills me to the bone. "We shared a womb, you and I. You're my only true sister, but you're a fool if you think we'll ever share anything again. I don't compromise."

"Are you really so afraid of me that you're planning to gun me down on a runway?"

Judica's eyes flash. "I'm not scared of you, but I won't let your Consort kill me either. I challenged you and you didn't have a Consort then. I wouldn't have agreed to a delay if I knew it would shift the stakes."

"You've been misinformed. I haven't named a Consort," I say, "and I won't be doing it any time soon. If you really are brave enough to fight me, I'll promise to give you the ring if I lose."

Judica sets her jaw. "If you lose, you're dead. Corpses can't keep promises."

"I'll leave you a letter that tells you its location."

"Why am I not surprised to learn you lied the night Mother died?"

I shake my head. "I didn't know then. Mom sent me a message at Alora's on the day of her death that disclosed the truth." I watch her to see whether she knows what I'm really saying. That I know about Sotiris.

Her face doesn't even twitch. "Which means you may not even know where it is. You haven't verified that information."

Frederick catches my eye and inclines his head almost imperceptibly.

"I know where it is."

"Mother sent you the location." Judica's voice is flat.

"Mom trusted me," I say.

"You're implying she didn't trust me."

"No one trusts you," I say. "This is a surprise to you?"

She scowls.

"I could have you executed for treason in my absence, you know." I signal Frederick and another line of guards run out and surround Judica's. "Or had you forgotten that I'm the real Empress? Maybe that's your excuse for ordering a hit on me, too."

"I didn't try to assassinate you," Judica says.

"You didn't send the Recluse to kill me?" Could Alora have hired them to shove suspicion on to Judica? My heart cracks, but I can't spiral, not now.

Judica glares at me. "Inara promised she had a formal request for an Inquest regarding Mother's death with the Five prepared that would be filed if you were assassinated. I'm not afraid of them, but I don't welcome that kind of interference either. I didn't raise a finger against you."

I can't decide if I'm more upset about Alora's incompetent attack, or relieved that at least she didn't betray me to Judica.

"I know you're planning a missile launch against China. You will promise not to give that order, whether I win or lose."

Judica smiles. "Why would I agree to any requests?"

My heart constricts. I want Judica brought to justice if I die trying to defeat her, but I care more about the people who are still alive. I'm sorry Mom. It's the only way I can think to guarantee that my people survive and Judica doesn't bomb China. "If you agree to my terms, Inara will sign away her right to request an Inquest as your Heir. But only if you swear not to order a missile launch on China, and you promise not to kill or punish Edam, Lark, Inara, or any of my other supporters if you defeat me. Including Alora."

Inara tries to protest, but a guard smashes her in the face, breaking her nose.

"It's okay," I tell her. "I'm more worried about keeping everyone safe than pursuing justice if I die."

Judica smiles. "I will agree not to order a missile launch on China after our duel."

That was almost too easy. "I want it in writing. And what about my supporters?"

She laughs, but it's an ugly laugh. "You're bargaining for

their lives when you die?" She looks around the landing strip. "This is your Empress? She's so sure she won't win that she's negotiating your release when she fails."

"Do you agree?" I ask her.

Her eyes are still laughing, but I refuse to be embarrassed for planning for my loved ones, including those who hurt me.

Finally, she says, "I agree. Although, I don't make any promises regarding exile." She glances behind me at Lark. "Especially for traitorous mutts who aren't even supposed to be alive."

"Done," I say.

"I need proof that you've located the ring before the fight," she says. "Larena can help with that. And I don't want you wearing it during the duel."

Edam's eyes widen, but Inara meets my gaze steadily. We both know why Judica doesn't want me wearing it, and I don't blame her. I wouldn't want to be torched during a fight either. Now that I'm here, facing Judica down, I want to cry. Poor Mom. Her greatest fear realized, her daughters fighting one another to the death. "Agreed."

Judica sighs heavily, almost like she's dreading this as much as me. "Well, then, blood of my blood, shall we fight?"

Blood of my blood? Judica's always been ridiculously melodramatic. "Let's go."

When we reach the main hallway, a familiar barking draws my attention. Duchess flies down the hall like an arrow. Mom's dog was immaculately trained. She didn't bark, she didn't jump up on anyone, and she waited to come until she was called. This Duchess has lost quite a bit of weight and she leaps up once she reaches me, placing a paw on both of my shoulders and nearly bowling me over.

Edam draws his sword.

I wave him off and crouch down to eye level. Duchess

licks my face, and when I start to cry, she licks my tears away. "I know," I whisper into her ruff. "I'm hurting too." Finally, I stand up and give her one more pat.

The guards who supported me upon my landing have joined my small force. I'm shocked by how many came to my defense. I look for Inara and find her, tripping along behind the two guards who brought her here.

"Wait," I yell. "Release Inara."

"Feeling guilty?" Judica asks.

I shake my head. "I didn't do that. You did. But she's our sister, and she deserves to walk on her own."

Judica snorts. "You're exhausting." She turns to her guards. "Take her to a holding cell below pending the resolution of our disagreement."

I consider arguing, but I've exhausted my leverage. At least I've secured Judica's promise that she won't harm anyone if I lose. "Draw up the papers and send them to my room. Once they've been signed and witnessed, I'm ready to fight."

"Delightful," Judica says. "Bring the ring, or all your extra terms are off."

Frederick and Arlington lead the way, and my procession passes the training room and continues on to the throne room. The arena is already set up inside, the raised dais prepared and illuminated with the barriers erected, the majesty of Mom's throne rising behind it. People are already assembled in rows to watch. I could have used the support of some of them back on the airstrip. Balthasar sits on the front row, and I wonder how he justified sitting over here during my plane's landing. Maybe they didn't know Judica planned to eliminate the need for this challenge. Or maybe they simply didn't have the gumption to object.

I worry for my people. How could Balthasar choose between us? He trained Judica for years, but he's known, and I believe loved, both of us. If he's torn, how could any of my people *not* be confused and hurting?

Judica tosses me a white training uniform embroidered with our family sigil. A circle of thorny vines surrounding the sun signifies light in the face of adversity. Judica walks toward her room, ostensibly to change, and I head toward mine too. I sure hope I'm right about Mom's ring.

Just before her party, I saw Mom leaving my room. She left the gown on my bed, but she could have had a servant do that. She almost never went into my room without me, and when I changed into that gown, the melodics training flute case I used as a young child but haven't touched in over a decade fell off my bed.

It can't be a coincidence. Right?

Noah, Edam, and Lark follow me to the door, but I ask them to wait outside. As soon as the door closes behind them, I race to my closet. It's been ransacked, so I dig through pile after pile without luck. At the very bottom of my closet, underneath a pile of clothing, there's a long, heavy object wrapped in brown paper. I slide it out, curious. It's clearly not the flute case or the ring. But what it is?

I open the paper to reveal a sword in a black scabbard. I slide it out and admire the clean, smooth hilt, the sheen carrying all the way to the end. I check the balance and it's as perfect as I expected. A few words are scrawled on the brown paper I discarded. I recognize the blade. It's Inara's.

Until you have your own.

A tear springs to my eye. She must have hidden this when she realized Judica wouldn't allow her the freedom to support me, but if I use it, my twin will know with certainty that Inara stayed to help defend me and my position.

This blade would certainly help me win.

And ironically, if I lose, it would seal my older sister's fate. I could never do that to her. I wrap the blade back up and place it where I found it, minus the part of the paper with the message scrawled on it, which I shred into tiny pieces and flush.

After I resume my search, it takes a moment, but I find it under a disheveled box of papers. A small black case, tattered and worn. I carry it over to my desk and set it down. I open it, and as I expect, the only thing in the case is a wooden flute. I pull a knife from my bedside table and slice the side of the case, peeling away the worn black velvet. It resists more than it should for such an old case.

Because it was re-glued last week.

I pull and tug and peel and it finally separates. I remove the wooden shell from the top of the inside of the case and then I can see it, stuffed on all sides with fiberfill so it won't rattle around in the frame.

Mom's staridium ring.

The cause of this whole nightmare. Instead of putting it on my finger, I set it on my desk and change into the white tank top with the sigil and matching fitted pants. A knock at my door startles me, and I toss a throw blanket over the ring.

"Enter," I say.

Edam opens the door, his eyes darting around the room. "Larena is here with the paperwork you requested."

I sigh and wave them inside. Edam insists on standing next to her, as though Larena might suddenly attack me instead of boring me to death with paperwork.

"Here's what I want to know," I say. "Does this give the Five a mandate to step in if Judica violates these promises?"

Larena nods. "They'd have the excuse they need to consolidate their forces and move against your sister if she doesn't honor them."

"Good enough." I sign the paperwork and stand up. It's the best I can do. "I'm ready."

"Not quite," Larena says.

"Excuse me?" Edam asks.

Larena lifts the lid on a box underneath the paperwork. It's solid glass, hollowed out in the center. "I need the ring. It will sit on a platform in front of the dais. Winner takes it. That's your consideration for this contract."

I shake my head. "I'll place it in the box in the ballroom, in front of Judica."

Larena shrugs, gathers her things and leaves.

Edam takes my hand. "Are you ready?"

"Accept the world as it is," I say.

"Or do something to change it." He takes my hands in his and squeezes them.

I look at Noah and he smiles at me. "No frowns and fear from me. You'll make the right choice when it's time. I have faith in you."

Lark doesn't say anything, but she pulls me close for a long hug. When she finally releases me, her eyes swim with unshed tears.

It's nice to see that a few people, at least, have faith in me. I walk toward the duel, trailed by my strongest supporters. When I reach the room, I hold Mom's ring over my head. "I hold Enora Isadora Alamecha's ring, the largest shard from Eve's staridium. I will leave it here, to await the winner of this duel."

By rights, the current Empress should wear the ring for the duel, but if it makes Judica nervous, well, I can't fault her. Besides, this isn't about a rock, and it never should have been. Mom made a mistake there.

Judica stands in the center of the arena. "Well met, sister. Select our method."

I can't stomach a hand-to-hand battle to the death, so I name the only viable alternative. "Blades."

Judica smiles. Mom gave Judica her own blade on her tenth birthday, and she had another made for her when she turned sixteen. I don't own one myself, and I couldn't bring myself to implicate Inara, which means I'll have to use one of the unclaimed practice blades. I look at the rack and trail my fingers down the length of the hilts. They vary in length, weight, and style. Curved blades, double edged, blunt tipped, decorative, simple.

I walk toward the far end where the small, light blades rest. One catches my eye. It's mid length, thin, double edged. It's simple, but gilded Hebrew letters are worked down the length of the blade and tiny black stone chips run down the center line. The letters in the blade almost glow. "Failure is a choice," they say, a motto I know well. Mom's personal motto. I lift the blade and shift it from one hand to the other.

I turn to face Judica, but before I can step into the arena, Balthasar touches my arm. "Do you know that sword?"

I shake my head.

"It was your mother's wedding gift from my brother."

Of course. It would have been her motto, even then. It seems fitting, to slay Mom's murderer with her own blade, like an act of vengeance from beyond the grave.

I ascend the steps to the arena, walk inside, and pull the half wall closed.

Judica salutes with her much larger, much nastier sword. "It's a good day to die."

☙ 32 ❧

"Accept the world as it is," Judica says.

"Or have the courage to change it," I say.

"Marks," Judica calls out.

The arena teems with Alamecha evians: men, women, and children. They murmur softly, shift from foot to foot, and glance flightily from Judica to me and back again. Many of the young ones have never witnessed a royal duel, but if this goes badly, there might be more as soon as this ends. The last royal challenge was when Melina fought Mom. Now, not even eighteen years later, the cause of that duel brings it full circle. Maybe Melina was right—Mom should have killed me.

I breathe in through my nose, close my eyes, and picture my mom. She'd be devastated to see her daughters killing one another, but not surprised. The first clap rises from all the evians gathered around me like the crack of a whip. Humans are always clapping, but evians only clap en masse for two things: beginning a duel and acknowledging a new monarch. I open my eyes on the second clap and exhale through my mouth on the third.

A millisecond after the third clap, Judica's sword flies

toward my neck. I drop below her swing at the last second and slash at her legs with mine. My sword arcs faster than any I've ever used, as it if were made for me. I'm surprised when I nick her leg. Judica gasps, probably more from shock than pain, and leaps back nimbly.

She circles me in the arena, buying time to heal her wound. I let her, because I'm not sure how to attack yet. I should be hearing her melodic line, but I'm not. My mind is blank.

I cycle through the videos Inara sent and close my mind to doubt, fear, and hate. I open it to the music around me, the slow beating of hundreds of hearts, the quick breathing, the shuffling of feet and the shifting of arms and hands.

I tune in to my twin, narrowing my focus to her breath, sucked in and released. I react to her movements reflexively, ducking and deflecting her parries, jabbing back to watch how she responds, and I finally hear it, her melodic line. Faint, but there. Clear, dire, straightforward in life, sideways in battle.

I think back to our childhood. She didn't physically attack me when we were nine, but she tried to poison me. She acts forthright and then comes at you sideways when she means harm, almost as if inflicting harm shames her. But she baked the poisoned cookies herself. I should watch for attacks that come from her directly, but in unexpected ways.

If I'd had the thought a second later, I'd be dead. I named blades, but I didn't specify the number. I assumed we were limited to one or I would have chosen a short sword as well. But I never stated the limitation. She pulls a short sword from behind her back and throws it at me. No wonder she was circling, biding her time. She didn't need me close; she just needed to distract me.

I drop to the mat just in time, and my hand snaps out as the short sword flies over my head, my fingers closing over its hilt. It's much lighter than my blade, and now I have the two I wanted. She couldn't have known that I fight better with two weapons, because I didn't know myself until a few days ago. Mom's presence surrounds me like a balm, like even now, even here, she's guiding things.

Judica scowls but recovers quickly. She leaps across the entire arena and lands inside my guard, her broadsword slicing downward like a hammer to an anvil. I twist left, under her sword arm, and slam the hilt of my mom's blade into her elbow. I smile when I hear the crunch this time, until Judica's blade slices down into my foot, pinning me to the mat, just like she speared my hand with that fork. It feels like that interrupted breakfast on the day the staridium responded to me took place a lifetime ago. Everything has shifted since then.

And I'm different, too. This time I'm not frozen by shock or fear or righteous indignation.

I pull backward with all my strength, forcing the blade through the bones, tendons, ligaments and muscles of my foot. Blood sprays the mat and the audience beyond, and I collapse to my knees as the pain rips through me. Judica thinks she has won. She tosses her sword into her other hand, her lip curling into a grin, sure that I can't move well until I heal. I've never fought through the pain, because I never understood it. She was right. But she changed all that when she killed our mother.

This time, after years of giving ground, after years of playing defense, I'm done. I won't defend any more.

I will attack.

When she comes for me, I fall back like she expects, but then I roll and come up with both blades out. I cross swipe with them, and my mother's blade catches Judica's shoulder. Her eyes widen and her face flushes, and she rains blows down on me. But I leap to my functioning feet and meet her blows in a staccato rhythm.

For the first time, I hear my own melodic line, and I revel in it.

When Judica slices at me, I block and launch an attack of my own. I feel her next move and wrap my own around it, dancing with her in a complex and undescribably beautiful interchange. We trade blows for several minutes, but I'm not gaining. She stays a few milliseconds ahead of me, which means I'm still missing something.

But what?

Judica's angry, ambitious, and what else? Could the thing I'm missing be guilt?

"Do you regret it?" I block her advance with the short sword and jab at her left knee with Mom's.

She frowns at me. "Do I regret what?"

"Killing Mom."

Judica's eyes flash and the intensity of her strikes deepens. I'm missing something. Something big. She slices my left arm, and then my right leg. "So you don't."

Judica roars, "I didn't kill her!"

"You're lying." I practically spit the words. "You must be."

Judica slams her sword against Mom's and the clang reverberates through my right arm. "How can you be so sure?"

"Because Mom told me everything in her letter."

"What does that even mean?" Judica pulls back and yanks a dagger from a slit in her sliced pants. She must have worn a thigh sheath. Now we're both armed with two blades, except Judica holds her dagger in her right hand and I use my short sword in my left. "It's not like you need to gloat about how much more she loved you. I know already. Everyone knows."

Something about this moment seems surreal, as though I'm momentarily looking down on us from above. Mirror opposites locked in combat against our will. We look the same, but we're different in every important way. How could she kill our mom? How could she kill our little sister *in utero*?

"I'm not gloating, Judica. It broke my heart," I say.

"We lost the same person," she says. "But you're such a martyr about it." Judica lands a glancing blow on my shoulder.

I jump backward. "I actually cared about her, even though I didn't know her. She might have fixed things between us, you know."

"What are you rambling about?" Judica straightens, pausing her attack momentarily.

"Our sister," I say. "Mom was pregnant, and you killed her for it."

Judica's face blanks and her hand loosens on the hilt of her sword. Even the tip of her dagger dips downward.

She didn't know.

She stumbles backward a step and opens a window. I could incapacitate her now, maybe even kill her. But I can't do it, not like this, not using Sotiris' existence as a weapon.

My voice is shrill and cold when I say, "You poisoned her when you found out."

Judica doesn't deny it. She's too dazed to say anything at all, and I'm horribly worried it's because she wasn't lying. My heart aches at the thought, but what if she didn't do it? Could Judica be hurting as badly as me? Or even worse, since Inara, Alora, and Edam all sided with me?

For the first time, her bone crushing despair, the soul-wounding sorrow that weighs her down becomes clear to me. In Judica's mind, Mom never loved her. She never thought I loved her either, and then Edam dumped her. Finally, the one thing she had, Mom's throne, was pulled out from under her feet when I reacted to a lump of black rock.

Then I throw Mom's pregnancy at her like a bomb.

Mom told me, not her. Mom loved me, not her. Mom chose me, not her. Alora chose me. Edam chose me.

Everyone chooses me.

I could hear parts of her melodic line, but I've been missing the most basic notes. The anger, the frustration, and the jealousy form a descant that rises above and surrounds a framework of aching, bone-crushing desperation. Judica's not the dragon I always took her for, no. She's a wounded animal, lashing out at her attackers. She's taking on the entire world alone, and screaming her rage in its face.

Her song echoes all around me as we dance. Cross, parry, strike. I back in a circle while she rains blows on me, right and left. Finally she falls into a very predictable pattern. Strike, hold, strike, hold. I can almost hear my mother whistling with her little wooden flute. A simple run. C minor to an F minor triad. My mother's phantom playing fills my ears. Instead of merely defending with my left arm, I begin to use it on offense, an intervallic relation to replace lone notes.

Judica falters.

She doesn't understand why or how I leveled up.

She steps back, resheathes her dagger, and grips her sword with both hands. She swings at me again, then feints and swings from the other direction at light speed, a key change. I catch her sword with both of mine, crossing my arms and throwing hers back in her face. She stumbles back and I'm on her, slashing with the short sword and striking with my mother's sword intermittently. She falls back, blocking and turning to evade my attack. I press my advantage. Ambient sounds drop away and only our melodic lines, accompanied by Mom's flute, every strike a note, every block and spin a run, envelop us. My opening appears when Judica's pants catch on an outcropping of the arena I backed her into, slowing her slightly.

I jab with her own short sword and it slides into her ribs, impaling her a hair below her heart. One upward thrust and she'll have catastrophic damage to repair. The kind of damage that would incapacitate her for a kill shot. And she knows exactly what I've done.

Her eyes flash. Not with anger, but with resolution. "Finish it, then."

A flick of my wrist and I'll slice her heart in two. She'll finally feel the way she made me feel every day, every week, every year of our lives. The way she rent my heart when she killed Pebbles while intending to murder me. The way I felt when she stabbed me with a fork and laughed. The way I felt when she taunted and mocked me, belittling me and attacking me over everything that made me different.

I should end this. I should spare everyone in China, and everyone else she will threaten if she continues in her destructive, selfish, ferocious path. But if she didn't kill our mother. . . maybe it's not too late for her.

I can't undo death. Nothing has become more clear to me since Mom died.

A scarlet tear wells in her left eye. "Stop prolonging this and do it!"

Is she begging me to end her suffering the way I'd put down a wounded horse? Has she been in unbearable pain this whole time? Was she lashing out because she can't heal the injuries she has sustained? I stare into her deep blue eyes, eyes that remind me so much of our mother. My eyes are the same, but seeing them staring at me from Judica's face, I know beyond a shadow of a doubt.

Even if she killed Mom, even if she's the devil everyone sees, I can't kill my own twin.

Alora and Edam and Inara all explained why she must die. Even Noah, a human, understands why I should end her. I wonder how many people explained to my mother why I had to die. How many people did she ignore when she spared me? How much did that decision cost? When will the payment for her mistake end?

If I don't kill Judica, the Five will see me as easy prey. They'll attack Alamecha. Judica will remain a threat, maybe forever. And most of all, I know Judica wouldn't hesitate to kill me if our situations were reversed.

I still can't do it.

I know me, and my strength is not in death or destruction. My power does not derive from hate. I want to build and heal. I want to right the wrongs of the world, not create more injustice and more devastation.

Judica sees my weakness for what it is.

Even with a sword rammed in her own chest, she brings all her strength to bear and swings her sword around and down on mine, chopping the short sword in two. The blow tears her chest open in the process. She reaches down and drags the end of the blade from her body, slicing her palms, but freeing her chest to heal. Her maniacal expression causes me to slide backward, putting some space between us. I throw the hilt of the short sword to the edge of the ring and bring mother's sword up and around to protect me. Before Judica can heal her hands and grab her sword, I press the razor sharp edge against her throat.

"I don't want to kill you," I say.

"No, you *can't* kill me. You're too soft." The effort of speaking makes her cough, and she sprays blood all over my shirt.

I shove Mom's blade forward, slicing into her neck. "Yield."

"Never," she says. "I won't, I can't yield. I was born to rule."

"You've chosen badly, Judica."

She snarls. "What do you know about my choices? You don't know me at all."

I clench my hand on the hilt, trying to convince her

that I can do it. I need her to cede the loss. It won't keep her from challenging me again tomorrow, but at least for today, she must back down. I don't realize how long I've delayed until I see skin spread across her exposed abdomen.

When I look back up at her face, she smiles again, but there's no joy in it.

She leaps backwards and throws her feet up at the same time, knocking the hilt of Mom's old blade from my hand. She catches the end of it, blood spraying outward. She slams it down behind her and it sinks several inches into the wooden floor of the room below, outside of the raised arena, out of bounds. Judica tosses her head at me and grins bitterly as she stands.

"You can't do what needs to be done," she says. "You never could. Mother saw it and she protected you from me, but she's not here anymore. You can't even keep hold of your sword."

She looks pleased, and she should. She's facing me armed, while I have nothing. The next moment is a blur of pain and destruction as I block with my forearms and shins and heal the damage as quickly as I can. I listen for her melodic line but hear nothing. I'm scrambling, desperate to locate some kind of pattern, but I'm too busy deflecting death blows into maiming ones. She comes after me like a dervish, her sword flashing, raining jabs and slices down on me with murderous glee. Judica's toying with me like a lynx with a wounded robin.

"You've improved, Chancery." Judica pauses. "You heal much faster. Maybe faster than me."

"I didn't understand pain before."

Judica barks a laugh. "You think you do now?"

"We've both suffered in the past week."

Judica lost her mother, only to discover that Mom had betrayed her, assigning her birthright to another. Then she challenged me and spent a week assuming I'd return with her old boyfriend to kill her. At every turn Judica has been beaten, abused, and rejected. She must be strong, because otherwise she is nothing. Now that I see her for who she is, I'm overwhelmed by her beauty.

I would have curled up and died in her place. The weight of her despair would have leveled me.

How might we have changed if she had a chance to be anything but the bad guy? How have our circumstances carved us into the mirror opposites we have become?

If I want to heal Alamecha, I need to start at home.

Judica redoubles her efforts, tearing into me like a ravaging beast, lashing out at me as retribution for all the pain she's in. Her next strike slices through skin and sinew and shatters my collar bone. A kick spins me to the right and when I try to correct my position, she brings my head down against a knee strike.

But all of this was never about rage or anger. It was always about a deep and abiding pain, an unfathomable suffering. In the very nanosecond she launches her final strike at me, her enormous broadsword arcing toward my unmoving neck, I drop, insanely fast, to the mat. My hands come together and slam into the bottom of her fingers where they clasp the hilt of her sword, knocking it free. I slap it with my full force and send it flying from the arena. It lodges in a side wall, inches away from a child's shocked face.

The next few moments are a series of strikes, kicks, and punches. I'm almost an observer, my body moving easily, quickly, methodically. Judica rushes to catch me and regain her position, because she doesn't comprehend what has happened. I've finally found peace. I can't let her die without ever knowing joy or experiencing love.

I'll set things right.

I pull her up by her hair and punch her square in the

face, knocking her back and breaking her nose. I leap from the arena and grab Mom's sword. I jump back in just as Judica regains her feet.

"Mom always loved you," I say. "Just as much as she loved me. A new baby would not have changed how she felt about us. It would not have destroyed you. That baby would have set both of us free."

Judica's lips draw back. "You don't know anything."

"Mom loved you to the end, and so do I," I say. "That's why I will not kill you today. I don't care whether you yield. Today, I yield to you."

I close my eyes, then, and picture my mom. Judica rises from the mat and advances. I open my eyes and lift the sword to her, one of my hands under the hilt, one under the blade.

"Kill me," I say. "If that's what it takes for you to forgive Mom and me, then do it. I'm so sorry I let you down. I love you."

I close my eyes again and wait, but the blow never comes.

When I open my eyes, tears stream down Judica's face. She drops the sword and sits down in front of me. "No, I yield."

No one moves or says a word. I collapse next to Judica and take her hand in mine. She doesn't resist.

I only gained Judica's acceptance through offering her what she wanted. Because in that moment, she realized it wasn't what she really needed at all. My gesture won't heal a lifetime of wounds, but it's a step in the right direction. I may have to fight her again and again. She may challenge me every single time we disagree, which I'm sure will happen frequently, but I'm confident that I did the right thing for today.

For the first time since Mom died, my world is better in this moment than it was the day before.

I glance around and the audience is kneeling, every one of them. Edam, Balthasar, Larena, Noah, they're all kneeling, waiting on me to speak. Every ruler needs a motto, a personal quote. You usually select it at the investiture, but mine comes to me in this moment.

I raise my voice so it rings from the rafters. "The smallest light still vanquishes darkness."

I reach over and grab Mom's ring. When I slide it on my finger, there's absolute silence as the ring fills with power, almost as if my people can sense something is happening. Then the ring flashes brightly enough to flood the room with light. Thankfully, I don't set off any fires or release any EMPs, but a lot of astonished faces stare back at me.

For a moment, I stand in utter silence. Then applause fills the room.

33

"Bring us chains," Edam says.

Rope won't contain evians. Most metal won't either. Titanium bindings are expensive and hard to work with, but they're the only thing you can count on. I guess there's a reason most of our sentences end in exile or execution. Imprisonment is impractical in the long run.

"No," I say. "I won't imprison her. She's my Heir, and she will be free."

"Do you believe me?" Judica asks. "Finally?"

"I do." My voice drops to a faint whisper. "Marselle said someone named Nereus bought the poison that was used on Mom." I don't see Balthasar, so I call out his name.

"Why do you want him?" Judica asks.

"I need to tell him to cancel any plans to bomb China."

Judica frowns.

"What's wrong?" I ask.

Judica sighs. "It's too late."

"But you promised," I say. "You promised not to bomb them."

"I agreed because I'd already launched the jets. Two

nuclear bombs were en route to a tiny town outside of Shanghai before your jet landed."

I freeze. "From where?"

"Alaska obviously," Judica says. "But they're Russian planes, older tech, and no one will be able to trace them to us."

I close my eyes and think. "When?"

"I gave the order right before your plane landed."

It's only been a few hours. I might be able to catch them if I take a fast enough jet.

"I gave them clear orders, sister. I sent three planes, two to protect the one carrying the nukes. They've turned off all communications and are not to abort for any reason. They'll shoot down anything that comes after them."

But she said it herself, they're old Russian tech. If I act fast, I can do something without anyone even knowing what Judica did.

"You should've killed her," Noah says. "She doesn't deserve your forgiveness."

Balthasar reaches my side. "Who doesn't deserve your forgiveness?"

"Judica," Noah says.

"She's Heir to the throne of Alamecha." Balthasar scowls at Noah and quiets, clearly listening for Noah's heartbeat. "Whoa, you brought a pet human?" His eyes widen at me.

"He doesn't understand," I say. "He wasn't being disrespectful."

"And he's not a pet." Noah splutters indignantly. "I mean me. I'm not a pet."

"He shouldn't be here," Balthasar says, ignoring Noah entirely.

"My mother isn't Empress anymore." I stand a little taller. "I am, and I'm eliminating the ban she had in place on humans on Ni'ihau."

Judica's eyebrows rise. "Already shaking things up with the hot human boyfriend."

My face heats. "It's not like that, but in general, I don't feel like Mom did about humans."

"What does that mean?" Balthasar asks.

"It means I like them."

"Great." Judica smirks. "I've been out of a job for five minutes and the family's already headed for total ruin."

I don't have time for this. "I need all the information on these bombs immediately," I say. "Bring it all to my room." There must be something we can do, some back door to crawl through that will stop this.

Balthasar opens his mouth, probably to argue, but then he clicks it shut. Wise man.

I walk toward the door, but before I can leave, Judica says, "I've done you a favor, whether you want it or not. You wouldn't do it yourself, but I've gift wrapped China for you. This will set the tone for your rule and keep Alamecha safe from attack and encroachment by the Five. You should thank me."

I ignore her.

"I need to make a call," Noah says.

I point at Edam. "Go below and free Inara. Take Noah with you and detain him there. He's a friend and after this is resolved, we'll set him up somewhere safe, but for now." I shake my head. "I can't trust him not to do something catastrophically stupid."

Edam beams at me. "With pleasure."

"You can't be serious," Noah says. "You have to let me help, or at least let me warn my family."

"Your family isn't anywhere near Shanghai."

"I have family and friends there, but that's not the point."

If his family has pull with the government, they might

be able to issue warnings, or maybe even shoot down the planes.

"Let him call his family as long as he tells them he heard this from a tip that came from a classmate with ties to Russia," I tell Edam. "I can't have this blowing back on us if we can't stop it. Once he's warned them, detain him."

Judica looks at me as though she's never seen me before. When she smiles at me, a chill slides down my spine.

I turn on my heel and walk away from both her and the crowds who seem to think celebrations are in order. I have too much to clean up before I'm ready to breathe a sigh of relief, much less party. Frederick trails me as I leave the room. I walk down the long corridor, head held high as I pass the people I grew up with. They all bow as I pass, kneeling before me one-by-one until I reach my room. I throw open the door and stride inside. Devereaux, one of my mom's old guards, catches me at the entrance to my room and hands me a manila envelope. It should contain all the information we have on the planes.

"Thank you." I clutch the envelope in my hand and close the door, leaning against it. My knees wobble and I slide to the floor, sitting in the middle of the carpet to review the information. I look over the paperwork until I have the rudiments of a plan worked out.

When I open the door, I expect to see Frederick, not Edam.

"Oh hi," I say.

Edam doesn't smile, but his eyes sparkle at me and he cocks one hip. For some reason a thrill runs through me from my toes to my nose.

Which is so inappropriate right now.

"I need our fastest jet. Fuel it up and have it ready to leave immediately," I say

"Where are you going, Your Majesty?" Frederick asks from behind Edam.

"New York," I say. "I have some pressing business to take care of there. Alora betrayed me and if she doesn't have some convincing explanations, she may be taking Inara's vacated cell."

Frederick's eyes are sad. "Yes, Your Majesty."

Edam's brow furrows. Once Frederick's out of earshot he asks, "Should that really be our top priority right now?"

I jog toward the ballroom by way of answer, and Edam runs right alongside me. Many people have filtered out after the fight, but dozens are still milling around. I raise my voice. "I need something witnessed and attested. I must see to some urgent business in person. Edam ne'Malessa ex'Alamecha is named Prince Regent in my absence. You will all do exactly as he says. If he is unable to handle a situation for any reason, Inara Alamecha is named Princess Regent, and she will speak for me."

The evians around me cross their arms over their chests, hands fisted, and bow. "Heard and witnessed," they say when they straighten.

I march down from the arena and back out through the doors with Edam. I walk immediately out to the landing strip and he follows without saying a word. I look up at the plane and say, "Wait, why are we using Noah's jet?"

A wiry man I've known my entire life runs the airstrip, Filomeno. "Your instructions were for the fastest jet, Your Majesty. It's a passenger aircraft, but it's very fast." He wrings his hands.

"That's fine," I say. "Thank you."

I step up the stairs to the plane, but Edam grabs my hand. "I don't understand. Did I upset you somehow?"

"I'm going to deal with Alora," I say, my voice wobbling convincingly. I really am upset about her betrayal, and I still don't understand it, so he should hear the truth of that in my words. "I need you to take care of things until I return.

Only Alora can tell me why she betrayed me and to what extent. I need to know, Edam."

"What about the bomb?" he asks.

"What about it? You heard Judica, and her paperwork confirms it. She didn't build in a cancellation of any kind. There's not much we can do about it now, other than send relief afterward. I wish it wasn't so, but I won't spend any more time dwelling on things I can't change. I've done enough of that for a lifetime."

"Shouldn't we call the Chinese government and warn them?" he asks. "Or was one call to Noah's family all you're planning to do?"

I chafe at the judgment in his tone. "Any real warning would create massive panic, and of course, even with back channels, it could destroy any benefit we otherwise stand to gain. Besides, the Five would perceive that as weakness at best, and as in-fighting at worst. Judica never should have sent that bomb, but it's done now. If anyone hears I surrendered to Judica, this strike might save my reputation and mitigate the risk to Alamecha."

Edam holds my gaze for a long time before he finally bows. "As you say, Your Majesty."

It stings that he believes me capable of abandoning all those people so quickly, but I need him to buy it, so I walk up the steps and onto the jet without looking back.

My fight with Frederick and Arlington takes longer, but I finally succeed in convincing them I'll wait while they assemble a new team. Then I close the door myself and call out to my pilot. "Hello? Who's up there?"

"Paul, Your Majesty."

He's my favorite pilot. Filomeno remembered.

I wish he hadn't.

"I expected Noah's people."

"No, Your Majesty, we sent them to rest. They're not safe to fly right now, so I volunteered," he says.

"We need to go, now. Like, this second."

"We haven't been cleared yet," he says.

"I'm the Empress, or hadn't you heard?"

Paul grins. "I heard. But what about your guards?"

"I'm instructing you to take off without them."

Paul's eyebrows rise.

"And I have a minor detail to clarify."

"Yes, Your Majesty?"

"We're changing our final destination."

"We aren't going to New York?"

"No, we're headed for Shanghai, or more specifically, somewhere over the sea of Okhotsk."

I pull out my envelope and flip to the flight information. I take it up to the cockpit and hand it to him. "We need to interrupt this flight, and hopefully come down behind them by surprise."

Paul confers with his co-pilot Davi, who I also really like. Which makes this much worse. They listen precisely and I tell them to shut off the radio once we're in the air.

Paul looks over the documents on the strike Judica sent once we're in the air. "They're flying high, very high, to avoid detection."

"That's good, right?"

He shrugs, "It is what it is, but we aren't equipped to take them out. We don't have anything but basic defensive anti-aircraft artillery. You said fast, not tactical."

"That doesn't matter. I brought everything we'll need."

Paul tilts his head and presses his lips together, but he doesn't argue.

"Can we catch them?"

Paul studies the documents and nods. "They're ahead of us, but they're using old tech. That means we're much faster than they are. But I need to know more about what you're planning to figure out the best approach. If they see us, they'll take us down immediately. They have pretty clear orders, and this will be sort of like going after a tank and two Humvees with a Porsche."

"I know." I tap my hand on the seat in front of me. "I brought a weapon. Try not to worry about that part overmuch. I'm going to take all three planes down at the same time."

"How?" Paul eyes me with understandable skepticism.

"The critical part," I say, "the part I'm relying on you to ensure, is that we intercept their flight path in the middle of the ocean, without anyone else around."

"We aren't coming back from this, are we?" Paul asks.

I glance down at my mom's ring. It sparkles in the light. "I doubt very much whether we will."

"Oh, heck no." Noah pops out of the bathroom at the back of the jet. "I knew I was right to come. You sound totally crazy."

"You're supposed to be in a holding cell." I raise one eyebrow.

Noah rolls his eyes. "Oh please. I'm human, not mentally deficient."

"You took out an evian guard?" I can't quite keep the disbelief out of my voice.

He snorts. "Let's not get carried away. More like, he saw what he expected to see, and I specialize in the unexpected."

"Was anyone injured?" I ask.

Noah rolls his eyes. "Thanks for the concern for my fragile human person, but I'm fine."

My voice is flat. "I meant my guards."

"Relax. They're fine, and I'm only here to help."

"What exactly are you going to do?" I ask.

He shakes his head. "I obviously don't know yet. I need to see the information you have and hear your full plan. But I'm an excellent problem solver."

Paul clears his throat. "Well, I'm sure you'll figure out

something brilliant with *his* help." He raises his eyebrows at me. "But if you can't come up with anything better, why don't you let me execute your plan for you. I can air drop you anywhere along here and send a message to home base so they can come and retrieve you."

Paul's offering to die in my place.

"I should airdrop you." I'm ashamed I didn't think of that. "Or at least one of you. I doubt I can fly the plane *and* execute my plan at the same time."

"It is an honor to serve you, Your Majesty." Paul seems absolutely serious.

I cross to where he's standing and put a hand on his shoulder. "You've always been kind, and brave, too. I appreciate your offer. But I have to do this myself."

His eyes glance down at my ring, probably thinking about the weight of ruling, or maybe about the fact that if we all die, the ring is lost again. Who knows, though? Maybe he has guessed that I plan to use the ring, somehow.

"Well, I'll be thinking things over in the cockpit," Paul says. "If I have any ideas, I'll let you know."

As soon as Paul's gone, I turn to face Noah. "I wish you hadn't come."

Noah sinks into one of the plush seats. I think about the last time I was in this plane. I was preparing to die then, too. I can't catch a break today.

"Have you heard of origami?" Noah asks.

"Uh, folding paper cranes? Yeah, I've heard of it."

"I've been practicing origami since I was four. I've probably made ten thousand paper boxes, so trust me when I say I'm an expert at thinking outside of most any shaped box."

"Speaking of boxes, there wasn't time," I say, "to equip this plane with a Faraday box."

"So your weapon's an EMP?" Noah asks.

I nod.

"How does it work?"

I glance down at my mom's ring, and Noah follows my gaze.

"Last time we had trouble, you used your necklace. So, what? Your ring turns into an arrow and you shoot it at the other planes?"

"Something like that," I say.

"I have totally been getting my mom's Christmas gifts at the wrong places. I need the name of your jeweler."

"Here's the thing, Noah. If anyone else could use this particular weapon, I'd let them. But only I can make it work. And if I weigh my life against that of thousands of humans—"

"I bet a lot of your friends wouldn't come to the same conclusion as you do about the relative value." Noah folds his arms.

"They wouldn't, no. They'd put a billion human lives up against one evian, probably, but I'm not them. Your family matters to me, as do all the other people living in the area being bombed. I'm so sorry this is happening."

I hand him the file.

While he looks over it, I think about my doubt before I fought Judica. It didn't help me. In fact, it kept me from seeing the truth for longer. And I need to see the truth of what to do here right away, because if I fail, Judica isn't the bad guy for sending these. I am for failing to fix it.

"It's noble of you to be willing to trade your life for people you don't know."

"Thanks," I say.

"You know what's even nobler?"

"What?"

"Not dying. Live *and* save people. That way you can fix all those things that are broken with your family."

"Thanks Confucius. Great tip."

Noah sits down next to me and rests his hand on mine. "Tell me what you're doing, exactly. How does it work?"

"I don't really understand it myself."

"Well, start at the beginning."

To my surprise, I do. Maybe it's because Noah's going to die with me. Maybe it's because he's human. I tell him everything. I tell him about my mom's death, and how awful it was. I tell him I don't know who killed her or why. I tell him about Sotiris. I tell him about what happened before she died, and how I reacted to the ring. I even tell him about the prophecy.

How it ruined my life. And how it's obviously wrong, since I'm about to die.

"So you're sick to death of the guilt?"

"Excuse me?" I ask.

"You tried to get your sister to kill you earlier. Now you're sacrificing yourself to save these people because your mom died for this secret. It must have a purpose, right? If you save these people, then your mom's death wasn't such a waste. And your sister, your poor, hurting, misunderstood sister can finally have what she always wanted, a sparkly crown all to herself."

I frown. "You don't get it."

"Oh, I think I do."

"Look, I've always thought there must be a God. And if there is, and he gave me this gift that ruined my life, there must be a reason. Maybe it's so I can right this tremendous wrong. Maybe all our decisions lead to others and there's a purpose behind each of them. If I'd come back sooner, Judica wouldn't have sent this yet, but I didn't. So here I am, fixing my mistake."

"Dying without cause is cowardly. The Chancery Alamecha I've been watching isn't a coward."

"You suck, Noah."

"I want to save that town full of people too, okay? I'm

on board with that. It's the dying horribly part where you lose me. There must be some way for you to use that ring without knocking out our plane at the same time."

I think about it. Isn't that what my mom wanted? For me to master the ring and be able to direct the projection of the EMP?

"The problem is that I focus my energy, and it just bursts out of the ring. I'm not sure how far, but it wiped out our entire island and part of a neighboring one the first time."

"That's a pretty hot blast," Noah says.

"Yeah."

"There was a second time?"

"My mom made me practice a little."

"How'd that go?"

"Not so great," I say. "Near the end, I directed the pulse so that it took out everything in front of me first, before the electronics beside me shorted."

Noah thinks for a moment. "Maybe the problem is the goal. We're imagining that we'll fly up behind the planes, right? Zoom down behind them and zap all three, right?"

I nod. "Basically."

"And if we do that, when our electronics are fried, we all lose altitude at the same time, and the bomb will be triggered below a certain altitude and BOOM, we all die, right?"

"Yep."

"So instead, how about we fly at them head on and pass them. Then you stand at the back of the jet and take them out. We'll be headed in opposite directions, so if you send your pulse out in just one direction—"

"Best case, we don't fry our plane, and worst case, we're already heading away from the other planes when we do. The warhead detonates at altitude, but they're flying west and we're flying east," I finish for him. "We might get far enough away to survive the blast."

Noah smiles. "I've heard you heal pretty well. I mean, as a human, I'll still be toast, but you might pull through."

I punch his shoulder. It might work. It's better than my suicide plan, except for two things. "If we pass them, they'll see us, and they'll shoot and kill us."

"Let's talk to Paul, but if we pass them way below or way above, then drop precipitously, maybe it could work. Maybe they won't see us."

"Even if we work that out, if we pass them first, before I use the pulse, I'll only get one shot. What if I mess up?"

"Don't."

"Very helpful."

"You have to think about directing the pulse. I saw you use your little necklace bombs before." He points at my chain. "You're really good with it. Think of the EMP as a slingshot. If you focus on throwing the pulse away from us..." He shrugs.

I talk to Paul about the logistics and we work out the kinks in Noah's plan. Paul thinks we can sneak past them. It helps that we have all the details on the planes, and they're dated. Plus, Noah's plane is a commercial one, not a fighter jet, so they might not automatically suspect us.

Once I work all that out, it's time for the part Noah is going to hate.

"Now that we might survive this," Noah says, "I think we need to get a message to our boy Edam so he knows where to come looking for us."

"I didn't want him to try and stop me," I say, "but now that we might make it home, yeah, you're right."

I grab Noah and before he has time to react, I wrap both his arms behind him. Paul helps me bind him up, and we prepare for an emergency airdrop. Noah shouts and hollers and squawks.

We ignore him.

Once we have Noah bound and ready to drop, with a parachute he can release and a raft with a homing beacon, I dial up the in-flight phone and call the palace. "I need to speak with the Prince Regent."

"Did you just say Prince Regent?" Noah groans. "That's a ridiculous name, and I can't just let that pass, but also, that old man is going to be even more insufferable after this."

"Shut up." I kick at Noah, but he hops out of the way.

A voice in the receiver distracts me. "Hello?"

"Edam?"

"Why did you leave without guards?" he asks. "And why did you shut the radio off? I've been debating whether to send a strike force after you."

"Do not send a strike force. I'm fine. I had Paul shut off the radio and I left before the guards could board on purpose."

Edam sighs. "I expected something like this. You're headed for China."

"I'm somewhere over the Pacific right now, yes."

Edam curses. A lot.

"I couldn't let them die," I say.

"There's nothing you can do! I thought you understood that."

"There is something," I say. "My mom's ring is a weapon. It caused that EMP the day before she died. *I* caused that EMP with it."

He swears even more creatively. "If I'd known, I'd have tied you down in your room until that bomb went off."

"And that's why I didn't tell you. I'm keeping you from committing treason. You're welcome."

"You'd be surprised what I'll do to keep you alive, Chancy."

"Well, then I'm glad you didn't know, because I need

your help. I have a stowaway, and I'm about to airdrop him and send you the coordinates. Please send someone to fetch him quickly. And in about half an hour, it's quite likely my plane will go down too. We'll turn on tracking so you can, hopefully, find us as well."

"I'll come myself."

"The Prince Regent absolutely cannot leave the island," I say firmly.

"Then why did you name Inara as my backup?"

I grumble under my breath, but I knew he'd do this before I called. "Accept the world as it is."

"I hate that stupid motto. Have I ever told you that?"

"No." I smile. "I'm not surprised, though. I've hated it for years."

"It should be, 'Accept the world as it is, or order troops to change it while you're safe at home, because you can't do every single little thing yourself'."

"That's not very snappy," Noah says.

"Wait, Noah's with you? I dropped him off downstairs myself."

"We definitely need to look into that upon our return," I say. If I return. "I have no idea how he escaped and snuck on."

"How did you manage to leave without Frederick?" Edam asks.

"Uh. . ." I say. "I sent Freddy to run an errand."

"He wouldn't tell me how you slipped away, but he's not happy about it."

"I'm low on time." I give Edam the coordinates and signal Paul to open the escape hatch.

It creates a lot less wind than I expected, which is good because I have to cut the ties on Noah's hands. Then I shove him out the door before he can argue with me any more. No matter how great his plan, no human could survive a plane crash coupled with a nuclear bomb. He needs to get out now, while he has a chance to survive this.

"Wow, who knew it was this fun to shove someone out an escape hatch?" I ask.

Paul is busy with buttons and knobs, but he tosses a grin back at me. "I'll look into that."

If we survive.

I head for the back so I don't distract him. But with Noah gone, it's eerily quiet. Paul and David prepare for the final course corrections, and I review my plan in my head. The minutes drag without Noah's jokes. I hope he's okay in the middle of the ocean. I hope Edam doesn't have any trouble finding him. I hope my plan stands a chance of working.

I review the plan for the rendevous over and over in my head. But finally, it's time.

Paul clears his throat. "Your Majesty?"

"Yes?"

"They're getting close, up ahead."

I walk to the cockpit and squint. I can barely make out three aircraft, two smaller ones flanking a larger plane below.

I walk to the back of the jet and buckle into the chair at the very back. I wish it swiveled around. "Open the emergency doors," I shout.

He does. The wind whips my hair around my face and tugs on my clothes, but I remain focused. Which is why I see the jets peel off.

"We've done everything we planned," Paul yells, "but I think they saw us. They're not going to let us fly past."

I undo my buckle and run toward the cockpit, staggering and grabbing chairs and railings to claw my way forward.

One of the MiGs fires something at us.

David presses a button. "Flares."

The missile zooms down below us.

"This might be a good time for you to do whatever you're doing," Paul says.

Duh.

The other MiG shoots off a missile as they close on us. It's now or never.

So much for my EMP pulse from the back of the plane. I focus on the lights flashing in Mom's ring and think of my anger, my hatred for Nereus, whoever he or she is, and what it's done to my family. I imagine my little sister, the little sister I'll never hug or kiss or sing to sleep. I take all that anger, that hatred, that fury, and I imagine I'm putting it all in a slingshot and shooting it at the planes and the missile and BAM, it tears out of me.

The second missile explodes in front of us and we fly through the debris, Noah's jet lurching and shuddering, but the planes don't alter their course.

"Did it work?" I ask.

I watch as the jet and MiGs fly past us, seemingly unharmed.

Oh crap. I got the missile and missed the real target.

I race to the back of the jet, flipping head over heels and flying past a dozen seats in the wind whipping through the jet before I grab one of the side railings. My heart throws somersaults in my chest. The jets are specks on the horizon, but when I poke my head around the corner of the emergency door, I can see them. Barely.

And the cup in my head is finally full again.

This time I don't try to aim or direct anything. I fling the power out of me and at the three aircraft with the full force of my rage, loss, despair, fear, and hope. A fireball flies through the air, and a strange sort of vibration blows past it and outward.

I squint up ahead to see the wave hit the three aircraft. I breathe a big sigh of relief when they all begin losing altitude at an alarming rate. I scream for Paul's help closing the emergency doors. When we return to the cockpit of our plane, I'm relieved to see lights and dials still whirring and beeping and flashing.

"You did it," Paul says. "You sent the EMP to them. Our controls still work."

"Now we just need to survive the fusion bomb." Five hundred times stronger than the original bombs Mom detonated before. Ugh.

"One thing at a time." David pulls on a lever and the jet accelerates. "Let's put some distance between them and us."

"Please go sit down and buckle up," Paul says. "Any minute the blast will hit us. You need to brace yourself."

There's a sound like my ears popping and then a bump like no turbulence I've ever felt, and then the world goes black.

34

Buzzing fills my ears and my head is stuffed with cotton. I shake my head and yawn, and I open my eyes. Edam and Noah are arguing directly in front of me. I focus on the movement of their mouths and realize there is an echoey reverberation that matches their voices faintly, behind the buzzing.

"Of course, you idiot. It's not like I didn't think of that." Edam's fist is clenched, and he towers over Noah menacingly.

"Then why are you standing there stupidly?" Noah asks. "Get a syringe! Her body might need a boost."

"You're pushy for someone whose blood would not only be useless," Edam says. "It would probably also give her hepatitis."

Noah's shoulders straighten. "I've had just about enough—"

I focus on my ear canals and drums, and the buzzing dissipates, leaving only an underlying humming. It could be the sound of rotors. "Hello?" My voice is raspy. It doesn't sound like me.

A split second later, both their faces swim over mine.

I blink and blink and blink until they both come into focus. "Where are we?"

"On an albatross, which is a friggin' seaplane." Noah rolls his eyes and jerks his thumb at Edam. "This one's idea of rescue."

"I am so happy to see your gorgeous, blue eyes," Edam says.

"They're blue again?" I blink more.

"Your retinas must have burned off in the blast, and they always regrow their original color." Edam shudders. "There's a phrase I wish I didn't need to say."

"I like them better this way," Noah says. "They almost match mine."

"How do you have blue eyes, anyway?" I ask Noah.

"Can we focus on relevant facts?" Edam asks.

"You're the one who brought up the eye color," Noah says.

Edam glares at him but doesn't yell or throw any projectiles. I think it's progress.

I roll my newly blue eyes at them. "I'm relieved to see you both. I worried Edam might leave Noah floating in the ocean forever."

"The thought did cross my mind," Edam says. "Some shark would be desperate enough to eat him eventually."

"I'm glad he survived," I say. "Because I think I'm going to need Noah to call his parents and tell them the tip was bad. We don't want to cause some kind of incident now that it's been defused."

"Sure," Noah says.

"Or, we can give him a replacement jet and send him home," Edam says. "He can tell them himself."

"Not a terrible idea," I say. "He does need to get back. He can't stay here, amidst all this madness."

"I think returning me should be low on the priority list. You broke your neck in the crash," Noah says. "And most of your skin and face were...” He cuts off and shakes his head like he wants to erase the memory. “They were burned off.” He gulps.

“That sounds really gross.” I move my neck back and forth and touch my face. “But I feel fine now.”

“It was kind of cool to watch you healing, but it was slow. A lot slower than during your fight with your sister,” Noah says.

A terrible thought occurs to me. “If I broke my neck...” What about Paul and David? “Did the others...” I can’t bring myself to ask.

Edam shakes his head. David and Paul were both Selah’s boys. Evian families grow quite large, with such long lifespans and so many displaced heirs. Selah’s my first cousin, daughter of my aunt, and her boys served the family long and well. I wish I could blame Judica, but this solution was my decision.

“I’ll call her when we reach home,” I say. “Selah deserves to hear it from me.”

“A true ruler understands the responsibility that comes with freedom,” Edam says. “Your mom would be proud.”

I wondered how Edam would react if I survived the fight with Judica. I hoped he’d be pleased, but I haven’t had time to interact with him at all, really. And I lied to him right after appointing him my Prince Regent. He could be angry, very angry.

“Noah?” I ask. “Can you give us a minute?”

Noah doesn’t joke or poke or anything else. He nods and walks to the far end of the plane. When he’s far enough away that he can’t see us very well, I look at Edam.

He meets my gaze for a long moment before he says, “I was so afraid. Worse than when you fought Judica, because I couldn’t even see whether you were okay.”

“I had to do something,” I say.

"It's who you are. But don't ever do anything like that again without telling me. Please."

"I'm Empress of Alamecha." I'm surprised my tongue doesn't stumble over the words. I'm surprised I don't choke on them. But somehow, they sound right. I'm Empress. No big deal, I just rule a sixth of the world. "Danger's part of the deal, Edam, and it always will be."

He shakes his head. "You'll never run from a fight, and that's one of the things I love about you. People see your mercy as weakness, but they're wrong. Being a good person doesn't make you a weak person."

"Then you understand."

Edam closes the space between us and takes my hand. "I understand you, but I need you to understand me. You can't leave me back at home to stand watch over your throne and polish your crown. You can't do that. Because I don't care about the throne, and I care a great deal about you. So the next time you leave to pursue some harebrained scheme, promise you'll take me with you."

I can't breathe.

"I've been supportive, Chancery. I'll always stand with you." The next words sound strangled. "No matter who you eventually choose for your Consort, I'll always defend and protect you. I think you will be the best ruler Alamecha has ever had, but that's not the only reason I'll stand by you." His voice drops almost an octave and it does something to my stomach. Something shivery. Something not quite comfortable. "I love you Chancery. I love your mercy and I love your strength. I love your humor and I love your intensity. I love your reticence and I love your boldness. Those things aren't opposites, they're complimentary. You're complex and caring and unique and a world without you in it feels unbearably bleak to me. Let me place you first, and we'll be fine. Can you do that?"

"I think so," I whisper.

"And you should know that I didn't only offer to be your Consort to keep you safe. I did it because nothing would bring me more joy."

I open my mouth, but Edam places a finger over it.

"You're not ready to make that kind of decision and I respect that. You're so young still, and I'll never rush you. But I want you to be utterly positive about where I stand. Say the word tomorrow, or next week, or in a year or in a hundred years. I won't change my mind."

As I look into his eyes, so full of longing, I want to say yes. It would be so much simpler to have someone to rely on, someone to share this load with. I trust him, and I believe what he told me, but a part of me isn't ready to choose a Consort. Besides, I need to be strong now, and immediately choosing a Consort doesn't seem like the action of a person who can manage things alone. I may be young, but I'm not a little girl who needs saving.

"I can't," I say. "Not yet. So I'm saying no, but I'm not saying never."

Edam brushes his lips against mine. "I'll take it." He straightens and takes a seat and I think our conversation is over. I barely hear his next question. "Is it because of my sister?"

"I don't think so." I shake my head. "But I don't know."

He looks away again and this time, I don't say anything else because there's nothing more to say.

When we get back home, the palace in Ni'ihau looks like a kicked anthill.

Balthasar's waiting at the bottom of the stairs. He pulls me down and into strong, familiar arms. "Welcome back and congratulations, Chancery. You deserve it. You could've won the traditional way, but what you did was even harder. Knowing their opponent is something very few people manage to do. Your mother would be so proud of you.

You've grown into the woman she always wanted you to become."

I wipe away a tear and squeeze him a little tighter. I never knew my dad, but I've always imagined he'd be little bit like Balthasar. Tough, handsome, knowledgeable, and gruff, but always speaking the truth. "Thanks."

He releases me but still looks at me warmly. "Now we need to talk about setting up your personal guard."

"Tomorrow," I say, "will be soon enough."

"Who will keep you safe tonight?" he asks.

Noah and Edam both take a step closer. I try not to roll my eyes. "I'm keeping Frederick as head of my personal guard."

Balthasar raises his eyebrows. "Do you trust him?"

I nod. "Yes."

He sighs. "Okay. But what about these two?" He doesn't even pretend to whisper. "One of them is a human, and the other is Judica's ex-boyfriend. Hardly a suitable support team."

I don't roll my eyes, and I won't roll my eyes, because it's not respectful. "I'm okay with it."

"I'll inform Frederick of his position and ask him to coordinate our process for establishing your guard and the rotation."

Larena, Mom's chamberlain, finds me next. "Your Majesty, welcome back. Agents of the Five have all contacted us to extend congratulations, and they're all asking when the investiture will take place."

"Monday. We've waited long enough."

She nods. "Alora has requested permission to visit and extend her congratulations."

I ought to order her to come. I should drag her here in chains. "Granted." I should set up a trial, but I can't bring myself to do it. Not with Alora, at least not until I know exactly what she did and why. Shades of gray. Why are there so many?

Of course that's not everything. Larena, whom I plan to keep as my chamberlain, has a million other questions, but I'm too tired to answer them all. I've nearly reached my room when Inara stomps into view. Seeing her hale and whole in front of me warms every chamber of my heart. I run toward her and she pulls me into a tight hug.

"I watched the video feed," she says, a tear in her left eye. "And you were absolutely brilliant."

"Thank you," I say. "Do you think I made a mistake?"

"Sparing her life?" Inara asks.

I swallow.

"Probably, but you're not Enora, and you're not me, and you're not Judica. You have to do what you think is right."

I smile at her. "Thanks."

"Did you find the sword I left you?"

I bob my head. "I am sorry for what you went through here alone. So sorry. And it was so generous of you to offer me that sword, but I couldn't risk your future if I lost."

Inara's smile is sad. "And you found Mother's old sword, and you did a beautiful thing with it. I'm so proud of you, little dove."

"Proud enough to step in for me?" I ask. "Because Larena has a lot of questions and I'm about to collapse from exhaustion."

"Of course." Inara bites her lip. "But before you go to sleep, I have news."

Nothing good, judging by her expression. Noah and Edam both inch a little closer to me as if they can protect me from it.

"Um, you do know this one's human?" Inara eyes Noah like she'd eye a McDonald's hamburger, or Payless shoes.

"I do. It's fine."

"I'm not at all saying this as an 'I told you so.' I think

what you did was brave and merciful, and that's sort of your brand. But sometimes mercy isn't warranted."

"Just tell me what happened."

"It's Judica," she says.

"What about her?" I ask. "Did she set her room on fire? Or she's on a hunger strike? What?"

"She's gone."

The End

If you enjoyed Displaced, you can grab book two, unForgiven, right now. (And book three, Disillusioned, as well!)

If you don't want to miss my new releases or promos, sign up for my newsletter at www.BridgetEBakerwrites.com. As a bonus, when you sign up, I give you a FREE FULL LENGTH E-BOOK!!

Finally, if you enjoyed reading *Displaced*, please, please, please leave me a review on Amazon!!!! It makes a tremendous difference when you do. Thanks in advance!

35

BONUS: FIRST CHAPTER OF UNFORGIVEN

I've never believed in God. Mother mentioned that my father bought into all that nonsense, but I've always been far too practical. On top of that, the Bible is a human record, which means it isn't very reliable. Which is why, when I slam the door to my room shut and one book falls off the edge of my bookcase, I don't read anything into the fact that it's the Bible. It could just as easily have been *The Art of War*, the Quran, or *Quantum Physics*.

I stoop to pick it up so I can slide it back into the empty slot, but my hand freezes over the page. It's open to Genesis chapter 25, which is nowhere near the middle of the book where I'd expect it to fall open.

31. And Jacob said, Sell me this day thy birthright.

32. And Esau said, Behold I am at the point to die; and what profit shall this birthright do to me?

33. And Jacob said, Swear to me this day; and he sware unto him: and he sold his birthright unto Jacob.

34. Then Jacob gave Esau bread and pottage of lentils; and he did eat and drink, and rose up and went his way. Thus Esau despised his birthright.

A chill runs up my spine. I've read the entire Bible as

part of my human studies coursework. This isn't a new passage to me. Jacob and Esau aren't even the only twins in the Bible. But in their tradition, Esau had the birthright, which meant he'd inherit all his father had as the older twin.

And he sold it to Jacob for a bowl of mush.

I don't pick up the book. I walk across the room to my bed instead, sinking down into the covers with a stifled cry of anguish, one hand clutching the figure eight necklace hiding under my tattered shirt.

My mother is dead. I fought my twin and lost, and what's worse, all of Alamecha witnessed my failure. First they saw me snatch victory from the jaws of defeat, and then they saw me hand it right back to her.

Why did I do it?

Why did Esau do it? He couldn't have needed a bowl of stew that badly. There has to be more to the story. But that line at the end is strange. I don't recall paying any attention to it before. Esau *despised* his birthright. What does that mean? I close my eyes and try to recall my human studies class.

In Ancient Near East tradition, all sons received a birthright, a share of the father's wealth, but the oldest received a double share, or something like that. בָּזָה in Hebrew, means to regard lightly I believe. My tutor told me it meant that he cared more about his physical well-being in the moment than for the spiritual blessings the birthright from God would promise him.

But now I wonder whether perhaps he hated the idea of being the head of the household. Did he realize he would agonize over every single decision, rationing the seconds of every single day like a miser, eaten alive constantly by the stress of perfection? Perhaps forgoing his birthright for that bowl of stew felt inevitable to him, if he hated it so much.

Was relinquishing his birthright the best thing Esau ever did?

If so, maybe humans and evians aren't as different as I've always been taught. Because my hands begin to shake, and for the first time in my life, I take a breath, a deep, unconcerned breath. I don't care whether my heart races, or my expression wobbles, or my enemies are hatching plots based on the information they gained from the wobbles and the racing.

I'm still Chancery's heir for a while, but ultimately she will move along, and the burden of Alamecha will shift off of me.

My life will be my own.

For the first time in eighteen years, I have no idea what I'll be doing ten years from now, or even six months from now. I flop back on my bed and close my eyes. What is it Chancy's always doing? Listening to music or watching stupid stories play out about fake people on a television screen? Reading even more insipid tales about the lives of humans? Pah.

I can't waste my time like that.

A tap at my door rescues me from tipping head first into a black hole. I sit up and brush off my blood-stained pants. I really should have spent the past few minutes showering instead of lying on my formerly clean bed. At least my covers are black and unlikely to show blood stains.

"Come in."

The door cracks and Roman's head peeks around the corner. His tawny golden eyes assess the room like he's looking for a bomb or a landmine. I suppose dealing with me may have scarred him permanently.

I flop back on my bed with a groan. "What do you want?"

"Just making sure you're alive." He grins, his big white

teeth bright against the dark brown skin of his face, and the mahogany bristle of his beard.

I flinch. "I'm alive. Now leave."

Roman walks inside anyway and closes the door.

I bolt upright, my shoulders too stiff. I force them to relax. "You still have to obey my commands. I'm still Heir."

Roman grins. "Yes, Your Highness. Of course, Your Highness." He crosses the room and sits down next to me. "I thought you might want to hear the news."

"What news?" I arch one eyebrow.

"Your sister has left, no one was told where, and Edam has been made Prince Regent in her absence. He doesn't appear to be handling things very smoothly."

She still hasn't named him Consort, which is bizarre. What is she waiting for? Is it possible she's holding off to try and spare my feelings? If so, she's an even bigger idiot than I thought. "Is that all?"

"That's all."

"Then you can go."

"I think I'll stay for a while." He shifts on the bed so he can see my face while sitting next to me.

"I lost." I throw the words up like a shield. Back off, Roman. I'm not in the mood to deal with you right now.

"I saw."

"I know you saw," I practically growl at him. "What I want to know is what you're doing in here, right now. I don't want to talk to anyone. Was I unclear on that?"

"Sometimes what you want and what you need aren't the same," he says.

I roll my eyes. "Thanks, Gandhi. Appreciate you dropping pearls of wisdom, but I don't need or want you in my room."

Roman puts an arm around my shoulders and pulls me against his chest. I consider stabbing him with the knife I keep on my bedside table. Or a good jab to his solar plexus would remind him that I'm still his commander, even now, even after I lost to my pathetic sister. But I don't do either of those. Instead, it's like the inside of my chest splinters and I collapse against him, sobbing.

How much must he hate me, to force me to cry on his beautifully sculpted chest? Am I to have no shreds of pride left intact? No matter how much I want to pull away, I can't. Not for a long time. My tears mix with the dried blood on my face, my neck, and my shirt, and stain the collar of his polo. The sight of fat, red drops of bloody tears splattering against the fabric of his shirt pulls me out of my temporary despair. I fist my hands in the fabric covering his chest and drag in deep breaths.

I finally stop crying and wipe my face on my own shoulder.

"I'm sorry about that," I say.

Roman's face closes off. "I protect and serve, now and always."

He has always been my most devoted guard. I shouldn't be so hard on him. "I know today was embarrassing for you," I say. "I'm sorry for that, and for breaking down in front of you just now."

Roman leaps to his feet. "You were real out there, Judica, for three seconds. You let your guard down. You looked at Chancery like a person, you eased up. I thought maybe—"

I was real? I want to shred something. "I *eased up*?"

"Yes, you could have killed her, more than once, but you didn't. You let her win out there. I thought. . ." Roman spins around and stares at the wall, hands clenched, back muscles straining.

"You thought I had, what? Completely changed in every single way?" I stand up. "And that made you hopeful. Does everyone despise me that much?" But I want to ask whether he despises me that much. I know Edam does, but

Roman has been my closest friend for a decade. If he hates me, too, I don't know what that even means.

"You know I don't despise you," Roman says. But he doesn't turn around. He doesn't meet my eye.

"Are you disappointed?" I ask. "That you're head of the guard for the Heir, still?"

Roman flips around to face me so quickly that I stumble back, bumping into the bed and nearly sitting back down. "Nothing about you ever disappoints me. How can you not know that?"

I lift one eyebrow. "I know you support me. You always have, and I appreciate it. I don't tell you that often enough."

"You've literally never told me that."

I lift my chin. "Well, I'm telling you now. Thank you for always being there for me."

"I don't want to be here as your guard." Roman makes a choking sound.

My heart skips a beat. "You're quitting? Why? Because I lost?" He just said he'll always support me.

He shakes his head, his jaw working. "You're probably the most gifted strategist I've ever met. Half the time I don't even understand what you're saying until I've spent some time analyzing it. You're three steps ahead of everyone else, and you show no mercy. How can you be so obtuse about this?"

"About what?"

"I'm in love with you, Judica. I've loved you for years and years. I'm not quitting. I'll never quit, but it's time you know, because I'm sick of watching you flirting with Edam, or Havel, or Xander or anyone else."

I knew Roman wanted to be my Consort. I knew he wanted to rule. Of course he did. They all do. I even knew he respected me, and he's always been unfailingly loyal. But no one loves me, not really. I'm cruel, merciless, and intense. Edam fled the second he saw an opening.

I don't even blame him.

No one wants to kiss a copperhead. No one dreams of snuggling up next to a tiger.

"You have nothing to say?" Roman asks.

I open my mouth, but no words come out.

"I expected that, but it still hurts more than I thought it would." He swallows and nods at me. "Well, don't let me keep you any longer, Your Highness. I'll be outside if you need anything."

I walk to my bathroom after he closes the door like a robot. I toss my bloody rags into a pile and shower all the blood and gore away, watching the red water circle the drain and then disappear. I wish sometimes that my doubt, my anger, and my sorrow could be washed away so easily.

Every time I close my eyes, Roman's face swims in front of mine. His golden eyes sad, his heart in his face, plain to read.

I'm lying to myself. I've known Roman was in love with me for a very long time. And maybe for a while I thought. . . Maybe. . . But he's never been a real option. Not for me.

Because I'm a better strategist. I'm a better fighter. I destroy him in linguistics. He doesn't bring enough to the table to be my Consort, and he never will. Thinking about it makes it hard to breathe, but it doesn't change the facts, not in the slightest.

I wipe away another round of unwelcome tears and dress quickly. I can't cower in my room. I'm not sure what I should be doing, but something. Anything but hiding.

A tap at the door sends my heart hammering up to my throat. I breathe in and out once, then twice. I can't let him know that his declaration had any impact on me at all. Once I'm in control again, I say, "Come in."

When Angel steps through the doorway with a tray, I'm

strangely deflated. I didn't want to see Roman. I can never be with him, and now that he said what he said, well, some space is a good idea. Even so, I'm not so deluded I can't admit to myself that I'm disappointed.

I wanted to see him again. I want to see him all the time.

"I'm assuming you're starving, Your Highness," Angel says.

She doesn't typically bring food herself. "You're a delivery girl now?"

Angel ducks her head. "I wanted to make sure you're okay. After today, but really, after the last week and a half."

Things have been strange between Angel and me since her release, but I had to know whether she killed Mother. I doubt she'll ever forgive me for my threats or how hard I pressed, but she understands. If anyone understands, it's her. I don't regret any of it, though. I never regret the awful things I do to protect the family. Alamecha is what really matters, and it's more than one person.

"I'm fine," I say.

"You need to eat. With all that regeneration your body has done, you must be famished."

I can't quite stop myself from frowning. She's basically shoving my face in how many hits Chancery landed on me, but I think she means well. And the smell coming from the tray she brought is heavenly. Angel was chef for the most powerful person on earth for centuries for a reason. The lady can cook.

"Tikka Masala, naan, watermelon, and a brown butter raspberry tart," I say. "All my favorite foods. What did I do to deserve this?"

Angel sets the tray down on my desk. "You've been dear to me since you were born." Her eyes soften. "And your mother." She shakes her head. "I wanted to show you that I harbor no ill feelings toward you for suspecting me, but I would never have harmed a hair on your mother's head. I've lived to serve Alamecha my entire life, and your mother was the embodiment of the family. You're her miniature, you know."

I do. "Thank you."

"She would be very proud of your actions today, and those of Chancery. She loved you both, and you made a hard decision, but I believe it was the right one."

My nostrils flare, but I manage to hold my heart rate steady and show no other expression on my face. "I appreciate your support." Now get out of my room.

When she leaves, I don't slam the door. I'm actually relieved to have successfully navigated the first of the gloating well wishers. She won't be the last. Chancery really might be more diabolical than I give her credit for. She's punished me far more effectively with this 'spare my life' nonsense than killing me ever would have.

I sink into my desk chair and breathe in the aromas I love most. I remember the first time Mother served Tikka Masala, warm and savory, with a tangy aftertaste of yogurt. I absolutely will not cry twice in one day. I shovel in a large bite of food to stave off the crying jag threatening to rip through me. The flavors burst over my tongue, triggering memories of dinner with Mother I didn't even realize I'd been blocking.

I'm still furious that she left me.

I inhale the food until all that's left is the brown butter tart. The crust is a combination of chewy and crunchy that I've tried several times to recreate without success. It's still warm enough that when I dump the vanilla gelato over the top, it begins to melt. The combination is so amazing that I don't taste the difference until my last bite.

There's a faintly metallic aftertaste.

I try to leap to my feet, but my body isn't working right. My arms feel heavy, so heavy. My eyes won't focus.

"Roman," I try to yell. The word emerges as more of a croak than a shout. I wrap thick fingers around the edge of the table and force myself upright.

But then my traitorous knees buckle and I collapse on the floor. My eyes won't focus on anything, and all I can see is the tufts of my rug. I wonder if the floor in front of her is the last thing Mother saw, too. A pang of fear for Chancery surprises me, but if someone has taken out both me and Mother, she's next.

As the world goes black, I think of Mother's face. Wherever we go after we die, I hope Mother's there, waiting for me. I close my dry, achy eyes, ready to find out.

ACKNOWLEDGMENTS

But the biggest thank you must be split, as always, between an amazing mother and a superlative spouse. Those two behemoths of support cannot ever be thanked enough. Truly, from the bottom of my heart.

My editor, Peter, is amazing. My cover artist, Christian, has outdone himself. And Alyssa (Plehn) Packard! Your face would launch a thousand ships, and I hope it launches this book into the stratosphere. Thanks for sharing it.

And Linsey, my AMAZING photographer. THANK YOU. To Esther, for being the consummate cheerleader, many thanks. And to my children for being so patient while I stared at a computer screen, I am so appreciative.

My readers are the REASON I keep writing. Your reviews, your comments, your notes to me, your recommendations of my books to others, they make this entire thing worth it. They keep me going when my confidence or my energy are flagging. THANK YOU. Now and forever, thank you.

(PS: I would be remiss if I didn't thank my agent. We parted paths, but she helped me to clean up the mess that was the rough draft of this story. And the many editors who rejected it merely firmed my resolve. Even the publishing houses who *almost* bought it helped strengthen my story.)

ABOUT THE AUTHOR

Bridget loves her husband (every day) and all five of her kids (most days). She's a lawyer, but does as little legal work as possible. She has two goofy horses and spends too much time riding and not enough time writing. She makes cookies waaaaay too often and believes they should be their own food group. In a (possibly misguided) attempt at balancing the scales, she kickboxes daily.

So if you don't like her books, her kids, or her cookies, maybe don't tell her in person.

ALSO BY BRIDGET E. BAKER

Sins of our Ancestors YA post apocalyptic Series:

Marked

Suppressed

Redeemed

Almost a Billionaire (clean) romance series:

Finding Faith

Finding Cupid

Finding Spring

Finding Liberty

Finding Holly

YA romantic suspense:

Already Gone (FREE IF YOU SIGN UP FOR MY NEWSLETTER!)

Birthright Series YA fantasy:

Displaced

unForgiven

Disillusioned

misUnderstood -coming March 15, 2020

Disavowed - coming May 15, 2020

unRepentant - coming summer 2020

Destroyed - coming fall 2020

Yes, you caught me. I overuse parentheses. (Whoops.)

CPSIA information can be obtained
at www.ICGtesting.com
Printed in the USA
LVHW010210200620
658570LV00012B/1617